The critics on Stephen Coonts

Fortunes of War

'A stirring examination of courage, compassion, and profound nobility of military professionals under fire. Coonts' best yet' *Kirkus Reviews*

Flight of the Intruder

'[Coonts'] gripping, first-person narration of aerial combat is the best I've ever read. Once begun, this book cannot be laid aside' *Wall Street Journal*

The Red Horseman

'One of the most thrilling post-glasnost thrillers to date' *Publishers Weekly*

Under Siege

'Mr Coonts knows how to write and build suspense. His dialogue is realistic, the story line mesmeric. That is the mark of a natural storyteller' *New York Times Book Review*

The Minotaur

'A fast-paced, graphic thriller with harrowing insights into the thankless, razor's-edge world of the navy test pilot and the labyrinth of superpower espionage' *Washington Post*

The Intruders

'*The Intruders* is another surefire Coonts novel, filled with plenty of action and adventure' *Baltimore Sun*

Fir

'Coonts goes back to putt
describes the sights and so
a master of that art'

By Stephen Coonts

Non-fiction
The Cannibal Queen

Novels
Wages of Sin
Deep Black: Biowar (*with Jim DeFelice*)
Deep Black (*with Jim DeFelice*)
Liberty
Saucer
America
Hong Kong
Cuba
Fortunes of War
Flight of the Intruder
Final Flight
The Minotaur
Under Siege
The Red Horseman
The Intruders

As editor
Victory
Combat (*short novels*)
War in the Air

Stephen Coonts is a former naval aviator who flew combat missions during the Vietnam War. He is the author of fifteen published novels. A former attorney, he resides with his wife and son in Las Vegas. He maintains a website at www.coonts.com.

Jim DeFelice is the bestselling author of two thrillers, *Coyote Bird* and *War Breaker*. But he is best known for his collaborative work with, among others, Dale Brown. *Dreamland*, which he wrote with Brown, was a *New York Times* bestseller.

Stephen Coonts'

DEEP BLACK: BIOWAR

Written by Stephen Coonts
and Jim DeFelice

ORION

An Orion paperback

First published in Great Britain in 2004
by Orion
This paperback edition published in 2004
by Orion Books Ltd,
Orion House, 5 Upper St Martin's Lane,
London WC2H 9EA

A CIP catalogue record for this book is available
from the British Library.

ISBN 0 75285 952 8

Printed and bound in Great Britain by
Clays Ltd, St Ives plc

Author's Note

The National Security Agency, Central Intelligence Agency, Space Agency, Federal Bureau of Investigation, National Security Council, Centers for Disease Control, U.S. Special Operations Command, Air Force, and Marines are, of course, real. While based on an actual organization affiliated with the NSA and CIA, Desk Three and all of the people associated with it in this book are fiction. The technology depicted here either exists or is being developed.

Some liberties have been taken in describing actual places and procedures to facilitate the telling of the tale.

1

Athens, New York, was founded in the great rush of enthusiasm following the Revolutionary War, when Americans first came to understand that their destiny in the world involved more than religion and capitalism. Its inhabitants saw the experiment in freedom and democracy as a link with the great Greek and Roman republics, which had produced not merely riches or military might—though both were important—but intellectual and artistic achievements unparalleled in human history. The men and women who settled in upstate New York were as optimistic as any. If, like the majority of their countrymen, their lives tended more toward hardscrabble than polished marble, they nonetheless were aimed in the right direction.

This Dr. James Kegan firmly believed, and had told Charlie Dean often. It was why he had decided to relocate to the small town, buying and restoring a dilapidated Federal period house perched precariously on a cliff just off the main drag. He could see the Hudson River from his porch. He would sit there some nights and gaze at the glittering reflections in the distance, reminding himself of man's potential and nature's power—or so he told Charlie.

Dean tolerated his friend's starry-eyed philosophizing for two reasons. One, he'd known Kegan just about all his life and, even though they hardly saw each other more than once or twice a year, still counted him among his best friends.

Two, he figured Kegan meant pretty much everything he said, whether or not Dean understood it—and most of what the microbiologist said Dean didn't understand.

Kegan and Dean had grown up together in Missouri in the late 1950s and early '60s. While in many ways the two men could not be more different, their friendship had endured the many twists and turns of their convoluted and complicated lives. Kegan—more often "Keys," a nickname earned during their first jayvee basketball practice a million years ago—was one person Dean felt he really knew. Their many differences somehow encouraged their friendship. Dean was relatively taciturn; Kegan was always talking and making friends. Dean had, if not a skeptical view of the world, at least a somewhat hardened one. Kegan remained an optimistic do-gooder, despite the fact that his early forays into altruism had ended badly.

Two years ago, Kegan had been diagnosed with cancer. But he'd come through it okay, survived the chemo with his optimism intact. He talked it about it matter-of-factly, didn't bullshit about it—he hit it straight-on, just like he played basketball. It was one of the things Dean liked about him.

Dean turned off Route 9W, driving his rented Malibu through the tiny downtown as he hunted for the crossroad that led to Kegan's. He missed it and had to turn around; as he waited for a bus to pass he saw an old phone booth and thought of calling his friend to make sure he was home. But the trip had begun as a surprise, and it seemed ridiculous to spoil it now, five minutes from his driveway. He made the U-turn and went back, cutting down toward the river and driving slowly so he could find the sharp cut that led to the house. The Malibu dipped and groaned as he took the switchbacks on the gravel lane.

Dean's attention was attracted to a large car carrier making its way upriver to Albany past a pack of Sunfish sailboats. He jerked his attention back on the driveway just before he would have sideswiped an eighty-year-old maple. He corrected and took the next switchback, avoiding the temptation to look down the rock gorge to his left. One more turn and he reached the macadam that ran around the back of the house to the garage and barn. Dean pulled around the side of the barn, glad to see Kegan's Saab; he made sure as he parked to leave enough space for the afternoon of hoops he anticipated.

A wooden porch extended around three-fourths of the building. Dean jogged up the steps and rapped on the wooden portion of the large front door—the house did not have a bell and Kegan refused to add even a wireless one.

"Hey, Keys, it's Charlie!" he yelled before rapping again. "Surprise, Keys!"

Dean glanced at his watch. It was a little past 9.00 A.M.; Kegan was a notorious early riser. He rapped again. Kegan rarely locked his front door; there was less need to here than back home in Missouri, and there was little need to do so there. Sure enough, when Dean tried the handle, the door opened.

It was possible—just—that Kegan was upstairs bedding some nubile lab assistant. Dean hesitated on the threshold, caught between wanting to be discreet and sensing the inherent humor of just that sort of situation. In the end he settled for cracking the door open and calling in.

"Hey, anybody home?" Dean yelled. "Any verifiable biology genius scientists at home?"

Kegan didn't answer. Dean pushed the door open and took a few steps inside to the edge of the Persian rug—authentic though not an antique.

"Keys! Keys! Hey, it's Charlie! What, are you in bed?" He took a step toward the wide staircase, which began about halfway down the hallway. "Keys, get your butt out of bed! I'm going to make some coffee. Then I'm going to whip your ass in a game of b-ball. Happy birthday, by the way."

Dean heard something move in the rooms to his left. He stepped back toward the large front parlor, his eyes glancing from the restored nineteenth-century claw-foot couch to the large brick fireplace with its early-twentieth-century spark catcher. The floor immediately before it was made of brick, arranged in an elaborate quadruple-fan pattern, and it was this symmetry that made it easy to spot the leg lying on one corner of the bricks.

"Jesus." Dean took a step toward the leg but stopped as the noise sounded again. He spun, heart pounding; in the same motion he reached to the back of his belt for the hideaway weapon his new employer had insisted he carry.

The tiny Glock felt like a toy in his hand. Dean took a step toward the kitchen at the rear of the hallway.

"Come out slowly with your hands where I can see them," he said.

There was no reply.

Dean went to the doorway, flattening himself against the wall, listening. Slowly, he lowered himself into a crouch. Just as he started to spring he heard the sound again, but it was too late to stop himself; he twirled and pointed his gun into the kitchen, both hands steadying it, ready to fire.

His heart jolted as a cat jumped down from the counter island. The cat was as startled as Dean and bolted from the room.

Casper, a kitten Keys had picked up at the shelter about a month or two ago. He'd mentioned him in an E-mail.

Dean dropped to his knee, listening, waiting for what seemed like hours before convincing himself he and the cat were the only ones moving in the house. He rose and walked back to the parlor.

"Keys. Keys," he repeated. "Is everything okay? Keys?"

A pool of blood extending out from the fireplace to the rug told him it wasn't.

2

William Rubens rose from his desk and unfolded the gray security blanket, draping it over the work surface with the same precision that he brought to every task he undertook. The corners had to be positioned just so over the shallow baskets at the corners; the creases were lined so they cut the large desk into an exact chessboard. Rubens smoothed the surface with his fingers, running them down the sides in the same manner his tailor used to set the seams on his pants. The National Security Agency's regulations called for the blanket to be used to cover sensitive papers on a desk whenever an NSA employee left his or her office. Rubens rarely left any papers, sensitive or otherwise, on his desk, but he would sooner neglect his personal hygiene than fail to place the blanket when leaving the building. Attention to detail was the only thing that allowed the mind to make order from chaos, and in his job as the number-two man at the NSA— and the head of the agency's ultra-high-tech covert "Deep Black" force, known officially as Desk Three—delineating order from chaos was William Rubens' prime concern.

Desk covered, chair positioned, Rubens stepped to the wooden credenza at the side of the office, double-checking that the drawers were locked. Finally, he reached to his stereo—hand-built by the agency's technical division to prevent the possibility of bugging devices—and turned off the Schumann midmovement.

Rubens had nearly reached the door to his office when the secure satellite phone in his jacket began to vibrate. The sat phone was one of two he carried; the other he might not have answered, as the number could be reached by anyone in the agency and quite a number of people beyond. But this phone was used exclusively for Desk Three operations, and so with a sigh he sat down in the chair near the door and entered the code to accept the transmission.

"Rubens."

"Mr. Rubens, this is Charlie Dean."

"Charles."

Dean was an ex-Marine foisted on Rubens by the White House for a recent mission. Though considerably older than most of Rubens' operatives, he had proven so capable that Rubens had added him to Desk Three's operations team. A Vietnam veteran who'd spent the last days of that war as a sniper, Dean brought a certain maturity to the job that Rubens appreciated.

"I have a bit of a problem here," said Dean.

"I thought you were on holiday," said Rubens, who had given Dean and the rest of the team from Russia a few days off.

"I came up to New York to see a friend and, uh, I found a body in his house."

"Your friend?"

"No, he's not here. I don't know where he is."

Rubens stared at the painting on the wall across from him, noting the subtle use of the green shades.

"Where is your friend, Charles?" he asked again.

"Haven't a clue. I was wondering whether I should call the police."

"By all means, you should call the police."

"If they ask what I do?"

"You're a government employee, Mr. Dean. It need go no further than that. Who is your friend?"

"James Kegan. He's a scientist."

The name registered in Rubens' brain, but he could not decide why. He knew Kegans and Kagans—Tom Kegan in at the Pentagon, Kagan at State, the historian, of course. . . .

"Do you think he murdered this person?" Rubens asked.

"I don't—I wouldn't think so."

"Are you there now?"

"I'm standing over the body."

How inconvenient, thought Rubens.

"Alert the authorities. Keep me informed." He glanced at his watch. He was due for his weekly haircut in forty minutes; after that he had a session with his yoga master. "Charlie, you were right to call me. For the next few hours I'll be tied up. If you need anything, speak to Marie in the Art Room."

"Yes, sir."

Rubens clicked off, entering his security codes as required to disentangle the phone from the system. He rose and went to the desk, pulling the blanket back from the corner so he could pick up the secure phone that tied to the Art Room—Desk Three's control room, where Marie Telach was on duty as supervisor.

"Marie, I'd like you to find out what you can on a James Kegan of New York. He lives in—" Rubens slid his thumb over the buttons on his phone to retrieve the GPS location that Dean had called from.

"Athens, New York," said Telach. "We're on it already. Charlie talked to me first."

"Very good."

"Listen, boss, you're going to want to take a look at this."

"Why would that be?"

"He's some sort of expert in germ warfare. His name is on our file as a potential consultant."

Rubens considered the painting once again. Green faded to gray; gray merged with black . . . shadow blurring to shade, shade to shadow: the perfect representation of the world Rubens and his people operated in.

"Is Mr. Dean aware of this?" Rubens asked.

"I don't think so. He knows he's a big-shot scientist, but when I spoke to him I hadn't run the name."

"I will be back in the building no later than eleven-thirty. Please have the details waiting in my queue."

3

"You found him just like this?"

"Haven't touched him. You can see where the blood is. I would have to have stepped into it."

"How'd you know he was dead?"

"Well, I guess in theory I don't," Dean told the plain-clothes investigator.

"All right, let's go outside. ID people have to go over the place."

"ID?"

"Crime-scene guys."

The state police investigator put his hand out in the direction of the door. Dean walked out to the front of the house and followed down toward the driveway, which was now filled with several troop cars, an SUV, and an unmarked Bureau of Criminal Investigation sedan.

"You mind showing me your license?"

"I went through this with the trooper."

"Yeah, I know." The BCI investigator didn't sound particularly apologetic. "You right- or left-handed?"

Dean held out his arms so the investigator could look at his sleeves himself. "You want to dust me or something?"

The investigator stared at Dean's arms and hands. Probably he was trying to decide whether Dean was smart enough to wash and change his clothes after firing a gun, so there were no traces of gunpowder.

Or blood.

"How 'bout that license?" said the investigator, looking up.

"Your name again was—"

"Achilles Gorman. License?"

Dean took out his wallet and handed over his ID. He'd already put his pistol and its holster in the car—not hiding them, exactly, just trying to avoid unnecessary questions.

Gorman called in the license information, then copied it in a small notebook he'd taken from his pocket.

"You live in California?" the detective asked.

"I'm in the process of relocating."

"Up here?"

"Maryland."

They went back and forth like that for a while, the investigator gathering useless background information. Even if Dean hadn't been working for the NSA, he would have stuck to one-word answers. He didn't particularly like being questioned, and while he'd come to respect police officers during his days as the owner of a string of gas stations, he resented the fact that Achilles Gorman treated him more like a suspect than a witness.

"So Mr. Keys, where does he hang out?"

"I just call him Keys. His name is Dr. Kegan."

"Where does he hang out?"

"I don't know. When I was here last we went into town. Some place called Maduro?"

"Like the cigar?"

Dean shrugged. "I guess."

"It's not there now."

"Don't know what to tell you."

Casper the cat came out, mewing loudly. Gorman stooped down, scratching the animal's head. He licked Gorman's fingers as if they were covered with catnip.

"Dr. Kegan—he a rich guy?" asked Gorman.

"He's got some money, but I wouldn't say he's rich."

"Pretty big house. A lot of property."

"Guess it depends on what you mean by rich."

The BCI investigator smiled. "Let's go over your arrival again from the top."

"Again?"

"You know, Mr. Dean, the thing is, this is a pretty serious felony here."

"Yeah?"

"Be better if you cooperated."

"You don't think I did this, do you?"

"Be better if you cooperated."

Eventually, Charlie Dean found himself back at the troopers' barracks, giving his statement for the third time. Gorman used two fingers to pound it into his computer. At three o'clock, as they waited for the printer to deliver a fresh draft, the investigator picked up his phone and sent one of the troopers to the deli for some sandwiches. That signaled the start of a short interval of nice-cop behavior; the investigator got a cola from the soda machine in the lobby and even offered Charlie a plastic cup to use. Charlie stuck with the can.

Gorman claimed he had a relative who worked for the GSA in Washington, and wanted to know which government agency Charlie worked for.

"I'm just a government employee and let's leave it at that," he said, and the nice-cop routine came to an end.

They went over the statement twice. Around four, the investigator's boss came in, a Lieutenant Knapp. Short and so muscular that the bullet-proof vest he was wearing looked like a flat baking pan, Knapp asked Charlie exactly two questions after looking over the statement:

This true?

You think your friend did it?

He answered "yes" and "no," respectively.

"You're done here. Make sure Gorman has a phone number where he can reach you."

"He does." Dean started to leave.

"If Kegan contacts you," said Gorman, "we'd appreciate knowing about it."

"Sure," said Dean.

Gorman frowned but said nothing else.

4

Rubens spread his forefinger and pinkie apart, nudging the key combination to kill the program. He sat back as the screen blanked, letting all that he had read settle into his brain.

The premonition of something truly awful lurked in the corners of his consciousness. He sensed that Dean—and thus Desk Three—had inadvertently stumbled upon a conspiracy with the gravest possible consequences. And yet the actual evidence would not have persuaded a logical man that anything more than a sordid murder had taken place. Rubens, a mathematician by training, prided himself on being logical. But he was also the descendant—now some generations removed—of a famous painter, an artistic genius, and as such Rubens could not deny the validity of emotional intelligence and intuition. It was important now to combine the two, to balance premonition with cold analysis.

To block out fear yet be aware of it.

Kegan had missed a scheduled contact visit with an FBI agent a day before. That was suggestive, especially since Dean's latest account made it seem the murder had likely taken place then. Autopsy information would not be available for some time, and the state police had apparently been uncooperative when a local Bureau liaison tried to get an update. But the FBI was extremely interested—worried more likely—and had already assigned an agent to find out where Kegan had gone.

Kegan, according to the information Marie Telach had retrieved on his behalf, was an expert on viruses and bacteria. While that in itself was not particularly noteworthy—many doctors might make similar claims—his area of expertise involved bacteria, and to a lesser degree viruses, that could be weaponized. He had served, briefly, as a consultant to the Pentagon some years before.

Was this connected to the murder?

Possibly. As best Dean and Telach could gather, the dead man had carried no identification. Officially he was a John Doe, an Asian—or Asian-American—in his twenties, no weapon, no apparent reason to be in the house. The murder sounded like a robbery gone bad: doctor comes upon an intruder, shoots him in the head, then panics when he realizes what he's done.

Telach had asked about the possibility of something more titillating: a homosexual affair gone bad. Dean discounted that, pointing out that Kegan had been married three times; Rubens decided that was not necessarily a disqualifier.

So more than likely, the murder had nothing to do with Kegan's profession and skills.

And yet, a connection could not be dismissed. Kegan was due to attend a conference in London on viruses in just two days, a conference that the NSA had in fact already been asked to monitor. This was merely routine; the science and technology section often gathered information for a variety of government agencies, and in this case the Agency's involvement amounted to providing a tape recorder for a Centers of Disease Control expert who would be attending the sessions. The agency would then transcribe the information, which would in turn be disseminated to the CIA and Defense Intelligence Agency as well as the CDC.

The conference concerned penicillin-resistant bacteria, an area where Kegan had not published. It was an area of interest, however, especially for someone interested in getting government grants, so it wasn't completely out of the ordinary that he would attend.

Of more interest was a contact by a company supposedly

unknown to Kegan but tracked by the NSA to a firm named UKD. UKD was a Ukrainian pharmaceutical company with links to a Polish "entrepreneur" named Radoslaw Dlugsko. Dlugsko had made a fortune selling surplus Polish arms to third world countries. UKD, meanwhile, had been communicating with the Research Institute for Viral Preparations in Moscow, which itself had connections to the Russian military's germ warfare program.

Connections, links—but no firm evidence of anything. Shades and shadows of great interest, but no precise forms.

Kegan had reported the contact, apparently because of a provision in one of his government contracts requiring him to note overseas contacts that might be of a suspicious nature. Rubens had the contact report on his computer—there was no mention in the report about why he thought it suspicious. And it was apparent from the processing that the people who had reviewed the report, including a low-level FBI official, had no idea, either. But the agent had at least been savvy enough to tell him to pursue the contact and then report back. Kegan had therefore sent a note saying he would be at the London conference and could be contacted there.

And into this mess walks Charles Dean, Kegan's friend since high school.

Coincidence?

Surely.

An unexplained murder at the home of a biology expert who had been contacted by possible terrorists—precisely the sort of situation Desk Three had been created to investigate.

Well, not precisely, but the executive order establishing the organization was suitably vague. Rubens picked up the phone and dialed the FBI.

5

Kjartan "Tommy" Magnor Karr walked up to the two men dressed in black and stretched out his arms.

"Maybe I can fly," he told them.

The men didn't laugh. As a general rule, the National Security Agency's men in black didn't have much of a sense of humor, and the select few who manned security at OPS 2/B—also known as the Headquarters/Operations Building National Security Operational Control Center Secure Ultra Command—were about as given to laughing as the hand-built supercomputers in the basement.

Besides, they'd heard that one many times.

The two men waved two small wands over Karr's body. One of the devices checked for electronic recorders and bugs; the other was a metal detector sensitive enough to detect the paper clip Karr had inadvertently forgotten about in the change pocket of his jeans.

"Just testing you, guys," said Karr, handing it over.

The two men resumed the scan. A second snag would mean a trip to a room around the corridor where, shoeless, Karr would be stood in the middle of a chamber that simultaneously conducted X-ray and magnetic resonance scans of his body; the search wasn't painful, but it would make him even later for his meeting downstairs. The blond, blue-eyed Scandinavian-American giant waited silently, forgoing his usual kidding around in hopes that the Black Suits would quickly clear him through. The men were efficient but not particularly quick, and they stuck religiously to the security protocol, slowly running their scanners over every inch of his six-seven frame.

"Mr. Karr," intoned his boss when he finally made it down to the conference room. William Rubens pushed back his suit jacket sleeve to expose his Hermes watch; Karr smiled and took a seat next to Charlie Dean.

"Where's Lia?" he asked Dean.

"She's on assignment," said Rubens. "If we may continue."

Karr reached for one of the 7UP cans on the table, then slid back in the seat. The NSA spent billions of dollars a year on high-tech computers and other gadgets; the table, for example, had flat-panel video screens that rose on command from the glass surface and could be tied into any number of inputs. It seemed as if no expense had been spared for Desk Three, which had its own satellite network, a small but potent air force, and hand-built weapons and sensors. But there were priorities: the seats arrayed around the table were so cheap the plastic nearly bent over backward under his weight.

Then again, Karr wouldn't have been surprised to find that Rubens picked them purposely to make sure everyone stayed awake during his interminable briefings.

"Dr. Lester is from the CDC," said Rubens, introducing everyone. "Bill Westhoven is with the FBI. You've already met Dean. Tommy Karr is one of our best people. Chris Carter, Joe Tyler, are experts in germ warfare."

Rubens clicked a small remote control in his hand.

"This is Dr. James Kegan. He's regarded as one of the world's preeminent experts on bacteria and viruses, though his expertise is fairly wide-ranging."

As Rubens spoke, the video panels began to rise. A picture of a fiftyish, ponytail-wearing man in an open-collar shirt filled the screens.

"Dr. Kegan has consulted with the FBI, CDC, and various other government agencies on facets of germ cultivation and weaponization," said Rubens. "Recently, he was contacted by persons apparently unknown to him, contacts that he had questions about."

Karr sipped his soda, waiting for Rubens to get to the punch line. He'd been called back to duty after only a few days of what was supposed to be a two-week vacation, so he knew something serious was up. But Rubens wasn't exactly the explaining kind—or rather, he did explain, but always in his own way after an interminable lead-in.

Dean shifted in his seat next to Karr. He cocked his eye toward the older man, who seemed unusually uncomfortable.

It was more than just the chair. His face had tinged red.

"Dr. Kegan was due to attend a conference in London two days from now," continued Rubens. "The FBI had hopes that the people who tried contacting him would show up. Dr. Kegan apparently did not know who it was who had contacted him. It's not clear why, therefore, he thought it suspicious. We've been able to track the contact to a Ukrainian company named UKD," continued Rubens. "Their purpose is not entirely clear. UKD, however, is connected with both the international underworld and the Research Institute for Viral Preparations in Moscow, which has some interesting intersections with the Russian germ warfare program."

"So what's the punch line?" Karr asked.

"The punch line is that Dr. Kegan has disappeared," said Rubens, "after someone was found murdered in his house."

"A John Doe," said the FBI agent.

"Kegan's disappearance presents us with a problem checking this connection out," said the FBI agent. "We don't have enough time to develop another source. So we were hoping that with your technology, you could fill the gap."

"What are we going to do, clone him?" said Karr. He smiled at the scientists, but their expressions remained somber.

"What they have in mind is sending a replacement who can claim to be his assistant," said Dean. "Someone who knows a lot about him."

"Like who?" said Karr.

"He was a friend of mine," said Dean. "I'm the one who discovered he was gone."

"And the body," added the FBI agent.

"And the body," said Dean.

"You think your friend shot this guy, Charlie?" asked Karr.

"I don't know," said Dean. "Probably not."

Under other circumstances, Tommy might have laughed and said something funny, something to get everyone to relax. But Charlie was too serious, and even Karr fell silent. He'd only met Dean a short time ago. The two men were very different; Dean was more than twice as old as the twenty-three-year-old Karr and even under the best of circumstances considerably less easygoing. But the danger they'd faced together had drawn them close; Tommy felt sorry for his friend. Dean had obviously learned something he didn't want to learn about someone he'd thought he'd known.

"Kegan wouldn't kill anyone," said Dean, folding his arms. The room remained silent for a moment.

"So all right. When are we leaving for London?" Karr asked finally.

"Mr. Dean will spend the next day being briefed on some of the areas that Dr. Kegan was working in," said Rubens. "Lia DeFrancesca is already en route to London to prepare for surveillance there. The FBI is in the process of obtaining subpoenas to check on the lab work that Dr. Kegan performed at a variety of institutions; we should know if there's anything unusual in a few days."

"What about me?" asked Karr.

"For the moment, I'd like you to go to Dr. Kegan's home in New York and take a fresh look at it."

"Poke through the garbage cans, huh?"

"I believe the garbage has already been inventoried."

6

While Lia DeFrancesca was in a general sense en route to London, the route was rather circuitous and included a climb down a nearly sheer cliff at a nature sanctuary in New York's Hudson Valley. The cliff itself wasn't much of a problem for Lia, who had done much harder climbs with full combat gear during the Army Special Forces Q, or Qualifying, Course, which she was one of the few (if not only) women to complete. But Lia was making her descent in decidedly unmilitary attire—a skirt that stopped some inches above the knees, and a pair of black heels, which went well with the skirt but not the rocks.

It did not help that her runner—a Desk Three officer monitoring her progress via a satellite link from the Art Room, Deep Black's special situation center deep within OPS 2—thought the situation rather humorous. Lia could hear Jeff Rockman's high-pitched giggle in her ear as she shifted her weight on one of the ledges, her backpack leaning precariously off her arm.

"I'm going to put you in a skirt and see how you like it," she growled at him.

"You're the one who didn't want to wait for the next guard change, when you could have walked right down the main road," said Rockman. " 'Let's take the shortcut,' you said. 'Bring it on,' you said."

Lia glanced to her right and saw a middle-aged man and

woman walking down the path toward her, at the moment oblivious to her. She continued to descend, unable to do anything to reinforce her modesty. As she stretched for a fresh foothold, she heard the faint yet distinct sound of over-stretched panty hose giving way.

"Son of a bitch," she complained as the stockings ran halfway up her left leg.

"Well!" said the woman, stopping just below her.

Lia looked down. She was now only eight feet above the path. "Get the hell out of my way," said Lia, kicking off her shoes.

"What?" demanded the man.

"Move or catch me," Lia told them as she leaned down. She intended to grab onto the footholds but missed and so did, in fact, practically jump on them. She rolled as she hit the ground; naturally her skirt hiked in the process.

Disgusted, she got up and reached into her backpack for a substitute pair of panty hose.

"Hanes Her Way. Satisfied?" she snapped as she reached up to change.

The couple started to back away. Lia rolled off the panty hose, exposing her sensible cotton to the fauna. She put on her shoes and began walking up the trail, which led to a gravel road.

"Turnoff in another hundred yards," said Rockman.

Lia could hear him through a small device implanted in her skull just behind her ear. His voice was like a whisper in her head, audible only to her. The microphone and an antenna array were embedded in her jacket.

"Any more surprises?" she asked. "And I'm telling you, I'm not swimming a moat."

"There's no moat," Rockman assured her. "Just the cameras and the physical security, plus the fence."

"Yeah, yeah, yeah."

Lia continued up the path, slipping her handheld computer from her jacket pocket and using its GPS function to find the exact point where she was to go in the woods. The small computer looked like a Palm PDA, the sort of device a traveling businessman might use to keep his schedule and contact information. But the NSA version had a wide range of capabilities, thanks to its capacious onboard memory and four processors that, ten years before, would have been found only in a supercomputer. It hooked into the Desk Three communications system, allowing it to accept downloads of satellite views and other information. The Art Room beamed her a situation map showing her position overlaid on a diagram of the facility she was approaching. She got her bearings and returned the handheld to her pocket.

Lia could see the security wall of the research building through the trees on her left as she turned. She had to walk along a very precise path about five feet wide—the gap in the coverage of the facility's perimeter cameras. Fortunately, the woods were cleared, and even with her heels on she found it easy going.

"There poison ivy here?" she asked Rockman as she got near the wall.

"Got me. Leaflets three, let it be," he added.

"Learn that in Boy Scouts?"

"I doubt there's any poison ivy," said Telach. "Hold at the wall. There's a jeep just starting a sweep."

Lia leaned against the smooth concrete, listening. Rockman had tapped into the facility's security system and was watching the video feeds as they were presented to the security desk. The high-tech system was controlled by a computer, which had made it relatively easy for the NSA snoops to break into.

Not that they wouldn't have found a way if it were more difficult. The FBI was still at least twelve hours away from obtaining a subpoena allowing it to review all of Dr. Kegan's experiments here. In the meantime, Desk Three's standing mandate to preemptively gather intelligence against potential terrorist threats would be used to covertly examine the facility's computer records for anything untoward.

While she waited, Lia took what looked like a bunch of small, flat spoons and a lipstick holder from the inside pocket of her jacket. Unscrewing the top of the lipstick holder, she slid one of the spoons into the slot and held it against the wall. As the truck roared past, she pressed the end of the lipstick holder and fired the spoon into the wall about head high. When the truck was gone, she used the small handhold to hoist herself up and then over.

"What's going on?" Rockman asked.

"What do you mean?" she asked, taking out her compact and lipstick—the real one—and seeing to her makeup.

"What are you doing?"

"I'm smoking a joint."

"The patrol will be back in two minutes. You want them to see you?"

"God, Rockman—why the hell do you think I'm wearing a skirt?"

Lia walked in a diagonal across the perimeter road toward a garage building, once more treading in a black spot of the compound's defenses. At the building, she opened the pack and took out her tiny Kahr, a custom-built pistol so small it could be palmed. Removing her handheld computer and a package of cigarettes, Lia took off her jacket and rolled it into a ball, sliding it into the backpack. Then she slid the ruck into an empty garbage can and put the lid on.

"You hear me?"

"Barely," said Rockman.

Lia adjusted her belt. The com system sent its signal from the belt to the jacket; the signal was low-power and worked in discrete bursts so that it was extremely difficult to detect.

"Now?"

"Still low."

"All right, hold on." She took the backpack out and put it behind the garbage can rather than inside. "How's that?"

"We'll fix the levels here," said Telach. "Get into the building. You have three minutes."

"Stay to the left of that driveway," added Rockman.

Dating from the early seventies, the Drumund University Research Site/Hudson Valley Division Laboratory had been designed to be heated by solar energy. Two years after it opened, however, the trustees belatedly realized the system maintenance and electricity for the pumps cost five times the amount an old-fashioned gas-burning furnace would. The high-tech system had been scrapped in favor of an oil burner, but the large roof arrays with their water panels remained. Lia headed toward one now, climbing up a narrow metal access ladder to a mechanical door at the outside. There were two locks on the door: the first took five seconds to pick; the other was considerably more stubborn, giving way to her small file in just over thirty.

Lia pulled the door open slowly, checking to make sure no one was there—the area wasn't covered by the security cameras. Stepping onto the metal catwalk inside, she pulled off her belt and stuck it in the door, maintaining her connection with the com system.

"I'm inside," she said.

"Yes," said Rockman. "All right. You want that stairwell on the right."

Lia walked quickly to the stairway. The top of the stairway was clear, but the landing was covered by one of the video cams. Rockman had to blank the feed as she passed— a three-second blip. He had already gotten the security people used to the short blips over the past forty minutes; they had checked out the areas twice and now had a call in to their tech people about the problem.

Actually, they thought they had a call in. Rockman had erased it from the voice mail system.

"Ready?" Lia asked.

"Hold just a second," said Rockman.

Lia took a long breath. "Find me a bathroom soon, all right?"

"Should've thought about that before you left home," replied the runner. "On my mark. Ready, set—"

Lia pulled the door open as Rockman gave her the cue. She took three steps down the stairs, then vaulted over the side rail onto the next landing and repeated the procedure, deeking past a second camera.

"Impressive," said Rockman.

"I'm impressed that your shoes held," said Telach. They had watched her through the uncorrupted portion of the feed, shunted down to the Art Room.

"Where's my bathroom?"

"Join the visitors first," said Rockman. "Door to your left, don't forget your smokes."

"And your badge," said Telach.

Lia had almost forgotten to take out the badge. She slid it from the inside of the cigarette pack, still wrapped in a foil wrapper. Once unwrapped, the badge would set off transponders in the building that were used to help track authorized personnel. Lia had to unwrap outside in the courtyard where people went to smoke, so she didn't suddenly appear in the middle of the building.

As she stepped toward the door, it swung open. Lia froze for a second—she had expected to be warned if anyone was coming—but quickly recovered, plastering a smile on her face. A good-looking Ph.D. fellow, roughly her age, stood in the doorway, gawking at her.

"Thank you," said Lia, starting past.

"Um."

"Just having a smoke," she told him, showing the cigarettes. "Care to join me?"

"You new here?"

"I'm trying to decide whether to accept a fellowship." Lia cocked her head slightly. "Maybe you could answer a few questions."

"Um, you should uh—you have to wear your badge," said the scientist. His eyes were boring holes in her breasts.

"Oh." She poked at her chest; a button magically slipped open. "I must've left it on my jacket."

The biologist's glance moved southward toward her legs.

"Yes," he murmured.

"So is it a good place to work?"

"Absolutely."

"Come on and have a smoke. Tell me about it."

"No, really I can't," said the man, glancing at his wedding ring. "Maybe later."

"Later," she said, sliding out the door.

"Smooth," said Telach when she made it outside.

"Next time I'll just shoot anyone who stops me," she said. Lia reached beneath her skirt and secured the gun beneath a thick garter strap.

"Just gave the security people an eyeful there," said Rockman.

Lia pulled her badge out of its wrapper. "Where's the rest room?"

"Cross your legs," said Telach.

"Should I pee right here?"

"There's one in the corridor you have to go in," said Rockman. "Light up."

"Oh yes," said Lia, pulling out one of the three cigarettes in the box along with the disposable lighter. She had had to bum the cigarettes off the helicopter crew earlier.

The first hit of tobacco set her off coughing uncontrollably.

"Giving your lungs for your country," said Rockman.

"Can it, runner boy." She tossed the cigarette. "All right, which door? The one on the left or the right?"

"I can't see you here."

"You know where I am; left or right?"

"Left," said Telach.

Lia reached for the door just as Rockman started to warn her not to.

It was too late. The door slammed open so fast it smacked her hand and sent her stumbling back. One of the two men who'd come out reached for her, trying to keep her from falling.

She didn't, but he did—surprised, Lia reacted instinctively, catching the man by the forearm and sending him tumbling over her to the pavement. Before the second could react, her elbow had dropped him to his knees.

"Jesus," said Rockman. "They're security."

Oops, thought Lia.

"You bastards," she said loudly. "You touch me again and I'm turning you in. I don't care if you are security—I understand the need for security. But I'm not going to be frisked by a man. No way. Searched by a woman, all right."

A gray-haired professor and two middle-aged women came up behind her.

"If this is the way guests are treated," said Lia loudly, "I can only imagine what happens to staff. He was trying to touch my breasts."

"They have no right to search you," said one of the women. "That's not right at all. No one else is searched."

One of the security people started to rise, reaching for his walkie-talkie.

"Call your boss," said Lia loudly. "Call him. This is the second time. The second time."

"The second time?" said the other woman.

"I'm sure it's just a misunderstanding," said the professor.

"Get going," warned Rockman.

"I'll bet it was a misunderstanding. I'm going to report this," said Lia, whisking around into the building.

"Left up the stairs. Move," said Rockman.

Lia took the stairs two at a time. At the top, she turned into the first room she saw—which just happened to be a rest room.

Men's, but times were desperate.

Lia went quickly to the far stall, her heels making a rather distinctive sound on the tiled floor. A pair of sneakers two stalls down jumped up and quickly retreated.

"Not good," said Rockman.

"I'm inside, right?"

"This isn't a shopping mall," said Telach.

"Yup." Lia peeled off the badge, realizing it would now be a liability. "Plan B. Where do I go?"

"End of the hall, make a left, then a quick right. The lab is down the stairs."

"Talk to you there," she said.

A potbellied virologist stopped dead in the doorway as Lia emerged from the stall. She smiled at him, then washed her hands.

"The women's room is down the hall."

Lia pointed at him. "Don't get any ideas," she said, drying her hands.

While she followed Rockman's directions to the lab, the Art Room launched an attack on the facility's security communications network, disguising it as a circuit blowout. This delayed the alert about the encounter with what the slowly recovering guards termed a psychotic visitor.

"How are you going to get into the lab area without your tag?" Telach asked as Lia headed down the stairs.

"I'll just wait for someone to come by and slip in with them," said Lia.

"We chose this lab because there's hardly anyone who uses it," said Telach.

"So open the door for me," said Lia.

"We can't without the tag."

"Right," snapped Lia, but when she reached the door it did indeed fail to open. A metal shield prevented anyone from slipping a nail file into the latch and prying it open—which would have been Lia's next choice. Before she could decide on Plan C, she spotted someone coming down the hallway toward the door.

"Rarely used, huh?" she muttered to the runner as she reversed course and started back up toward the stairs. She turned into the stairway as the person cleared the door, then waited on the steps. As the man—a twenty-five-year-old doctoral candidate who specialized in the study of RNA replication—turned into the stairwell, Lia skipped down and collided with him.

"Oh, Jesus," she said, falling against him and then away, her blouse somehow popping open in the process.

"Sorry," said the Ph.D. candidate.

Flustered, Lia helped him up, apologized, slipped down herself, scooped up a folder that had fallen, apologized, laughed at herself, and continued quickly to the automatic door—which opened thanks to the man's ID card, which Lia had palmed.

"Excuse me, excuse me," said the man, trotting toward her.

Lia turned at the door. "Oh my God," she said, staring at the folders in her hands.

She was still unbuttoned. Her bra, not nearly as sensible as her panties, provided a more than ample diversion as she dropped the folder on the ground. His badge tumbled with it; she apologized again, retreating down the lab hallway.

"Smooth," said Rockman in her ear.

"Never underestimate the power of Intimate Moments," she said.

"Or male lust," said Telach.

"You even got me hot," said Rockman.

"Before you melt down, tell me which of these doors I want," she said.

"Any one on the left," he told her. "Um, better get moving—the guys you kneed in the courtyard are at the supervisor's desk."

"I didn't knee anyone," said Lia, opening the door into a long, narrow room dominated by flat-panel computer displays mounted on benchlike desks parallel to the hallway. Lia walked to the back of the room, remembering the layout she had seen on her computer. She entered a second room, where a row of servers sat behind a locked panel. Ignoring the servers, she went to a PC at the far end, sat at the chair in front of it, and pulled off her right shoe. She removed a small keylike device with a USB plug from the cavity below the heel. The plug's USB interface, common on all PC-style computers, allowed the hardwired program on the device easy and immediate access to any machine it was plugged into. The Desk Three ops called the device a dongle. They had named it after software protection devices that plugged into early computers. The name was easier to use than the official nomenclature, which referred to the device as the "Universal Access Interface, A54, WIN mod 2, 3.7."

After placing the dongle into the proper slot, she hit the keys to reboot the computer; as soon as the PC checked the USB drive the worm program lodged in her dongle slipped inside the system.

"So?" she asked the Art Room.

"Give us a minute," said Telach.

"I'd rather not be caught here," said Lia.

"Odd time to start worrying about that," said Telach.

"I do have a plane to catch."

"These things take time."

"Guards in the hallway," warned Rockman.

Lia ducked down, waiting while the NSA-written code infiltrated the lab's computer system. The system was physically isolated from the outside, unlike the other systems at the lab, which had been compromised by Desk Three earlier. The small device Lia had plugged into the port was now communicating with the Art Room via the com system contained in Lia's clothes. The physical compromise of the system was not without risk—the agent might be caught, after all—but it would supply the Art Room with a complete copy of the data on the hard drives.

"Okay," said Rockman. "Go—they're going for your rest room upstairs. Go. We're set here."

Lia pulled the device from its socket and stomped on it, crushing it beyond recognition or use. Its memory had already been erased, and it was now just a useless piece of silicone and metal, which would be unnoticed in the garbage. She found an empty soda can and threw it inside, shocked that the scientists didn't recycle. Then she made her way outside the hall, where she once again confronted the closed door.

"Can you take the door out for me?" she asked Rockman.

"The alarms will go off. They'll lock down."

"Didn't you just tell me we were in a hurry?"

"You want the video cameras off, too?"

"Not yet," she told him, since that would mean he wouldn't be able to see what the guards were doing.

The lights in the facility blinked off. Lia grabbed at the door, pulling it open as the emergency beams came on. The lights came back, but a fire alarm was sounding. Lia trotted up the steps, intending to either find her way back to the roof through the mechanical section or go outside with the rest of the scientists, then slip away. But just as she reached the main floor hallway, one of the guards she had kneed earlier appeared near the doorway, helping herd people out of the building.

Ducking her five-four frame behind two researchers in long white lab coats, Lia pretended to sneeze as she passed by the door. The guard said something as Lia slipped past, but she didn't hang around to see if he was referring to her. She made it outside, walking quickly from the bricked area to a gravel walkway that skirted around the corner of the building. She turned the corner and quickened her pace, aware that she could be seen on the surveillance cameras. She retrieved the cigarette pack, squeezing one of the cigarettes to make it look like a marijuana joint. With the garbage pails in sight just at the edge of the black spot in the surveillance net, she stopped, made a show of looking around, and then lit up. She stepped out of the camera area, tossed the pseudo-blunt, and ran toward the cans and her backpack. She'd leave the belt; its function wouldn't be obvious, and as far as she was concerned it wasn't worth the risk retrieving it.

As she was unzipping the ruck to retrieve her jacket, she heard the security Jeep approaching. She pulled out the cigarette pack and took out the last cigarette, lighting it just as the Jeep pulled up.

"Excuse me, ma'am," said one of the security people from the truck.

Lia turned around, holding the cigarette out as if she were embarrassed to be discovered. There were two guards in the truck, a man and a woman.

"You really have to be back in the gravel area," said the man.

"I'm sorry."

"Hold on a second," said the woman as Lia started away. "Who are you and where's your badge?"

"Corina Jacobs," whispered Rockman in her ear. He had undoubtedly chosen the name from a roster of legitimate visitors, but Lia realized it was an unfortunate choice—she was Asian-American, and she undoubtedly didn't look anything like a Corina or a Jacobs.

Then again, she didn't look like a DeFrancesca, either.

"Jacobs." Lia patted her blouse as if looking for her name tag. "Must've left my jacket inside."

"Jacobs?" said the woman.

"I was adopted," said Lia. That much of her story was true, though the particulars she spun from it now were fiction. "Chinese Jew, New York City, over-the-hill hippies, yada-yada-yada. Pretty interesting around the holidays. Let's not tell anyone I smoke, okay?" She stomped on the cigarette. "Please?"

The name was on the list the guards had; Lia saw the woman frown when she spotted it.

"That's how I got into viruses," said Lia. She walked toward the truck. "Because, see, my birth mother was HIV positive, which was why I was put up for adoption. I think she might have been a prostitute or something."

The female guard rolled her eyes and prodded her companion—whose eyes had been pasted on Lia's chest the whole time—to resume the patrol.

Lia took out her handheld computer as the Jeep drove off. She put her thumb on the sensor at the rear, waiting for the machine to recognize its owner and wake up. When it did, two taps on the menu in the left-hand corner brought up the map of the site with the black spots of the surveillance net and her own position marked out. She turned, still on camera, made as if she were going back to the courtyard, then twisted back into the clear area.

"They're coming back," hissed Rockman in her ear. "Probably make you repeat the whole story."

In two steps, Lia had reached the wall. With the third, she had vaulted to the top, grabbing on the ledge and swinging upward. She nearly lost her balance but managed to slide her other arm far enough over the top to pull herself up and over as the Jeep returned. Lia fell to the ground, cursing, but sustaining no bodily injuries.

Her panty hose remained intact as well—her luck was starting to change.

"All right. Have the helicopter at the rendezvous in fifteen minutes," she said, starting back toward the nature area.

"Better make it twelve," said Telach. "You have less than a half hour to get to Kennedy Airport."

7

Rubens made it down to the Art Room just in time to see Lia board the helicopter, a "sterile" civilian Sikorsky S80 leased by the NSA for domestic travel. The helicopter had a cam in the passenger compartment, which Rockman was feeding onto the large screen at the front of the situation room. The camera was mounted low enough to provide a tantalizing glimpse halfway up Lia's skirt.

"Still keeping a prurient eye on our people, Mr. Rockman?" said Rubens as he walked toward the row of desks at the front of the room. The room had two levels; at the back were three rows of computer consoles and other communications gear used to tie into various systems during complicated operations. The front section of the room, arranged stadium-style, had three rows of desks with machines devoted directly to the agents in the field, although they, too, could be tied into the backup and support systems. It was possible to obtain real-time intelligence on nearly any spot on the globe here. Some came from in-place sensors; the Art Room could tap directly into the NSA's exhaustive resources, looking or listening to raw radio transmissions, for example, or piping them through automated (and not always completely accurate) computer translators. It had real-time access to satellite data from the military reconnaissance office known as DEF-SMAC (for the Defense Special Missile and Astronautics Center) and the Air Force Space Command, as well as a system of Navy satellites used to track ships on the ocean. More important, Desk Three could launch its own "temporary" sensors from in-place satellites or drone aircraft stationed around the globe. These were controlled via a satellite system in a suite across the hall, eliminating the logistics problems the CIA had encountered in its earlier Predator program.

For Rubens, improving what the CIA did was absolutely critical; he considered the agency his primary rival, a bigger enemy on any given day than terrorists or a foreign government. Desk Three had been carved out of traditional CIA real estate, and the agency constantly looked for ways to reclaim it.

"Do we have Kegan's files yet?" Rubens asked Telach.

"Working on it," Telach answered. "May take a bit of time to see what, if anything, is significant."

"Mmmm," said Rubens. He was due for a meeting in Washington, D.C., in an hour.

"Tommy Karr is on his way to Kegan's house," Rubens told Telach. "He should arrive at Stewart Airport in Newburgh in a few hours. He's already contacted the state police who are handling the case."

"I still think the FBI should have gone with him," said Telach. "This is more their field."

Rubens frowned at her but said nothing.

"My bet is a lovers' quarrel," said Rockman from his desk at the left-hand corner of the front row.

"A twenty-two in the back of the head isn't a spur-of-the-moment thing," said Telach. "Besides, if they knew each other, we'd know who the victim is. Which we don't."

The Art Room supervisor continued, updating Rubens on what at the moment was a baffling and open-ended operation. Immigration records as well as missing persons reports were being checked, but Rubens didn't think that the dead man would be identified anytime soon. At the moment, finding Kegan remained the best bet for finding out what was going on. The NSA, with some help from the FBI, and vice versa, was scouring financial records and checking on Kegan's various associates and assistants. One man appeared to be missing—a D. T. Pound, who at twenty-two held not one but two Ph.D.'s. A multidisciplinary team of researchers headed by an eccentric mathematician—John "Johnny Bib" Bibleria—was hard at work scouring intercepts, reading papers, and thumbing through databases in an effort to track him down.

"Very good," said Rubens finally, convinced that Telach was doing her customarily thorough job. "If you find any information, as opposed to theories, that will be useful for Tommy, let him know. I have a meeting in Washington."

Roughly two hours later, Rubens stepped from his nondescript Malibu and headed toward the side entrance of a building on K Street in the shadow of Capitol Hill. Looking slightly dowdy in the row of fancier accommodations devoted to lobbyists, the building bore no outward sign of its importance, though a true insider would realize instantly that its very ordinariness was a dead giveaway. A pair of men in rumpled brown suits watched Rubens enter and, though they knew him by sight, nonetheless directed him to the large desk at the center of the lobby, where he was asked to look into a retina scan and speak his name. A light on the desk shielded from his view blinked green, and Rubens was allowed to proceed to the row of elevators at the side. Rubens pressed the middle button next to the middle door, holding his thumb there long enough for the scanning device inside to get a good read of his thumbprint. It matched it against the retina and voice information recorded and checked earlier and then delivered the car to his level.

The K building—it had no other name—had been taken over by the Office of Homeland Security some months before. It was used primarily for high-level meetings of the type Rubens was now late for, though there were also a number of offices upstairs belonging to different departments in the country's newest bureaucracy.

Rubens did not particularly care for Homeland Security. While the lower rungs of the department were generally effective, he found the upper echelons amateurish and lacking in clout. In short, they were no threat to the NSA or Desk Three. He intended to do everything he could to keep it that way.

The elevator doors opened on the basement conference level. A security guard shanghaied from the Coast Guard stood at ramrod attention across from the door, not even acknowledging Rubens as he passed down the hall to a maze-like entrance to the main conference room. The baffle was but one of the myriad protections against bugging installed in the room; it was a low-tech precaution against laser or other direct beam communications. Copper shielded the entire level; there were a variety of passive detectors to find clandestine transmissions as well as active disruptors or jammers in place to defeat them. Even Rubens' encrypted phone connection with the Desk Three network would not work here.

Not that Desk Three couldn't have bugged the place if Rubens ordered it to.

"Mr. Rubens. We've been waiting you." Sandra Marshall was the Deputy Director of Homeland Security and generally rated as the heir apparent to Greg Johnson, who was spending less and less time in Washington as he tested the waters for a run at the Texas governorship.

"But that's not a problem," Marshall added. "We told your secretary the meeting was a half hour earlier than it really was, knowing you'd be late."

This was a joke, and Rubens deeply resented it. But he smiled and sat down, pretending for the others that he was both good-natured and a regular guy. He feigned interest in the chitchat nearby, then watched Marshall as she called the working group on Internet security recommendations to order and began the meeting.

Marshall had made a small fortune in Silicon Valley before joining the President's campaign as a consultant on high-tech industry. She had parlayed that role into a post at the Pentagon, hopping from there to State and on to Homeland Security in a matter of weeks. For a woman of thirty-three (she gave her age as twenty-eight, a modest and passable fib as such things went) her body remained well toned. She was not conventionally beautiful or even pretty, but of special interest to Rubens were her eyes; in his experience, every woman in Washington, even the young ones, had thick, puffy eyes from overwork and lack of sleep—or from partying, depending on the woman in question. Sandra Marshall's eyes were smooth and clear.

"I had breakfast with the President last Thursday," said Marshall, "and he mentioned how very interested he is in our project, and he specifically endorsed something to apply to all computers at all times. Something radical, and something that will provide the highest level of security to all people. To individuals, not just to the people downstream, the servers and companies."

"The initiative should end identity theft as we know it," said Griffin Bolso, who was representing FBI Director Robert Freeman.

"Exactly."

Rubens had heard various proposals to improve Internet security for individual users over the years. With a few notable exceptions, most were either unworkable or futile. A few were both. His mind drifted; he began thinking of the Kegan operation until the words "portable biometric identification is the future" fluttered across the room.

"There are many applications," Marshall continued. "And just as many ways of selling it to the public. I hope we can move ahead then with the report. Obviously, we'll need a full-blown technical study. That's the next step. Perhaps my staff can pull together a report and present it to the working group next week?"

Until this moment, Rubens had seen his involvement on the committee as necessary—his boss had assigned him to attend—and potentially beneficial, inasmuch as it allowed him to hear what other elements of the government were up to. But this was something else again.

"What you're suggesting is a scheme that would eliminate on-line privacy completely," he said.

"Scheme? That's such a difficult word," said Marshall.

"I don't think it would do that," said Bolso. "Do we even have complete privacy now? Of course not. Server addresses are routinely recorded. E-mails can be identified."

"That's not the same thing as knowing a user's precise identity every time he signs onto the Net," said Rubens. "The American public won't go for it."

Marshall's eyes met his.

"There will be arguments, yes. But nodes on the Net are tagged now, and it is possible to identify who is doing what at any given moment," said Marshall. "Your agency does so routinely."

"Not without proper authorization," said Rubens.

"A voluntary program to aid in authentication would greatly increase confidence in transactions, and that would be the place to start."

"There would be many ways around it," said Rubens.

"Not with the proper devices."

"Then it would not be voluntary."

Bolso took up the argument. Rubens—somewhat appalled that an official who ran a secret spying agency had to argue for personal privacy rights—considered pointing out the uproar that had ensued when it was rumored that the FBI asked libraries for lists of books that patrons took out. But then he reconsidered.

Why not let Marshall and the others push the idea further along before squashing it? People were always suspicious of the NSA, calling it Big Brother and whatnot. How better to counter that image by opposing this sort of plan as obtrusive?

A public relations coup.

Not that the NSA was interested in public relations. But if an opportunity like this presented itself, could it be ignored?

Let this dumb idea move along a bit, then start discreetly leaking information about it, along with the all-important tidbit that the NSA had found it necessary to oppose the initiative?

Yes.

Ultimately, such a proposal was unlikely to get beyond the study stage. But that only argued in favor of letting it proceed for now.

"So, we'll give it to my staff," said Marshall, with a note of finality. "All agreed?"

A vote. Or a quasi-vote. In any event, it would be a record of his position.

Rubens snapped up straight.

"I have to go on record as recusing myself, and the agency," he said, leaning over the table as he smiled at the secretary who was presiding over an automated transcription machine at the far end of the room. "Any involvement would be inappropriate, given the executive order governing our formation."

It was a rather shabby demurral, and Rubens half-expected that the others would point that out—or follow his lead and propose their own excuses. But no one else spoke up.

"Very good then," said Marshall, as cheerfully as if he hadn't spoken at all. "We're unanimous. Until next week."

Marshall managed to slip up next to him in the hallway.

"I hadn't expected you to oppose the initiative," she said. "After all, it's just a study."

"I don't know that we have any opinion, really. We've just taken ourselves out of the debate."

He expected her to argue, but instead she reached out and gently squeezed his arm. "We should discuss it further."

"I don't know if that would be useful," he said.

"Useful?" She tilted her head back ever so slightly. "Pleasurable at least."

Is she trying to seduce me? wondered Rubens.

"Perhaps over lunch?" she added.

"My lunches are generally not my own."

"Well, neither are mine," she said. "But are you going to the benefit for the Kennedy Center Thursday?"

She was trying to seduce him.

Hardly. Her purposes were surely political.

On the other hand . . .

"As a matter of fact, I am going to the benefit," said Rubens, knowing he could call on one of his many relatives for a ticket. "Yourself?"

"Yes. Perhaps we can talk then."

"I'll see you there."

"Maybe something to eat afterward?"

"Perhaps."

"I'll look forward to it," she said.

8

Karr had seen bus stations bigger than the airport he landed in at Newburgh, New York. But that made it easier to spot the state Bureau of Criminal Investigation agent waiting to meet him.

"Hey." Karr pointed at the detective as he approached, his voice booming in the low-ceilinged room. "I know you, right?"

Achilles Gorman stopped a second, temporarily puzzled. The NSA agent threw his arm around him without breaking stride, leading him toward the door.

"I'm Tommy. Whole name's too long to worry about. Let's hit the road."

"You're here from Washington?"

"That's what the sign at the airport said."

"You're NSA?"

"Say that out loud again and I'll have to kill you."

The doors snapped open and the two men headed across the parking lot to a green Impala. The double antennae and grille lights made the unmarked car so obvious Karr wondered why they bothered. The Deep Black op paused next to the car, stretching his arms back as if he were stiff but actually taking the opportunity to make sure they weren't being followed. Karr got in the car and pushed the seat back as far it would go, his legs still bumping against the dashboard.

"I'm sorry about inside," said Gorman. "My boss said you were NSA and he didn't make it sound like—"

Karr laughed. "Hey, don't sweat it. I'm just busting your chops. I'm working for CDC as kind of a loaner on this. Communicable diseases—because the guy who's missing is a disease expert. Germs. They told you all this stuff, right?"

Gorman nodded grimly.

"You all right?" Karr asked.

"Stomach's giving me trouble."

Gorman was silent until they found the Thruway, which took about five minutes.

"I didn't recognize you at the airport," said Gorman. "I expected someone in a suit."

"Hey, these are my best jeans," said Karr, who hadn't worn a suit since giving up the black one he'd worn, briefly, as a member of the NSA security force. "You named after the heel or the hero?"

Gorman looked at him with the pained expression of a man who had wandered into an insane asylum and couldn't find the exit.

"So tell me about Kegan," Karr said.

"We're looking for him," said Gorman. "I was hoping you'd tell me about him."

"All I know is he likes bugs." Karr laughed, but the BCI investigator didn't. "You think he killed the guy you found?"

"He's the number-one suspect," said Gorman.

"You find a murder weapon?"

"No."

"ID the victim?"

"No."

"Motive?"

"Unknown."

"Not much of a case."

"No kidding."

Karr had spent part of the flight north reading the preliminary reports on the investigation, as well as news reports and some background on Kegan and the investigators themselves. The state police's Bureau of Criminal Investigation handled homicides in most jurisdictions outside of cities north of New York; they had a decent track record in closing up homicides, but this didn't look like it was going to be closed anytime soon.

The victim's identity remained a mystery even to Desk Three. The man was around twenty-three years of age, of Asian descent, in decent shape, unarmed when he was found. He had no wallet, no jewelry, and no watch. His clothes could have been purchased in any Wal-Mart across the country. He had been shot once in the back of the head, execution-style, with a .22-caliber pistol. The pistol had probably been equipped with a silencer, according to the BCI's ID division, which handled the forensic end of the investigation. The man's prints didn't match any the FBI had dug up, nor did they match those recorded of known foreign agents, at least not according to the common agency files that Desk Three had double-checked.

It occurred to Karr that the victim would have been better suited to have been the executioner.

"Kegan's car was on the property," said Gorman. "We think he drove away in the victim's car."

"Makes sense."

"About the only thing that does."

A uniformed trooper sat in his patrol car at the side of the driveway. Karr smiled at his disapproving glare as they came up the drive.

Big old house, in very good repair. Great view, but nobody was just wandering up here without having some sort of reason.

The NSA op got out of the car and walked up to the porch, letting himself in ahead of Gorman. He walked down the hallway to the office and stood in front of the scientist's two computers. One had a DSL link as well as a wireless portal for other devices; the second wasn't hooked up to anything, physically firewalled from the rest of the world.

That was the one he was interested in. Karr knelt down to the CPU, sliding a disk into the floppy drive.

"Whatcha doin'?" asked Gorman.

"Snooping around," said Karr, hitting the power switch.

"We've already looked at the machines," said the BCI investigator. "They're clean."

The investigator meant that literally. There was nothing at all on the two hard drives of the machine Karr turned on— the program on his floppy revealed nothing more than assembler-level zeros. Which meant it either was brand-new or had been scrubbed by a low-level formatting program sophisticated enough to defeat Karr's snooper.

"I want to send the drives to my guys," he told Gorman, pulling the computer out from its shelf beneath the desk. "Be easiest just to send the whole computer."

"I guess that's okay," said Gorman. "We haven't found anything. I'll just need a receipt. We have a form—"

"Whatever paperwork you want is yours."

Karr went to the other computer and once more slipped his boot disk in. This one had the latest version of Windows, along with an intact file structure. Besides the system programs and files, Office, three different organizer programs, Quicken, and Turbo Tax accounted for most of the used space. Karr quickly recovered the deleted files; most were just Internet sites routinely deleted.

A calico cat came into the room, meowing as he curled against Karr's leg. Tommy reached down and patted him; the cat licked his finger.

"Nice cat," he said, wiping the cat slop onto his pants.

"Just hungry." The detective shrugged. "No more cat food in the house. Gave it some tuna last time I was here. I don't know if there's any more left. Thing comes and goes. Probably somebody in the neighborhood feeding it. Hopefully they'll adopt it."

"No ASPCA?"

"Only take dogs in this county, not cats. Too many, I guess. I'd adopt it, but my wife's allergic," added Gorman. "Thing loves to be petted. Slobbers all over you so much you'd think it was a dog. What's all that stuff?" Gorman asked, pointing at the screen.

"Things someone was looking at the day before the body

was found," said Karr, flipping through the recovered files on the second computer.

"Anything interesting?" asked Gorman.

"URL for a page showing what time it was in Asia. Couple of them." Karr keyed up the DSL dialer to connect to Desk Three, which would siphon the contents for examination. Gorman watched him for a while, scowling but saying nothing.

"Mind if I take some pictures?" Karr asked after the modems connected.

"Of me?"

"Hell no—you'd break the lens."

"Go ahead then."

Gorman scooped up the cat and brought him into the kitchen, looking for food. Karr took out a small digital camera, sliding it into the base of his satellite phone. He walked to the next room, which was a library, and began scanning the shelves with the camera. The books were mostly related to science and medicine, though several shelves were devoted to period homes and furniture. When he was done he unhooked the camera and spoke to Rockman over the phone.

"You got it all?" Karr asked.

"Lot of books," said Rockman.

"I'm just doing what I'm told. Gonna have to ship you the lone computer. Disk was scrubbed pretty well."

"Well, that's interesting."

"Yeah."

"Maybe he backed up onto a CD or something."

"Not in the inventory that I saw," said Karr.

"Look at the music collection. Maybe he stuck it in there, you know, hiding it kinda."

"You see that on *NYPD Blue*?"

"Murder She Wrote," said Rockman. "We'll crack this case." His tone changed, becoming more serious. "We should have data from his work computers soon. We'll buzz you if it's important."

Karr sat down in one of the leather club chairs at the side of the room. He settled his hiking boots on the floor. The carpet was thick and, though Tommy wasn't an expert, looked handwoven and very expensive. It was the sort of thing that would go for thousands, probably.

He looked at the furniture and furnishings a little more carefully. There were a lot of antiques in solid, showroom shape.

"So you think this murder is related to his work?" Karr asked Gorman when the investigator returned.

The BCI man gave him a blank stare.

"Angry student or something?"

Another blank stare.

"Robbery? Guy comes here; he turns the tables, kills him, then panics and runs off?"

Gorman finally blinked. "I doubt that. There's no sign of panic. Everything except the body is perfectly in place. There was even food for the cat."

"What about the guy who found him?"

"Not a suspect," said Gorman.

"No?" asked Karr.

"FBI ruled him out. Just some friend who came up on a lark. Works for the government. They didn't say who, but I thought CDC for some reason."

"I don't know. I don't think CDC," said Karr, realizing that Gorman was talking about Dean. Karr had been instructed not to lie—but also to avoid stating Dean's affiliation, if at all possible. It was the sort of bureaucratic reflex, bordering on paranoia, that made little sense to the op— they'd told the state police that Karr was from the NSA, after all, even if they clouded the affiliation by claiming he was working for the CDC—but obviously the people who were paid to worry about the agency's public image had thrashed it all out. Karr was just here to follow orders.

Gorman gave him a funny look.

"They don't tell me much," claimed Karr. "Except where to go." He laughed and propped his elbow against the arm of the chair and leaned his head on his hand. The BCI investigator was easy to read—he didn't like Tommy and probably resented the fact that he was parachuting in to work on his case.

"The FBI working hard on this?" Karr asked.

"Hard as they usually do."

Gorman apparently didn't mean it as a joke. Before Karr could ask anything else, his phone buzzed.

"Hey," said Karr, pulling up the antenna.

"Mr. Rubens wants you to go to Bangkok," said Telach. "You found that Web page with Bangkok's time equivalents."

"And?"

"There were two E-mails from the missing lab assistant on the lab system Lia compromised that we traced to Thailand," said Telach. "One of them has a date in it. Five days ago."

" Okay."

"D. T. Pound. He's twenty-two years old," said Telach. "Text of the E-mails is minimal. Just describes the weather. We're getting pictures, tracing his credit cards—but we're working on the theory that he's over there in Thailand and Kegan went to see him. That jibes with your Internet pages."

"This sounds suspiciously like a wild-goose chase, Marie." Karr looked up at Gorman, who was pretending not to eavesdrop.

"Maybe. Go to Albany Airport. There'll be a ticket waiting."

"Aw, come on."

"Tommy—"

"Can I get some lunch first?"

"No. We may be under a time constraint here. We just don't know what's going on."

"You're out of your mind, Marie."

"Not my mind. Mr. Rubens'."

"You're out of his mind, too."

9

By the time Charles Dean got off the 767 at Heathrow Airport, he had received the equivalent of an upper-level biology survey course on microbes and related phenomena. Armed with a mini–DVD player, he had worked his way through a collection of lectures that began by explaining the difference between viruses and bacteria. Viruses consisted of RNA or DNA surrounded by a protein shell and required a host cell to replicate; bacteria (the plural of bacterium) were single-cell microorganisms, much larger than viruses but in general able to replicate on their own. From there the lectures had proceeded to explain some of the various subtypes and how they caused disease; the final series demonstrated the rudiments of their replication and manipulation in the laboratory.

In sum, Dean learned enough to know that he would never in a million years fool anyone in the field.

But if they wanted an expert, they would have sent a scientist. Rubens wanted someone who could handle a difficult situation if things got complicated. And he wanted someone who knew Keys.

Did he know him, though?

He knew a lot of facts—Kegan was a great pool player, loved old houses, and at a shade past fifty could still play a hard game of hoops. He'd beaten back cancer and jogged about three miles a day. He could make women fall in love with him very easily, but inevitably they fell out of love just as fast.

He'd been a decent basketball player, a better outfielder, and a halfback so quick he might have tried for a sports scholarship if he hadn't broken his ankle in his senior year.

But what did he really know about Kegan?

Kegan's mother and father had died when he was in college. They were poor people, even poorer than Dean's family. Kegan had had to work his way through school, even though he'd gotten a scholarship that covered his tuition.

What did he *really* know?

Kegan had been altruistic enough as a young man to volunteer to work for the World Health Organization. He'd been sent to Southeast Asia—Myanmar, then known as Burma. He'd returned older and wiser, but no less altruistic.

What did he really know?

That James Kegan wasn't a murderer.

What did he really know?

That once his good friend had had a hell of a jump shot.

The long flight had left Dean's knees stiff and he had a kink in his back. He felt creaky all of a sudden, making his way into the terminal like an old man.

Dean adjusted his glasses—he had not yet been implanted with the Desk Three com system and wasn't sure he wanted to be. The glasses contained a tiny speaker that focused sound waves so that only he could hear them. There was a microphone near the nose bridge. The glasses connected to a transmission and antenna system in his belt, which was studded with metal.

"So I'm here," he told the Art Room.

"Go through Customs like everyone else," said Rockman. "Take a taxi to the Renaissance Hotel near Covent Garden. Lia will trail you there."

Dean followed a pair of college girls through the terminal building to the long hall in the basement where his luggage waited. He picked up the big brown bag and snapped out the handle to wheel it along. The suitcase beeped at him, telling him that while it had been prodded and dropped and kicked—a large black smudge on the side near the base attested to this rough handling—it had not been opened or tampered with.

Dean pulled it along through the hall to the customs area, where he took a spot at the end of the snaking line. Dean surveyed the crowd, casing it to see if he had been followed. In his brief stint with the NSA he'd learned that paranoia could be extremely healthy, but he'd also learned that picking a really good trail team out in a crowded place could be next to impossible.

If he was being followed, it was at least being done by pros.

"Let's move along now," said a female customs agent at the front, opening a new station. Dean pulled his luggage up and took out his passport, which was in his name. He handed it and the questionnaire to the clerk.

"Business or pleasure?"

"I'm here for a scientific conference," said Dean. "But I do hope to get a little pleasure in."

"Science, really?" said the woman. "What of?"

"Biology," said Dean. "Bacteria and viruses."

"I see." The woman looked as if she might start quizzing him, and Dean wondered about the timing of her arrival—she'd opened up a station just as he got to the head of the line. Had she been sent by Desk Three to test him?

Or was something else going on?

"Yeah," said Dean, noncommittally.

"Thick glasses," said the clerk.

"Trifocals," said Dean. He smiled apologetically and held them as if adjusting his vision. "Getting old."

She took his passport and looked at it under a special lamp to make sure it was authentic—or in this case, an authentic forgery. The two college girls he'd followed earlier were now at the station on his left. One made a joke when the customs agent asked why they had come, and they were given a lecture about the employment situation in Great Britain. (Not pretty, according to the agent, who noted that Her Majesty's government could not have illegal workers "mucking about" and taking jobs from legitimate citizens.)

"That way," said Dean's customs agent, clearing him through.

Lia stood next to the line for the ATM, watching the escalator up from the lower level. British intelligence had an operation going to track the arriving scientists—she'd seen them pick up on a pair of Russians earlier, tagging their luggage with a small locator bug and then following them onto the airport shuttle into the city. For some reason they hadn't tagged Dean—whether because he was American or hadn't been listed on the original list of conference attendees wasn't clear.

Lia had one of the ops in sight. They were easy to spot, lacking luggage and knowing far too much about where they were. The man made no move as Dean walked past, nor did he touch his ear to use his radio.

"You're going to lose Dean," warned Rockman in her ear.

"That'll be the day," she said, circling around the escalator. She paused to adjust her shoulder bag, moving the strap button so it focused on a brunette near the coffee seller.

"What's Sylvia doing here?" said Rockman.

"My point exactly," said Lia.

Sylvia Reynolds was a former CIA officer who did contract work for the FBI and occasionally British MI-6 and MI-5, respectively the external and internal intelligence organizations of the United Kingdom. Lia watched as Sylvia paid for her coffee, then began walking toward the terminal entrance. It wasn't obvious that she was following Dean, which of course made Lia suspect immediately that she was. Dean had found his way to the taxi queue and was standing about twelve fares back.

"Tell him to go downstairs and take the express," said Lia. "Let's make sure she's on him."

"Good idea," said Rockman.

Lia went back inside, spotting a pair of Russian SVR officers coming through the door lugging their bags. There were going to be more spies in London than scientists.

The Russian foreign service agents were veteran holdovers from the days their spy agency was known as the KGB. Lia put her hand to her face as she went through the door, nearly bowling over a bleary-eyed American tourist who was carrying a baby in a backpack. Dean, meanwhile, had given up on the taxi line and was waiting for an elevator to the basement level, where he could take the shuttle to London.

Lia circled through the large shop area, trying to avoid giving the airport security cameras a good shot at her face. Sylvia Reynolds had followed Dean to the elevator; Lia saw her get in the car with him.

"He know she's following him?" Lia asked.

"We didn't tell him."

"Why the hell not?"

"He'll be more natural if he doesn't have to act natural."

Typical Art Room logic, thought Lia.

She went down the stairway, coming out as Dean walked through the hallway into the shuttle tunnel. Tickets were sold at a machine on the wall, but as she approached it, Rockman warned her that the train was arriving. Lia veered toward the tunnel, deciding she'd have to buy it on board.

The train came in just as she reached the platform. She slipped into the last car, holding her carry-on luggage and watching through the glass as Reynolds found a seat in the next car up. She couldn't see Dean, but Rockman told her he was in the next car as well. The com system blanked as the train started; it was supposed to provide complete coverage to a depth equal to two basement levels, but there was a gap between supposed-to and reality.

Lia took out her handheld and clicked on the transmission detector mode; there were no signals being sent in her car. She had started to get up to check the next car when Rockman came back on the line.

"I'm going up to the next car," she told him.

"Sylvia may recognize you," he said. "Hang back."

"She'll see me sooner or later. Did you figure out who she's working for?"

"It's not really a big deal at this point."

"You don't think she's his contact?"

Obviously the idea hadn't occurred to them, because there was a long pause. Telach came back on the line.

"We may be able to psych it out on this end without announcing that you're there," she said. "There's no reason to think she's involved. The contact will come at the conference."

"Why?"

"Because we haven't answered the E-mails; we just registered him as Kegan's last-minute replacement."

"Like she wouldn't have accessed the information already?"

"Lia, she's working for the Brits. Just stay in the background for now, all right?"

"Suit yourself."

Lia reached into her large bag and pulled out a tourist guide. The book contained eight pages of detailed maps of the area and hotel they'd be working; while she had the same information on her handheld, there was a certain quaintness to using the guidebook. It also saved on the battery.

In a few moments they were outside of the airport tunnel, hurtling toward London. And then, not. . . .

The train slammed on its brakes, and Lia, caught by surprise, found herself flying into the Plexiglas liner of the luggage compartment.

Dean braced himself as the brakes slammed on, warned by a change in the sound of the train's wheels—a benefit of having grown up in a town where trains ran through regularly.

"Trouble," he whispered to his runner.

Dean was sitting next to an emergency exit and eyed the bottom of the glass as the train screeched to a halt.

"We're with you," said Rockman in his ear. "There's a woman following you named Sylvia Reynolds. Brown sweater, brunette hair, about forty. She's with the Brits but we're not sure why she's trailing you. She's in your car."

Dean adjusted his glasses, clicking the small tab at the

back near his left ear. The tab opened a video feed in the lower portion of the glass; another click and the screen displayed a view from a microscopic lens located at the back of the glasses, allowing Dean to see the woman who was tailing him without actually turning around. She looked as surprised as any of the other passengers. He tapped the feed off and craned his head to the left, looking through to the next car. A conductor and two policemen were moving through the car, glancing at the passengers. Dean slid back in his seat.

"Your passport, sir," said one of the policemen after Dean presented his ticket.

"Sure," said Dean. He took out his passport and gave it to the policeman.

"You just landed in London?"

"Yes," said Dean.

"Where are you staying?" asked the bobby.

"Go ahead and tell him," whispered Rockman.

"Renaissance Hotel," said Dean. "What's going on?"

"Official business," said the officer, handing the passport back. He pointed ahead and they moved on, stopping near the end of the car and questioning another man.

"They seem to be looking for someone," Dean told Rockman after they left the car.

"We figured that. Not clear what they're doing. May have nothing to do with us."

"The woman you said was tailing me is getting up," said Dean, watching her. "She's going after them. Should I trail her?"

"Negative," said Rockman. "You're just Kegan's assistant, remember? Stay where you are."

It was nearly twenty minutes before the train started moving again. Rockman had tapped into the local radio network in the meantime and determined that the police were looking for a man they called Sand. The name did not appear to correspond to any of the outstanding notices or warrants, but in one of the transmissions they mentioned an MI-5 operative; the operation appeared unrelated. Sylvia Reynolds, meanwhile, had gone back to her seat.

"It's possible they think you're Sand," said Rockman. "Might be a terrorist thing."

"If so, why didn't they arrest me?"

"If they really are looking for someone who's a terrorist, odds are he won't look like you. Relax. We're working on it."

Dean slid back in the seat. The Art Room was *always* working on it. In his experience, they had a tendency to figure out things about five minutes after they'd be truly useful to know.

"Your tail only went to the ladies' room," Rockman told him. "Lia doesn't think she spoke to the police."

"But we're not sure."

"No. Was she close enough to hear you when you told the policeman where you were staying?"

"Maybe. I'm not sure."

"Okay, don't sweat it."

Once the train resumed moving, the ride into Paddington took only another twelve minutes. Dean got out and, directed by Rockman, tucked around to the right to the outdoor cab stand. Sylvia Reynolds no longer appeared to be following him. Lia had been spotted by Reynolds—it had been impossible to hide when the police came through—and she stopped trailing Dean, though Rockman assured him she was close enough to back him up if something happened.

"Who's backing her up?" said Dean.

"She can take care of herself," said the runner. Then he added, "Not that you can't."

"Thanks."

There were members of at least two different intelligence agencies in the giant train station—British and Russian. Guided by Rockman, Dean steered a seemingly haphazard path away from them, heading toward the taxi queue outside. There he joined the line, pulling his bag up as the line moved steadily. It was just after morning rush, and there was a steady flow of large black cabs, punctuated by newer models in green, blue, and red. Dean got into a black one in the far lane, swatting the car on the rear window before getting in. He told the driver his destination only after he was inside, then settled back as they waded into traffic.

His swat on the window had not been for good luck. The Desk Three op had placed a penny-sized wide-angle cam on top of the chrome. He took out his handheld computer and turned on the transmitter, which would work for forty-five minutes, then fry itself beyond recognition with one last burst of energy.

He fed the image into the lower portion of his glasses as well as relaying it back to the Art Room. But after a few minutes he found the fish-eyed feed of the traffic behind him distracting and turned it off. The Art Room claimed he was no longer being followed.

The Renaissance was a luxury hotel near Holborn and several blocks from the conference itself. Not using the conference hotel made it easier for surveillance and, more important, kept him away from the British intelligence network already set up there. Three different rooms had already been reserved in the hotel for him under different names, and as he rode through the morning traffic the Art Room checked the hotel's reservation banks to see who had booked near them. They went with a large room on the sixth floor, wiping the others off the system.

Three doormen sprang to attention as the cab pulled in under the archway into the courtyard at the front of the hotel; Dean pulled a twenty-pound note from his pocket and stuffed it into the cabbie's hand.

"Too much of a tip, guv," protested the cabdriver paternally, but Dean waved him off.

"How much did you give him?" asked Telach.

Dean ignored her, following the doormen to the front desk, where the clerk found that his room was ready, despite the early hour. When Dean was alone in the elevator Telach hissed at him not to go overboard in tipping again.

"Rubens will have your head."

"He already has the rest of me," said Dean. "So where's my friend?"

"She switched off and started following Lia," said Telach. "Must be doing contract work for MI-5."

The Art Room supervisor explained that British intelligence would routinely collect dossiers on various experts, a preemptive "just-in-case" operation. Dean would have attracted some attention because, cover story or not, he was new to them. The fact that he was covered by a rent-a-spy meant he was considered small potatoes.

"As long as I'm not mashed," he told her.

"We're inside the hotel's computer, which has a link to the video system, so we'll see her or anyone else if she comes in. So far we don't have any indications of agents there. It may be that she wants to see what Lia's up to now—whether she was trailing you or someone else. We're betting that she was only supposed to find out where you were staying, which she would have been able to do when you spoke to the police. She hung with you long enough to make sure you were headed in that direction, then went after the lead that seemed more interesting."

"Yeah, but I could go anywhere in the taxi."

"True, but they don't know that you're up to anything particularly interesting. But an American op shows up, that's different. Lia's worked with the British before, and with Sylvia. So she's a hell of a lot more interesting. Don't get offended," Telach added.

"I'm not. I'm beat. I want to take a nap."

"No time," said Telach. "We need you go to a store near Charing Cross."

"Why?"

"We've recovered the E-mails that led Kegan to file the contact report. They're pretty bare, but the last one mentioned the Mysterious Anderson bookstore. You're supposed to be there at ten. It's close to your hotel. You can walk."

"I'd like to catch some rest," protested Dean.

"Next lifetime," said Telach.

As soon as she was sure Dean had gotten into his taxi, Lia watched Reynolds come back inside and get into the Heathrow Express back to the airport; obviously her job was done, at least for now. Lia waited until the train left, then took her own circuitous route in and out before ducking down a Tube entrance and making sure she wasn't followed.

Lia rode the Circle line to the Embankment stop a short distance away. Aboveground, Rockman directed her over to the Charing Cross bookstore Dean was heading for. Rather small, it specialized in mystery and crime books; the shelves were fairly disorganized by English standards, with books pushed in every which way and stacked so tightly that it was hard to take them out.

"When's this meeting taking place?" Lia asked.

"Supposed to be in a half hour," said Telach.

"Plenty of time."

A video camera sat at the rear. Lia asked the more sympathetic-looking of the two clerks if there might be a rest room she could use; in a minute she was being led past haphazardly arranged piles of books to a small, rather fetid room about the size of a closet. Lia went inside, waiting a respectful moment before taking out her small computer and using it to find the shielded video cable running along the edge of the floor at the near wall. From her purse she took out what looked like a button with a metal clip; she attached it to the cable, then left. By the time she thanked the clerk, the Art Room was viewing the video feed from the store system. Lia walked down the street in search of a tea shop, waiting for Dean to arrive.

The sun glinted off Dean's sunglasses as he turned left out of the hotel, walking down High Holborn toward Shaftesbury Avenue. Besides blocking the sun, the mirrored finish of the glasses provided a good backdrop for the viewer portion of the lens at the bottom, which made them much more practical to use than the clear set, at least outdoors. Dean was able to project a GPS map and locator system on the left screen; he found the map a good deal less annoying than Rockman's directions, which made him feel like little more than a robot.

Rockman barked at him when he came to Cambridge

Circus, telling him he should turn left; Dean ignored the runner, waiting against the rail for the light and then crossing, walking around near the Palace Theatre before going back toward the river. That meant he had to cross the street again, but the zigging course made it easier for him to check if he was being followed. He found the small store and went in, wandering for a while as if truly looking for something to read. He found the recent Ian Rankin and picked it up. He moved farther back, then paused over the true crime section, which turned out to be dominated by American authors. He pulled a book at random—*Lobster Boy* by Fred Rosen—and cracked it open.

"So?"

"Browse for a few minutes more," advised Rockman.

Dean wandered back and forth for about ten minutes before finally going to the register with the two books. As the clerk put Dean's credit card through the machine, a short Asian man came in, glancing in his direction before heading toward the back. Dean signed for his books, then left the store, walking down the street slowly. Sure enough, the man came out of the store—but went immediately in the other direction.

"Not following you?" asked Rockman.

"No."

"All right. Go on back to the hotel and let's see what happens."

"Maybe I can take a nap," muttered Dean.

As he reached the end of the block, he decided not to go back the way he had come. He took a right and nearly knocked over a man about his size who'd been studying a newspaper.

"Sorry," said Dean, moving around him.

The man pulled the newspaper away, revealing a gun. "Onto the Tube," he said, pointing with the barrel.

10

Rubens had placed his best analysis team on the virus project, but he had not made the decision lightly. The team was headed by Johnny Bib, a genius mathematician and a remarkably brilliant leader, at least in the eccentric world of the Deep Black analytic section. But Johnny brought a certain annoyance factor to any enterprise he was involved in. He was eccentric even by the outsize ruler the NSA used to measure eccentricity.

At the moment, for example, he sat in Rubens' office holding a red apple in his hand, glancing at it and shaking it, without explaining either the apple's significance or, more important, what he had wanted to talk about.

"Johnny, what did you want to tell me?" Rubens asked.

"Fauna."

"I assume that means something."

"Fauna," repeated Johnny Bib.

"Why, Johnny? Why?"

"Yes. I haven't decrypted it yet. Yes. Yes. Pictures, though. JPG format; any PC could view them."

Frustrated and confused, Rubens just barely controlled his anger, stifling the urge to yell. He made his voice very quiet instead. "Is that all you wanted to tell me?"

"Does he have a garden?"

"Who?"

"Dr. Kegan."

"Why is that important?"

Johnny Bib took a bite of the apple and then began talking. According to the material they had recovered from the computer linked to the Internet, Kegan had downloaded considerable information about plants in the past few days.

"Why?" asked Rubens.

"Yes," said Johnny triumphantly.

"What about the reformatted hard drive?"

"Very good work. We haven't gotten anything from it yet. Very, very good work. The plants, though. Why?"

"Okay. *Why?* Does it have to do with plant bacteria or viruses?"

"Yes," said Johnny Bib, who had an annoying habit—a mathematical habit, it must be admitted—of acknowledging the validity of the question before actually answering it. "No. Not apparently. Funguses in a few cases, but mostly plants. So: Does he have a garden?"

"I don't know," said Rubens. "We can find out. Have you checked the images for code?"

"Yes. No."

Rubens really wondered if perhaps the best approach might be simply to throttle him. "Talk English, Johnny."

"There are no fractals, none of that sort of thing," said Bib, referring to a type of encryption that used complicated formulas as keys, inserting the information in what looked like data for something else. "And we looked at the originals. But maybe they are code for something: *apple* for anthrax, that sort of thing."

"A substitution code?"

"Primitive, but effective if you can't sample a large message. And we can't." Johnny Bib handed over a page of names that the team had pulled off the computer. "Some of these are exotic."

"Are they real?"

"Oh yes."

Rubens looked at the list. The names were all in Latin, with explanations about the species next to them.

"There is one point of intersection," said Johnny Bib.

Rubens realized that the analyst was testing him, trying to see if he caught on. He glanced through the list; he didn't recognize any of the words.

But he would sooner go home than lose a game like this to the likes of Johnny Bib.

Come to think of it, he really ought to go home. What was it, two o'clock in the morning?

He glanced at his watch—past four. Good God.

"They're all from Asia." Rubens was guessing—he truly couldn't think of any link at all. But his tone was assured.

Johnny Bib's face fell. "Yes."

"Why, Johnny? Why? That's the question. Was he working on plants?"

Johnny Bib shook his head. "I don't know."

"So what do we do next?"

"I, uh, there were several zoological books in the library that Mr. Karr surveyed," said Johnny Bib. "We'd like to take a look at them."

"Yes, certainly," said Rubens. "We'll have to work with the local authorities to get them—the New York State Police, I think."

"Unless he has a garden."

"I don't know if he has a garden—"

Rubens' direct line to the Art Room rang, interrupting him.

"Yes?"

"They just contacted Dean," said Telach.

"I'm on my way." Rubens rose. "Figure it out, Johnny. That's your job. Whatever it takes."

Johnny Bib nodded.

"And, Johnny, please don't play those coy little guessing games with me anymore. They're so . . . obvious."

11

Lia watched Dean on the handheld as he went through the store, following the video that was being fed from the bookstore's security system. The view switched to one of the video flies she had planted as he started outside; she moved across the street and retrieved it, a good three-quarters of a block back when he was approached.

"They told him to go to the Tube," said Rockman.

"Can't even spring for a taxi?"

Lia turned the corner and saw Dean and the thug just going down the steps. Another man was following them, obviously a backup.

"They showed a gun," said Rockman.

"Why?" Lia asked.

"Not clear at the moment."

"Let's play along," said a new voice on the line. It was Rubens.

"Why are they flashing guns if it's a voluntary meeting?" asked Lia.

"Dean can take care of himself," said Rubens. "That's why he's there."

"I'm not worried," lied Lia. "I'm just wondering what they're up to."

"So are we."

"We're going to lose him down in the subway," warned Rockman. "Can you get closer?"

"Yeah."

Lia squeezed past the tourists, moving quickly but not running, for fear of drawing the attention of a second trailer or the bobby who was standing on the other side of the turnstiles. Lia fished for a ticket as she approached the stiles; she had to step aside to look in her purse for it.

"We're going to lose him," said Rockman. "Jump the stile."

"Yeah, right, asshole," she said, finally retrieving the ticket.

Dean's instincts prodded him to make a play for the gun as he reached the bottom of the escalator. He decided that would jeopardize the mission, telegraphing to the people who had made contact that he wasn't the meek scientific type. So instead he walked calmly ahead, turning to the left and passing a white-tiled wall that opened to the tracks.

Keys wasn't a meek scientific type. Granted, he was fifty now and hadn't had the benefit of twenty years in the Corps to keep his body in tune, but he could still probably take Dean two out of three in a game of hoops.

So would his assistant be a wimp?

There were about a half-dozen people on the platform. As Dean stopped near them he realized he was still wearing his sunglasses. He took them off and replaced them with the clear set he had in his pocket.

"Our train coming soon?" asked Dean.

The man who had met him on the street ignored the question. Another man walked up near him; obviously they were a team.

Dean rocked his shoulders gently as he waited for the train to appear. His body was still on Washington, D.C., time—it felt cranky, like it ought to be turning over in bed somewhere.

Next to Lia would be nice. He spotted her walking past an archway in the hall that ran between the lines. Dean stared at the space as she passed, pretending not to notice.

A train rumbled in on the opposite platform. The goon who had shown Dean his gun poked him in that direction but then reversed course as another train came in on their line.

"Where?" Charlie asked.

"Here," said the man, finally sliding into the train.

Lia waited—the men with Dean seemed unsure of which direction to take. Finally, they got on the line headed toward Leicester Square. She pushed in, elbowing a pensioner aside as the doors closed, then opened again. She saw Charlie and the two men at the next door. The man on the right of him moved backward—they were getting off. Lia tried to follow but found her way blocked by the old man she'd pushed aside, as well as a pair of women with a baby carriage. She threw her hand forward to grab the door, but it was too late; she pounded the door so hard and cursed so loudly that despite the roar of the train as it left the station, everyone in the car turned and stared at her.

"What, you never missed your stop before?" she barked, and they all looked away.

12

Both Desk Three ops were so far underground that they weren't shown on the locator map. Rubens stepped back from the consoles, considering Johnny Bib's earlier question regarding plants.

A substitution code?

Surely not. The fact that they were all Asian was surely significant.

Plant-eating bacteria, perhaps? Or a virus that lived within a plant host?

He might talk to one of the biology people on the off-chance.

Except there were none.

"Where the hell are our biology experts?" he snapped at Telach.

"It's a little early."

"You're here. I'm here. What happened to the CDC people? Lester promised around-the-clock coverage."

"They still haven't passed all the lie detector tests," said Telach. "The conference isn't for another two days."

"Get them here now," said Rubens.

"But procedure requires—"

"Get them down here. Blindfold them if you have to, but get them *now*."

Telach touched the phone on her belt and turned away to talk.

This was how things screwed up down the line, Rubens realized. A small slipup that escalated. Not even a slip—just slavish adherence to standard operating procedure.

He had invented Desk Three to avoid the tangle of standard operating procedure, and here he was, ambushed by it.

Did he have to attend to everything himself?

"They're on their way," Telach said. "I'm sorry. I messed up."

"Yes."

Telach frowned. Rubens frowned back.

On the right side of the room, Sandy Chafetz was keeping tabs on Tommy Karr, who had caught a military flight en route to Japan, where he would transfer to a civilian airliner for the final leg to Thailand.

"We're still trying to get resources lined up," Chafetz told him. "Satellite allocation is getting stingy because of the situation in Cambodia. There's been some skirmishing now with the Thai military, and they're asking for support. Meanwhile, Special Forces Command locked up the visual satellites for a campaign in Malaysia against the insurgency that starts in another eight hours."

Rubens folded his arms. They were dealing here with a situation of far greater import than a minor border conflict. It wasn't Telach's fault, of course—she was merely the messenger.

"Do we have leads on Kegan or Pound yet?" he asked.

"No. We have a hotel where Kegan stayed in the past. But nothing definitive. It may be that Pound went into the country under a different name. We're trying to run down some of the possibilities, eliminate them before Tommy gets there."

"Johnny Bib found a list of various plants that Kegan was checking on," said Rubens. "Could they be a link?"

"Plants?"

"Check on the disk contents. You'll see the pages."

Chafetz turned back to her computer console and brought up the information, looking at the Web pages that had been found. "Pretty basic stuff. You sure he didn't have a garden or something?"

"I'm not sure, actually," admitted Rubens.

"Did he work with plants?"

"Admittedly, it does appear a red herring," conceded Rubens. "But keep it in mind, in case there are any intersections."

Chafetz nodded. "I'd like to be able to call on some military assets if things get tight."

"Tight?"

"They're practically at war with Cambodia. We don't know where this is going."

"What exactly do we need?" he asked.

"I won't know until I know."

"Talk with USSOCOM," he said, referring to the military's Special Forces Command, which oversaw special operations personnel and missions.

"I have."

"And?"

"That's why I'm talking to you."

Rubens frowned. "Have Marie allocate assets from Space Command," he told her.

"I already have a platform," she said. "I'd like an RS-93, some—"

The RS-93 was a remote-controlled space plane that could provide stationary surveillance over any spot on the globe. But it was enormously expensive to operate and required a large support team. Even if he could justify it, it would never be ready in time. Besides, he might need it later on.

"No," said Rubens. "Not at this stage."

"The CIA has a Huron under contract. It's in-country already."

The Huron was a turboprop aircraft dressed to look like a civilian but equipped with high-resolution digital still and video cameras as well as a side-looking ground-imaging radar. Tasked to work with the Thai military in patrolling the border area, the Huron mostly sat around at Chiang Mai International Airport. But using it meant talking to Collins, the Deputy Director of Operations at the CIA.

She'd be only too happy to help, of course.

"Boss?" said Chafetz.

"All right. I will get the Huron," grumbled Rubens.

"And for fire support—"

"What fire are we supporting?"

"If we need it, how about F-47Cs? Or a Puff?"

The F-47s were robot fighter-bombers. Puff was the nickname for the A-230, an unmanned gunship that was like a downsized AC-130.

"Why are we going to need assets like that?" asked Rubens.

"Do you want me to be prepared or not? As it is I'm running him with just embassy backup."

"We don't need the CIA's help."

"Except for the Huron."

"Except for the Huron."

"There are a few Marines and a freelancer we can call on."

"Very well." Rubens sighed. "If we have the need, we can have the A-230."

"I have to have it flown in from Manila."

"Position it," Rubens told her. "Go ahead."

"Thanks, boss."

He feigned interest in something on one of the systems' tech screens. The systems technicians—two sat in the row immediately behind the runners—were jacks-of-all-trades who spent most of their time breaking into various computer systems during the operation and providing data to the runners.

"Something's up," said Rockman.

Rubens went down and joined her at Rockman's console, looking over her shoulder at the large flat panel displays. The one on his left showed the ops' positions against a grid map. Both were purple, indicating that they hadn't been updated in at least ten minutes. Suddenly one of the markers went green, appearing in the next grid. Rockman pressed his headset to his ear.

"It's Lia," said Rockman. "She lost him in the Tube."

Rubens bent over the screen, trying to correlate the grid to the city. The Thames ran along the bottom edge of the map; Lia had gone one stop to the left of where she had gotten on, emerging aboveground in Leicester Square. The radioactive isotope system they used to track their field ops was undetectable by monitoring devices, but it had its limits—roughly six meters belowground, a distance exceeded by the London Tube.

"Cursing up a storm," said Rockman.

"Just tell her to relax," said Rubens. He looked at Telach, whose bottom lip had curled in on itself.

"They did show a gun," said Rockman. "That's the part I don't get."

Rubens straightened, reminding himself of advice a yoga master had given him many years before: There were long moments in life when chaos threatened to intrude, and at those times one must tap energy from the kundalini, a point somewhere near the lower spine that the master believed was the center of Rubens' personal, transcendent soul.

Rubens held his breath for a moment, then exhaled silently, summoning and exuding calm for the rest of them.

"Here we go," said Rockman, pointing to the screen. Dean had surfaced at Bank near the Thames on the eastern side of the city. Rockman worked his keyboard as he updated Lia, trying to see if there were any obvious destinations in the area. Dean was still in the terminal above the subway level; Rockman told the op not to move yet, since it wasn't clear where he was going.

"I'm not getting any audio," said Rockman. He backed the grid map out one level, getting a larger view of the city. The subway and rail lines as well as the streets were marked. "Maybe he took his glasses off."

"They're definitely doing something in the station," said Telach. "There's another rail line here, Docklands. They may be taking that."

"Get Lia over there," said Rubens. "She can pick up the trail from there."

Telach glared at him as Rockman gave the order. It wasn't

that she disagreed—she would have said so—it was that the direction should have come from her.

Not a time to be temperamental.

The green diamond showing Dean began to move to the left of the screen, following the ghosted gray map of the Docklands light-rail line. Rockman brought up a screen showing the line's path, looking for a place where Lia might be able to get on. She was too far away to get to the rail line quickly enough to take the same train; she'd have to follow along as best she could.

"Get back on the Tube," Telach said, giving her directions to the line. "Call us when you get to Monument."

"Dean's audio's back," announced Rockman.

"Conference it," said Rubens.

The sound of machinery flooded through the speakers, then faded.

"I don't think so," said Dean, his voice muffled slightly.

"Oh yes," said someone with a light German accent. "You will or you will be killed."

There was a muffled sound, and then the audio died again.

13

Lia jumped from the train, striding quickly to the left up a short flight of stairs that led to the escalators. They were out of order, and the only way to the surface from here was the stairs or the elevators at the far end, which already had a thick queue from an earlier train. She pushed through the doors to the stairway, ordinarily used only in emergencies. Even Lia, who was in exceptional shape, started to lose her breath about midway up the seemingly endless spiral of metal stairs. Her legs started to stiffen, but she pushed on, angry not so much at choosing the steps or even at losing Dean but at being so out of whack about it. If she were just following someone else, even Tommy Karr, she'd be her normal calm, disgusted self. But Dean—she liked the son of a bitch and was truly worried about him.

Loved, maybe.

Lia emerged from an emergency access closet into the station vestibule, striding across the pedestrian tunnel just ahead of a surge from the nearby elevator.

"Well?" she asked Rockman. "Which way?"

"Get on the light-rail. You have to hurry. It's coming."

"Which direction?"

"Take a left."

"I mean, the train."

"East."

"How far? Moscow?"

"If I tell you to," snapped the runner uncharacteristically. Telach or Rubens must be on his back because they'd lost track of Dean.

A bobby eyed Lia as she went to one of the kiosks to buy her ticket. Lia forced herself to smile for the clerk at the window, then sauntered toward the train. The policeman's interest seemed to wane; obviously his interest had been purely prurient.

"Shuttle bus—he's going to London City Airport," said Rockman in her ear.

"Mmmm," said Lia, silently cursing. The city airport had connections with much of Europe.

"All right, go along. We'll work up the flight—there's something up with his com system. We think one of the thugs hit him with a shot of something, because he's not talking, just breathing."

"Mmmm," said Lia again.

Charlie should have gotten the stinking implant.

Sissy. This would show him.

As she turned toward the track area, two women in rather dowdy polyester pants cut her off.

"Excuse us," said one of the women, pulling out an ID card. "We'd like to speak with you a minute."

"Oh?" said Lia.

"What?" asked Rockman.

"Who exactly are you?" Lia asked.

"We'll discuss that with you," said the other woman.

"I think you ought to do that right now," said Lia.

"Scotland Yard," said the woman.

"Oh, bull," said Lia.

"MI-5," said Rockman.

The woman on the right took hold of Lia's purse.

"You're going to let go of that right now," said Lia.

"You're going to come with us," said the woman.

As they'd been speaking, Lia had shifted her right arm up against her shoulder, which allowed a small canister of pepper spray to slide down her sleeve. She moved her other hand on the bag as a distraction, and when the second woman came close to her, she pulled her right hand up and palmed the dispenser.

Then she raised her arm and nailed the evil sisters in the eyes.

With two strides, Lia reached a small group of tourists. By the time the two British agents reacted to the pepper spray—one screamed; the other cursed and grabbed for the radio in her purse—Lia was almost to the station doorway.

"You hit them with the pepper spray?" asked Rockman.

"Ground decision," said Lia. "Which way is the taxi stand?"

"Left," said Rockman.

Lia saw a policeman starting for her as she reached the door. She turned right on the street, took three steps, then broke into a run. Another entrance to the Tube was just ahead, but as she reached it a double-decker bus loomed on the left. Lia leaped onto it.

"Where am I?" she asked the Art Room.

"In the wrong place at the wrong time," answered Rubens. "Why did you gas the MI-5 people?"

"Because they were there?"

"I don't appreciate inappropriate sarcasm."

"I'm here to display initiative, right? Besides, why did they stop me?"

"It appears you were acting eccentrically and caught their attention," said Rubens. "In any event, they're our allies."

"Then you can apologize," said Lia. "In the meantime, get someone to tell me the best way to the airport."

14

The blow to the side of Dean's head had been meant to persuade him to cooperate, not to knock him out. But Dean decided that he might learn more about what was going on by playing possum and had collapsed against the side of the railcar. This generated an argument between his two abductors in what Dean thought must be German. The thug who had hit him propped him up and tried reviving him; Dean remained slumped over even when the car stopped. After a brief discussion, his abductors produced a bottle of whiskey and poured some onto a cloth, rubbing it in Dean's face. The sharp stench turned Dean's stomach, and he began mumbling, then decided the time was ripe to come to before they drenched his clothes.

"Cooperate," hissed one of the men as Dean shook himself. "You won't be harmed."

"Let go of me." Dean pushed his shoulders back and walked on his own. They took a turn and headed onto a moving walkway. At the edge of the terminal was a bus, just taking on passengers.

"Where are we going?" asked Dean.

"No questions."

Dean hadn't heard from the Art Room since his abduction. He reached up and adjusted his glasses, pressing the right side rim twice, which was supposed to send an alert back to the runner—basically asking for instructions. But nothing happened. Dean tried again.

"My glasses," said Dean out loud.

"What about your glasses?" said one of the thugs.

"They seem crooked or something."

"Get on the bus," said the man.

Dean climbed up, shuffling toward the back. He tried to think about the character he was supposed to be. How would a lifelong lab assistant act?

Geeky. Scared, or at least apprehensive.

Geeky was tough, but he could do apprehensive. He got on the bus, jerking his head back and forth, wondering how close Lia was.

While Lia made her way to the airport by taxi, Rockman worked on figuring out where Dean was heading. He located the booking by guessing that it had been made in a block of three seats; he tapped into the reservation systems at the airport and got an answer so quickly Lia suggested it was a ruse: a Lufthansa flight to Hamburg boarding in ten minutes.

"If it's a blind, at least I have a credit card and names," said Rockman. She could hear him pounding the keys, entering different databases at will—some with permission, some decidedly not. The men came up as Irish nationals with no known files at Interpol or anywhere else, but the credit card they used was from an active account in Austria, and Rockman began plumbing for information about it.

"They're going to Alitalia," said Telach.

Lia, stuck in traffic a good distance from the airport, fumed.

"Wait—here they go over to Lufthansa," said Rockman. "You owe me five bucks, Marie."

"Just tell me where to go and shut up," Lia snapped.

The taxi driver turned around.

"I wasn't talking to you," she told him. "I'm Joan of Arc. I hear voices. Now get me to the airport before you start hearing them, too."

Lia arrived at the terminal ten minutes after the plane

cleared the runway. She booked a seat on the next flight to Hamburg, which didn't leave for another two hours.

She started to walk away, then came up with another idea. Lia reached into her pocketbook and pulled out her satellite phone, pretending to use it so she wouldn't be grabbed as a bag lady.

"I can take a flight into Austria," she told Rockman. "It boards in ten minutes."

"Austria?"

"That's where they're going."

"How do you know that?"

"The credit card."

"I doubt it," said Rockman.

"They probably chose Austria because of the banking laws," explained Telach. "The records are held in strict confidence. The red tape's incredible."

"If I'm wrong, I can catch another plane from Vienna. It'll be faster than waiting around here."

"Not necessarily," said Rockman. "By the time you change planes and—"

"I got to go," she said, spotting a bobby at the other end of the waiting area.

The policeman walked off in the other direction without noticing her, but Lia realized there was no way in the world she could wait here for two hours. Taking a chance on Austria seemed to be a better idea than getting detained in London. So she went to the counter and bought a ticket, handing over a credit card. She was relieved to get it back— she had half-expected Rockman to kill the account on her so she couldn't take off.

15

Lia's run-in with MI-5 had several consequences. Not the least of these, as far as Rubens was concerned, was the need to personally brief the National Security Advisor first thing in the morning. Since it was already past 4.00 A.M., Rubens had to wait until George Hadash was awake.

Rubens gave him until 4:55, knowing from experience that Hadash's alarm was just about to ring.

"I need to go over the biology problem," said Rubens. Both men preferred euphemisms even though they were on a secure phone.

"William." His name in Hadash's mouth sounded halfway between a sigh and a lament. "You woke me up."

"Yes."

"This is the Kegan project?"

"Some very important tangential issues. I can tell you now or—"

"Meet me for breakfast at the White House," said Hadash. "Six-thirty."

Hadash's office was located two doors down from the Oval Office, with only the room used by the President's appointments secretary intervening. Not even this physical proximity caught the actual closeness of the President and Hadash, who as National Security Advisor ran the National Security

Council (NSC) and shaped much of the administration's foreign and military policy. The two men had worked together in various capacities for more than twenty years. Hadash's background was split between government and academia, while the President's had been exclusively political. Their personalities, however, couldn't be more different. Rubens saw Hadash as something of a nervous Nellie, while the President—a naval officer in his salad days—was the sort of man who would stand calmly on the bow of a destroyer as it dodged through a minefield at flank speed.

Hadash was on the phone when Rubens came in. A tray of coffee sat atop the papers on the National Security Advisor's desk; Hadash gestured for Rubens to sit, then poured him a cup of coffee as he continued the conversation.

To Rubens' surprise and consternation—much more the latter—the conversation appeared to be about the Internet biometrics proposal. Even worse, Hadash seemed to think it was a good idea.

"Well, thank you, Senator, I appreciate hearing from you," said Hadash finally. "Yes, we'll speak later on in the week."

Hadash hung up the phone, then rose and refilled Rubens' cup.

"So what went wrong?" asked Hadash. The blunt greeting was completely in keeping with his usual style; he would play the distracted host one second and the impatient taskmaster the next.

"Nothing," said Rubens. "But the situation appears considerably more complicated than we first believed."

The opening statement was necessary to lay the background for the real purpose of his appearance—damage control for Lia's run-in with MI-5. The overall context must be firmly established before the diplomatic incident was trotted onto the stage and shown to be the ridiculous diversion it was.

"How complicated?" asked Hadash. He sat down in his seat, his brow beginning to knit.

"Well, they've kidnapped our operative for one thing," said Rubens. "Mr. Dean."

"Kidnapped?"

"Dean is fine. I was told on the way over that he's on a flight to Vienna from Hamburg. We've lost direct contact with him, but we have one of our best people on his tail. After some difficulties."

That was meant as a cue for Hadash's sympathies, but the National Security Advisor didn't take the bait.

"Vienna? I thought you connected this to a Polish arms dealer."

Radoslaw Dlugsko operated throughout the world, and there was no reason he couldn't be in Austria. But pointing that out would do nothing to help Rubens ultimately—and besides, the fact was Vienna didn't exactly bolster the theory that Dlugsko or UKD was involved. In truth, there was much, much work to be done.

"We're still gathering information," said Rubens mildly.

"The programs that Kegan was working on—were they compromised?" asked Hadash.

"He hasn't worked on germ warfare programs for years," said Rubens. "But the FBI is reviewing what sort of exposure there is."

"Why was he contacted?"

"We're still working on it. There's nothing new since yesterday," conceded Rubens. "His lab work over the last few years has mostly dealt with recombinant DNA. There's a project to breed a bacteria that will eat PCBs and other pollutants. It's possible that this is about that."

Hadash made a face. Rubens himself did not believe that, but throwing out different possibilities emphasized the difficulty of the situation. Thus when the problem was solved, those who had solved it would receive sufficient credit.

It would also put problems into the proper perspective.

"We've been concentrating on finding him and, more important, tracking down the people who were trying to contact him," said Rubens.

"And you have nothing new?"

"Hints, but nothing solid."

Hadash took a long gulp of his coffee. "How serious is the threat?"

"Potentially, extremely serious," said Rubens.

"Potentially?"

"That's the best I can say."

"You've tracked the E-mails back?"

Rubens realized where the NSC head was going and sank back in the chair.

"The E-mail messages you recovered?" added Hadash.

"Yes."

"You tracked them?"

"As far as we could, yes."

Rubens could offer nothing else. Hadash began talking about the proposal that would provide biometric IDs as part of every Internet activity.

"This makes a good case—an almost airtight case," said Hadash. "If the biometric ID was in place, you would know."

"It could easily have been spoofed."

"Not if it's properly constructed. At a minimum you would have a starting point to work from."

"We have starting points now."

"Not as extensive as Internet DNA," said Hadash.

Internet DNA. Good God, what a sound bite.

"I don't believe it's a good idea," said Rubens. "And this case certainly isn't an argument in its favor."

"Your task force is recommending it be studied."

"It's not my task force," said Rubens quickly. "It's Homeland Security. Sandra Marshall's. And I've already gone on record as recusing the agency from the recommendation."

"Recusing or opposing?"

A tactical error, Rubens thought—he had been far too cautious. He should have opposed.

Unless Hadash was pushing it. Which he seemed to be.

"I don't believe the proposal is in anyone's best interests," said Rubens. "Not the government's, not the NSA's, and certainly not our citizens'."

Hadash frowned. Rubens put the conversation back to its original track.

"Not to change the subject, but British intelligence was apparently a little too aggressive in tracking arrivals at the conference," said Rubens.

"How so?"

"They attempted to detain one of my agents while she was following Mr. Dean's kidnappers. They were rather adamant about it, and I'm afraid there was an incident."

"What did she do?" asked Hadash.

The remark tipped Rubens off that Hadash had already been informed, undoubtedly by the State Department, which would have given him the British version.

"She responded in kind," Hadash told him.

"Spraying them with pepper gas was responding in kind?"

"Given the circumstances."

"The British are upset."

Rubens reached into his suit jacket pocket and took out a printout containing the text of a British protest. "They're to deliver this protest later today."

"This wouldn't have been poached from the British embassy phone lines, would it?" asked Hadash.

"Of course not. The Russians intercepted it and we stole it from them."

Hadash shook his head. "Why were the British following her?"

"Apparently they were surprised to find Lia in London. We believe it was merely a coincidence. The MI-5 agents happened to be in the station, trailing someone else. They may have thought she was interfering with their project."

"Quite a coincidence."

Rubens didn't trust coincidences, either, but this one did appear to be just that.

"I hope you've given this enough priority," said Hadash.

"Absolutely."

Rubens rose to go. Hadash stopped him.

"William, the Internet DNA thing. You should know the President has expressed interest."

"It's absurd," said Rubens. "To waste money on a study that will tell you it's technically unfeasible and politically suicidal?"

The corners of Hadash's mouth flickered, but he said nothing.

16

Karr bounded off the plane into the airport, pushing through the knots of medical and sex tourists whose pace slowed as they realized their moment of decision or indiscretion was finally near. A potbellied American in a perfectly tailored silk suit stood at the right of the funneling line; Karr made a beeline for him, pointing to him as he came close.

"Deavor, right?" said Karr.

The man nodded. He was a military advisor to the ambassador, tasked to meet Karr and take him into the city. Karr pumped the man's limp hand, then reached over and grabbed the hand of an associate who'd been trying to act nonchalant in the background. There were two other men nearby, all part of the security detail and undoubtedly thinking they were passing incognito in the mix. Karr didn't bother saying hello to them, as it would break the unwritten rules of etiquette— never tell your host how incompetent he was.

They paid the briefest of courtesy calls to the back room of the Thai customs agency, then went to a pair of waiting cars. A light rain was falling, casting the city in a gray shroud.

"So you're with the CDC," said Deavor, leaning over the front seat.

"I'm kind of a consultant for them," said Karr.

"You're a doctor?"

"Why? You got a broken leg?"

"I have this numbness in my pinkie every so often."

"You smoke?" asked Karr.

"What's that got to do with anything?"

"If you don't want my advice, don't ask for it," said Karr.

"That's caused by smoking?"

"Not necessarily. You try sex?"

"Now I know you're putting me on."

Karr laughed at him. "You could have a screwed-up disk, or just the muscles pulling it are out of whack. Massage'll loosen it up. Or sex. Those don't work, see a chiropractor."

Deavor looked at him, trying to figure out if he was on the level or not.

"Thanks, Doc," he said finally.

"Don't mention it."

The embassy put Karr up in a house occasionally used by Marines assigned to the security detail. Karr knew it would be bugged, but he was surprised to find not only American and Thai devices, but a Chinese pair as well—an interesting fact that Rubens would no doubt relish passing along as a less than subtle dig against the CIA, which would have certified the lodgings as clean.

The sheer array of bugs was impressive, but none presented a real problem; he disabled them all, then fired up his handheld and retrieved the latest dossier prepared by Desk Three.

The NSA had found an old credit card account, since closed, that Kegan had used on a visit to Bangkok about a year before. They had also been able to connect Pound, the lab assistant, to a $300 cash withdrawal from an ATM in the arrival hall of Terminal 1 at Don Muang Airport two weeks ago; he'd used his mother's account. But so far they hadn't been able to locate any records indicating what he had done after that. His mother, in a nursing home in Kentucky, didn't know where he was. An Alzheimer's patient, she didn't really know where she was.

One of the E-mails Pound had sent to Kegan had been

posted from a kiosk in Bangkok a few blocks from the hotel Kegan had stayed at. The other had been tracked to a small Thai military unit on the border with Myanmar.

A wild-goose chase, but one with promise.

Karr had never been in Thailand until today. Had he been asked what he expected, he probably would have drawn a verbal picture of small huts and rickshas in crowded, muddy streets. The streets here were crowded and there were rickshas—here called *samlors*. But there were also a variety of motorbikes, slightly larger motorcycles (though still small by American standards), *tuk-tuks* (three-wheeled motorcycles with roofs that had no real counterpart in the West), cars, truck-buses (pickups with double-deck standing-room-only spots in the rear), ordinary buses, and a range of delivery vehicles and trucks. There was also an elevated rail system called Skytrain and any number of ferries and boats plowing through the waterways that crisscrossed the city.

Karr stared at the city through the front seat of his car, rented with a driver by the Art Room through a fictitious account. Luc Dai, the driver, was a former freelance newspaper writer who'd found it much more lucrative to rent out his car than his typewriter. A Vietnamese national who'd spent considerable time in America, Luc Dai was exactly the sort of person who'd be "rented" by various intelligence agencies, though if he was working for any, the Art Room hadn't told Karr.

The light rain that had greeted him at the airport was gone. They threaded through the congested streets and found the Bangkok Star Imperial Hotel, which was among the most expensive in the city. Karr told the driver he'd be inside for a while, then hopped out as a uniformed doorman reached for the door.

The hotel had some claim to its fame, or at least its high cost. Outrageously ornate, its ceiling glowed with a thick layer of gold leaf, showing off what was said to be up to a million dollars' worth of precious stones and jewels encrusted in a design that imitated the visible constellations. Below the stars an elaborately designed handwoven rug depicted the earth as a mythic kingdom of gods and dragons. The carpet was not merely spotless but also seemed to have been woven only the day before. The hotel desk sat beyond several groupings of lushly upholstered chairs, its massive beak like the hull of a boat. The wooden trim and accents were inlaid and highly polished.

Karr walked to the young man at the far end of the desk and in English asked for "my good friend Mr. Bai." The man bowed his head, then led the way through a paneled hallway to a room that looked decidedly more utilitarian than the lobby; its whitewashed walls provided the backdrop for three banks of nine-inch television sets offering a uniformed guard with a view of the hotel environs as well as the lobby, elevator, and upstairs hallway. The young man muttered a hello—it was definitely English—to the guard, then knocked at a metal door at the far end. A few words flew back and forth in Thai.

"Mr. Bai has much work," said the man when he returned.

"Great," said Karr. He remained planted in place.

The man frowned and returned to the door. More Thai flew around until finally the door opened and a short man in a brown silk suit emerged to shake Karr's hand as if he were an old friend.

"Bai," whispered Sandy Chafetz, the runner in the Art Room. They'd tapped into the hotel's security system; she could see everything that was happening.

"A friend in D.C. sent me," said Karr.

"Oh, very good," said Bai, ushering Karr inside as if he'd been expecting him half the day.

Old enough to be Karr's father, Mr. Bai had escaped from Burma as a young man, then joined the Thai Army. As an officer he'd had some dealings with the American military in the seventies and eighties, and he still had occasional contact with the embassy, though mostly now as an expediter for the hotel. He accepted Karr's hints without question or elaboration, ordering tea and nearly insisting that Karr have something stronger. But for all his jovial hospitality, Mr. Bai showed no sign of recognizing Kegan or Pound when Karr showed him the photos.

"They're not among our guests, are they?" asked Mr. Bai.

"You tell me."

Mr. Bai studied the photos again, then shrugged. "If they were guests they did nothing to attract attention."

"You think you can look up some names in your computer?" Karr asked.

Desk Three had already run the same check—Karr was asking not only to see how cooperative Bai might be but also to emphasize how serious he was about finding the men.

Mr. Bai's expression grew grave. "The privacy of our guests is extremely important."

"Oh, I'm sure of that," said Karr.

He smiled at the hotel security chief, who soon enough reached for the keyboard of his computer. The names were printed at the bottoms of the photos.

"No," said Mr. Bai.

"How about recently?"

"How recent?"

Karr shrugged. "Ever, I guess," he said offhandedly.

Bai frowned.

"Three years?" offered Karr.

"Two is all I can manage."

"Go for it." He'd been prepared to settle for one.

Mr. Bai hesitated, then clacked a few more keys. "Doesn't look like it."

"Ah well, life's like that, you know?" Karr got up, sliding a business card on the desk. It listed the CDC as his employer, giving a local number that would be intercepted by the Art Room and rerouted to Karr's sat phone's voice mail. "If something rings a bell, you can get me through the embassy."

Bai smiled and, once more the hospitable host, led him back to the lobby.

"So are those real jewels or what?" Karr asked as he shambled past the reservations desk.

"What are you talking about?" asked Chafetz.

"The ceiling," he told her.

"I haven't a clue," she said. "Why are you talking to yourself? Aren't you afraid people will stare at you?"

"Nah. They see big blond crazy Americans all the time." Karr smiled at a pair of elderly European women who were, in fact, staring at him. "Part of the image, Sandy. I'm supposed to be a lovable, nutty bear."

"Well, you have the role down well."

"Except that I'm smarter than the average bear, right?"

"You said that; I didn't."

"Yuk, yuk." Karr twisted around. He'd managed to pick out all of the security people and was confident that no one else inside was watching him. "So does Bai know something or what?"

"He's not using the phone or the computer. We'll activate the fly you left once you're out of the building."

"He definitely recognized the picture of Pound. I don't know about Kegan."

"All right. We have the shops Kegan went to the last time he was here. They're up in Chinatown. Why don't you head over and see if anything shakes out? Expect to be followed," the runner added.

"Really? Bai's people?"

"Not sure. Somebody's watching you near the entrance. Their security camera doesn't have a good view."

Outside in the car, Karr took out his handheld computer and consulted his map of Bangkok.

"We need to get down by the university," he told the driver. It was a good distance from Karr's actual destination.

A few blocks later, Karr noticed that the driver was paying an inordinate amount of attention to his mirror.

"Problem?" Karr asked.

"We're being followed."

"Really? How 'bout that."

Karr consulted his map and found a bridge about a mile from the area he'd just given the driver. As he did, the driver took a turn up a main street, entering a thick flow of bicycles.

The street narrowed for a small bridge ahead, and the bikes and cars mixed with a flood of pedestrians coming in from the side.

"Wait a bit at the university, then drive around and end up at the bridge we just went over," Karr said, slipping his handheld back in his pocket. "It'll be a while."

"What's going on?"

"Just doing some sightseeing," he said, cracking open the door.

The NSA agent barely missed bashing two women on precariously balanced bikes. His pursuers were some distance back in the throng, and while they could see what he was doing, there was no way for them to follow without making it obvious that they were doing so. He slid against the traffic flow, reached the side of the bridge, and bolted over the railing, swinging his legs around and hooking into the gridwork. His bulky frame made for an awkward fit through the closely placed girders, but he managed it anyway, dropping near the base at an embankment on the eastern side behind the car following him.

A warren of small buildings began where the bridge ended, and Karr quickly trotted into a back alley, climbing up onto a roof and looking back toward the bridge. His pursuers were stuck in the clog and if they wanted to follow him, would have to opt for the only decision that made sense, sticking on the car.

"Good work," said Chafetz. "We'll see if we can pull some IDs on them."

"Bai's people?"

"Not clear. He didn't talk to them. We think one was watching in the lobby when you came in. We'll get the car registration, then track it down. They're sticking on your rental, so we'll see sooner or later. You worry about yourself."

"What? Me worry?"

Karr cut through another alley and then back in the opposite direction, finally finding a main street. Within a few minutes he found an empty pedicab. He had himself cycled twenty blocks to an area of small shops nestled at the foot of a mountain of apartments just on the outskirts of Bangkok's Chinatown. He got out in front of a twenty-story high-rise, pulling a piece of paper out as if consulting the address. Karr walked down the block as if checking to see where he was, not only waiting for the driver to leave but also checking to make sure he hadn't been followed. When he was reasonably sure he was clear, he found a basement stairway and descended a few steps, scanning his body to make sure he hadn't inadvertently picked up a tracking device. As he dialed up the program on the handheld, a quartet of eyes appeared above.

"Hello," said Karr as the faces disappeared.

He adjusted the program and did the sweep—he was clean—then hunted around his pants pockets for the roll of Life Savers he'd picked up at the airport back in the States.

"Hello," he repeated as the eyes emerged on the other side of the steps. They were accompanied this time by a pair of giggles, and when Karr rose he saw two children, five or six years old, studying him as a curiosity. He reached out with the candy, but the two girls didn't immediately realize what it was and took a step backward. Tommy started to crouch, trying to make himself less threatening, but as he did a piercing wail broke through the hum of the surrounding buildings and nearby traffic. The children's minder—probably their grandmother—appeared from around the corner, yelling as if Karr were the devil himself. The kids froze, suddenly petrified, though it would be hard to say whether they were scared of him or their keeper.

"Just some candy," said Karr in English, smiling at the old woman, who was now lecturing him indecipherably. He laughed, put the roll of Life Savers on the ground, and went back to the street.

"Masher," whispered Chafetz in his ear.

"I was only giving them candy."

"That's what they all say."

"You should have told me what to say in Thai."

"You would have been arrested."

"What was the old woman saying?" he asked his runner.

"Among other things, she has a very tasty recipe for your liver." Chafetz's voice changed. "You're still five blocks away."

"Just making sure I'm not being followed," Karr told her. "Anything on Mr. Bai or my shadows?"

"Nothing new on Bai. The people following the car aren't military and they're definitely not TAT," she added, referring to the special unit of Thai tourist police.

Karr walked a block and a half, then turned toward his destination, a row of small shops near Nakorn Kasem, the "Thieves' Market" a few blocks outside of Chinatown's central core. His first stop was a house shop that sold a variety of statues. Karr looked around for a minute or so, then showed the photos to the short woman who had been watching him from near the counter. The woman wanted nothing to do with the pictures and the agent didn't press it, smiling at her and leaving a twenty-dollar bill near the register before walking out. He moved down and across the street to a tailor shop.

"Maybe I'll get a suit of clothes and charge it to the agency," he told Chafetz as he crossed.

"I heard that," said Telach.

"Hey, mama, how's it hanging?"

"Your mix of metaphors boggles the mind," said the Art Room supervisor.

"You know, Marie, you sound more and more like Rubens every day," he said.

The tailor also did not recognize Kegan from the picture. Karr laid a bill on the counter, slipping a fly down as well. If he kept a file on his customers—some tailors did—he didn't consult it after Karr left.

Two stops later, he came to a restaurant. This time Karr showed cash up front, supplementing it with a few sentences of Thai from the Art Room translator. This got him immediately to the manager, who studied the photos Karr fanned out on the table nearly as intently as the hundred-dollar bill below them.

"Two days, three," said the manager, who spoke English.

Karr nodded as if he'd expected this. "Both men?"

"Just this one," said the manager, pointing to Kegan.

"He used a phony credit card," said Karr matter-of-factly. He reached into his pocket for supplemental funding. "We'd like to make sure you get paid. But we have to find him to do that."

Concern was now evident on the manager's face, but the financial incentive did not produce a receipt or a better memory. But this was enough for a start: the Art Room would pull the restaurant's records from the local credit card service— no subpoena was required to tap into the foreign processing unit—and grab a list of credit card numbers. They could then start examining those accounts to see if they could backtrack to Kegan.

Assuming, of course, that Kegan had really used a credit card.

Karr left another hundred on the table and started to leave.

Then he got a better idea.

"Mind if I have some lunch?" he asked.

"You're running behind," said Chafetz.

"I wasn't talking to you," he said, smiling at the thoroughly confused manager as he pulled out a chair.

17

Dean's years in the Marine Corps had convinced him that patience was the most important innate skill a sniper could have. A steady hand, good eyes, perseverance, guts, instinctual knowledge of the way people behaved—Dean didn't know a sniper who made it through training without these qualities. But the real diamond, the most difficult gem to find in the deep mine of human consciousness, was the ability to wait. You couldn't just sit—you had to sit with your eyes and ears and nose open. You sat ready, and you sat like that for hours and hours and days and days.

It had been a long time since Dean was in the Marine Corps—four or five lifetimes, it seemed. But he was still very patient, or could be when the circumstance required it. As it did now.

They had landed in Hamburg, taken a taxi to a house where he'd been fed and blindfolded, then driven around for a while longer before arriving back at the airport, where they'd boarded a flight apparently for Austria. Dean assumed the elaborate arrangements were meant to give his escorts a chance to see if they were being followed, but it was also possible they were trying to skimp on plane fare—the thugs hadn't bothered to enlighten him.

The airplane they were flying in was an Airbus A320, a two-engined commercial airliner that in this case accommodated 150 passengers, though only three-fourths of the seats on the flight were filled. The CFM International turbofans had a throaty hum that reminded Dean of the sound a dentist's drool sucker made as it pulled saliva from a mouth during drilling—assuming that sound was amplified a hundred times.

Most of the people on the plane were businessmen and -women, though there was a mix of students and a few tourists as well. Dean didn't recognize any of the accents as American, nor did he spot anyone whose face looked familiar and who might be part of a trail team.

After they landed, the men prodded Dean to move quickly through the terminal; one handed him a passport that claimed he was Canadian. Dean adjusted his glasses, clicking the alert on, though by now he realized the com device had been broken. He considered taking out his sunglasses as they came outside, but the afternoon sky was overcast and threatening to rain and he thought it would be too suspicious. The Art Room would be tracking him and Lia would be behind him somewhere; it was best to just be patient and see how it played out.

It always came down to patience.

A blue Mercedes met them outside the terminal. As the driver reached over to open the door, Dean caught a glimpse of a holster inside his jacket. Dean slid in between his two minders. They spoke in German to the driver, whose tone sounded somewhat dismissive, though Dean had no way of knowing precisely what they were all talking about.

Five miles from the airport, the Mercedes pulled over. Another car, this one a station wagon, stopped behind them.

"Out," said the man on Dean's left as the other one opened the door.

"What's going on?" asked Dean.

"We want to search you."

"In the middle of the road?"

"Just get out," said the man, adding something in German before pushing him toward the door.

Two men from the other car patted him down, looking for a weapon. When the search was over, one of the men went back to the station wagon and returned with a small suitcase.

He opened the case, producing what looked like a long, thin microphone. After adjusting a knob on a control panel in the suitcase, he began running the wand over Dean's body, looking for a transmitter.

The NSA techies had assured Dean that the com system couldn't be detected. Its transmission circuits shut off in the presence of magnetic fields produced by devices such as the one that was being used now to scan him, and the extremely low current used in the device mimicked the current inherent in a human body. But all the assurances in the world didn't make Dean's stomach rest any easier as he waited for the men to finish.

"Very good," said the man back by the suitcase.

Dean waited as they packed up the equipment. One of the two men who had met him in London went and spoke to a man in the front seat of the station wagon. He nodded and took an envelope before going back to the Mercedes. Dean began to follow, but the man who had wanded him put out his hand.

"Professor, no. Your ride is on its way."

"I'm not a professor," said Dean. "I work in a lab."

The man smiled but otherwise remained silent. A few minutes later, a second Mercedes drove up. A short man in khaki pants and a gray T-shirt got out and walked over, holding a folder in his hand. He spoke English with an accent that sounded German to Dean.

"You're not Dr. Kegan," said the man.

"Dr. Kegan is busy."

"Where?"

"I work for him, not the other way around," said Dean.

"Where?"

"Drumund University, Hudson Valley Division, primarily," said Dean. That was the lab Lia had visited; Dean's name was now listed on the security files as that of a visiting fellow with all access privileges. "Actually I'm paid by him directly under one of his grants; I'm not exactly sure which."

The man frowned and opened his folder. "The University of Albany?"

"What about it?"

"The name means nothing?"

"Of course it does. I did my undergrad work there. I lived in Indian Quad."

"A state school."

Dean shrugged. "So? Some of us weren't born rich."

"Your grades were not impressive."

"I didn't realize I was being interviewed for a job," said Dean.

The man smirked and closed the file. "*E. coli* one-three-five-six-E."

Dean stared at the man. It was obviously some sort of test, but what?

He touched his glasses, trying to make it look like a nervous tic—eminently believable.

Now he wished he had the sunglasses on. But maybe they wouldn't have worked, either.

"One-three-five-six-E."

"I'm not really sure I know what you're getting at," said Dean. "There are many strands of *E. coli*. Are we talking about protein synthesis or hamburgers?"

The man frowned, but something in the answer satisfied him, for he signaled to the other men. "I'm sorry, but we're going to have to blindfold you. It's a precaution. You won't be harmed."

"I'd like to get something to eat," said Dean.

"You will be treated well once you arrive at your destination."

"Let me take my glasses off first."

"Go right ahead."

One of the men slipped a hood over Dean's head, holding the fabric gently to keep it from hurting his ears. Dean let himself be led to the car—he guessed from the distance that it was the Mercedes—and sat back as the driver got in and pulled away. An opera began to play gently in the background as they drove. Dean cleared his mind, trying to count and keep track of the time.

He estimated that they drove for fifteen minutes. As he

got out of the car, he heard the sound of a helicopter approaching, then felt the wind whipped up from its rotors as it landed nearby.

"Keep the hood on, please," said the driver. "And duck your head."

Dean hunched over, trying to feel his way into the helicopter as the door was opened for him. The driver of the Mercedes came around the other side once Dean was in and helped him fasten his seat belt.

"Where are we going?" said Dean, shouting over the rush of the motor as the aircraft took over.

He asked twice more before realizing that he was alone in the back of the aircraft.

Lia had picked him up at the airport, hoping to find a way to bump into him and attach a fly so the Art Room could monitor what was going on. But they'd moved through too quickly, and she'd had to follow in her car. She drove past them after they pulled off; before she could backtrack she heard a helicopter in the distance.

"This is moving too fast," she told Rockman. "We have to pull him out."

"Relax."

"He doesn't have any backup," said Lia. "If they start asking him questions, they'll know he's a phony."

"Charlie can handle himself. Relax."

"You're out of your mind if you think they're not dangerous." Lia gunned the car back toward the spot where they had pulled off.

"These are just scientific types," said Telach, coming on the line. "Dean's resourceful. That's why he's there."

"Damn easy for you to say," said Lia.

The Mercedes pulled back onto the highway as she approached. There was another car—and the helicopter, its rotors spinning in the field to the left.

"Where is he?" demanded Lia, slowing down.

"Just take it easy, Lia," said Rockman. "We're going to trail him."

"The car or the helicopter?"

The helicopter whipped upward. Lia slapped her hand on the wheel.

"You need to turn around," said Rockman.

"Damn it."

"Relax, Lia."

"Tell me that one more time and I'm going to shove my fist down your throat."

Dean remained motionless in the seat after they landed, not quite sure what he was supposed to do next. Finally the door on the right side opened and he was helped from the aircraft. He smelled perfume and realized that he was being guided by a woman, though she remained silent. There was at least one other person with her, another woman, he thought, though she didn't come near enough for him to tell.

Inside another car—this was a much smaller vehicle than the others—Dean asked where he was.

"You are in Austria," said a woman. "We'll be at the castle soon."

"Castle?"

But the woman said nothing else. Dean began counting to himself, more because he had nothing better to do than as part of any tangible plan to figure out where he was. After about ten minutes, the car began driving up a steep hill, leveled off, and then began climbing again, this time in a circle. He heard the sound of gravel popping between the tires, and then the car stopped.

"We are here, Professor," said the woman as the door opened.

"Actually, I'm not a professor," said Dean. "I really don't like to teach."

"No?"

"Some people just don't like it."

The woman helped him from the car, then removed the hood. The woman smelled nice, but her face could have stopped a tank.

"This way," she said, gesturing toward a stone arch before them.

A concrete walkway began at the arch and led around a wall made of yellow-brown bricks. As he approached the wall, Dean looked up and saw a castle looming at his left, perched at the top of a considerable slope that seemed to be made of sheer rock. There were steps on the other side of the wall made of thick slabs of limestone, the centers worn down by millions of soles sliding along their surface.

Dean stayed a step behind the woman, who seemed nonchalant in her attitude toward him; she wore jeans and a knit top over a blouse. It was possible she was armed, but Dean thought that he would have had no trouble overcoming her if he had to. He didn't spot any obvious cameras or other devices, though he knew from his short stint with Deep Black that this was no guarantee of anything.

"Are you tired already?" the woman asked. He had fallen several steps behind.

"A little," Dean lied. "Long flight of steps."

She smiled at him and, if anything, started walking faster.

"How old is the castle?" he asked.

"Oh, not as old as it looks," she answered.

"My name's Charlie."

"Yes, I know who you are."

"And who are you?"

"Just a friend."

At the third landing, there was a large metal door off to the side. The woman went to it and opened it, swinging it back easily, though to Dean it looked ponderous.

"Good-bye, Dr. Dean," she said, gesturing for him to enter.

"You're not coming?"

"No. Good-bye now."

Dean stepped into the narrow, dark passageway. The rock walls seemed sheer and solid; they were lit by a string of dim red lights about knee-high bolted to the stone and connected by a run of wire. Dean ran his hand along the stone as he walked. It seemed too smooth to have been cut by hand, and he remembered the woman's comment that the castle itself was not as old as it looked. He came to a corner and turned; a large freight elevator gaped at him. He walked to it and got in. Before he could touch the control panel, the doors closed and it began to move upward.

"Going up," said Dean.

By rights, it should be Keys being transported. Would he have been nervous?

No, because he'd undoubtedly have a better idea what was going on. Maybe he had a deal with these people.

A deal to do what?

Supply the bastards with a germ that could kill millions?

That wasn't Keys, thought Dean. He wasn't a traitor.

Then again, Dean didn't think he was a killer, either.

Dean let his arms drop to his sides, relaxing his body. He'd bluffed his way past the E. coli question, but it was unlikely he'd get off that easy again.

Kegan had done some work with E. coli, but the answer Dean had supplied had come not from the briefing but a high school biology class about a billion years before. Dean smiled at the memory of his old teacher, Wayne Guernsey—Guernsey, like the cow. Rumor had it that you could judge the difficulty of the lab by how far his thick oily hair stood out from the sides of his head.

The door opened onto a dimly lit corridor. Dean took a breath of the dank air as he stepped out of the elevator onto a stone floor. Two men with Steyr Para 9 mm submachine guns stood across from him, their faces covered by hoods. Dean stepped forward and someone stopped him from behind, tugging gently for him to stand in place. He was searched for a weapon once again, quickly and efficiently. The hands then took hold of his shoulders—he guessed he was being held by a woman, though he had only the lightness of the touch to go by—and nudged him two steps forward, then held firm. A light flashed in his face as the entire space was lit by powerful floodlights. Blinded, Dean put up his hands, then remembered the sunglasses. He gestured with his thumb that he was going to take them out; when no one reacted, he did so. The lights were so powerful that he had to keep his hands near his eyes, continuing to shield them.

"Who are you?" asked a voice that sounded as if it were generated by a machine.

"My name is Dean. I work for Dr. Kegan as an assistant. He asked me to come to the conference for him."

"Why are you here?"

"I was brought here."

"Tell me about Baltic flu," said the voice.

"A bluff," said a voice in his head. "Kegan has never worked on flu viruses."

The Art Room—*finally*.

Dean shrugged. "Flu viruses aren't my thing."

"What variety of smallpox did Dr. Kegan work with?"

"Aralsk," said the voice. "It's named after a city in the old Soviet Union where there was an outbreak."

Dean sensed that there was more to the question than that. Someone who was trying to bluff his way in—as he was—would be expected to have detailed knowledge; he'd just memorize everything he could. An intelligent interviewer—and someone with a setup like this had to be intelligent—would be looking more at his behavior than his answers.

"Dr. Kegan doesn't work outside the law, if that's what you're getting at," said Dean.

The voice laughed. "Smallpox," it repeated.

"Unpublished paper. Two of them," the expert in the Art Room told him. "Nineteen-ninety-one and nineteen-ninety-three."

"I haven't been with Dr. Kegan that long," said Dean. He took a step forward. "Truth is, he kind of adopted me as a project. He's helping supervise my dissertation. It's written."

"You're rather old to be working on your Ph.D."

"I'm not that smart," said Dean.

The lights shut off abruptly. Dean wanted to keep the glasses on, sensing that the interview was far from over, but he knew that would give him away. He folded them up slowly;

his eyes had trouble adjusting to the darkness. The room was filled with shadows.

"What's your dissertation on?"

Dean had memorized the dissertation topic, but he decided again that his behavior was what was in question. He was supposed to be a technical person—more drudge than scientist. He'd gotten to work with Kegan because he was useful, not a genius.

"It demonstrates the propagation of bacteria in mouse tissue," said Dean. "It's not particularly advanced."

"No?"

"Frankly, Dr. Kegan is interested in the techniques I used to culture the cells. They're not in the paper because he said we should keep that proprietary."

"We?"

"I owe him a great deal."

"And how did you culture them?"

"Well, it wasn't really that tricky." Dean smiled. "But if it's something that's worth money . . ."

"Do you like money, Dr. Dean?"

"I don't refuse it. By the way, I'm not a doctor." He smiled. "Though everybody I meet seems to think I am."

A man in a red ghoul's mask stepped from the shadows at the left. He was dressed in black, and for a moment he looked as if he were a real ghoul, emerging from the depths of hell. Dean gathered that was the idea.

"Where is Kegan?" asked the man.

"He sent me to the conference in his place. He said something had come up. I assume he's back in the States working."

"Where's the antidote?"

"First of all, I want to know exactly where I am," said Dean.

"You have the mistaken impression that you have some influence on what happens next."

"I'll gladly admit I'm confused."

"Your employer owes us the antidote. He has twenty-four hours. *You* have twenty-four hours. Tell him that."

"Then what happens?"

The lights flooded on again. Before Dean could repeat his question, a dart shot into his back. His neck felt paralyzed for a second; his mind seemed to leave his body, and he saw himself falling to the floor. Then the lights slammed off and he lost consciousness completely.

18

Fortified by a serious lunch—and still lacking any real information about Kegan's or Pounds' whereabouts—Karr decided the next order of business was to find out about the men who'd trailed him in the car earlier. He circled back to the spot where he'd told the driver to meet him, discovering that the goons had split up, with one now on a motorbike. Obviously they were quick learners.

"Hey," said Karr, jumping into the car's front seat.

"You're back," said Luc Dai.

"Told you. Drive ahead."

"Then?"

"Find a tourist trap where I'm likely to be ripped off," Karr said.

The driver twisted his head. Karr smiled at him, then reached down and pulled up his pants leg. He loosened the strap that held the gun there, sliding in the handheld behind it. Modesty prevented slipping the computer down his pants to his thigh, where the second of the three guns he carried was secreted.

"You want to be robbed?" asked the driver.

"Just mugged. Doesn't everyone?"

They'd gone about a half-mile when Karr spotted a broad avenue that would do perfectly. He told the driver to let him out, then meet him on the other side of the block. Luc Dai shook his head but pulled over nonetheless.

"Get ready," said Chafetz as Karr closed the car door and turned toward the street vendor selling trinkets.

"Born ready." Karr could hear the high-pitched whine of the motorbike in the distance. He stepped over to the stall and pointed at a trinket, taking his wallet from his pocket just in time to have it snatched from his hand by the thief.

Karr shouted and grabbed for his assailant, making sure to just miss. When both the bike and the car were gone, Karr made a show of gathering himself, then walked down the block toward the spot where Luc Dai was to meet him. He had the driver take him to a spot where he could rent a motorbike, then dismissed him for the day. With the Art Room tracking the thieves, Karr took the time to haggle over the rental fee for the largest bike in the inventory, which he still dwarfed. By the time the deal was completed, the goons had stopped at a building several blocks from the hotel.

"We think it's a warehouse," said Chafetz, giving him directions. "Did the CIA draw these maps or what?"

"Taking the name of the competition in vain?" Karr asked.

Chafetz guided him through a maze of tiny alleys in the capital city, tracking the thugs into a district thick with sweatshops, some ultramodern, some that would have seemed out-of-date in 1700. Finally he got to within a few buildings of the factory. If you ignored the vegetation peeking out from the torn macadam and the relative lack of graffiti, the area could have been the backside of any American city, with dilapidated buildings and rusting wrecks of trucks.

Karr parked the bike and leaped up on a Dumpster at the back of a low-slung concrete-block building, climbing up on the roof and then mounting the ladder of a water tower to look at the warehouse where the goons had stopped. He reached into his pocket and took out a small pair of folding opera glasses, along with a wire to hook the feed into his handheld and ship it back to the Art Room. The optical portion of the glasses was capable of 20X magnification; the unit could also use an infrared, or IR, sensor roughly twice as powerful as

Generation 3 military units. Karr selected infrared to try to look through the thin wall of the warehouse; he saw two figures near a window at the front but wasn't positioned well enough to see farther into the facility. Neither of the figures had guns.

"We're running down the owners of the warehouse," Chafetz told him. "But I doubt that's significant. Can you get close enough to get visuals on the people as they come out?"

Karr craned his neck toward the building. He could hop from one roof to the other.

"Doable," he told her. Then he hopped from the ladder, took a short windup, and jumped to the next roof. A taller building sat next to it; he could just barely reach high enough to pull up and get over. This one had a good view of the warehouse and the alley in the back.

He moved his glasses around, scanning the warehouse. Most of the interior was empty, but a small part of the front corner of the building had interior walls and thick insulation, probably so it could be air-conditioned efficiently. This made seeing through it problematic, though the Art Room was able to find and enhance five shadows, IDing four as people and the fifth as a cat.

A Toyota was parked in the back. Karr reached to the back of his belt and took out one of his flies, a small eavesdropping device that could fit on a fingernail. From his left pocket he removed a device that looked like an old-fashioned Pez dispenser. Instead of candy, however, the device dispensed a sticky plastic that Karr rolled into a ball. He placed the fly at the top, then tossed the wad gently on the roof of the car. It splatted, looking like an odd bird dropping. He keyed his handheld to wake up the bug, got a beep indicating it was working, then went back to scanning the warehouse.

"Duck," said Chafetz suddenly.

The kids who had followed them and stolen his wallet came out the front, scootering away. Two other men got into the Toyota and backed quickly out of the alley.

"You want the Toyota," said Chafetz.

"Great. Keep tabs on it for me while I go get my wallet," said Karr.

"Uh . . ."

"Uh what?"

"They threw it in a barrel and lit it on fire. I'd guess it's pretty crispy by now."

19

Malachi Reese grooved on the Blink 182 cut, bouncing at the edge of his seat as he guided the tiny spaceship toward its destination. Called a "vessel," the craft looked like a foot-long section of copper pipe, the sort you'd find in a home water system. It had steering fins that were "ignited"—in layman's terms "extended"—by a small canister of hydrogen, allowing Malachi to steer it with the aid of the keyboards in front of him. In some ways, the vessel was nothing more than a ridiculously expensive space-launched dump truck; in about thirty seconds Malachi would hit a red button on his console and shower his target with motion and sound sensors about the size and shape of a flattened penny. Once deposited, the sensors would transmit their data back to the Art Room for the next four hours.

"How are we doing?" asked Telach.

"We're just about on target."

"I have a man in there and he's been knocked out," said the Art Room supervisor, her voice strained. "I need to know what the hell is going on."

"Hey, like, I'm doing six times the speed of sound, you know what I'm saying?"

That was an exaggeration—the vessel was actually moving at about Mach 4.

Malachi was a ReVeeOp—a remote vehicle operator or, more bureaucratically, "flight control specialist class three," the highest designation below supervisor status—controlling the spacecraft from a bunker a short distance from the Art Room. He made a slight course correction, then got ready to pickle his sensors.

"I'm sorry," apologized Telach.

"Not a prob, Mom."

He checked his course again, jacked the volume on the Mp3, and watched his screen for the cue.

"Baby," he said as the timer nailed down to one. His fingers danced quickly on the board.

"Got a good spread," he told the Art Room through the headset sitting over the buds for his stereo player. The vessel had dumped its load of sensors on and around the castle where Dean was being held.

"What's that in the background?" asked Telach. She reminded him of his third-grade teacher.

"Christmas carols," said Malachi.

"You're a bit ahead of the season, don't you think?"

"Never too early to celebrate."

He tickled the buttons, monitoring the vessel's flight on the pseudo–3-D terrain map at his right. He wanted to crash the now useless pipe into a wooded hill about two miles from the target, which was a large castle on a hill in northern Austria. The course had been preset, and as soon as the computer beeped to confirm they were on beam, he went back to the keyboard at the extreme left of his work area, punching the two preset keys at the right. The screen above the board changed, putting up green dots and squares to show whether the sensors were good.

He had a full board. Kick butt.

Had to be the music. Blink ruled. From now on, Christmas songs every flight.

In July. They'd love that.

"Malachi?" asked Telach.

"You're up and good," he said, punching the bar at the very bottom of the board, giving control of the feed over to the Art Room.

20

As the Toyota drove out of the city, oblivious to the bug on its roof, Karr decided the time had come to gear up. He headed for an equipment cache stored in the basement of a store that sold Buddhist shrines and related paraphernalia. After he purchased two small envelopes of incense from the rail-thin girl who worked at the register, an old man with a long white mustache appeared in the doorway.

"I'm Sam's friend," Karr said, adding a line in Mandarin Chinese, not Thai, that told the man he had come to worship his ancestors.

The old man bowed, then smiled, showing that he was missing several teeth at the front, and led the way into a back room, pulling a rug off the floor to reveal a trap door. The wooden steps bent severely with his steps, the rickety stairway creaking and swaying as he made his way down. The man stopped and lit a match, then picked up a torch from a bucket nearby. Flames shot upward when he ignited it, scorching the rafters; Karr followed as the old man brushed aside spiderwebs, walking past a collection of wooden boxes toward an area lined with shelves.

"How many bodies you got buried down here?" Karr joked.

Chafetz had claimed he didn't understand English, but a moment later the proprietor stopped and held the torch over a skeleton in the corner.

Karr laughed, then stooped down and gently pushed the skeleton to the side, pulling out a large footlocker next to it. The locker held a variety of light weapons and equipment available for Deep Black ops and had to be opened in a certain way or the plastiques it was largely made of would explode. With his right hand still on the red diamond at the top, he reached with his left hand and undid the latches. Then he removed his hand and yanked it open—the locks had to be cleared within five seconds of being undone.

He took one of the rucksacks at the side, debating whether to take the light armor as well. He finally decided against it; though the carbon-boron vest was relatively light and flat, it would still be bulky under his shirt and provided incomplete protection. He helped himself to a number of different grenades, then took one of the large flat cases at the bottom of the locker. The flat case held a special NSA-issue rifle called the A-2. A gas-operated assault weapon similar in most respects to the German Heckler & Koch G11, the weapon had virtually no recoil and was extremely accurate. At the same time, its thirty-inch length made it more compact than an M4, the standard assault gun preferred by American airborne troops because of its small size and weight. The A-2 actually looked more like a box with a pistol grip than a rifle, but its magazines held 102 rounds.

The old man held the torch out but looked away the whole time, as if he were afraid of intruding on a woman's modesty. Karr repacked the locker, closing it with a thud. Upstairs, he left a few bills with the girl before leaving.

"What do you have?" Karr asked Chafetz.

"The car is owned by an employee of a silk exporter in Chiang Mai. We're trying to flesh that out."

"I don't think this is about clothes."

"We're working on it. There's no connection to the hotel or to your friend there. Or to Kegan for that matter. The Toyota's a few miles north of Don Muang, the airport. Head in that direction and we'll see what comes up."

"You sound more like Rockman every day."

"Be nice."

By the time he reached the highway, the Toyota had stopped at a building owned by an American company that had gone bankrupt several months before. The silk exporter—the name in English meant Silken Rose—had done business with the American firm, but the Art Room had otherwise been unable to obtain any useful information about whom they might be dealing with, let alone what the connection was with Kegan.

Karr followed Chafetz's directions, turning off the highway, rumbling past a housing development, and then through an industrial park onto a less-developed road. He drove for about a mile until the macadam turned into hard-packed sand; the ruts made him slow down but he was still doing forty when he passed the building. He trucked on a bit, pulling off about a half-mile away after the road bent to the north enough to keep from casual sight.

"They're in the building," Chafetz told him. "We can't hear a thing."

"I think I'll use the Kite," Karr told her.

"It's daylight, Tommy."

"Sandy, anybody ever tell you that you have a habit of stating the obvious?"

The Kite was an unmanned aerial vehicle or UAV. The NSA had a variety of the robot planes for use in different situations. This one contained video and bugging equipment and was small enough to be carried and launched by one person. It could stay aloft for roughly an hour and was quiet enough to use in the countryside. But it did have a drawback—intended for night-time use, the Kite was painted black. It would be fairly visible in the bright sky. Karr knew from experience that the aircraft often could escape detection; most people saw only what they were looking for. Still, it was a risk, and one he should avoid unless the situation clearly warranted it.

The warehouse property was marked off on his left by a barbed-wire fence; Karr walked toward it, trying to get a look inside. There was another row of fencing beyond it, with a line of seemingly abandoned trailers parked nearby. He couldn't see the Toyota. He took out his binoculars and scanned the area, making sure he was alone. The trail he'd taken ended a hundred yards farther east in a large swamp, and there were no signs of anyone nearby. He stuffed the binoculars back in the ruck and took out his IR viewer, scanning the area close to him again just to be sure.

"All right, so we're not hearing anything from that fly on the car?" Karr asked Chafetz.

"If I were hearing something I'd tell you that, wouldn't I?"

"Maybe you'd want it to be a surprise. How come the warehouse is made out of concrete block?"

"Is that a trick question?"

"I didn't see any other warehouses around here made out of block."

"You're a building inspector now?"

"By birth."

Tommy's father had been a master carpenter in Scandinavia before emigrating to the United States, and among his many lessons was the fact that a building's construction always told a story. The story here, or at least part of the story, was that the material was difficult for the infrared sensor in the glasses to see through. In fact, he wasn't getting any heat signature through the walls at all—which probably meant a great deal of insulation on the inside as well.

"Could be a freezer," said Chafetz.

"Send me the blowup of the satellite image," said Karr, taking out his handheld.

The image showed no external heating or air conditioning unit. These could be buried or disguised, of course, but a similar infrared scan from an earlier series gave no indication of that either.

"You think it's shielded?" asked Chafetz. "If so, it could be a bio lab."

"Well, let's find out," said Karr. "I'm going to launch the Kite."

"Risky."

"Better than knocking on the front door."

Telach came on the line as he pulled the knapsack over and took out the Kite.

"Tommy, you're moving kind of fast for us," said the supervisor.

"Thanks."

The robot airplane looked very much like a miniature box kite, with a sausage and propeller in the middle. It carried video sensors and could be rigged to drop sensors. Though nearly silent, it was intended for night use and painted black, which was why Chafetz had been objecting.

Karr slid a drop package onto the nose area opposite the battery-powered motor. The entire aircraft was about the size of a shoe box.

"Tommy, if there are a lot of people in there, you're going to be outnumbered," said the Art Room supervisor. "Wait a bit and we'll have the CIA airborne resources on-line."

"How long's that going to be?"

"Thirty minutes tops. It's flying up from the south."

"The Toyota's not going to hang around. Don't sweat it, Marie."

Karr keyed up the robot aircraft's control program on his handheld computer. Unlike the UAVs used in both Gulf Wars and Afghanistan to supply visual images of the enemy, the small robot drones used by the Desk Three ops could be flown by a single person, either in the field or back at NSA headquarters.

"All right, you have a point," said Telach. "Just remember we have no backup if you get on the hook. You're on your own."

"Understood," he said, tapping the bottom of his handheld computer. A compass and a slidebar popped into view. He nudged the slidebar upward, pushing his power off neutral to two-thirds. Then he picked up the aircraft and hooked its nose into a thick band of rubber attached to a slingshot and launched the $50,000 spy plane like a child's toy.

Though he could navigate with the bird's-eye view screen on his computer, Karr found it easier to watch the plane and adjust the controls as he went. He tapped his stylus against the side of the screen, where a small compass showed the plane's heading. The computer translated the taps into a complex warp of the box wings, adjusting them to stay on course as the proper bearing was met.

Karr flew the Kite a half-mile to the east, away from the perimeter of the factory, started a turn, then popped up the sensor map, which thoughtfully interpreted the magnetic field anomalies that the device detected. As he'd suspected, the perimeter was protected by a series of video cameras and motion detectors—and a minefield around the sides and back. But he couldn't see inside.

Karr pushed the aircraft onto a course to take a direct overflight, deciding at this point he might as well go for it. As he'd feared, the top of the factory was as shielded from the infrared as the side; his sensors were simply not powerful enough to see through. He guessed that metal shielding had been used to help guard against bugs as well, though the field indicators didn't come up with anything.

Interesting, but hardly informative.

Karr spun the Kite around a second time. This wasn't getting him anywhere; it was time to fall back on a favored NSA tactic: provoke a response and see what happened.

Before he could decide exactly how to do that, the large garage door at the side of the building opened and two men with rifles emerged. Karr swooped back, pushing the Kite toward the open door and nailing the throttle.

"Tommy, what the hell are you doing?" asked Chafetz as the Kite plowed through the opening. He lost its feed; three seconds later, he heard a muffled explosion as the Kite executed the kill command, blowing itself up. By then, he was on his bike, hoping to escape the two pickup trucks that had barreled out of the building just as the Kite exploded.

21

Lia sat in the car two miles from the castle where Dean had been taken. It had been more than ten minutes since he'd apparently been knocked out, and they were just now getting a full eavesdropping net on-line.

She wanted to throttle Telach personally.

Or Rubens. They should have had more people in place when the operation began—or they should have just skipped the meeting in the bookstore.

"All right, we have it mapped," said Rockman finally. "I'm uploading the schematic for you."

"It's about time."

"You want to trade places, be my guest."

Lia put the car in gear, slipping back onto the road that ran near the gated entrance. The castle was owned by the state as a museum but was not open to the public. The main entrance was at the foot of a steep hill, more than 300 feet above the point where Dean had come in on the opposite side.

"The guards are moving," said Rockman. "They're going back into the building."

Lia pulled past, then drove down about a hundred yards to a point where the shoulder area off the road widened.

"No one's in front," said Rockman. He could tell where people were by looking at the input from the motion and sound sensors that had been spread over the site by the vessel.

"Can you hear what's going on inside?" she asked.

"We can hear some shuffling near Dean, but he's not moving."

"All right." She put on her lightweight rock-climbing shoes and tied down her jeans at the cuffs. As she walked, she fastened a body-hugging knapsack across her chest. Besides her gun and computer, it held a number of bugging and tracking devices, a very thin but strong nylon rope, and anchors that could be inserted into the stone wall of the castle to aid climbing. Just as she reached the fence, she put on a skullcap, smoothing back her hair.

Lia jumped up on the fence and pulled herself quickly over the pointed stakes at the top and then dropped down. The security system was not tied to a computer, or at least none that the Art Room could find, and so she was relying on their analysis—more like a guess—of the likely coverage area they'd mapped out after spotting the video cams with their sensors. Rockman directed her through a swath of uncovered area that, conservatively, measured three feet wide. Lia sidled through it to the camera itself, a shoe-box-sized video job that had a pair of shielded wires running into its mount. She took out a large coupling piece from her back pocket—it looked a bit like a sawed-off section of garden hose with hinges—and clamped it around the top wire. She had to then fit a transmitter onto the top.

"Easy," said Rockman. "You're going to jiggle the image."

Lia pushed her thumb into the activator slot, trying to use as little pressure as possible.

"So?"

"We're working on it. This is an old-fashioned system; one monitor per unit. We have this one knocked," said Rockman. "But we'll have to work around the rest."

"Great."

She started walking toward the castle wall, stopping precisely eight feet from the wall, just short of the spot where the analysis predicted her shadow could be seen by another video camera. There she took the rope from her pack, tying a plastic gripper onto the end. With a heave Lia reared back and tossed it up at the stone cutout on the wall twelve feet above. She wasn't so much worried about hitting the cutout precisely as tossing the rope high enough to reach the walkway behind the rock ledge; otherwise it would flop back down and with her luck fall through the video coverage area. She made it and with two flicks of the wrist caught the loop in the rope.

"All right," she told Rockman.

"Hold on. We think we have a workaround on the video system. It'll take another ten minutes."

"Way too long," she said. "We're going to have to risk it. Worst case, my shadow will only flicker across."

"Yeah, okay, you're right. They're moving around a lot inside," added the runner.

"Is there anyone on that level?"

"Negative, but there's a door at the far end of the walkway."

Lia took a step back, curled her hand on the rope testing the weight, then leaped forward, gliding to the wall. She tugged upward, quickly climbing to the top.

"Clear?" she asked, but before Rockman could answer she started over, realizing she couldn't be seen because of the way the wall angled.

"Why are you asking if the coast is clear if you're not going to listen to me?" complained the runner.

"I do nothing *but* listen to you," she whispered on the other side. "Which way?"

"The stairway on your left."

The outer wall of the castle was irregularly shaped, extending around three sides of a courtyard, which was set off from the keep by another wall. That wall was fifteen feet higher than the one Lia was on; the main part of the castle towered another twenty-five feet or so. There was a guard post beyond the steps, though Lia couldn't see into it from where she was huddled. She took out her handheld, scanning for security devices, even though the Art Room had already analyzed satellite data and found none. When she confirmed that the area in front and below was clear, she began moving toward the steps.

"Helicopter coming," said Rockman as she reached them.

"Yeah, I hear it."

"They'll be able to see you from above."

"That guard post?"

"Yeah, it's empty—go!"

She went back up the steps and trotted along the wall to the guard post, which covered an angle in the outer wall. While the roof was open—there would have been boards there during the castle's active days as a fortress—a thick ledge of stone blocks provided an easy place to avoid detection from the air.

The helicopter, meanwhile, had grown louder and louder.

"I think that chopper's going to land here," she told Rockman.

"People moving in the main building."

"Dean?"

"No. Wait—he's going in the opposite direction. Lia, stay where you are."

She froze, seeing the shadow of the helicopter as it circled above, only a few feet from the courtyard. It was descending—a close fit. The sound reverberated against the wall behind her, and dust flew into her face. She crawled backward, getting out of view.

"Careful," hissed Telach.

"I'm going to blow up the helicopter," she said, sliding against the stairs and unzipping her pack.

"No," said Rockman.

"We can't let them take Charlie."

"They're not taking him," said Telach. "There are two people who are going to get aboard the helicopter. We want you to take their pictures."

"Shit."

"Lia, we need you to try to get pictures of the people boarding the helicopter," said the Art Room supervisor. "Dean is being brought back downstairs."

"Where are they taking him?"

"Don't worry about that. Get the pictures. We need to figure out who these people are," insisted Telach. "Then we'll decide what to do."

"I have to help Charlie."

"Dean is fine. Even if they did take him, it's part of the operation. Don't let your hormones screw with your brain."

"Give me a break," said Lia.

"They should be up there now," said Rockman.

Lia pushed her handheld and its camera in the direction of the helicopter and crawled back toward it.

"Got it. Two good faces," said the runner.

The helicopter engine revved. Lia scurried back to the sheltered spot, waiting as the aircraft rose and circled the castle before heading back to the east.

"Where is he?" Lia asked.

"We want you to look over the castle. You can get down through the courtyard, that door we pointed out on the right near the corner," said Rockman.

"Where's Dean?"

"He's being carried down the steps by two men. There's someone else with him."

"I'll check it out."

"No, by the time you get there, they'll be gone. Go inside the castle," said Telach. "It's empty now. Have a look around."

She hesitated.

"It's all right, Lia," said Rubens from the Art Room. "We share your concern. Mr. Dean will be fine. They're taking great care with him."

"All right," said Lia, lingering a second more before going back to the steps.

22

Karr's bike wasn't going to be confused with a Harley, and even the dinky Toyota trucks following him soon began making up the distance. As the first rounds of gunfire chipped up the road in front of him, the NSA op hit the brakes and went into a power slide. Misjudging his momentum on the unfamiliar machine, he hurtled off the side of the roadway, losing his pistol in the process. He rolled to his feet, grabbing for one of the flash-bangs—special grenades that produced a loud bang and a flash of light, designed to stun or surprise people rather than kill them—that he'd tucked into his pocket. But he didn't have a chance to thumb off the tape holding the trigger, let alone throw it—the driver in the lead truck jammed on his brakes and sent the two men with M16s in the back flying across the pavement.

Karr grabbed his backup Glock from the back of his belt and shot at both, hitting one square in the head but missing the second, who managed to take cover behind the truck. The driver slumped behind the wheel, temporarily dazed.

The other pickup stopped about fifty feet away in the middle of the road on Karr's right. This one had two men in the cab but none in the back that Karr could see. For a second everyone stood frozen.

Karr tossed the grenade toward the second truck, then spun and fired two rounds through the bed of the other pickup, taking out the gunman. By the time the grenade exploded, he had grabbed his bike, restarted it, and hustled away.

He headed toward a cluster of buildings near the intersection of the road and the highway. Just before the highway Karr found a narrow alley and whipped down it, zipping past a pair of doorways and then a pile of rotting vegetables before running out of alley. He abandoned the motorbike, jumped a fence, and ran into a backyard where several children were playing. The NSA op shooed at them with his hands, trying to get them to go inside or at least run away where they couldn't be hurt. When they didn't react, he raised his arms and roared at them like a wounded bear, finally succeeding in scaring them.

He saw another alley and went up it, coming out at the front of a row of small shacks.

"Hey, Chafetz, how we doing?" he asked, leaning against the side of one and catching his breath.

"You tell me."

"We're tired but intact. You find out what's in that building?"

"We've gone over and over the feed. It looked empty except for the trucks and two cars."

"Jeez, Louise, are you sure?"

"You want to check it out yourself?"

"As a matter of fact, I do," he told her.

Karr reached back into his pack, taking out two smoke grenades and two flash-bangs. He slipped them into his pockets, then climbed up over the fence and began tracking back toward the warehouse.

"What are you doing?" Chafetz asked.

"I told you, I want to see what's going on. Besides, I left my Beretta back there."

"Forget it," said Telach, coming onto the line.

"Easy for you to say. Rubens'll make me pay for it out of my own pocket. That's a five-hundred-dollar pistol—more if I have to pay government prices."

"We'll get the Thai military to check out the building," Telach told him.

"That's a joke, right, Marie?"

"We have no backup for you," she hissed. "Come on. Call it a day."

"You're just being overprotective," Karr told them.

"There is a time for caution," the Art Room supervisor told him.

Rather than arguing, Karr changed the subject.

"Did you know that a lot of people come to Thailand for sex change operations?" he asked.

"Tommy, sometimes your wisecracks just aren't appropriate," said Telach. "I'm concerned for your safety."

"I'm safe," he told her. "And that was serious. I didn't know."

"Are you suggesting you're coming back here with tits?" asked Chafetz.

"Just giving you a heads-up, that's all."

His pistol lay in the dirt at the side of the road where it had fallen, but the truck and the two men he'd shot were gone. There was no one outside the warehouse.

They'd left the garage-style door open. Karr checked for booby traps with his glasses and handheld. He found none.

A wire grid had been used in the building as a protection against bugging devices. It was relatively primitive but still good enough to render Karr's com system unusable inside. He had to go back outside to talk to Chafetz.

"Hey, I found Pound," he told the runner.

"We'll have a chopper there in ten minutes."

"Uh, hold on a second," said the op. "Half the back of his head's missing. Stinks pretty bad in here, so I think he's been dead awhile."

23

Rubens glanced at his watch, waiting as Lia made her way down into the castle. On the floors above him, two dozen intelligence analysts were combing through databases of intercepts, using the castle and location as nexus points in a comprehensive search to turn up information about who had contacted Dean. The problem wasn't so much getting information as sorting through it. They *knew* UKD must be involved—and yet they had no direct link. As for Dlugsko, the NSA had decent information that he was in Kraków.

Taking a sauna with two young assistants of the nubile persuasion, actually.

"They researched Kegan pretty well," said John Gides, one of the NSA scientists tasked to act as Dean's advisors. "The work he did on flu viruses is pretty obscure."

"Actually, they did a very superficial job," said Rubens. "They knew nothing about Mr. Dean. They never tested his cover story."

Rubens considered what this meant. The operation had money and resources, and presumably they had done *some* checking on Dean, found him listed in the databases. They hadn't gone beyond that for one of two reasons—either there wasn't time or they had dealt with Kegan enough in the past to trust him, at least at a minimal level.

More likely the latter than the former. If so, then Kegan

would have money from them somewhere that had not yet been discovered.

His people would have to work harder to find it.

"Did the way the questions were asked suggest anything to you?" Rubens asked the scientist.

"What do you mean?"

"Were they read, or memorized, or something a man such as yourself might ask at a chance encounter?" Rubens realized the scientist hadn't considered that. "Replay the conversation and consider that. There would be a limited number of people who would be able to ask such a question and understand an answer, correct?"

"Dean didn't really answer."

"Yes, but that suggests that the person listening was looking for more than the simple information, which to me suggests that he does know the scientific information very well, and he asked the question more to see how his subject responded—as you would if you were asked to judge whether a person was authentic or not. On the other hand, someone working with a checklist, as it were, would make sure the blanks were filled precisely."

Gides nodded, though Rubens could see he wasn't completely following.

"The interrogator already believed Dean was authentic. He had checked his background while he was being transported," explained Rubens. "But he knows the subject matter. Or rather, he's familiar with the subject matter, but perhaps not the real details. So once he senses familiarity, he has no need to go further—he's looking for results. This suggests a scientist, but perhaps one whose specialty is in a slightly different area. A problem."

"Why?" asked Gides.

"A problem for us in that it widens the pool of possible candidates. A problem for them in that they might not know precisely . . ."

Ruben's thoughts trailed off as his words did. Of course they weren't the experts Kegan was; that would be the whole point of dealing with him. He **had** a small piece, tantalizing but not a real fit.

Rubens turned and saw Telach, raising her hand at the front of the room.

"Keep thinking, Doctor," he told the scientist. "Something will occur to you. Perhaps the subscriber lists of the journals where the articles were published."

"Can we get those?"

Rubens smiled indulgently; scientists could be such children. "We can get anything. Talk to Johnny Bib."

Telach paced uncomfortably at the front of the room.

"Is it UKD or someone else?" Rubens asked her.

"Oh. We're not sure," she said, slightly distracted. "The helicopter was leased. We're trying to figure out by whom. That should give us an answer."

"You can't trace the connection through the castle?"

"As far as we can tell, no one asked permission to use the castle. It's owned by a state museum and they seem to use it solely for functions and whatnot."

"See if it's been rented in the past," suggested Rubens. "Maybe there would be a connection. A mention in a local newspaper. Scan for stories, then have someone chat up the editors or reporters. They might know. A society page. Or business," said Rubens. "Give it to Johnny Bib's people if your staff is too busy. It's more strategic information anyway."

Rubens checked his watch. He was due upstairs to talk to the Director.

"Tommy wants a word," said Telach. "He's found the lab assistant who was working with Kegan."

"Excellent," said Rubens. "Finally, something useful."

"Not really. He's missing a good part of his head."

Rubens sighed, then punched himself into the circuit. Karr's relentlessly cheerful voice greeted him.

"Bodies falling all over the place," said the op. "Hey, you know, Thailand's kind of an interesting place. Little on the warm side, though."

The op had determined that Pound had been killed elsewhere and moved quite a while ago, "judging by the stench." He wanted Rubens' okay to alert the Thai authorities.

"Let us do it from here, anonymously," said Rubens. "How did he die?"

"Bullets all through his body. Something's been eating him, though, so it's hard to tell exactly what. Getting kind of dark over here, too. You want me to grab a bullet or something?"

He might have used the same tone to ask if Rubens wanted a cheerful souvenir of the visit. The interesting thing about Tommy Karr, thought his boss, was his relentless good humor, a trait that did not seem to come from artificial stimulation of any kind. Perhaps they should conduct some tests to understand it.

"That won't be necessary," Rubens told the field op. "Return to Bangkok and get some rest."

"On my way."

As the line snapped off, Rubens realized the advice might apply to him as well; it had been well over twenty-four hours since his head had touched a pillow.

The need to sleep was an absolute annoyance. The NSA official had reduced his quota to four hours per twenty-four and could shift them around within a forty-eight-hour block without impairing his performance. But without using drugs—a remedy he studiously avoided—there was no effective way to reduce this quota. Short power naps, caffeinated drinks, dogged determination—all were ultimately useless.

If he was willing to accept subpar performance, of course, he could go nearly four days without sleep. The question was whether it was worth it—a question made pertinent by the reminder on his calendar that he was supposed to go to the gala at the Kennedy Center this evening.

Where he would see the lovely and highly connected Ms. Marshall, who had somehow managed to convince George Hadash to support a ridiculous and useless proposal.

Why?

As yet an unanswerable question, which meant it was doubly in his interests to go.

Assuming he could stay awake during it.

"Segio Nakami has an update on the people who were following Tommy," said Telach, interrupting his train of thought. Nakami was an expert cryptologic mathematician who ran the team in Johnny Bib's place; he was considerably less eccentric than Johnny Bib, though in fairness he was also much younger.

"Segio? Where's Johnny Bib?" asked Rubens.

"He went to New York."

"What?"

"He wanted to check the books in Kegan's library. Something just doesn't fit, and since it was too much trouble to get the books here, he decided to go himself."

"What? When did he leave? What plane is he on?"

"Johnny wouldn't fly. He took Amtrak, I'm sure."

Rubens remembered his yoga, forcing his gaze to remain calm and purposeful.

"Should I speak to Segio?" he asked Telach.

She shrugged. "They have a connection between the silk exporters and an Islamic guerrilla group known as the Crescent Tigers. The Tigers have a long history, stretching back thirty years, most of it in Myanmar. At one time they were pretty potent, but they've been losing ground to newer fanatics. They may even have dispersed. In any event, there doesn't seem to be a connection between the hotel and this group. They may have staked out the hotel looking for Kegan."

"What about with UKD or the people who took Dean?"

"Nothing yet."

"All right," said Rubens. "I'm going upstairs. Update me if you get anything new."

"We will."

When he reached his office Rubens was still debating whether he might be best off going home and sleeping. He had just lifted the blanket from his desk when his external phone buzzed.

"Rubens."

"This is Dr. Lester over at CDC."

"Doctor, good morning," said Rubens. "I'm afraid we don't really have anything new yet. If you care to check back in a few hours—"

"I have something new, something important," said Lester. "We have two people sick in an upstate New York hospital with an undiagnosed disease. It has some flu symptoms, but it's accompanied by what look like bruises or welts to the body. One of the internists thought it was *E. coli* food poisoning and then Rocky Mountain spotted fever, but so far the tests have proved negative and we're still working on figuring it out."

"*E. coli?*"

"I don't think that's a good bet myself. They've looked at Coxsackie B virus as well, but the tests haven't come back. Many times these sorts of reports turn out to be overblown. Personally I'd think it was just random food poisoning except for this: one of them is Achilles Gorman, the BCI investigator who was handling the Kegan case. And the other is one of the crime-scene people who went over Dr. Kegan's house. Both men have run fevers over one hundred and five. It doesn't look good for either of them."

24

Dean heard birds—thousands and thousands of them.

Pigeons, cooing.

They fluttered into the air, then landed again.

Cooing, a short flight, cooing.

He woke up and found himself sitting on a park bench, head hanging backward on his shoulders. It hurt when he raised it; his eyes couldn't focus—the world had gone gray. He started to get up, then stopped, feeling his face. The sunglasses were perched at the very edge of his nose; he took them off, breathing slowly, regaining his consciousness. A clock began to gong in the distance. It was 7:00 P.M.

Dean slid his head down beneath his knees, letting the blood rush in, waiting out the fog in his brain. He adjusted the glasses but said nothing, unsure whether he was being watched or not.

Pigeons flocked nearby, attracted to the crumbs thrown by an elderly woman at the next bench over.

He got up, still unsure where he was, and began walking to his left. A large group of people were gathered at the intersection of two paths, listening as a tour guide described the significance of the statue at the intersection. Dean began to move to the left when someone bumped into him so hard he spun back and knocked into someone else; together they fell down.

"Um Verzeihung bitten! Entschuldigung!" said a short

Asian woman, helping up the person he'd knocked over. "I'm sorry, I'm sorry, please excuse me."

Lia.

Dean adjusted his glasses, listening as she spewed out a long string of German at the woman, whose expression indicated she hadn't a clue what Lia was saying.

"I apologize," said Lia to him. He could tell she wanted him to act as if he were a stranger.

"It's all right."

"Did you drop that?"

He looked at the ground. There was an envelope. He picked it up, turned it over. There was handwriting on it, Lia's:

YOU'RE BEING FOLLOWED.

"I don't think it's mine," he said, handing it back.

"It's not mine," she said. He tucked it in his pocket. "You're American?"

"Yeah."

"You live here?"

Dean pushed the glasses, waiting for someone to say something in his ear.

"No," he said finally.

"Oh," she said, as if losing interest. She turned to go.

"Wait."

Dean caught her arm. Lia turned at him and gave him a look that would have withered a mugger.

"I, uh—want to get some coffee?" he asked.

"No thanks," she said, smiling and shaking her head.

He watched her start away, not sure exactly what he was supposed to do. Then he decided to act naturally, as if he really were trying to pick her up. He loped after her and grabbed her arm from behind.

She swung around, her arms pulled back defensively, an inch short of flattening him.

"Look," she said loudly. "Leave me alone. If you want coffee, you go get it yourself. There must be a million coffee shops on that boulevard where you can pick up some lonely tourist. Get out of my face."

Lia swung around indignantly and stalked off.

She's good, Dean thought to himself.

Then he realized that her tirade had drawn the attention of others nearby. He held his hands out apologetically.

"I wasn't trying to pick her up or anything," he said.

Half of the dozen or so people nearby nearly choked with laughter. The rest looked as if they might take him on themselves.

Dean ambled in the direction that Lia had given him. He found a coffee bar but realized he had no Euros, only a few pounds and dollars. He went back toward the corner, where he had seen the outside kiosk for an ATM. As he reached into his pocket for the wallet, he found the envelope Lia had dropped. There was an address in the left-hand corner—27 Sitzung.

Sitzung was the name of the street he had just crossed.

He stuffed the envelope in his pocket and went through with the transaction, withdrawing fifty Euros. He walked back along the street, looking for 27. Just as he reached number 25, two men came barreling out of the doorway, yelling and cursing as they shoved each other. Dean tried to avoid their fight, pushing toward the building as a siren sounded down the street. Two men nearby ran up to stop the brawlers, but this only resulted in a bigger tangle, and Dean had to duck quickly to escape being bashed. As he spun around, a hand grabbed him and yanked him into the building. Before he could say anything, a hand slapped itself over his mouth.

A woman's hand. Lia's.

Dean felt her pull off his shirt, tugging at his buttons. He helped her, sliding out of it, and doffed his shoes as well when she pointed at them. She pushed him down the hall, where a man in a suit was waiting near a doorway. Inside, Dean found himself in the fitting room of a tailor.

"God, you're thick," said Lia, coming in behind him. "If I didn't have half the embassy working for me, you'd still be out there." She shook her head. "Being tracked by a bag lady, no less."

"My clothes were bugged?"

"I just like seeing you naked."

She stepped aside as Dean lowered his pants to put on the suit that was waiting for him on a hanger.

"I didn't know you spoke German," he said.

"The Art Room claims I messed up the tenses, but I think they're full of it. They want a full report when you're dressed."

"About what?"

"What happened in the castle, et cetera. By the time I got inside they'd cleared out."

"You were there?"

"You think I'm letting you out of my sight, Charlie?" She whistled. "Nice pecs for an old dog."

"You weren't there," he told her.

"I was on the wall when they carried you out," said Lia. "I had to clamp my mouth to keep from laughing. Just like now."

"Hey, watch it or I'll bench-press you."

"Anytime, big man."

She leaned up and gave him a light kiss on the lips, pulling away long before he wanted her to.

"Who are they?" asked Dean.

"We're not exactly sure," said Lia. "Which is the scary part. Get dressed; we're going to dinner. Then you're getting your ears bobbed."

"What?"

"Eyeglass com systems are too fragile, especially when they get smacked against a hard head like yours."

25

The taxi pulled away before Johnny Bib could ask about being picked up again. He stood at the edge of the hilly driveway, momentarily paralyzed.

Attend to your business, whispered one of the voices in his head.

"Yes," said Johnny Bib, and he began walking up the driveway. Johnny kept exactly twenty-nine voices in his head—twenty-nine was a particularly beautiful and useful number—and while he did not always take their advice, he did in this particular instance, following along to the back of the house and looking around for a garden. A number of tomatoes grew on stakes in a raised bed about twenty feet from the house; there were cucumbers as well and a few stunted pieces of spinach suffering in the summer heat. None of the plants had been watered now in several days, and the tomato vines had begun to yellow.

The fact that Kegan kept a garden did not mean that Johnny's hunch of a substitution code was wrong, but he nonetheless felt disappointed. He wanted Kegan to be using a substitution code. Not because he'd thought of it, but because there was something archaic and romantic about the idea. Modern-day encryption had moved too far from the personal, Johnny Bib thought; it had become simply a mathematic problem to solve. Oh, there were still beautiful wrinkles to be discovered, surely, and untangling a scrambled fractal embedded in an encrypted video stream—well, there were still things that could thrill a mathematician's heart. But the real romance and intrigue were gone from the profession. The heady atmosphere of the days of World War II and Enigma, the Japanese wind codes—where was that glory now?

The use of a simple substitution code—simple and yet, if properly executed, nearly impenetrable—surely that was a thing even Turing himself might have appreciated.

Johnny Bib had come here not hoping to break the code Kegan was using (if it even was a code he was using, as opposed to an encryption). What Johnny really wanted to do was get a glimpse of the romantic era of genius, to touch it and in that way partake of it. What more could a mathematician really ask for? Johnny Bib had reached the age when a mere solution to pi no longer thrilled him. No, he wanted not to solve Fermat but to understand *why* a right triangle was in fact *right*. He longed to cross the mystic threshold.

Had Kegan? The man worked with microbes and DNA. What was DNA but a marvelously effective and powerful encryption? Surely the intersection of math and biology would yield something stupendous, something soulful, something . . . *Godlike* was the only word.

And so now, directed by another of his inner voices, Johnny went to the back of the house. He avoided the crime-scene tape on the porch and tried a rear window, which he found unlocked. Johnny stepped through, nearly tripping on the curtain but finally maintaining his balance enough to hop into the center of the small room, a sort of den at the back of the house opposite the kitchen.

The house had a central hallway running down the middle, dividing it perfectly in half—an excellent condition, Johnny thought, walking to the library at the right side. He noticed that the wainscoting in the corridor divided the wall precisely at the three-sevenths spot; if this was significant he couldn't decide, but it certainly felt like a good omen, and he practically bounced into the library. He knew from the photos that there were over 10,000 volumes here, but his immediate interest was confined to a small section of the third shelf from the window on the right side. Johnny walked to it now, tilting his head slightly to survey the titles on the spines. He was just pulling the book out when his voice directed his attention to the right.

The shelves at the bottom, said the voice.

Johnny had heard this voice before. It had a slightly French accent; he thought of it as Descartes, though of course he was not so crazy as to believe it was *really* the great French philosopher and mathematician.

One of his students, perhaps.

"These shelves?" Johnny asked aloud.

At the bottom, repeated the voice.

Johnny bent down, then realized that the voice was referring him to a small section of books one case over. There were three books on cancer and its various forms. Next to them were much older texts, collectors' items from the looks of them. He slid along the rug and started to tug one out; when he did he realized there were several books behind them, along with a three-ring binder.

The books were battered. One was an old herbalist encyclopedia. Two were written in French and appeared to be alchemy texts. The last was a book by Aleister Crowley on magic spells.

"Superstitious garbage," said Johnny Bib. "What do we make of this?"

None of his voices responded. He opened the notebook and began to read.

26

The helicopter bucked toward the green blanket of fronds, its nose ducking down as if the pilot had decided to try landing on the top of the trees. Karr, sitting in the ancient Huey's right front seat, watched with growing curiosity as a cleft opened ahead. A waterfall spewed off to the right, a stream dropping a good hundred and fifty feet. The newly risen sun flashed off the water, its glare making the liquid seem like fire flowing from the white heart of the earth. The chopper pivoted and followed the path the water had taken, wrenching itself to the northwest, heading for the border with Myanmar.

"Nice morning," said Karr.

"Buh," said the pilot.

"Lot of trees," said Karr.

"Buh," repeated the pilot. He seemed to speak neither English nor any of the known dialects of Thai. In fact, based on their conversation since leaving Chiang Mai about a half hour ago, Karr had come to the conclusion that the man's vocabulary consisted of exactly one word: *buh*.

"Military camp far?" asked Karr.

"Buh."

"Just ahead, huh?"

"Buh."

"You from around here?"

The pilot didn't answer. Instead he pushed hard on the

yoke and threw the Huey into another sharp turn, descending at the same time. The helicopter seemed to move backward, then straight down, then both together. The skids brushed up against some of the treetops. Red clay appeared before them. The noise of the engine caught up and dust flew in a fine mist; the helicopter had touched down.

"You were beginning to make me think I oughta put on my seat belt," said Karr.

"Buh."

"Nice flying with you," said Karr. He held out his hand to the pilot, who looked at him quizzically. Karr gave him a shoulder chuck and popped open the door, sliding out into the dust storm with his two rucksacks of gear and a long case containing his rifle. The two Marines he'd borrowed from the embassy at Telach's insistence pushed out of the back of the helicopter, gathering their own gear. Both men were dressed in plain khaki uniforms that did not have insignia, though anyone looking at them would spend all of three seconds guessing they were American.

And maybe another millisecond more figuring they were Marines.

The Huey revved and left them standing in the swirling dust.

"Put two of these landing areas together and you'd have almost enough room for a half-court game of hoops," he said.

"It's forward base. What'd you expect, O'Hare?" asked Chafetz.

"Have a good nap, Sandy?"

"Dreamed of you the whole time."

"Where's the reception committee?"

"Clearing up ahead, on your right. They're watching you."

He turned and glanced at his Marines, who'd shouldered their rucks. The men carried early-model M16s identical to the weapons the Thai forces used—another bit of fussy misdirection that would fool no one, but Karr had decided there were better things to do than waste his time arguing with the Marines' captain, who, after all, was himself only following someone else's orders.

"You guys ready?" Karr asked the Marines.

"Locked and loaded," said the shorter of the two men, Horace Foster. Both men were lance corporals, but Foster had enlisted a few days earlier than his companion, Jason Gidrey, and therefore considered himself spokesman for the unit.

"Locked and loaded is the only way to travel," said Karr.

"I thought these guys were friendly," said Foster.

"*Friendly*'s a relative term," said Karr. "Smile; we're being watched."

Karr walked through the gap in the trees, treading down a path too narrow for a good-sized horse. He saw movement on his right, then in front—a pair of kids in fatigues totting M16s jerked up to challenge him.

"Heya," he said. "Yo, Chafetz, what are my words?"

A linguist back in the Art Room relayed the Thai phrase for "hello," which sounded something like *"sa-wut dee."*

It had about as much effect on them as *buh*. The two men, members of the Thai Army, squared their rifles. Foster and Gidrey twitched behind him.

"You sure I didn't say, 'Shoot my butt off'?" Karr asked Chafetz as he walked toward them. He edged his hands out in as universally nonbelligerent a manner as possible.

"Their major's en route," said Chafetz. "It'll be okay."

Another Thai appeared behind the two men as Karr sauntered down from the landing patch. Though the man wasn't wearing any insignia, he was clearly a superior—older and with a more purposeful frown.

"I'm Tommy Karr," said Karr in English.

The man said nothing as Karr approached, but the Deep Black op interpreted the fact that he hadn't been shot at yet as a good sign. The Art Room had sprinkled a vessel's worth of bugs around the jungle camp before sunrise and was also getting an optical feed from a CIA Huron "Eyes" asset; they'd at least know who to come after if he got waxed.

"Tommy Karr," the agent repeated when he was close enough for the M16s to poke him in the chest. "These are Foster and Gidrey. How's it goin'?"

"Commander Karr," said the Thai officer in a thick accent. "I am Major Sourin."

"Major." Karr dropped his gear and stuck out his hand, but Sourin didn't take it. Instead, he spun on his heel and headed into the thicket.

"Here we go," Karr said to his Marines. "Keep your eyes open for a steak joint. I'm starving."

Sourin's camp consisted of two huts, a large tent that appeared to be American surplus circa 1945, and a number of dug-in positions. He had forty-five men divided into two platoons, with a handful of aides serving as a headquarters or command unit. His weapons were old and had seen considerable use before most of his soldiers were even born. Sourin's force had nothing heavier than 60mm mortars dating from World War II.

One thing it did have, however, was two command laptops and a supposedly secure connection back to the Thai regional command. The unit's node had been used to send the E-mails found on Kegan's system—but did that mean the message had been sent from here, or that the system had been compromised? The laptops used dial-up modems over the command's fiber optics landline, which ran through the jungle back to the territorial capital, which meant that the Art Room had to wait until they were physically connected to look at them. Thus far, only one of the computers had hooked in, and then only for a few seconds, so the Art Room hadn't had enough time to completely search the hard drive.

Karr had a solution—a dongle that would plug into the modem ports and flush the drive back to the Art Room via a satellite connection. The only problem was getting it onto the laptops.

Karr spotted the units sitting on a small folding desk next to the briefing table in the command tent when the major led him inside; one of the major's orderlies sat a few feet away, and there was no easy way to grab it without doing so in plain sight.

An option Karr considered but rejected for the time being.

"The guerrillas have camps in the mountains all around us, on both sides of the border," said Major Sourin, who'd received orders from above to brief the American "terror specialist." The instructions included a line that might be politely translated as: "Make nice but not too nice to the buffoon before sending him on his way."

"The guerrillas aggressive?" Karr asked.

Sourin shrugged. "Most are more interested in each other than fighting the Myanmar government," said the major.

The Thai officer explained that his government's view toward the guerrillas varied depending on their exact affiliation. Because the Myanmar government was a repressive regime and, more important, was at odds with the Thai government, groups genuinely opposed to the Myanmar regime were viewed fairly benignly. But some of the guerrillas across the border were simply pirates, preying on anyone they could, and most of their victims were Thai citizens. It angered Sourin that he did not have the resources to properly deal with the guerrillas.

What Sourin didn't say but what Karr had already gathered from his briefing, was that the lack of formal control and governmental infrastructure in the jungle to the northeast meant that anyone with a few weapons and iodine pills to purify the water could operate there. Four or five of the guerrilla camps just over the border were known to shelter radical Islamists, who though opposed to the Myanmar government, were on American watch lists because of their connection with international terror groups. At least two of these had long histories of violence against Westerners and had, in fact, operated in both Thailand and Myanmar for over two decades.

Sourin also didn't say that with all the activity going on near the Cambodian border, his sector had less priority than Fourth of July picnic planning the week before Christmas.

"Can you plot out the camps for me?" Karr asked. "As many as you know."

The major said something to one of his aides and a large

topographical map was produced. There were *x*s scattered around.

"We're not sure how many camps," said the major.

"Would satellite photos help?"

The major didn't answer.

"I can probably get some satellite analysis for you," said Karr. "Help figure it all out."

"Why exactly are you here?" said the major.

"There's one group I'd like to check up on," Karr told him. "I'd like to look at them up close. Probably they're not going to be very friendly. You help me. I help you."

"You're getting way ahead of yourself," scolded Chafetz. "We don't even know if they're on our side, for christsake. Let's check the computers before we start making deals."

The major said something to his aides in Thai. All three men left the tent. Karr thumbed the two Marines out as well.

"Why should I help you?" asked the major.

"My enemy is your enemy?" Karr smiled, hoping the major's English education had included all of the important clichés. "One hand washes the other?"

The major gave him a sarcastic smile. Karr expected a lecture in the realities of jungle warfare, especially for a unit stranded far from support, with limited firepower. But instead the major took a more direct approach.

"What's in it for me and my men?"

"Better weapons than you have now," Karr told him. "Minimis for starters—M249s. They're squad-level machine guns. Belgians make them."

"I know what Minimis are," said Sourin.

"GPS locator gear, night goggles, better computers. What are these, from 1960?"

Karr went over to the laptops and picked one up, glancing at the unit. He didn't recognize the make, but the plug on the side for the modem looked to be standard. There was a serial port, a parallel connection, and a USB bus. He'd have no problem connecting his dongle.

"Hey, you got Donkey Kong on this?" Karr pulled the machine open. "I love that old game."

The major put his hand on the cover, closing it.

"My commander told me to cooperate with you, but he did not order an attack."

The NSA op shrugged. "Your call."

Karr decided Sourin wasn't the type to suggest a direct monetary bribe and, in fact, was probably even a little put out at the offer of weapons. Which were good things, Karr thought, though they didn't particularly advance his current agenda.

"Let me ask you a question, Major," said Karr. He reached into his pocket for the photos of Kegan and Pound. "There a lot of white guys running around the jungle here?"

"Tommy, no," hissed Chafetz. "If he's working with them, you're cooked."

Sourin made a dismissive gesture. "How would they get up here?" he asked.

"Kinda what I'm wondering," said Karr. "I have a couple of places I'd like to check out, and your help would be useful."

"I'll have to talk to my commander," said Sourin.

"Great."

"Why did you show him the pictures?" demanded Chafetz.

"Got to find out whose side he's on somehow, right?"

"Jesus."

"So what did he do?"

"So far, all he's done is tell his commander that you're looking for some Americans who are apparently working with the guerrillas. That and he thinks you're crazy."

"I like him, too," said Karr. He continued walking along the camp's perimeter line, avoiding the area to the left that had been booby-trapped. Located on a slight rise, the camp commanded the only road through the border area, but in truth the deep potholes and ruts made it almost unusable.

"There are three possible camps, all connected with Muslim extremists according to Thai intelligence," said Chafetz.

"Which one do we hit first?"

"We're still trying to figure out which is our best bet. In the meantime, you need to tap into those computers before you get anywhere."

"Looks like I have to wait until tonight," Karr told her. "I may not even be able to get in then."

"Marie isn't going to go for any sort of armed reconnaissance mission over the border unless we're sure they're on our side."

"Not her call. It's Rubens'."

"I doubt he will, either."

"Oh, don't be such a pessimist. Listen, you sure you can't airlift some Mickey D's in? My stomach's rumblin'."

27

"It's not *E. coli* at all. Nor is it a morph of Asian SARS, which was also suggested, though we can't really rule anything out until we've been able to conduct better tests."

"There's no way it could be a virus, because other cases would have cropped up. It's probably just a coincidence."

"There may be a vector that we don't understand. I still vote for *E. coli*—where did these guys go for lunch?"

"*E. coli* with a seven-day incubation period?"

"You don't know it's seven days. You don't know anything, really," said Westhoven, representing the FBI.

Rubens furled his arms across his chest as the video conference continued. Though mindful of the fact that he was on camera, he had a difficult time maintaining a neutral expression. There was such a wide gap between math and biology—opinion too easily mixed with fact here.

A dozen scientists affiliated with the NSA, the FBI, the Surgeon General's office, and the CDC were debating exactly what, if anything, they were dealing with in upstate New York. Despite massive doses of penicillin and other drugs, Gorman was running a fever right around 104. He could not keep anything in his stomach, and his lungs were full of fluid. His body was covered with large purple welts.

The other man, a crime-scene technician for the state police, was in a coma. Two other cases in upstate hospitals were being investigated for similar symptoms.

A full battery of lab tests had thus far produced baffling results. The white blood cell count was extremely high, yet it wasn't obvious what the immune systems were fighting. Tests for everything from Rocky Mountain spotted fever to the mumps had proven negative.

Meanwhile, the FBI's investigation of Kegan's work had thus far failed to produce anything that could be potentially used for germ warfare; his work was primarily concerned with breeding bacteria that could literally "eat" pollutants.

"We need a wider range of tests, and more resources to complete them," said Dr. Lester finally, bringing the debaters to heel. "We need to define what we're looking for—we're not even sure whether it's a virus or a bacteria at this point. In the meantime, we need to initiate a quarantine until we understand exactly what's going on."

"I agree with the tests," said Westhoven. "I have a team that wants to look at potential crossover from Kegan's experiments—granted, a long shot."

"We can't rule out long shots," interrupted Lester.

"But I don't think a quarantine's a good idea," continued Westhoven. "It's premature."

"It's not your decision to make," said Lester.

"If this is related to the Kegan case in any way," said Westhoven, "then we have to proceed very cautiously."

Rubens understood the dilemma. On the one hand, the doctors wanted to corral this before it got out of control—if it hadn't already. On the other hand, Westhoven and the FBI were concerned that if the disease had been caused by something Kegan was working on, then a large-scale action by the CDC would demonstrate to anyone watching that he had a viable weapon.

Of course, publicizing it would also make the FBI look bad, which undoubtedly was in the back of Westhoven's mind.

Would the NSA look bad as well?

Of course not. They were called in after the fact, almost by accident, to straighten the mess out.

"We still have only two cases," said a doctor from the

Surgeon General's staff. "A quarantine would be premature—it's not even clear whom we would quarantine."

"The hospitals for starters," said Lester.

Rubens decided it was time to take control. "We can't jump to conclusions, but we do have to proceed cautiously," he said.

"Proceeding cautiously means not setting off a panic," said Westhoven. "Or jumping to conclusions. There's no evidence that Kegan either was sick or made something that could make people sick. Panic, on the other hand, and—"

"How much of a panic would a thousand deaths cause?" asked Lester.

"There have been no deaths yet," countered Westhoven.

"There are many considerations," said Rubens. "We have to face the possibility that this disease—may I call it a disease?"

"For want of a better term," said Lester.

"We have to face the possibility that this illness was caused by something Kegan had or has. If that's true—I stress *if*— then it may be that someone else has this virus or bacteria, whatever it is. We have to act in a way that's not going to encourage an attack, even as we stem the spread that we are already observing. Doing both at the same time does require a certain amount of delicacy, Doctor," said Rubens, realizing Lester was the only person he needed to convince. "So how can we combine both goals?"

"Well, a soft quarantine, strict rules on the present patients, their medical teams."

"You would do that as a matter of course, wouldn't you?" suggested Rubens.

"Yes," agreed Lester. "But if there are more cases—"

"How many more?" asked Westhoven.

A mistake, thought Rubens; best to leave the future ambiguous.

"Any more," said Lester.

"Do you know how it's passed?" Rubens asked.

"Well, the specifics really depend on the entity itself. Both of these people had contact with the dead man, and we're assuming that that's where they got it."

"But the dead man didn't die from it," Rubens pointed out.

"No," said Lester. "But he might have been carrying it. There's a reasonable assumption of a long incubation period."

"Or simply no connection at all," mused Westhoven.

"We should have some better information within twelve hours," said Lester. "We'll at least know whether we're dealing with a virus, as most of us suspect, or some sort of bacteria germ. I've also requested a full autopsy of the man who was found in Kegan's house, and we're flying in our people to perform it."

"I would suggest, if we're going to do a quarantine, we quarantine the people who have come in contact with that house," said the Surgeon General's doctor.

"Everyone?" asked Westhoven.

"It seems only prudent. Until we understand the vector, or the means of its transmission." The doctor began talking about the ability of various viruses and bacteria to survive on different surfaces for a long period of time. The SARS virus, for example, could live for at least four days on a plastic surface as long as the temperature never rose above seventy degrees Fahrenheit.

"We're back to a wide-scale quarantine," said Westhoven.

"Doctor, wouldn't it be prudent to contact the state police people involved who responded and check on their health?" said Rubens. "I would think that the reason you could give would be fairly vague—after all, you wouldn't want to rule anything out. In the meantime, that would allow you to observe everyone—what was the term you used before? First tier contact? Well, whatever, you could proceed with that, and in the meantime the house could be secured for further investigation. As it happens," added Rubens, "one of my people is already there."

Not particularly by my wish, he might have added, though he didn't.

"I don't know," said Lester.

"Well, I think that's best."

Lester visibly sucked air. The video feed from the CDC—he seemed to be standing in a lab area—was fuzzy and slightly out of sync with the audio. "Agreed."

"I still think this fuss is premature," said Westhoven.

"Perhaps," said Rubens lightly, aware that the stance only made the Bureau look as if they had bungled the matter when Kegan contacted them weeks before.

Had they, though?

Probably not. Surely this was just a bizarre coincidence.

On the other hand, image was everything in Washington, or nearly so.

"We're presenting the matter to the full NSC at six P.M.," said Lester.

"You are?" said Rubens, barely able to keep the surprise from his voice. "Mr. Hadash has already been informed?"

"An hour ago. Given the other circumstances, I felt it absolutely necessary to take this to the highest levels right away. I'm afraid I have to cut this short," added Lester. "I have to go over and see Sandra Marshall. Mr. Hadash recommended she be the point person at Homeland Security on this."

Rubens soldiered the muscles in his face into blankness and even managed a smile as the conferees signed off. Before he could decide how to proceed—before, really, he could recover from his shock at the new political fault lines appearing around him—the Art Room rang with an update.

"We have Johnny Bib on the line," said Chris Farlekas, spelling Marie as supervisor. "We've been waiting for your conference to clear."

"Put him through," said Rubens.

"It's an open line."

"Understood."

"Mr. Rubens?" Johnny's voice was uncertain, as if he'd never used a telephone before.

"Johnny—what the hell are you doing in New York?"

"I had a hunch that Kegan was using a substitution code and that I could find the codebook."

There were many possible replies. Rubens might have mentioned that this wasn't World War I—or, more accurately, any of the campaigns undertaken during the Roman Empire, which was about the last time that codebooks might be relevant. But instead he said simply, "And you discovered what?"

"My hunch was wrong," said Johnny Bib, with such enthusiasm that he actually suggested the opposite.

"I'm shocked that you made a mistake, Johnny. I will circle the date in my calendar and play it in the lottery tomorrow."

"You're being sarcastic."

"Very possibly."

"Well," said Johnny Bib. "Then perhaps I won't tell you what I've found."

If I get to pick my successor, thought Rubens, I will first scour the nation's elementary schools for a seasoned kindergarten teacher.

"Johnny, unfortunately, it turns out that I have a great number of things to do this evening, just as I have every evening. And morning. And noon. And night."

"More sarcasm?"

"I'd appreciate it if you could tell me what exactly you found. Expeditiously."

"He's looking at plants because he's trying to find a cure for rat-bite fever."

"For what?"

"Sodoku. It's an Asian disease that was brought back to Europe during the seventeenth and eighteenth centuries. There were apparently cures, and he's researching them."

"And you know this, how?"

"I have the books right here. Pages turned, things underlined. They were sitting right on the shelf. There are gardening texts and botany texts, historical references—it's a mother lode."

"A mother lode, yes. Have you talked to the scientists about it?"

"I passed it on to my team. I'd like to take the books down for them."

"I'm afraid that won't be possible. Do you have a digital camera?"

"Uh, no—"

"We'll get you one, along with a secure hookup. Those books can't leave the property," Rubens told him. "Nor can you. I'll get someone to ferry up the items."

"I can't leave?"

"I'll have one of the medical people call up to explain the technical details. You can tell him what you've found. It's probably just a senseless precaution."

He thought of Dean and Tommy Karr—they had been at the house and should be quarantined as well.

But he couldn't afford to lock them away for days. On the contrary.

"What should I do here?" asked Johnny.

"Keep reading. I'm told there's plenty of material handy."

28

"Nice night, huh?" Karr told the Thai guard outside the door to the command tent.

The Thai guard mumbled something in response.

"He's saying something along the lines of 'go away,' except it involves your relatives," said Chafetz. "We're having a little trouble with the volume."

"I'll ask him to speak up on the way out," said Karr, putting his hand up to push against the door.

The guard pulled his M16 up, ready to fire.

"Phone call," Karr explained. "I have to make a phone call."

Chafetz told him the words. Karr spoke several languages, including Russian, but Thai wasn't one of them. The word for "call" sounded like "rēē-uk," but the tone was difficult to get unless you were familiar with the language, and finally Karr found it easier to use English and pantomime. The guard frowned but finally pulled the gun back upward and let him pass.

There was a second guard inside. He'd been sitting on a small folding chair near several crates of papers and maps, probably dozing, but the conversation outside had gotten his attention. He met Karr with a drawn pistol.

"Hello," said Karr, letting the door bang behind him. "Phone. I have to use the phone."

"He wants to know why you're not with the major," said Chafetz.

"Because I don't want the major to see me breaking into his computer?"

"Tommy—"

"So give me the words again," he told the runner. He took his hand and made it into a phone, miming as he struggled with the language.

The guard said something with Sourin's name in it.

"Did the major give you permission?" translated Chafetz. "Sure."

"Chai," said Chafetz.

"Chai."

Tommy's pronunciation clearly puzzled the soldier—he said the word as if he were ordering Russian tea—but the man let him pass as he walked toward the communications center. Karr made sure to pick up the generic phone—it had a white receiver—that Major Sourin had allowed him to use earlier to talk to the embassy. The Art Room had already compromised the line, and Karr found himself talking to Farlekas.

"Thailand is a beautiful country," said Farlekas. The Art Room supervisor had served two tours in Southeast Asia during the Vietnam era—first as an Army medic and then as a CIA paramilitary. "Very ancient and proud."

"Reminds me of Scandinavia," said Karr.

"Oh, I can see that," said Farlekas. "We're ready here anytime you are."

"I'm working on it," Karr told him. He reached into his pocket and pulled out a pack of cigarettes and a lighter. He gestured to the Thai guard, who looked at him dubiously but then accepted a cigarette. Karr tried to light it for him, but the cigarette lighter wouldn't catch. He tried several times, the flint failing even to spark.

"Any second now," said Karr.

"Don't knock yourself out," said Farlekas over the phone.

The soldier reached into his pocket and pulled out his own lighter—a Bic with a picture of a bikini-clad model on it. He lit his cigarette, then handed the lighter to Karr. The op actually didn't smoke and turned away as he choked back a cough.

"Taking a while," said Karr as he handed back the lighter to the guard.

"Sure he got a good whiff?" asked Farlekas.

The guard's eyes began to close. "All right, here we go."

The anesthetic that had been in the phony lighter had finally knocked the soldier out. Karr put the phone down on the nearby table as he pulled the dongles from his pocket. He attached them to the laptops, then hunted around the desk for blank floppies. He didn't want them to boot into their normal C drives for fear that a security program would trip him up.

"Any disk will do," Chafetz reminded him.

He found a pair and booted up.

"Strike CONTROL-DELETE-D, all together," said Chafetz.

He had trouble settling his large fingers on the Chiclets-style keys but managed to get the combinations. The computer screens blanked.

"We're in—have them both," said Chafetz. "Uh-oh."

"Uh-oh for you or uh-oh for me?"

"Sourin's stirring."

"How long do we need?" Karr asked.

"Thirteen and a half minutes," said Chafetz.

"Pull 'em," said Farlekas.

"Nah. I don't have any more of the gas with me up here," said Karr. "This is our best shot."

"He's out of the tent," said Chafetz.

"Probably just taking a leak, right?"

"No—checking his guard position on the west flank. Can you get one of the Marines to divert him? Talk to him or something."

"Too late," said Karr. "Besides, he doesn't like them. He'd know something was up. Nah, we're cool. I can deal with him. Just keep the download flowing."

"Talking to the guard," said Chafetz. "Telling him to not play with his toes. Well, more or less. He's a little graphic for a Thai."

With 1:33 left, Sourin turned from the guard position and began walking toward the command tent.

"You can pull unit two," said Farlekas.

"Wait until he's ten seconds away," Karr told him.

"He's thirty seconds now," said Chafetz. The computer could calculate his progress based on his stride.

Karr reached to unit two, making sure he'd removed the floppy, then pulled the dongle.

Karr slid his hand over the back of the laptop as the guard outside snapped to attention and loudly challenged the major—probably as much to warn his fellow guard inside as to impress the officer.

The door to the tent flew open.

"Mr. Karr," said Sourin in English.

"Hey," said Karr. He put his hand on the laptop as if steadying himself. He had the white phone to his ear.

"What are you doing?" asked Sourin.

"Could you hold on a second?" Karr said into the phone.

"Pull it, Tommy," said Farlekas.

Karr smiled at Sourin, shook his head back and forth, then motioned to Sourin that he would be right with him. Sourin took a step into the tent.

"No, no, I really need you to hang on a second," Karr told the imaginary person on the other end of the line. He put the phone down.

"What are you doing?" demanded Sourin.

"Just calling in to check on that support you wanted." Karr glanced to his right where the Thai guard was dozing. Sourin's eyes followed—and then widened in rage. He began cursing—or at least the flood of words sounded like curses. The guard from outside ran in as Sourin's voice rose in a shout, and he dragged the unfortunate man out of the tent. Karr stepped back to the laptop and yanked the dongle out, palming it as the major returned.

"What are you doing in here?" the major demanded.

"Like I said, talking to my people to get you support."

"What's in your hand?"

Karr held it up, turning it over. "Helps me make a connection if I need one," he said. "I put my computer into it."

"No, Tommy," warned Chafetz.

But it was too late. Sourin came over and yanked it from his hand. "Show me."

"You're not cleared, my friend."

Sourin yanked his pistol from his holster and pointed it at the op's head. "Show me."

"Afraid I can't," said Karr.

Sourin extended his hand. His pistol was an older Colt model, a .45-caliber that would make a very artistic hole in Karr's head if fired.

"Tell you what—I'll show you on one of your computers if you want," said Karr. He reached over and picked up one of the laptops. "Plug it in like this."

He felt Sourin's gun press against his ear. "That'll be enough," said the major.

"Suit yourself," said Karr, returning the dongle to his pocket. "Mind if I finish my phone call?"

"It's finished," said Sourin.

"You want that gear or not?"

The major frowned at him but then holstered his pistol.

"I'm a crank when I don't get my sleep, too," said Karr, picking up the phone.

"You pushed that too far," said Farlekas.

"Yeah, no kidding," said Karr, smiling at the major. "So what time should we expect delivery? And can you include a steak?"

29

Dean felt the perspiration rise from his body as if it were steam, bubbling and running off into his clothes in rivulets. The bed seemed to have sunk in the middle, and his head buzzed; the inside of his stomach felt like scorched sandpaper, and the fire smoldered up his esophagus.

He pushed himself upright, breathing slowly to try to clear his head. Lia had taken him to a hotel several towns away from where he'd been dropped; she was sleeping in the next room. Security men—they were Air Force sergeants, borrowed from an Air Force base in Germany and dressed in plainclothes—were watching the floor, along with several people Lia had taken from the embassy earlier.

God, he was hot. He touched his skull beneath the back of his right ear where the com device had been implanted. A butterfly stitch bandage covered the incision.

Was his headache a result of the operation? It hadn't lasted thirty seconds.

More likely the beers.

Dean went over to the window, and despite the fact that he'd been admonished not to even look out, he opened it now, trying to get a full breath of air. His lungs rebelled, and he started to cough.

Dean settled back on the bed. He'd had a wild dream, and it came back to him now—he and Keys in high school, cutting a class and hanging out by the baseball field drinking a god-awful mixture of wine and whiskey Kegan had lifted from his dad's liquor cabinet.

Kegan leering at him, drunk. "We're cows," he said. "Cows."

Dean shook his head.

That hadn't happened. Kegan never cut class as a kid. Kegan was too serious about his grades, too committed—or too scared maybe.

Not scared. Serious. Very serious. Even in those days, he knew he was going to be a doctor. Dean figured he'd find a cure for cancer or something like that.

Kegan had predicted that, hadn't he? During one of their drinking sessions—they did have drinking sessions, though his memory was foggy about them now.

Dr. Kegan, the man who would save the world from the scourge of cancer.

That's how Dean thought of his friend.

Not as a murderer. Though the two things weren't necessarily contradictory.

Dean's stomach rumbled. He pushed himself up out of bed, stumbling toward the bathroom.

30

Sandra Marshall was the first person William Rubens saw that evening when he walked into the secure conference room in the White House basement. She was sitting just opposite the doorway, looking at something on the screen of the computers reset into the tabletop. Blue light reflected up from the screen, casting her face in a soft glow. The light was more than flattering, and Rubens was surprised by a twitch of lust.

He moved quickly to take a seat next to his boss, Vice Admiral Devlin Brown. Brown wasn't particularly happy that Homeland Security was involved; like most, if not all, Washington and military veterans, he had little use for the agency.

"Dr. Lester is from the CDC," said George Hadash, running the meeting in the President's absence. "He's going to give an overview of the situation, with input from the FBI and Desk Three."

Lester started his summary from the beginning, focusing on the domestic outbreak, thus far limited to two positive and twelve suspected cases. Thanks to a heads-up from Desk Three—Lester at least gave credit where due—the CDC was now focusing on a family of bacteria known as *S. moniliforms,* which were responsible for streptobacillary rat-bite fever. Ordinarily transmitted by rat bites, the disease was characterized by a high fever that would typically cycle on in two-to-four-day series randomly recurring over the course of months. A maculopapular rash that looked like a large bruise typically accompanied the disease, which also featured a variety of flulike symptoms, meningitis, and pneumonia. Maculopapular referred to the fact that the rash was both macular—a stain-like mark distinguished from its surroundings—and papular—having pupules or eruptions above the surface of the skin like pimples.

The symptoms fit *S. moniliformis* better than *Spirillum minus* or *Sodoku,* a very similar disease also called rat-bite fever but caused by a different bacteria, which was also under consideration because of evidence the Desk Three people had uncovered. But there was one problem in making the connection—both diseases were caused by rat bites. As far as they could tell, Victim Two had not been bitten by a rat.

Victim Two was Gorman, the BCI investigator. The other man had died an hour before.

"We're just in the process now of preparing the tests for the organisms," said Lester. "Rat-bite fever is very rare in the U.S."

"If you haven't done tests, how do you know that's what you're looking at?" asked Marshall.

"We've diagnosed it clinically," said Lester.

"But you just said it could be confused with half a dozen things."

Lester glanced at Rubens in exasperation.

A good sign, thought Rubens. He could count on the doctor after all.

"There are indications unrelated to the disease itself," said Rubens. "Intelligence indications."

"What sort of indications?" asked Marshall.

"Until we're really sure, I'd prefer not to get into methodology. We are assisting in the investigation, for reasons that the FBI can get into."

Westhoven's face blanched from sheen to high-gloss white. He began explaining the link with Kegan and briefly—very, very briefly—gave the scientist's background. A thorough review of his current work was ongoing, but at the moment there appeared no connection with germ warfare of any kind, nor was there an apparent link with rat-bite fever.

"So, what's the link then?" asked Marshall.

"None that we can ascertain."

"Well, the house," said Lester.

"The dead man there?" asked Marshall.

"As I intimated, rat-bite fever would not be something commonly looked for," said Dr. Lester. "The dead man will have to be examined for that. He was possibly a carrier."

"What was his contract work for the government?" asked Marshall.

"I don't have the exact contracts in front of me," said Westhoven. "But suffice it to be said that these bacteria were not involved."

"But he could have constructed them?"

"Well . . ."

"Could he have, Dr. Lester?"

"Not really my area," said Lester, demurring.

"I believe you might mean propagated them," said Rubens, stepping in. "If he did, there's no indication in any of the records anyone has found at any of his work areas."

"Which you've accessed?"

She meant that as a jibe, Rubens realized, but he ignored her, continuing on. Kegan's work with bacteria would permit him an opportunity for many things; the FBI tests of his labs would have to reveal whatever they could reveal.

"At this stage, the important thing to do is gather information," added Lester. "We don't really want to rule anything out. Because, frankly, the symptoms are very confusing. It's very open-ended, and if it weren't for the fact that Dr. Kegan was involved, we might not even be thinking in this direction at all."

"Which direction, exactly?" asked Marshall. "Candidly, Doctor, I feel as if I've come in on the middle of a conversation. I don't entirely understand what's going on."

"If the disease was caused by an engineered organism, which I emphasize we have no evidence of," said Lester, "then we'll need to study it very intensely. Is it penicillin-resistant?"

"Is it?"

"We don't know yet. Patient Two hasn't responded to the first course of treatment. Or the second."

Lester backed up and once more went through the basic situation, this time studiously using simple terms. Was Marshall really a notch slower than the rest, Rubens wondered, or was it an act to disarm the others?

What was she really after?

Westhoven had tamed his belligerence considerably in the few hours since the video conference. He didn't mention his opinion of what Lester called a soft quarantine—extensive tests of everyone who had been at Kegan's house. Instead, Westhoven concentrated on the investigations the Bureau had done. Thus far, there was no indication that Kegan had done any work on bacteria except for those involved in the pollution projects—but those were, indeed, engineered.

Perhaps, Westhoven hinted, something had morphed out of control. Perhaps it simply appeared to be rat-bite fever.

"But how would that account for the dead man in the house?" asked Marshall.

Westhoven simply shrugged. It wouldn't.

Marshall headed Rubens off at the door, reminding him that they had agreed to discuss the biometric IDs this evening. Trapped, Rubens offered dinner; he was hungry, he decided, so he might as well eat. She suggested Clancy's, a fancy restaurant considered the latest trend on the Potomac. Under other circumstances, Rubens would have suggested a much quieter place, but he realized that might send the wrong message—here at least people would surely see them and it would be clear that he had nothing to hide.

The food turned out be surprisingly good, if slightly pretentious, even by D.C. standards. Rubens ordered the most basic selection on the menu: lamb chops with foie gras and apple-pear chutney.

"Lovely man, Dr. Lester," said Marshall as they finished dinner.

"Oh yes," said Rubens.

"Do you work with CDC often?" Marshall asked.

"We work with whom we work." He paused, emphasizing the mystery. "But I would say rarely."

"Rarely?"

"We do adhere to our charter."

"Your operations are offshore."

Actually, he had meant that the NSA's primary concerns had little to do with the disease. Nor did the NSA charter specifically dictate that it conduct overseas operations only, a common misperception. But Rubens smiled in a way that he knew might suggest agreement yet leave things open-ended.

"I don't suppose we should really talk about business," she said.

"What would you like to talk about?"

"Oh, art. Are you really related to Peter Rubens, the Flemish painter?"

"Yes," he said.

This wasn't a secret, surely, but he was nonetheless surprised that Sandra Marshall—a California ladder climber—knew not only that his famous seventeenth-century ancestor was a great painter but that he had been a diplomat and almost certainly a spymaster as well. And Rubens was further surprised when she turned the conversation to the Matisse exhibit due at the Metropolitan in New York next month, discussing the early modern painter quite knowledgeably.

And then, before he could even ask how she had come by all this knowledge—an art history major in her undergrad years was his guess—she abruptly brought the conversation back on point.

"Have you thought of the Internet proposal?" she asked after the waiter had left them with a pot of coffee.

"Candidly, no," said Rubens.

Marshall's face flickered with disappointment.

"You really think it would be a good idea? Everyone gazing at a computer and embedding their ID in every keystroke?" he asked, trying to keep his tone light.

"You think we should use iris scans then?" she said.

"No, I was just throwing it out as a metaphor."

"The President was inclined toward something similar."

"Interesting. And George?"

He had debated how exactly to refer to the National Security Advisor. Rarely did he in fact call Hadash "George," even to his face, and it took a supreme effort to make it seem natural.

"George seems to favor a thumb monitor that would work via the keyboard," she said. "The specifics really are the realm of the experts. That's why we need a study. You still oppose it?"

"Formally, we have no opinion."

"But you think it's a bad idea."

Rubens had no point of safety to retreat to. He had to commit, or at least come as close as one did in Washington.

"Probably," he admitted.

"Yes," she said with obvious disappointment. And then she reached out and touched his hand. "I hope you'll keep an open mind for a while."

"First impressions are not always lasting ones," said Rubens. He glanced at her hand, noting that it was still on his forearm.

"Are the rumors true?" she asked, pulling her hand away.

"Which rumors?" said Rubens.

"That you're being considered for Secretary of State."

"I didn't know that there would be a vacancy," said Rubens, honestly. He hadn't heard of any rumors along those lines.

"Oh, there will be. You would be an excellent choice."

"Well, thank you," said Rubens, unsure what else to say.

Rubens' head was practically spinning as he drove to his safehouse to swap cars and go home.

Secretary of State?

Of course it was a post he coveted. Defense was so much less refined—not to mention weighed down by the pendulous bureaucracies of the services the office was supposed to supervise. At the moment, State was not particularly effective, but under his leadership—well then, of course.

But there were no rumors that he knew of about the post becoming vacant. James Lincoln was not only competent but also an occasional ally.

An important ally. The fact that Rubens couldn't stand him personally notwithstanding.

Secretary of State.

His Art Room phone buzzed. Rubens took it from his jacket pocket.

"Rubens."

"Boss, this is Chris in the Art Room," said Farlekas. "You ready for an update?"

Rubens listened as Farlekas detailed the data from the computers Tommy Karr had compromised in Thailand. The military unit appeared to be loyal to the central government, and there were no traces of penetration by the rebels. However, the Art Room had come up with three possible guerrilla cells operating nearby that might have penetrated the communications system. They were in the process of preparing missions to bug all three, sending vessels to land miniature flies in their area. Analysis of optical satellite data had turned up one interesting finding—there were pigs at one of the camps.

"The significance of swine would be what?" asked Rubens.

"Very useful for growing certain organisms," said Farlekas, explaining how pigs were used to create insulin as well as other materials. Pigs were raised all across Asia for food, and in fact there were wild swine in many places as well. But Islamic law forbade the eating of pork.

"Wouldn't the logical conclusion be that these are not Muslim guerrillas?" asked Rubens.

"Thai intelligence indicates that they are."

"Chris, we're looking for bacteria. All they need are petri dishes."

"The scientists raised the possibility that if they were to be using animals, the program would be very far advanced. They might have found a way to use the swine as organism factories. It's actually not as far-fetched as it sounds. Normal diseases, even the flu, can be harbored in animals. Any number of ailments have started naturally that way. The science section is very worried about this."

Rubens did not believe that terrorists could use such advanced techniques. Or rather, he didn't *want* to believe it. He thought the scientists had let their imaginations and fears run far ahead of reality, just as the Thai intelligence service had made a mistake about the guerrillas' fanatical religious affiliation. And yet the history of fighting terrorism was nothing if not a history of imagination, prodding the brain into the odd corners of the unexpected. The terrorists' few spectacular successes had come more because those fighting them had failed to anticipate—had failed to *imagine*—their capabilities.

As far as technology went, infecting a pig with a germ was hardly the cutting edge of science.

There was no downplaying the danger.

"Are these people connected to the Crescent Tigers?" asked Rubens.

"Not that we know, and not according to the Thai authorities. The Tigers seem to have fallen on hard times. Their Myanmar camp is abandoned. We've checked."

"On foot?"

"I have more than a dozen satellite photos and a new series coming in about two hours. No fires, no traffic, no anything. They're long gone. I have Johnny Bib's people trying to track them down. I'll put them at the top of the list if we find them, I guarantee."

"Very well. Send Tommy to take a look at the most likely camps, with this as the priority," said Rubens. "Have him go to the abandoned camp as well."

"He'll have to use the Thai military unit. They'd have to attack them."

"That's what the Thai unit's supposed to be doing, isn't it?"

"Their resources there are limited. Most of the firepower is on the other side of the country."

A series of zeros flashed before Rubens' eyes—the budget

line he was about to blow past. Even Deep Black had to deal with bean counters.

But so be it.

"Very well. Find out what we need. Expedite the process. We may be working on a time constraint here; the sooner we recover Kegan the better. Europe?"

"We still have no leads on the people Dean met with."

"Nothing?"

Rubens felt the steering wheel shake violently. He glanced down at the speedometer and saw that he was pushing the nondescript agency Malibu over eighty. He backed off the gas, trying to calm himself as well.

"Our resources are a little stretched. Johnny Bib is up in New York, and his team has been focused more on the information that he's looking into than the European end," said Farlekas.

"Well, correct that," said Rubens.

"I'm trying. They gave him twenty-four hours," said Farlekas. "So they'll be looking for him soon."

"Yes."

"I want to send him back out."

"And?"

"He wasn't feeling well."

"Describe his symptoms."

"Sounded like he ate something that didn't agree with him."

Rubens once more checked his speed.

"Boss?"

"Does he have a fever?"

"He says no. I'd like to have him checked."

Dean should be—*he had to be*—checked out, not only for his own health but also to find out exactly what the hell the infection was.

On the other hand, if he didn't keep the meeting, they would lose their best chance at finding out what was going on. If these people knew about an antidote, they had to be apprehended. For Dean's sake as well as everyone else's.

The enormity of the threat became a physical thing weighing against the back of Rubens' neck as he considered the implications of the two strands of their investigation: an incurable disease propagated in pigs, which could spread flu-like through the population and at the same time compromise the food supply, or at least a portion of it.

Rubens took a deep breath, centering himself. There would be a cure. They had no real evidence of a guerrilla connection, let alone any reason besides a scientist's paranoia that animals were involved.

Imagination had its uses, but it must be controlled. The intellect must be tempered by experience.

Aristotle's gloss on Plato, in a sense.

"Set up a very strong operation around Dean," Rubens told Farlekas. "We can't lose track of him this time, not even for a moment."

"If he has this disease—"

"If he has it, we have to find a cure for it. And right now, he may be our best shot at it. Prepare for that contingency, but the operation must move forward. There is no other choice."

Farlekas remained silent for a moment.

"One other thing, chief."

"Yes?"

"CDC confirmed ten of those cases they were looking at. Only one has a connection they can find to the Kegan house and victim. They have more to look into. A lot more."

"A lot more being how many?"

"Two hundred."

"I'll be back at the Art Room in about forty minutes."

31

"You don't look that good, Charlie Dean."

"Thanks, princess."

"Don't ever call me that." Lia stood up from the table, her chair legs screeching against the tiled floor of the hotel café. "Tommy calls me that and I hate it."

"You ever tell him that?"

"He's not important enough to tell."

"Sorry." Dean rubbed his eyes with his hand. His stomach had settled a bit, but he hadn't felt like eating anything. "It cold in here?"

Lia reached across the table and put her hand against his forehead. "You're burning up."

"I'm okay," he told her. "I'll be okay. Let's just get this thing over with."

"Charlie—this isn't going to be like yesterday. These guys are very serious."

He pushed himself up from the table and narrowed his eyes. "I'm fine. Just let's get going, all right? How does the com system work?"

Dean pushed away from the table, willing his legs to stop wobbling. He was chilled, as if he were getting a bad fever, but he'd been through worse, much worse, and he was going to get through this thing now.

Where the hell was Keys? He'd warned him about food poisoning once, more than once, gone on in great detail.

We carry billions of little buggers around in our stomachs all the time. Russian roulette—you're going to get nailed eventually. Bright side of it is, only a few can really kill us.

"Touch the back of your belt," said Lia.

"Specific spot?"

"Any spot. That turns it on. Has to be your finger—it keys to your personal magnetic field. If you turn it off, they can't hear you. Don't pay attention to what Rockman says. It's agent-controlled."

"You all right, Charlie?" said Rockman in his ear. The voice was even spookier than with the eyeglass system, a whisper that could belong to God, or at least a guardian angel.

"Yeah, I'm cool. Let's get this stinkin' show on the road, huh?"

Lia watched Dean walk out of the restaurant. Like nearly every man she'd met, he was a stoic asshole when it came to being sick.

Most likely, it was just food poisoning, something in the overly rich cream sauces that had been slathered over their food. But she couldn't dismiss the notion that Dean had been poisoned by the people who had kidnapped him, though why wasn't clear.

Outside the hotel, Lia watched Dean flag down a taxi. It was one of theirs, driven by a low-level embassy CIA officer she'd borrowed. A van manned by the Air Force people Desk Three had shanghaied from Germany started out after the taxi pulled away; two more Air Force security types were already in the park where Dean was headed. Lia got into her rental Renault and slid on a headset, which was connected to a small radio in her purse. The unit allowed her to tie into the military people, who were using Special Forces–style PSC-5 radios, with satellite phones as backups.

"All right, let's all check in," she said.

Two of the Air Force people spoke over each other.

"Let's keep the testosterone down, please," she snapped.

"Sean," she said, picking the team leader in the first van, "you're first."

As they drove toward the park, Lia took out her handheld computer and fired it up, switching into the surveillance net covering the area where Dean had been dropped off the day before. Small video cams had been placed atop the brick pillars that stood at the two entrances; between them they covered 96 percent of the park. A gussied-up Fokker with optical sensors—an NSA-owned "Eyes" asset—orbited to the south, providing real-time video and sharper-resolution, near-real-time digital still feeds of anything they wanted superior detail on, like license plates and faces. Operated by an Air Force Special Operations crew that did not officially exist, the plane had twice the capability of the CIA model it had been based on—a William Rubens requirement. It could fly between three and five miles away from a target and still provide reasonable surveillance, though it had to be careful about local flight rules.

"Dean's just getting there," Rockman told her. "Locator's working fine. Did he take his iodine supplements?"

"What am I, his nurse?"

"My, we're cranky today," said Telach.

Theoretically, the radioactive material used by the tracking system posed no threat—as long as it remained solid. If it broke up in his body—occasionally this happened—the iodine could be absorbed by his thyroid, which was why he'd been given supplements to block it.

"Dean's in the park, walking to the bench," said Rockman. "All right, everybody be real careful now. We don't want to get too obvious."

Lia ignored Rockman, leaning out the window to get a glimpse of the park. She saw Dean sitting at the bench; then her view was obscured by two old people feeding the pigeons.

"Go around," she told her driver. "I want to keep him in sight."

"That wasn't what you had laid out earlier."

"I changed my mind."

Dean felt the boards at the back of the bench slap into his back as he sat. His whole body seemed achy.

Maybe it wasn't food poisoning. Maybe it was the flu.

Good. Maybe he'd give it to these bastards.

His stomach pressed up against his esophagus, and for a second he thought he was going to have to find a bush. But it calmed, and he started to feel a bit better.

A husband and wife, obviously American tourists, stopped near him.

"Would you take our picture?" asked the woman, gesturing with a camera.

Dean hesitated, then reached for the camera. He felt slightly dizzy but managed to take the picture for them. When he sat back down, an old lady wearing far too much perfume had perched herself at the other end of the bench. She had a paper bag of popcorn, which she tossed out piece by piece to the pigeons.

Dean looked in the other direction, waiting for the goons.

Let's get this thing over with, he thought to himself.

Rockman switched the feeds back and forth, still unable to spot the contact people. He had a situation map on the main screen; Dean's position was marked with a green triangle and the two Air Force people in the park with squares. (They had old-fashioned FM transmitters.) Beyond the park were the three vans packed with military people they'd borrowed, Lia in her rental, and a pair of embassy Marines in plainclothes but with diplomatic plates and IDs, in case they had to deal with the local authorities. A pair of Army AH-6 scout helicopters borrowed from a unit stationed in Germany stood by at the airport available for their use; equipped with rockets, Hellfire missiles, and machine guns, the helicopters were a last resort if things got nasty.

They could always call on the local authorities, of course. But Rockman figured if things got that bad, they might just as well use the F-47Cs that were on the ground at Avino Air Force Base and nuke the place.

A figure of speech. The thermobaric bombs slung on the robot planes were designed to merely eradicate bunkers, not whole cities. The weapons ignited a mixture of solid fuel and air in a confined space, such as a bunker or a tunnel. The result was a kind of flash fire that created massive pressure to destroy the target.

"How we looking?" asked Telach, coming over to his console.

"Just waiting for them to show."

"Biology people ready?"

Rockman thumbed to the back benches where an NSA scientist named Bill Chaucer was sitting with another expert from the CDC. They had open lines to university labs around the country, as well as Desk Three's own research team and a vast database of knowledge.

"Wish I had that backup for my college chemistry class," said Rockman.

"I doubt it would have helped," said William Rubens, appearing behind him.

"We're just waiting for them to make contact," said Telach.

"How's Dean look?"

"I think it's food poisoning," said Rockman. "He does, too."

Rubens' brow furrowed, but he said nothing, slowly rocking on his feet as he gazed at the screens.

Dean pushed his shoulders back and let out a slight groan. His neck muscles were so tight he felt as if they were pressed between clamps.

"Genau das habe ich gesagt," said the old woman.

"I'm sorry, I didn't mean to disturb you," said Dean. "I think I have a cold coming on. Something like that."

She turned toward him. *"Genau das habe ich gesagt."*

"I don't speak Austrian."

"German," whispered Rockman.

"Genau das habe ich gesagt. Do exactly as I say."

Dean followed the woman's glance downward toward the bag. Rather than popcorn, she was holding a gun.

32

"He's got two platoons, no air support, nothing heavier than sixty-millimeter mortars that date to World War II," said Foster, looking at the plan Karr had outlined.

"I like a unit that travels light," said Karr.

Foster shook his head. The other Marine made a sound something similar to what a horse might make if sighing.

"You guys don't think they're up to it?" asked Karr.

The check of the computers showed that the Thai major had been pushing for raids over the border; all indications were that he was loyal to the government and Rubens had given his okay to proceed. The Art Room had made a decision on the first target, selecting the largest of the three camps it had spotted earlier. Satellite reconnaissance had detected pigs there; while there didn't seem to be any of the prerequisites an advanced bio lab would require—there was no electricity, for example—the animals conceivably could be used for experiments or even breeding germs. Most of the experts described that chance as "vanishingly small"—but they couldn't rule it out. For his part, Karr preferred to hit the largest camp first; that meant the others should be easier.

Assuming, of course, the tiny Thai force didn't get squashed.

"With a lot more firepower, maybe we could take these guys," said Gidrey. "Or, if we were talking two teams of Marines—"

"What, eight guys?"

"The right guys you could do it with four," said Foster.

"See what I'm saying?"

"Yeah, but these guys . . . I mean, no offense," said Gidrey, "but they're not equipped. And, uh, from the looks of the way they got this camp organized—"

"Got to work with what we got," said Karr. "Come on—there's not that many people at this guerrilla camp, are there? Dozen at most."

"They all got guns, though."

"First of all, to get to any of these camps, it could take more than a day of travel by foot," said Foster. He jabbed his hand at the map. "The terrain is torturous, and I'd bet there's lookouts, booby traps, mines maybe—all sorts of crap. Plus, you have to cross area here which is held by another guerrilla group. The woods are full of 'em."

"So we need a couple of helicopters. What else?"

"A gunship."

"Like an AC-130? What else?"

"You're going to get a gunship over here?" asked Gidrey. "From where?"

"Oh, I can get anything I want. My daddy's rich," said Karr. "Come on; help me draw up the attack. Don't forget half these warm bodies here are just pigs—the swine kind, not the human. They're going to have trouble aiming rifles."

33

"They're on A1, going in the direction of Vienna," Rockman told Lia.

"God, can't they make up their minds?" she snapped.

"Maybe you'll get some sightseeing in," said the runner.

Lia glanced at her watch. They'd been on the road now for nearly an hour, driving backward and forward. Dean was in the back of a black delivery truck, along with two guards who either didn't understand English or were pretending not to. Thus far, there had been nothing to indicate where they were going. The outskirts of Vienna lay about five kilometers to the east. Lia was on the highway about a half-mile ahead of the truck; one of the vans was three cars behind it.

"Turning off."

"What a surprise."

"You see the feed from the Fokker?" asked Rockman.

"No, I have my eyes closed." Lia zoomed out the display on her handheld computer. A black vehicle had joined the parade—a Mercedes that had been waiting by the roadside. A shadow arced nearby.

"Helicopter's watching—don't let the Fokker get too close," said Lia.

"Right, we're on it," said Rockman.

"They're slowing," said the team in van one, which was closest to the delivery truck.

"Pass them by," said Lia.

"Turning into an industrial park," said Rockman. "Maybe our target."

"Circle back," Lia told the driver. "And find a place where you can take a leak."

"I don't have to go."

"You will."

Dean's head felt as if it were about to explode. The package truck they'd put him in not only found every pothole or crack in the pavement, but the springs and shock absorbers seemed to have been removed. Sitting on a bare metal floor, he had a hard time maintaining his equilibrium. Now as the truck came to a stop he slammed against the panel so hard he felt his eyes smack against their sockets. Instead of the darkness of the back, he saw rivulets of yellow and white light.

"Out," said one of the men who had met him. *"Gehen."*

"Yeah, okay, out, go. Right," said Dean, pushing upward. One of the men grabbed his arm and helped him toward the back. Except for his grip, he was very gentle.

The sunlight blinded Dean temporarily. He waited for them to blindfold him, but instead they prodded him toward a brick building that sat behind a macadam walkway on his right.

"No blindfold?" he asked his minders, hoping the Art Room was listening.

The minders didn't respond. He walked ahead to the building as they trailed. The door opened just as he arrived, and a short, slightly overweight man of about sixty appeared, his thick glasses hanging off his nose and his oily black hair tousled as if he had left in a hurry. The man moved quickly, obviously anxious to get away—and then touched Charlie on the arm as he passed.

"You're with me," said the man. He spoke with what seemed like a British accent.

"Uh."

"This way now," said the man, already moving along the asphalt path.

Dean glanced at the two minders, but their faces were blank. Not knowing what else to do, he followed the man to a BMW. The man gestured toward the passenger seat. When they were inside, he said, "Dr. Dean, a pleasure to meet you."

"I'm a little confused."

"I understand that your employer did not fill you in before he sent you overseas. That is unfortunate." The man gestured with the ignition key, as if it were a piece of chalk and he was in the classroom. "Please put your seat belt on."

Dean complied and the man put his key into the ignition. The accent wasn't British exactly, but he had spent some time there, at least enough to wash the majority of the rest of his accent from his voice.

"Where are we going?" Charlie asked.

"To get the antidote."

"Draw him out," whispered Rockman in Dean's ear. "Ask him some questions about who he is."

"How do I know you're the person I'm supposed to talk to?" asked Dean.

The man chuckled. He had a squashed freckle the size of a ladybug on his right chin, a birthmark of some type and undoubtedly a good identifier. But Charlie wasn't equipped with a video fly; they'd worried it might be detected.

"Do you really think, Doctor, that anyone else in Austria would know who you were?"

"I don't know," said Charlie. "Maybe you're with the CIA or something."

"Hardly."

"Who then?"

"I'm a friend. Call me Hercules."

"Not too conceited, is he?" said Rockman. "Ask him, 'Why?' "

Good God, shut up, thought Dean. I'm not stupid.

"You're the second man I've met with that name. Knew a

fellow named Hercules Jones, little guy, feisty. His mother had no idea what she was doing when she gave him that name. He fought all the time as a kid. Plays a cello in an orchestra now, I believe."

"Please, Dr. Dean."

"I'm not a doctor. I don't have a Ph.D."

"Oh, that's a bit of ridiculous formality, isn't it? You could have your degree anytime you choose—Kegan hold you back?"

"I owe him a lot."

"Hardly."

"You offering me a job?"

Hercules chuckled. The man was about as far from being a hero of Greek legend—or any legend—as could be imagined.

"The antidote is where?"

"I have a place to take you to," said Dean. "But whether the antidote is there, I haven't a clue."

The man turned to him and smiled. "Tell me about the difficulty of cloning DNA that originates in bacteria."

"Uh, what do you mean? The technical aspects? Mapping?"

"Good," said a new voice in Charlie's head. He recognized it as the voice of one of the biology experts.

"I mean cloning bacterial DNA," said the man.

"Once it's properly sequenced," said Charlie, "I don't know that there's more of a problem with bacteria than with anything else. I'm not an expert and I'm not saying the process is easy, but in theory, DNA is DNA. The literature—I guess I'm not entirely sure what you want to know."

Hercules' face clouded.

"We use a dye process generally at the first stage to do the mapping," said Charlie. "Is that what you mean? Um, do you want me to walk through the lab process?"

"MegaBACE 4000:384 capillary DNA sequencer," said Chaucer. "They call it 'Marvin' at the Hudson Valley lab. There's a smaller set, too—Little Mo."

"You want Mo's blueprint or Marvin's or what?" asked Dean. "What are you looking for?"

Hercules put the car into reverse without answering.

"That didn't go well," said Lia, sitting in the car a mile and a half south of the industrial complex.

"It's all right," said Chaucer, one of the bio experts. "It's not clear what Hercules wants. He's got to be more specific. Dean is answering exactly the way I would."

"Oh, that's reassuring."

"Lia, we have a tentative ID on Hercules," said Telach. "I'm going to beam some of the information down to you. He's a Greek national, a scientist who's had some trouble with the government and his university—he's been working with a group of Georgians. The Soviet variety, not the Atlanta."

"Not SVR?" The Russian foreign intelligence service—the initials came from the Russian words—was a successor to the KGB's foreign spying operations. Among its important duties was the study of scientific breakthroughs; Lia had fenced with them before.

"I don't know. We're still sorting it out," said Rockman.

Lia keyed the handheld so she could get the photo, which had been taken by the Fokker at long-range. They'd obviously used the birthmark on the man's chin, to help cinch the ID.

"All right, they're pulling out of the lot," said Rockman. "Everybody get into position and we'll trail them again. Hang on—helicopter is coming around."

Lia heard Rockman tell the Fokker pilot to maintain his position in an orbit southwest of the city. She flipped back to her situational overview and saw that Dean was starting to move.

"Another helicopter," warned Telach. "Good, more lease data to get through—I need some registration numbers."

"Okay, everybody, keep doing exactly what you were just doing. Don't stop; don't react," Lia told her ground team. "They're going to spin around the block a few times and see if anybody moves. That's why there's another helicopter."

Lia got out of the car and went to the trunk. The driver

started to get out, but she waved him back in. "I can handle this myself. Just wait. Keep track of where they're driving around."

"Lia, they're back out on the highway, going toward the city," said Rockman.

"That's nice." She could hear the helicopter well to the north.

"Aren't you going to follow?"

"No."

"Why not?"

"Woman's intuition."

She popped the trunk and took out a large golf bag. Unzipping the top, she pulled out what looked like the body of a good-sized crow. The wings were contained in a small case; she slotted them into the indents and added the stabilizer, which looked like a fanned tail at the end. The robot airplane was powered by a battery-operated fan engine that fit on the top; it could only do about twelve knots, but it was difficult to tell from a real bird from anything over ten yards away.

Lia booted up the diagnostic program on her handheld, waiting for the aircraft's tiny computer to finish its own boot checks. Finally she got a green flash. Programming the Crow was simple—she designated the target and then punched one of the preprogrammed flight patterns, in this case an overlaid double-eight. Then she picked up the Crow, put her right thumb on the launch button—actually a detent on the right side of the bird's body—and took a two-step away from the car, throwing it into the air as she did. The Crow swooped downward, then began to soar.

"Why did you launch the Crow?" hissed Telach.

"They're coming back to the industrial park."

"How do you know that?"

Lia ignored her and got back in the car.

"Lia, this time you've gone too far. Lia!"

"Drive up the highway to this point here," she told her driver, showing him the map on the handheld. "See this fence here? I think I can get over it."

"That car in the corner there—we saw that in the briefing, right?" asked the driver.

"Right. That's one of the vehicles they used to shadow Dean after he was dropped off," said Lia. "It's covering the south entrance to the industrial park and it hasn't moved at all. The geniuses back in the Art Room missed it."

"Well, you could have told us that earlier," said Telach in her ear.

"I accept your apology," said Lia.

"Tell me about your days as an undergraduate, Dr. Dean."

"A lot of partying," said Dean.

"You're the same age as Dr. Kegan."

"Yes, I am. I lost a few years."

"So I've heard. Where did they go?"

"You want my life story?"

"After a fashion."

Dean's phony life story tracked his real one to a point, substituting the twenty years he'd spent in the Marine Corps for a gig as a high school biology teacher with a drinking problem. That allowed for the perfect intersection of his youth, which couldn't be conveniently altered, and gave him just enough of a sordid past to suggest he might be interesting. His phony teaching record, college transcripts, a few academic papers, and even two DWI convictions had been sprinkled surreptitiously into the official records by Desk Three.

"St. James?" asked Hercules.

It sounded familiar—was it a school Keys had gone to?

"Bluff," said the voice in Dean's head.

"Um, a church?" asked Dean.

"Chester High School," said Hercules.

Charlie laughed. His head pounded harder.

"I'm afraid I don't remember much of my time at good ol' Chester Central School District," he said. "Eventually I was informed that my services were redundant."

"Too much of the grape."

"Vodka, actually. Though for a bit there I wasn't all that particular."

"You don't look well."

"I don't feel that well," said Dean. "I think I ate something bad last night."

"Where did you eat?"

Was that part of the test?

"A restaurant, uh, Kingel or Kindel or something along those lines."

"If you're in Vienna again, I would recommend Zum Kuckuck," said Hercules. "Very nice. Expensive."

"Maybe you'll foot the bill, huh?"

Hercules leaned over in the seat as they drove, and tugged at Dean's sleeve.

"What?"

"Show me your arm."

Dean rolled up his sleeve.

"No bruises?"

"Bruises?"

"Welts anywhere?"

"He thinks you have it," whispered Rockman.

Have what? Charlie wondered.

"Not that you know," said Chaucer.

Charlie pulled his hand back. "I didn't realize I was supposed to get a physical."

"You may be feeling the aftereffects of the Demerol," said Hercules, sitting back upright. " Okay, let's go back."

"Back where?"

"I'm afraid that my associates don't quite believe you're who you claim to be, and so we have a little quiz for you to pass before we can proceed. Given the amount of money at stake, I'm sure you understand that we want to protect our investment fully."

"I don't know anything about money," offered Dean.

Hercules laughed. "You really are naive, aren't you, Dr. Dean?"

"I'm not a doctor," said Dean.

The complex consisted of two identical buildings covered with elaborate masonry designs, along with a smaller garage at the left end and a number of trailers in the back. Only one of the two buildings seemed to be occupied, at least if the Crow's sensors could be believed; it was possible that there was a basement level with activity the Crow couldn't see. A satellite was being directed overhead to provide a view.

The trailers were more interesting. Two appeared to have been set up as roving laboratories. The infrared images were being studied by the scientific teams; there were autoclaves, a fermenter, refrigerators, incubators, microscopes, computers—enough gear to keep a mad scientist happy for years.

"That's where we want to go, huh?" said Lia, looking at the images on the handheld.

"Dangerous, very dangerous," said Telach. "Let's let this play out a bit."

"I want to get inside the complex before they get back," Lia said.

"All right, but hurry. They're less than ten minutes away," said Rockman.

The infrared camera on the Crow gave Lia a good view of the complex. A pair of security cams observed the rear fence; they were static but had good coverage. One could be approached from the west without being observed. It had been situated in a recessed box in a stone pillar to prevent tampering—a not unreasonable approach, unless the person doing the tampering was a member of Deep Black.

Lia slid up to the box, holding what looked like a large tumbler in her right hand.

"They're coming," said Rockman. "Five minutes."

"Yeah, no kidding."

"Guards on foot can see you from that angle."

"You know what? You're making me nervous. Did you take control of the Crow?"

"We have it."

"Then come on yourself."

"It wasn't built for precision flying and we're controlling it from here, rather than Space Command."

Lia waited until the Crow fluttered toward the camera,

heading directly for the lens. Just as it seemed as if it would poke into the box, Lia moved the glasslike device quickly over the opening. The pseudo-tumbler was actually a sophisticated video screen, at the moment transparently projecting the fence. In twelve seconds Rockman would flick a switch that would substitute a loop of that image for a real feed.

"We still have the Crow," said Telach.

Lia trotted down the fence line. Once on the other side, she had to cross about twenty feet of open area before reaching the two vehicles parked at the side of the garage; this was by far the best spot to use to get inside the complex, but there was no cover from the fence to the buildings.

She tucked her gear into the small ruck attached to her belly. Except for her small hideaway pistols, her only weapons were a pair of tear gas grenades, flash-bangs, and a heavily customized Ingram Mac 11. The gun, which was loaded with 9mm slugs, had a carbon-fiber stock in place of the standard metal, and some of the metal in the body had been replaced with plastic or titanium for extra strength as well as lightness; a good number of water pistols were heavier. The modified Mac 11 retained the original's excellent balance and light kick; it could be fired adequately with one hand. Lia had several magazines in her bag, as well as a noise suppressor that worked considerably better than the standard "muffler," a scope, and a standard stock. The gun slipped as she started to climb; she nearly lost it and had to pull the strap awkwardly over her neck to get over.

She had just gotten down on the other side and pulled her computer back out for an update on where everyone was when Rockman hissed a warning in her ear.

"Two guards, with guns, coming from around the corner on your left."

As Lia turned to look, she saw a gun barrel and boot turning the corner and realized she'd never bring her own weapon to bear in time.

34

"Stinking Air Force is never on time," said Karr, glancing at his watch.

"First thing you said since you got here that I agree with."

"You know what your problem is, Foster? You look at a glass and you see it's half-full."

"I look at a glass and I wonder who was drinking out of it," said the Marine, who was sitting on the rocks next to the stream.

Karr laughed.

"What do we do if they don't come?" asked Gidrey. "These guys are going to roast us after all your promises."

"Wait. . . . Listen—"

"You talking to yourself again?"

"No, listen." Karr put his hand to his ear. The drone of an MC-130 could be heard in the distance.

Foster and Gidrey didn't react until the Special Forces cargo plane was nearly overhead. Guided solely by an on-board GPS system—Karr had fed the coordinates to them via the Art Room—the four-engined transport rode practically into the jungle canopy before rolling its load out the ramp at the rear of the plane. By the time the plane roared away, Karr and the Marines were hustling toward the crackling trees where the large skids of gear had come down. Six members of the Thai Army followed. One of the skids had landed at the edge of the water; the other leaned against a tree.

"Come on, let's get going," said Karr. "There's supposed to be steak in here somewhere."

Karr walked to one of the skids, taking out his knife to hack away the netting and plastic protecting the gear. Foster went to the other, and soon the Thai soldiers were donning body armor and passing out new weapons—Minimi machine guns and enough new M4s for everybody in the squad. The M4s were essentially short-barreled M16s, and the Thais had no trouble exchanging their older, worn-down rifles for them; the shorter length and lighter weight made them easier to handle and carry. The Minimis added firepower to the squads; though theoretically the weapons could be fired from the hip, as a practical matter the lightweight machine guns demanded either prone firing positions with the attached bipod or the use of a heavier tripod for accuracy. Gidrey gave a quick demonstration that emphasized the loading of the boxes that slapped into the underside of the gun; they held 200-round belts and were clear enough so a shooter could get an idea of how much ammunition he had left. Magazines from M16s could also be used in a pinch.

Meanwhile, Fisher and Karr continued sorting through the dropped supplies. There were several crates of M72 anti-tank missiles, night-vision gear, grenades, and radios.

And one sixteen-ounce porterhouse, packed in ice.

35

The Crow saved her. Its path took it back from the direction to the guards' right, and the two men stopped in their tracks at the corner of the building, watching it.

Lia leaped forward, dashing across the lot toward the cars about twenty feet away. She jerked up the Mac 11 as she ran, then held it close to her body as she spun and dropped down between the cars on her butt. There was barely three feet of clearance between the bumpers, but the close space helped hide her as she sidled to the left, sliding behind the small VW sedan.

The guards watched the Crow flutter away, then resumed walking, checking the fence line and jabbering in Austrian-accented German so quickly that Lia couldn't make out what they were saying.

"That was close," said Rockman as the two men turned the far corner, walking by the trailers.

"Why the hell didn't you warn me?" asked Lia.

"They came up out of the basement entrance at the side. We never saw them."

"Don't let that happen again," she told the runner. "You're supposed to be watching for me!"

"Really, Lia, recriminations are unnecessary," said Rubens in her ear. "I'm sure we can all find plenty of areas for improvement."

"Just make sure they're improved before I get fried," said

Lia. She pulled out her handheld. She had a sit map but no visual from the Fokker. "Where's Eyes?" Lia asked.

"The helicopters are too close. We have to keep the Fokker back," said Telach.

"Yeah, but I'm here, damn it."

"Your language, Ms. DeFrancesca, is hardly professional," said Rubens. "Focus on obtaining your objective. Mr. Dean is now entering the compound. Once he's inside and the helicopters back off, we should have an easier time of things. You're not in any danger."

"What sort of guns do the guards have?"

"Excuse me?"

"Those were Steyrs, right?"

"Very possibly."

"Just wanted to make sure they weren't cap guns."

"They're coming back," said Rockman.

Dean followed Hercules into the building they had stopped at earlier, walking down the corridor next to him. His head hurt too much now for him to keep track of where he was going, let alone to anticipate what would happen next; he wasn't quite to the point where he didn't care anymore, but he was getting close. Sweat poured from his body, and he felt as if he'd been pummeled by a dozen heavyweights.

"Through that door," said Hercules as they came to the end of the hall. A large metal door with a panic bar stood at his right.

Dean pushed outside. A wave of cold hit him; his teeth began to chatter.

"You really aren't feeling well, are you?" said Hercules.

"No," said Dean.

"Well, come then. This will be over quickly. One way or the other."

36

Rubens paced behind the consoles, suddenly worried about Dean and whether he could pass the test. He thought about ordering his crash team in. Made up of Desk Three paramilitaries—all of them Black Suits specially trained in hostage rescue and terrorist suppression—the team could have Dean safe within eight minutes.

Eight minutes would probably be too late.

Dean had been a Marine sniper in Vietnam; he was used to dealing with uncertainty. Rubens knew intellectually he'd be all right and yet couldn't shake the sense of dread and worry.

"There are two men in that first trailer, the one that has all the computer gear. That's where they'll take Dean," said Telach. "I think they're holding off the lab for later, if at all."

"Have you tapped into the trailer's computers?"

"Can't. They're not connected to anything. The only reason I know they're there is from the infrared on the Crow."

"Can Lia get into them?" asked Rubens.

"Not as long as there are other people in the trailer. Best bet is to get her inside the building once the guards complete their circuit. We'll see what we can do from there."

"The buildings are just for show, or just temporary," said Rubens, realizing how the operation was set up. "The trailers are the key. See if you can get registration data, that sort of thing."

"We're already working on it."

"Work harder," said Rubens. "We have a man under the gun there."

"And Lia."

"And Lia, yes," said Rubens.

37

Dean's legs wobbled as he went up the steel steps at the back of the large white trailer. From the outside, it looked like a generic trailer, the sort that would be used in the States to transport any number of things, the kind that clogged the nation's highways and byways. The only hint that it might be something more than a trailer was the second door behind the folded-out rear gate.

"Just turn the handle," said Hercules, behind him on the steps.

Dean fumbled with the inset steel ring. The door opened with a slight hitch, and Dean felt a rush of crisp air hit him at the side of the face. The cold air helped, and his legs steadied as he walked inside.

Natural-hue fluorescents filled the interior with a soft light. Dean stepped across the threshold into a paneled room that could have been a waiting area for a dentist. A tall young man with a goatee stood at the door opposite the entrance. He had a smirk on his face and said something to Hercules that Dean didn't understand.

"They're going to quiz you," said Rockman in Dean's head. "They're speaking Greek, but it's not their first language. It may be for Hercules' benefit, or it may be to cross you up since they know you don't know it. We're working on getting IDs here."

Dean coughed as an acknowledgment. Hercules looked at him with some concern, then led him through the door into a room with computers, through that room, and into another set up like a small classroom or lecture center, with a white board at the front and six student desk-chairs crammed together. Hercules gestured at the front row and Dean sat down. A clean-shaven man in his late twenties came out from a door at the end of the room; he had a large metal detector in one hand and a device to search for bugs in the other.

Hercules started to object, speaking quickly in Greek.

"That's been done twice," interpreted the Art Room.

The man continued anyway, ending by directing Dean against the wall and patting him down. Finally satisfied, he directed Dean back to the chair.

"Tell me about your work with viruses," he said.

"You don't work with viruses, you work with bacteria," said the Art Room specialist.

"What really are you looking for?" answered Dean.

"Perhaps you'd like something to drink," said Hercules. "Coffee? Tea?"

"Water'd be good," said Dean. "Boil it first, though."

The others laughed.

"Afraid of catching germs?" said the clean-shaven man.

"*E. coli*'s everywhere," said Dean.

The man smirked. "Any strand in particular?"

Dean suddenly felt angry at being jerked around. He was tired, and the fever that had started earlier now burned through him like a barn fired by kerosene on a hot July afternoon. He couldn't deal with this anymore.

"You want to talk about water, or you want the antidote? What the hell is it that you want? One guy asks me about *E. coli*, the other guy wants me to build him a DNA sequencer."

"We want to make sure you're not a spy," said the clean-shaven man. "We understand Dr. Kegan has already been visited by the FBI."

"Who says?"

"Don't act for us."

Dean held out his hands. "Do I look like the FBI? Would they send someone with a hundred-and-four fever?"

"Is your fever really that high?" asked the voice in Dean's head.

The clean-shaven man glanced over at Goatee, but neither man said anything.

"Dr. Kegan assured us he would be here himself," said the clean-shaven man. "And yet he is not. And he has not answered our E-mails."

"I'm not sure about his plans," said Dean. "He asked me to come to Europe in his place."

"Then how do you know about our business?"

"I don't," said Dean. "I don't know anything beyond what I've been told."

The clean-shaven man frowned. The two men started talking. Even before Rockman told him that they were arguing whether it would be better just to get rid of him, Dean realized he was in trouble.

"Let's take a guess," said the Art Room scientist, whispering in his ear. "*S. moniliformis.* Rat-bite fever."

Oh sure, you take a guess and I end up in the sewer, Dean thought.

"My fever's not part of your problem," Dean told the two men. "Unless there are a lot of rats running around."

The two men looked at each other.

"*Moniformis*?" said the clean-shaven man.

Dean looked at him, trying to puzzle out what the man expected as the answer.

"The bacteria is *S. moniliformis,*" said the voice in Dean's head. "He said it wrong. He's trying to trip you up."

Or it was an innocent mistake, thought Dean.

"*Mon-il-i-form-is,*" said Dean, sounding out the syllables. "You left out *il. Ill.*" He started to laugh. "Get it? Don't worry. I have food poisoning, nothing else."

"Moniliformis or spirillum?" said Goatee, in English.

"Different type, related disease," said the voice. "Both types of rat-bite fever."

"Why?" asked Dean, stalling.

"You can identify the type of disease by doing a blood culture," said the Art Room expert.

"Tell me difference."

"To me or the rat?"

"Moniliformis is a gram-negative rod; spirillum is a spiral," said the voice.

"*Spiril-lum*," said Dean, remembering part of the lecture he'd heard on the way over. "Spiral. See? You can tell the difference with a microscope. It jumps out at you, right away."

"How?" asked Goatee.

"They're no more than grad students, if that," said Rockman. "They're asking real simple questions, but they're looking for answers they've memorized. We think Hercules is the real expert, but these guys are working for the muscle people. They don't really understand what you're saying. Hercules is the one you have to worry about."

Dean had reached the same conclusion about the men's level of knowledge, but he didn't agree that he couldn't worry about them. On the contrary.

"I don't know how to tell you more clearly than that," he said to Goatee.

Hercules returned with Dean's water. Dean took it, nodding in gratitude.

"How can you tell the difference?" asked Goatee again.

"You can use white blood count numbers to diagnose the disease in a patient," said the expert in Dean's head, guessing what the man had been told was the answer.

But Dean played it beyond the crib sheet.

"Between bacteria that look like springs all wound up and others that look like pencils or little rods?" he said with exasperation. He looked at Hercules. "You know what I'm trying to say, right? They're both gram-negative bacteria. One looks like—a string of beads, maybe. The other—" He spun his finger as if demonstrating.

"The relationship between *S. moniliformis* and streptococcus," said Hercules. "That's the sort of question you should be considering."

"None," said the expert.

Dean knew instinctively that wasn't the right answer, even if the textbooks might declare it to be. He held Hercules' gaze. "If I could answer that as precisely as Dr. Kegan," said Dean, "then I'd be the genius and he'd be the assistant. But even to know that's a valid question means you're a step ahead."

Hercules smiled and pulled over one of the chairs. "No, he's far ahead."

"Penicillin resistance," said the voice in Dean's head. "Oh, wow—now I see what they've done."

"Let's get on with it," said the man with the goatee.

"Let's," said the clean-shaven man. "You will take us to the antidote now, Dr. Dean, or we will kill you."

"I'm not a doctor," said Dean as the man with the goatee grabbed the back of his shirt and pulled him out of the seat.

Lia watched the Fokker feed on the handheld while the guards who had trailed Dean and Hercules to the trailer settled into their posts below the steps, then ran around the side of the building to the door at the front. It was locked, and though the lock itself was easily picked, she wasted time checking for an alarm system—none—before she could get inside. By then, Telach was already telling her to hide because Hercules and Dean were coming in at the far end.

Hiding was not quite an easy matter—the door nearest the entrance was locked and equipped with an alarm system, as was the second. As the outside door at the end of the hallway opened, Lia threw herself down to the floor. This time, she had her silencer-equipped Mac 11 ready.

"In here, first," said Hercules in English at the far end of the hall. "Let's take care of nature."

Lia caught a glimpse of Dean as he followed the Greek into a room at the left at the far end of the hallway.

"Two more outside—they're coming," said Telach.

"The alarm system, have you compromised it yet or what?"

"It's not hooked into a computer. Use your stomper."

The "stomper" was a glorified alarm buster that could

figure out the circuit configuration and disable it, usually—
though not always—without detection. It was definitely only
a second choice, but there was no alternative now. Lia pulled
the cigarette box–sized device from the flap on her jacket
and pulled off the end, exposing a magnetic coupler. She got
up, slapped it on the door where the sensor was, and pushed
in as the indicator bar flashed.

"In," she said, sliding the door closed as gently as she
could. Footsteps approached; neither of the two men spoke.

She swung up the machine pistol, ready to fire.

Neither man stopped. She heard the door at the front of
the building open.

"Where's Dean?" she hissed.

"He's with Hercules at the other end of the building.
There's a bathroom there."

"I'm getting him."

"No, Lia," said Rubens firmly.

"Yes. You don't have an antidote. They'll kill him."

"We need to get as much information as we can," said
Rubens. "Mr. Dean is not our highest priority."

"Bull."

"We want you to look in the trailers and see if there are
samples you can remove. We've located what looks as if it's
an incubator in one of them."

"They're coming," said Rockman.

Rubens stood holding Chaucer's headset to his ear. He
looked down at the scientist, then covered the mouthpiece so
his voice couldn't be heard over the circuit.

"What is the antidote?"

"Well, assuming they're talking about a cure, ordinarily
it's penicillin. Rat-bite fever responds pretty well. But
they've found some way to make it resistant, either by breeding or, I think, recombinant DNA that combines elements
from a different bacteria. That's what the business of streptococcus was all about. Streptococcus is the same organism
that causes, among other things, strep throat."

"Kegan worked with that?"

"Twenty years ago or more. But the important thing is that we understand what he's doing now—he designed the bacteria. That's incredible. Even a designer virus—"

"So it could be amazingly contagious," said Rubens, cutting him off.

"Or not. It depends on what the characteristics are. We don't know what they might have done. We really need to examine the organism. The people who have already been infected—they're gold mines."

"Is it likely it's in the lab?" asked Rubens.

"I don't know," said Chaucer. His face clouded suddenly. "What if there is no cure?" he added, the situation finally dawning on him. "What if this can't be stopped?"

"Talk to Johnny Bib up in Kegan's house," said Rubens. He couldn't encourage pessimism. "Tell him what you've found. Let him babble on until he comes up with something."

Chaucer gave him a blank look.

"He's quite crazy," said Rubens. "But he's a genius at finding connections. And there's some sort of connection here between Thailand, these germs, and the odd books he's looking at."

"Okay," said Chaucer, clearly not convinced.

"Stay where you are, Lia," Rubens said, taking his hand from the mike. "Mr. Dean will be safe, I assure you."

"Fuck yourself."

Rubens sighed. "Such language from a professional."

"Fuck yourself twice."

Dean followed Hercules down the hallway. His headache had actually started to recede. The foreigner seemed genuinely concerned for his health, though Dean wondered from some of his reactions if he thought he'd caught whatever disease this was from Kegan.

Obviously Keys had been working on something very bad.

Evil. That was the word.

Keys? Evil? The guy who'd gone to the jungles of Asia to save people? When Dean went to kill people?

Actually, they'd both gone to save people. Keys was just more obvious about it.

"We're with you, Charlie Dean," said Rubens, the words seeming to echo in his feverish head. "Just relax and go along. You're going to drive into Vienna. We'll be with you the whole time; just follow our directions. We have a team working on preparing something for you right now. The more information you can get from them, the easier it will be."

Jesus, thought Charlie—we're not talking about a milk shake, for cryin' out loud.

His headache flashed back with the force of a freight train.

Lia stood poised by the door as they approached. It would take three seconds, no more—push the door open, step out behind them, blast Hercules in the head.

And then?

Grab Charlie and run down the hall, back to the room where he had just been. Out the window—no, go right out the door and wax the two guards, who were still in the back by the trailer.

Then over the fence, take out Beard Boy and Clean Face.

She could look in the trailers at her leisure.

Probably not. But it would be easier than sneaking into them.

Of course, whoever was behind this would know their operation was compromised.

So what? Would they move up their timetable, unleash some superbug on the world?

Maybe Charlie already had it. Maybe that was what Rubens was worried about.

The handheld computer showed they were three yards away.

Lia's hand was on the doorknob. She had been in the

Army—technically, she was still in the Army, just on semi-permanent loan to Desk Three. She was programmed to follow orders.

Sensible, legal orders.

Which these weren't. Sensible, that is. They were legal.

God, Charlie, I don't want you to die. I love you, baby.

It was that thought—the realization that she did feel for him—that kept her from saving him now. She knew it was possible that her emotions might be interfering with her instincts. She hesitated for that reason, and in the space of that hesitation, her chance was gone.

38

Dr. Kegan had an excellent stereo system, and while his CD collection favored sixties and seventies rock, there were seventy-three CDs devoted to jazz.

Seventy-three was an extremely interesting number. Not only it was it prime—which by definition meant it had power—but also in many Christian mystical systems it represented the union of Christ and the Trinity—"7" and "3." Seven alone—"4" equals man, "3" equals God. So it was 433—another prime. This filled Johnny Bib with a certain amount of awe, which merely compounded his excitement when he discovered that the first CD in the collection was a Thelonious Monk compilation. The music of Monk, with its complicated references and atonal digressions, was to Bib's mathematical mind an artistic precursor to the revelations of chaos theory. Or, more precisely, a statement of the underlying principles, which of course were anything but chaotic.

Johnny Bib slid the disk into the player and cranked it; the notes began to fill not only the library where he was working but the entire house, ported through an admirable remote arrangement. But just as Johnny began pondering the simple yet elusive rifts of "Ruby My Dear," the phone rang.

"Bib," he said, grabbing the line and answering as if he were in his own office.

"Hello. This is Dr. Chaucer. Mr. Rubens directed me to call."

"Yes?"

Johnny listened as Chaucer explained that they had developed new information regarding the targeted bacteria. It seemed as if it would turn out to be a penicillin-resistant strain built from the bacteria that caused rat-bite fever. Did that ring any bells?

A curious turn of phrase, thought Johnny as Monk's piano jangled in the back.

"Could the DNA itself be an encryption?" asked Johnny Bib.

"Well, we haven't gotten the DNA sequence itself," said the scientist uncertainly. "In any event, even with a bacteria, it would be exceedingly long."

"Chaucer, right? Any relation?" Johnny Bib had always wondered why there were 24 tales, or even the 124 contemplated. These were not auspicious numbers.

"I'm afraid I don't know what you're saying."

Monk slapped into "Well You Needn't." That said it all for Johnny Bib.

"What was your question?" asked Johnny.

"I, uh—is there anything that you've come across that might have to do with treatment-resistant disease, specifically rat-bite fever?" said Chaucer. "And . . ."

Plants—it was the plants!

". . . was there any evidence regarding something like penicillin, because there would have been—"

"Put on Mr. Rubens. I have important information for him," said Johnny Bib.

"Uh—"

"We can discuss your questions later. Please. This is of vital importance."

39

Lia slipped out the bathroom window onto the hard macadam and edged toward the corner. There were only two guards left at the facility. One had gone to the front of the building. The other had taken up a post at the rear, where he could watch the trailers. Less than ten yards separated her from this second man; she could pivot around the corner and empty her pistol into his chest before he had a chance to re-act. But that wasn't the gig.

"Go with the voice," Lia told the Art Room.

"Kommen," muttered a voice from inside the hall. Though somewhat clipped—it had been extracted from a longer sentence—the word was in the other guard's voice, which the Art Room had recorded and was now replaying through a small speaker Lia had left hidden in the rest room wastebasket.

Thinking he was wanted, the man began walking noncha-lantly toward where he thought his companion had called him from—the side of the building where Lia was crouched.

"Try it again," she said, watching on the handheld.

The Art Room replayed the voice, this time adding a snippet that seemed to indicate the guard was inside one of the rooms. The man changed direction.

"Had you worried there, huh?" asked Rockman as Lia trotted toward the trailers, the coast finally clear.

"You're lucky they didn't use their walkie-talkies."

"We're jamming them."

"And you don't think that would make them suspicious, huh?"

"Relax. They obviously don't think they're doing anything important. They'll be throwing back beers in a minute."

Lia reached the rear of the first trailer. Rather than using the door, she went to the back and climbed on top, moving quickly to a vent panel. She fished into her knapsack and removed a power screwdriver, diddling with the attachments to get the right hex head.

"Coming back outside," warned Rockman.

Lia lay down next to the vent and began unscrewing the screws by hand.

"Walking around, walking around," warned Rockman. He was watching a feed from the Eyes asset, which had been taken off the team trailing Dean because of the helicopters.

The first two screws were easy, but the next one seemed frozen in place. She pushed against it and almost lost the driver. Reluctantly, she moved to the next. This, too, was jammed.

"Going into the other trailer," said Rockman. "You can use the driver."

Lia got on her knees and switched the driver on. But its torque couldn't budge the two screws that had stuck. She got the rest off and then went back to them without any luck. Nor would the vent lift off completely with them in place.

"Going to have to drill them," she said.

"Do it," said Rockman.

By the time she had the new bit in, the guard was coming out of the other trailer. She waited, expecting him to come over to this one. But instead he went back to the post at the back of the building. He couldn't see the top of the trailer from where he was, but she couldn't get inside, either. All Lia could do was wait.

And wait.

Finally, the other guard came around the back to share a cigarette. The two men began talking.

"What are they saying?" Lia whispered.

"You don't want to know," said Rockman.

"What is it?"

"Uh, basically about porking girls. Except cruder than that."

"Cruder?"

"Lia, don't do anything rash," warned Rubens.

"What's your definition of *rash*?"

"Heads up," warned Rockman.

The two guards were walking toward the trailer. They continued to the back, right below where Lia was lying, and unzipped to relieve themselves.

The temptation to whack them now was almost too much to resist. But Lia managed, and eventually the two men began laughing and zipped up.

"They're going up front to check the perimeter," said Rockman as they walked away. "All right, go with the drill."

"What were they laughing about?"

"Uh, you really wouldn't want to know," said Rockman.

Lia once more regretted not taking them out. She drilled through one of the screws, then found she could wing the vent cover around. She slid in through the opening, standing on a large freezer-type machine as she pulled the vent back in place.

The interior was pitch-black. Lia pulled on her night-vision glasses, adjusting to the limited perspective. She was in a room about eight feet square. Most of the space was taken up by freezers, which had combination locks on them. Lia left them for later, going into the next room. This was set up as a lab, with three large microscopes attached to a set of computers. She found a USB port and plugged in a dongle.

"Don't fire them up just yet," said Telach. "Let's decide first what we have here."

"Looks like a college bio lab to me," said Lia. She went ahead to the next room, which was a small lounge area. Beyond it was another lab, this one with a variety of equipment, ranging from microscopes to refrigerator units.

"Is there a DNA sequencer?" asked Telach.

"You tell me."

She put a cam on the handheld and set it on top of the bench, feeding the video back home. While the Art Room was sorting out the gear, Lia bent to one of the refrigerators, looking to open it.

"No, let's not get inside that," said Rubens. "You're not adequately prepared yet."

"It's about time you started worrying about my health," said Lia.

She moved over to a set of workstations. Both were on and attached to uninterruptible power supplies. Neither had outside drives or cable hookups, though there were ports in the back. The Art Room debated briefly on how to proceed, then directed Lia to the USB ports. A few seconds after she connected the first dongle, she heard Rockman cursing in her ear.

"This part of the operation is sophisticated at least," said Rockman. "Wiped itself clean. Leave the other workstation."

"You can't figure out a way to get around it?" Lia asked.

"We're going to rethink this. Get out of the trailer," said Telach. "Go over to the next trailer and let's get into their computers."

"So this was all a waste?"

"Call it a gamble that has not yet paid off," said Rubens.

"Whatever," said Lia, wishing she had trusted herself earlier and saved Charlie when she had the chance.

40

Rubens stood back from the console, contemplating his options. Seizing the lab would naturally give them a lot of information, but it would also tell whoever was running the operation that they were on to them. Until he actually knew what was going on—and until he was confident he could take down all of the operation in one swoop—Rubens was reluctant to move.

On the other hand, the Austrians would surely catch on soon, and delay risked their moving without him. That would provide additional obstacles, even in the best-case scenario.

If there was an engineered bacteria in the lab, he had an obligation to shut it down as soon as possible. Every hour of delay—there was no way of knowing how long it would take to gather these various strands together—increased the risk that the bacteria would be used or escape his grasp.

However, if it already had escaped his grasp, if it wasn't here—and the low security argued strongly that was the case—then moving now would lessen the odds it could be tracked down.

Rubens' watch buzzed. He glanced at it, momentarily unsure what he had set the alarm for.

The Homeland Security working group on the Internet. There was a meeting in two hours.

Eminently missable.

"Mr. Rubens?"

"Marie?"

"Johnny Bib wants to speak to you."

"Now?"

"He claims it's urgent. He was speaking to Dr. Chaucer but insisted on talking to you."

"If this is another theory on Fermat's Equation, Marie, I am going to be less than overjoyed."

She held up her hands in a helpless gesture.

"Go ahead, Johnny," said Rubens as the circuit clicked in.

"Fungus."

Rubens sighed. "I'm afraid we must have a problem with the connection here," said Rubens. "I thought you said 'fungus.'"

"Fungus," repeated Johnny Bib.

Rubens finally realized what he was trying to say.

"Johnny, you're on an open line, aren't you?"

"Yes."

"The computers are still hooked in?"

"Affirmative."

"Type up the data. I'll have Ms. Telach—" He turned and saw the Art Room supervisor waving at him. "I will have Marie set up something on this end so we can see what you're typing."

"I need time to compose it."

"Take your time," said Rubens. He pressed the button on the headset control to kill the connection, then turned to Telach. "What?"

"We've lost Charlie Dean."

"What?" Rubens turned and looked at the screen where the op's position was supposed to be marked.

"They went into a tunnel and didn't come out."

"That's impossible," said Rubens.

"I know," said Telach. "That's why I'm worried."

41

While the guard pulled another inspection in the other trailer, Lia used her small digital camera to send pictures of the interior of her trailer back to the Art Room. There were no papers, no reports, not even any doodles in the lab that she could find.

The guards repeated their earlier routine, grabbing a cigarette and then going together into the building as they swept through the rooms there. Lia climbed up and out, slid the top vent back in place, then ran to the other trailer. The lock and alarm were easily defeated; she put her dongle on a computer in the first room and immediately the Art Room infiltrated and began copying the contents of the drive. This time, the security precautions were rudimentary and the computer was networked with the others in the trailer; as each computer booted, it gave itself over to the Art Room's probe without a whimper.

Lia moved into the back of the trailer. Unlike the other one, this facility looked as if it was used for administrative tasks or even as a classroom. There were no papers or anything else lying about.

"All right," said Rockman. "We've got it. You can get out."

"What's up?" asked Lia as she walked back to retrieve the dongle.

"What do you mean?"

"Something's wrong. I can tell from your voice. Where's Charlie?"

"Heading back to the city somewhere."

"Somewhere?"

"Lia, concentrate on your job, please. We want you to make the scene ready for a seizure operation. We need some flies planted. I have a list of locations."

"Screw off, Marie. What happened to Charlie?"

"We're having trouble tracking him."

Lia cursed. She couldn't get the dongle to disengage and had to push at the computer, leaning back awkwardly.

"Hide," said Rockman. "The guards are coming."

"Where should I go?"

"He didn't go into the back room on his last sweep," said Telach. "It's a rest room."

Lia pulled up her Mac 11 but retreated as Telach had suggested. The rest room was bare—a tiny sink and some sort of chemical toilet. It also stank. She folded against the corner behind where the door would open. She could feel the guard's footsteps shaking the trailer floor as he approached.

Belatedly, she realized that she hadn't had a chance to shut off all the computers.

The door to the rest room opened. Lia slid down the Mac 11, the silencer just over the doorknob.

The guard said something, then let the door go.

Lia started to exhale. Then something made her throw herself down. As she hit the floor, the doorway exploded with a spray of automatic rifle fire.

42

Dean continued through the corridor, following the driver as he walked down the narrow steps. They had stopped in the middle of a tunnel under the river, gotten out of the car, and then climbed into what had looked like a manhole for a sewer. Well-lit, the hole opened into a large, tiled expanse that made Dean think of a subway station, except there were no tracks. Hercules had prompted him to keep walking; the tunnel seemed to head ever-downward as they snaked first to the left, then to the right.

The stairway ended in a concrete-walled room with steel doors at both sides.

"Now what?" asked Dean.

"You tell me," said Hercules.

"I haven't a clue where we are," said Dean. "Am I supposed to know?"

"Where is the antidote?"

"I'm not going to just tell you," said Dean.

"I'm afraid you're going to have to," said Hercules. "Where is it?"

Dean shrugged. "I tell you now, you're going to kill me."

"If you don't tell me now, Hans will shoot you," said Hercules.

Hans, who'd been standing a step away, moved forward. He had a Glock in his hand.

43

Bullets spit barely over Lia's head as she lay on the floor of the rest room. The lead chewed up the thin metal and broke large hunks of ceramic off the toilet nearby. The Steyr AUG had forty bullets in its magazine, and the guard used a little more than half before taking a breath. Then he fired another half-dozen rounds, spraying these in a wider angle. It was only when he paused that Lia raised her weapon and fired.

The guard got off two more shots. Unsure whether she'd gotten him or he'd simply run out of bullets, Lia fired another burst of her own, then jumped up to pull the door back. It started to bend and fall out of her hand; she threw her momentum into the opening, firing the Mac 11 as she did.

Bullets flew by her head as she crashed into the room. Lia lifted her gun and this time, finally, hit her opponent square in the head.

"Where's the other one?" she asked Rockman.

"Coming on a dead run. You won't make the door."

Lia reached to her belt and took out two tiny balls of C4 intended to blow locks off doors. She started to rig them against the wall, thinking she could blow a hole in the side of the trailer to escape from.

"Lia—the trailers are rigged to self-destruct," warned Telach. "There's a routine on the computer we compromised."

"Peachy. Where are the charges?"

"We're not sure—don't do anything crazy to set them off."

"I'm going to blow a hole in the side and get out."

"No. Too risky until we understand what they've got. We're analyzing it now."

The other guard had reached the front and was shouting to his companion.

"Call him," said Lia.

"What?"

"Use the speaker I left in the building."

Rockman said nothing as Lia ran to the front of the trailer. The guard yelled again.

They reached the anteroom at the end of the trailer at the same time, both coming in from the other direction. Lia was the faster shot—the guard tumbled backward outside. As he did, his finger tightened on the Steyr; bullets sprayed from the rifle.

"Lia?"

"Yeah, I'm still here."

"Helicopter."

"Finally."

"Not ours."

"Damn it."

Lia got out of the trailer and ran to the side of the building, reloading as she did. She could hear the helicopter approaching, the heavy whomp of its rotors already starting to shake the ground.

"Have you found Charlie?" she asked.

"We're working on it," said Telach. "Are you all right? We're moving backup in."

"I'm fine."

"The helicopter's landing."

"No kidding. How many people?"

"What?"

"How many in the helicopter?"

"Two, I think. Yeah—hey, Lia, no, that's too risky. No!"

The helicopter slipped in over the fence, its tail spinning

around toward the building as it settled in front of the trailers. Lia bolted as it touched down, ignoring both the dust storm and Rockman's shouts. As the door to the helicopter opened, she pressed her finger on the trigger, running toward the cockpit at the same time, as if she were pushing the bullets into the man who was just getting out.

Something fell from the helicopter. A body appeared; she pushed more bullets in it.

The man slapped against the door, slid away. Lia threw herself forward, jumping onto the skid of the Bell 212 and wedging upward.

"You!" she screamed at the pilot. "Take me to the others!"

The man blinked at her. He didn't have a weapon.

"Take me to them," said Lia in German as she pushed herself into the seat, then pulled the Mac 11 up so it was very obvious. *"Schnell."*

44

"Let her play it as far as she can," Rubens told the runner in the Art Room. He wouldn't have ordered her to try taking the helicopter—it was suicidal—but now that she had they might as well take advantage of it. "Have you found Dean?" he asked Telach.

"I'm sure he's in that tunnel somewhere," said Telach. "It's just a matter of waiting. The crash units are ready."

"Very well."

"Lia went too far," said Telach. "She could have been killed there, easily."

"Yes, that is the problem with Miss DeFrancesca," said Rubens. "She always goes too far. Nonetheless, she does get results. And at the moment she's our best line to Dean."

"All right," said Telach.

"It's all right, Marie. I'll speak with her when the operation is over," said Rubens.

"If she's here to speak with," said Telach.

45

Dean and Hercules stared at each other. The driver was about three feet behind him to the right, the barrel of his pistol just visible in Dean's peripheral vision.

"Well, Dr. Dean?" asked Hercules.

"I'm not a doctor," said Dean, holding his hands out in apology. "I don't have a Ph.D. Remember?"

A faint smile curled at the corner of Hercules' face. He turned and nodded at the driver.

It was then that Dean struck.

Dean threw his leg hard into the man's chest, knocking him backward against the wall as the pistol went flying. Hercules reached quickly for his own gun, but Dean threw himself into the scientist, landing on him like a blitzing linebacker taking down an unprotected quarterback. With one hard smack against the floor he knocked Hercules cold; he rolled off and dived for the other gun as the driver came up from the floor. Dean grabbed the weapon with both hands, fumbling before pulling it around to hold it properly.

The driver threw his hands back, surrendering. Dean got up.

"Against the wall," he told the man. "Spread 'em. Do it."

The driver got the idea after a few gestures. Dean patted him down, careful about keeping the pistol positioned where the driver couldn't pull the same trick he had. He found a small revolver strapped to the man's ankle and slid it into his pocket.

Dean went to Hercules, intending to grab him and pull him with him. But as he hauled him up, the Greek's head flopped to the side; Dean realized with a shock that his blow had killed the man.

Voices were coming from the other end of the tunnel. Before Dean could react, the driver shouted, then lunged at him.

His first bullet grazed the Austrian's arm, but the second and third missed and the gun fell away. Dean wrestled with the man; though they were about the same size, the driver was perhaps half Dean's age. They gripped each other and twisted, stumbling back and forth, neither able to get an advantage. There were more shouts from the tunnel and the sound of three or four men running.

Desperate, Dean screwed up his energy into a final burst, hurling his assailant over his shoulder and then, in a blind fury, kicking him unconscious as the man dropped to the floor.

Dean scooped for the gun but dropped it.

The footsteps were coming. He ran to the door at the left and pulled it open, finding himself in another tunnel, this one lined with concrete. Dean began to run.

46

"Schönbrunn," said Lia. "Where is it?"

"It's a palace just outside the city," said Telach. "There's a lot of ground there."

"It is near where you lost Dean?"

"A mile away."

"Close enough," said Lia.

"They wouldn't land the helicopter there," replied Telach.

"He'll land it anywhere I want."

"My point is that they wouldn't have planned to go there. It's filled with tourists during the day. And there's all sorts of security."

Lia put her pistol to the pilot's head.

"Where the hell are you supposed to meet them?" she asked. She'd put on the radio headset to make it easier to speak.

"Schönbrunn," said the pilot. His voice cracked twice; Lia decided he was telling the truth.

"Lia, their other helicopter is headed toward the airport," said Telach. "We're just not sure what he's up to, but it looks like he's out of the picture, at least for now."

"That's nice." Lia pushed her gun closer to the man's neck. "What are the words for 'get the lead out'?" she asked Rockman. "I can never remember the idioms."

. . .

Unlike the first tunnel, this one was very poorly lit, and Dean kept stumbling as he went. He came to a Y intersection and ran right.

Within twenty feet the light gave out completely. With voices now echoing behind him, he decided it was better not to turn back, and so he kept going, resorting to feeling his way against the side of the wall.

After twenty or thirty yards, he came to a ladder. He was about five rungs up when the beam of a flashlight played across the space below. Dean froze, then reached for the small revolver he had taken from the driver earlier.

There were two lights, coming toward him from the distance. Dean watched and waited as they approached; he could get both bodies behind the lights, but it wasn't clear to him whether there was a third or fourth man behind the front two; his first shots would leave him an easy target.

More shadows—a third man, maybe a fourth farther back.

One of the lights swung toward the ladder. They were ten yards away.

Dean fired his first shot into the skull of the man on the left. One of the men in the rear began returning fire. Dean took down the second man with the flashlight and then fired into the flashing rifle; it took two slugs before the gunfire stopped.

The flashlight rolled on the ground. Gunpowder filled Dean's nostrils, mixing with the damp air and hot sweat pouring off him as he scrambled upward. Finally his arm smacked hard against something. He pushed; miraculously it gave way. He threw himself up as another gun began firing behind him.

He was in a tunnel.

A train tunnel.

There was a light behind him, and a loud rumble approaching.

. . .

Lia saw one of the vans that had been part of the Austrian contingent moving along Edelsinnstrasse, which ran roughly west–east at the southern part of the grounds.

"We see it, too," said Rockman. "All right, what was he supposed to do?"

Lia asked in German. The pilot pointed to the ground. Lia realized that he was supposed to hover until Hercules appeared. If he didn't come, then he was to return to the airport.

"Go over to the airport," said Rockman. "Let's get a line on that, see who else is working with them."

"No way," she told him. "If Hercules comes out and doesn't see the helicopter, he'll know something's up."

"Lia's right," said Telach. "Stay with him."

Thank you, Lia thought, though she didn't say anything. She looked through the windscreen, trying to see what the pilot was watching for.

"Is it the van?" she asked the pilot. "Van?"

The man shook his head.

"What then?"

Words sputtered from his mouth. He was looking at the Gloriette Monument overlooking the gardens. The massive stone structure looked like the ghost of an ancient castle.

"He's supposed to be on the lawn near the monument?" asked Lia.

"*Ja,*" said the man. "Yes."

"Go," she said. "Now. *Schnell gehen. Go!*"

For a moment, Dean wasn't sure whether to run or try to get back down the hole. Finally he saw a small ledge at the right side of the underground. As the subway train bore down on him, he threw himself over the rail and lay in the tiny coffin space between the track and wall.

The space had been carefully measured to provide clearance for workmen in case of an emergency. But Charlie didn't know that. All he knew was that the air rushing around him felt like a tornado thrust sideways against his face. He couldn't breathe, and even his heart seemed paralyzed from the shock of the train and the danger.

He heard the screech of brakes.

I'm dead, he thought to himself. I just got split in half and I'm dead. I'm seeing my own demise.

But no angel came for him. Instead, the train had cleared and gone on a few hundred yards to the station.

Dean unfolded himself, trembling, then started in the direction the train had taken. After two steps he began to run, realizing that his pursuers might still be after him. He could hear the train in the station ahead starting out, saw another track nearby. And then he was at the platform, pulling himself up.

He'd nearly gotten flattened in a subway in Moscow a week or two ago. Then Tommy Karr had been waiting by the steps. For some reason, Dean didn't think he'd be waiting to bail him out now.

47

Karr had just finished his steak when the first of the two helicopters began rumbling in the distance. Unlike the helicopter that had taken him up-country, these were large Chinooks,
massive troop carriers propelled by rotors at either end.
Temporarily chopped from a Special Forces assignment in
the southeast, the helicopters were so large that they had to
descend one at a time to pick up the Thai force, which had
been divided into half for the mission. Karr went aboard
with the first group, moving up to the cockpit to help guide
the pilots to the landing zone. The Thai major, somewhat in
awe to be receiving all this assistance, came with Karr, staying
a respectful distance as he popped his head next to the two
warrant officers guiding the big helicopter. One of the men
handed him a headset with large earphones so he could hear
above the roar of the engines as they lifted off.

"Pretty small airstrip," said the pilot, his Texan accent
nearly drowned out by the engines.

"Yeah, I was going to ask you to drop a bulldozer first,"
said Karr, "but I figured these guys would have so much fun
playing with the sucker I wouldn't get them to come along."

The flight over the border took less than fifteen minutes.
Major Sourin had picked out a field as a landing zone about
a mile and a half from the target camp; the helicopters had
an easy time getting in.

"We'll be back at nine, unless you warn us off," said the

pilot. "Things get dicey, you can call us back earlier, but we have to head all way back to Chiang Mai to refuel. Build that into your timetable."

The attack plan was relatively simple—one unit would swing around behind the camp while the other three groups approached from the southeast, splitting for the final attack. Karr's satellite reconnaissance photos revealed only two defensive positions covering the southeast; the guerrillas' real enemy, the Myanmar army, would approach from the north and the guerrillas had not unreasonably located their main defenses there. The photo interpreters predicted a force of no more than fifty men, with the likely number closer to two dozen; Sourin had guessed seventy-five, though this may have been a play for as much firepower as he could get. The attack was planned for first light, giving them three hours after landing to get into position before the air support arrived.

There were two small buildings at the center of the camp, more huts than houses. They'd seen the pigs near building two. Karr gave strict orders that the buildings themselves were not to be targeted and under no circumstances were the antitank missiles to be used against them. The Thai soldiers were also told to be on the lookout for an "Anglo"; as an incentive against shooting him, Karr offered a reward of $25,000 to the man who captured him, as well as a similar amount to the major.

Sourin's point people were all equipped with night-vision goggles and small radios. Each group also carried an AN/PSC-5(V), a twenty-pound multiband radio that could hook into satellite frequencies as well as UHF and VHF. Karr clipped a small radio onto his belt. He attached a headset with earbud headphones and a necklacelike mike that would allow him to talk to the others. The Marines did the same.

The Thai soldiers were well disciplined and used to working in the jungle; they moved toward their target area silently, stringing out along both sides of a small streambed. Karr adjusted his night-vision glasses—unlike the powerful but relatively clumsy AN/PVS-5 units supplied to the Thai forces, his were NSA-designed and looked more like extra-thick wraparound sunglasses than traditional night viewers. They were very powerful, however, and besides allowing the wearer to see in the dark provided up to sixty-four-times magnification, depending on the circumstances. Even the Marines, who were equipped with AN/PVS 14 monocles, were jealous.

"How we looking back there, Chafetz?" Karr asked his runner after they'd marched for better than two hours through the jungle.

"Satellite's just coming over the area now. We'll have a fresh series of infrared snaps for you in about ninety seconds."

He took out his handheld, waiting for the download. Besides his A-2, he was humping one of the Minimis and three see-through boxes of ammo belts, all he could fit in his second ruck. Just before joining Desk Three, Karr had done a short stint in Iran helping to plant a signal-stealing device array in the northern mountains; the brief but intense experience drove home one overriding fact of warfare—you can never ever have too many bullets.

The handheld screen flickered, then came up with a red-tinted window of the guerrilla camp. He had to stop so he could fiddle with the magnification. Sourin came over to look.

"Our target," Karr explained, holding the image up for him.

The Thai major had apparently never seen a handheld computer before and turned his head to look behind the device. Karr showed him how the screen image could be sized. By now the analysts back at the NSA had added information to the image; Karr toggled the overlay and showed Sourin that there were guards in both of the trenches they had spotted earlier. At least six men guarded the northeast line. The Desk Three people IDed two Russian DShKM heavy machine guns, commonly called Dushkas; the weapons were mounted near the center of the compound on a rise that gave them decent coverage to the south as well as the north. Though older than anyone on the assault team, the guns were serious weapons that fired 12.7mm rounds. Lighter machine guns, Russian-made RPDs, were mounted on tripods covering the Thai approach; there were two, along with a third, more curious weapon.

"Hey, uh, Sandy, my computer's got a glitch. One of the machine guns is being called a Stoner."

"That's what it is. Stoner 63 LMG. I may have to hose down the weapons guy. He's asking if you can take it home for him."

"What am I going to get in return?"

The Stoner dated from the 1960s; an American weapon, it was a versatile lightweight gun that had been popular with some Special Forces troops in Vietnam but never really caught on in the military at large.

"He's offering to trade a mint Winchester Model 1873, still chambered for .44-40."

"That a good deal?"

"Claims it was used to shoot at Wyatt Earp."

"Uh-huh."

"Malachi Reese is your air support liaison. His time-to-target is two-five minutes; you'll want to launch the Kite ten minutes before he's there."

"Sounds good," he told her. He started to set the buzzer on his watch, then realized an audible alarm might not be a good idea.

48

"We have him! He's in the subway—the metro. Heitzing—the stop is Heitzing," said Rockman. "It's right nearby. He's coming out."

"You don't have to shout," said Lia, turning to tell the pilot to fly there.

As Dean cleared the turnstile and went outside, he heard the pounding rotors of a nearby helicopter. He started to move along the sidewalk, disoriented by the rush of daylight and the press of the tourist crowd nearby.

People were pointing, saying something.

The helicopter was coming right over the buildings, literally close enough to knock them over.

Dean's headache instantly returned, and he felt his stomach revolting again. A swatch of green appeared on his right, trees, a massive park.

The chopper was coming for *him*.

Dean bolted across the street, running. People were staring, shouting.

There was a line of people, a fence, a gate.

Dean's head swirled. Everyone was looking at the helicopter, which was landing in the park nearby.

"Charlie," said the voice in his head. "Charlie, we can see you."

"Rockman?"

"Go to the helicopter. Lia's there."

Dean started to run.

Lia opened the helicopter door and leaned out as it came down. She could see someone running on the street toward her.

Charlie?

She lost sight of him as the helicopter descended. She yelled, but of course he couldn't hear—the engine was too loud and now they were yards and yards away, separated by a small run of trees as well as the metal fence.

She'd have to leave the chopper to get him.

"That van is coming back around," warned Rockman.

That did it. Lia leaped out, tumbling on the ground as the helicopter roared away. She ran to the park perimeter.

Dean was there, just reaching the fence.

"Get in here! Get over the fence—come on. Come on!"

Dean swung his head around, then started toward her in slow motion. Two men—policemen—were running toward her. Lia pointed toward the street.

"The van!" she yelled in English. "The van!"

Dean grabbed at the fence.

Even if the policemen could have heard her over the roar of the nearby helicopter, there was no van on the street. One of them grabbed her arm and immediately regretted it—Lia flipped him over and spun him back into his companion, both men sprawling in a tumble. Dean climbed the fence, hauling himself up over the pointed bars at the top.

The van skidded to a stop in the street as Lia tossed one of the smoke grenades onto the sidewalk. People began to run—she readied her gun but didn't fire.

Dean collapsed onto the ground. She ran to him, grabbed his shirt.

"What?" he said.

"What yourself. Come on," she said, pulling. One of the policemen started to rise but stopped as he caught sight of her Mac 11. Tourists threw themselves down or ran in the opposite direction as Lia and Dean began heading deeper into the grounds. They ran across the paths, cutting momentarily through some of the trees and then to Lia's left, skirting the large zoo.

"I can't keep going," said Dean. "I can't."

Lia turned. Dean had stopped running and was walking almost in a daze. His face had flushed red.

"Charlie?"

"I'm okay," he mumbled.

"You're burning up," she said, feeling his face.

"Yeah," he said.

They walked at a slower pace, making their way toward the Gloriette Monument and then down the large lawn toward the formal gardens at the very bottom. Lia folded the stock on the Mac 11 and held it tight to her body so that it looked almost—almost—like a purse. She could hear police sirens in the distance.

"What's going on, Rockman?" she asked the runner.

"Just your typical city riot."

"You getting us out of here or what?"

"Oh, *now* you want my help. Move on down the hill to the Fasangarten," said Rockman. "That would be the place with the flowers."

"You going to give me the history of the place next?"

"I may."

Dean continued beside her, walking slower and slower but still moving at least.

"What'd they do to you, Charlie?" she asked.

"Nothin'," he said. "We stopped in some sort of tunnel. They had somebody waiting to grab the car. Hercules is dead."

"They didn't drug you or anything?"

"No. I feel like death, though. All that food I ate yesterday."

"Then how come I'm not sick?"

"You eat like a bird."

Lia curled her arm tighter around his. They crossed a roadway to the back border of the garden, walking down a tree-lined path. She flinched as something ran out at them from the right.

Two brothers, maybe seven and eight, chasing each other in a game of spy versus spy.

"Rockman," she hissed.

"Listen for it."

All she could hear was police sirens.

"Have you told the Austrians we're on their side?"

"We're in the process of doing that. Listen for it."

The air had started to vibrate with the loud rap of rotors. Six Blackhawk helicopters circled out of the northeast. The choppers were dark green American birds.

"Finally," said Lia when she spotted them.

"I told you we had it under control," said Rockman. "You have to learn to trust us."

"I suppose you're going to tell me these guys have been here all along."

"They've been nearby," said the runner.

"I'll bet." Lia stopped at the edge of one of the large garden squares, which was laid out with colored flowers to form a pattern. "We're almost home, Charlie," she said.

"Yeah, roger that," he said, sitting down.

Lia expected the helicopters to land on the grass beyond the tree line they'd come through. But as she took a few steps in that direction, she realized that the two lead Blackhawks were coming toward the gardens. They had their wheels down, ready to land.

"Tell them they're going to ruin the flowers," said Lia as grit began to whip around.

"Just stay where you are," said Rockman.

Dean and Lia turned their backs and huddled together as the sandstorm increased. Finally Lia turned back toward the helicopter to look for her rescuers.

There were a dozen SF troopers, guns ready, fanning out around them. A few were carrying shotguns; the rest had M4s.

But that wasn't the weird thing.

All of the men had full hazard suits on—they looked like spacemen, bundled up against any contingency.

"What is going on?" asked Lia.

"Put down your weapons and come with us," said a voice from the helicopter over a loudspeaker.

"Rockman, what's going on?"

"Do what they say, Lia. It's for your own good."

"No way."

"We will use our weapons if necessary."

"What the hell?" said Dean.

Before Lia could react, a slug of nonlethal but very painful ammo from one of the troopers with the shotgun took her down at the knees. It was followed by a rain of small plastic pellets and, for good measure, a dose of tear gas.

49

Malachi Reese steadied the Puff/1 as it came over the ridge, fighting a wave of turbulence. After steering satellite-launched "vessel" space planes and Mach 2–capable robot fighters, flying the prop-driven robot was like stepping into a Model T. The two-engined unmanned aerial vehicle looked like a three-quarter-sized OV-10 Bronco, with a fattened central fuselage. In place of a crew cabin, the body contained two GAU-12/U Equalizers, 25mm Gatling guns mounted in turrets that could swing approximately thirty degrees in any direction. Adapted from their original incarnation as podded weapons in AV-8B Harrier II jump-jet attack planes, the cannons could put a hundred or so armor-piercing rounds through the skin of a medium tank or armored personnel carrier in a little over ten seconds. Sitting between them was a double-bank of nineteen-inch rockets, unguided missiles that had high-explosive warheads.

While the weaponry was relatively low-tech, the aircraft itself was not. Its wings and surface area were covered with LED panels that could project real-time background images across the aircraft, so that in the middle of the day it might look like a collection of clouds passing overhead. The engines were powered by fuel cell technology; they were about 15 percent as loud as normal turboprops. The power plants could drive the aircraft 1,200 miles and back without stopping for a refuel.

But Malachi couldn't get used to the slow speed. He had Feckboy jammin' on the Mp3 player, but 300 knots was still 300 knots. The big screen in front of him plotted his position on a detailed topographical map; he could see the squad members who were carrying radios as well as Tommy Karr, the Desk Three op on the scene. A timer drained off in the right corner, showing how long it would be before Malachi was within weapons range. His console displays toggled between four video feeds; two were infrared capable.

"Stand by for site feed," said Telach, over in the Art Room.

Malachi punched the function key and brought up the video, which was being supplied from a man-portable unmanned aerial vehicle known as a Kite. The small UAV was three miles from the guerrilla camp; the camp was a blurry gray-red image, jittering at top of the screen. The battle-analysis computer looked at the image and interpreted it, ID-ing the guard units.

"Hey, Malachi, what are we listening to today?" asked Karr over the sat com system.

"Feckboy," he told the op.

"That thrash rock or metal rap?"

"In that direction."

"You seein' what I'm seeing?"

"Two guards on that perimeter," said Malachi. "I'm on target in zero-five."

"I have only one request: Don't hit us."

Malachi snorted. He nudged his joystick controller left slightly, positioning Puff for a swing that would take it to the northwest of the site. Firing from that direction would have the advantage of confusing the guerrillas about where the ground attack would come from. It also put a little more distance between Puff and the ground forces.

Malachi began his prebattle checklist: instruments in the green, fuel steady, guns armed and ready, Mp3 cranked at 8, two full bottles of Nestlé's strawberry drink on standby, straws inserted and ready to go.

"Ready when you are," said Karr.

Malachi glanced up at the large screen, looking to see

where everyone was. The NSA op had moved to within five yards of the sentry line; he was planning on running right past the position as soon as Puff took it out.

"Sixty seconds," Malachi told him. "Careful where you're going."

Karr heard the light hum of the robot gunship about two seconds before it started to fire. The weapons didn't carry tracer rounds—the sighting was all done with radar data—and so the rattle seemed to come from the earth itself. Dirt flew upward; Karr hunched down behind the tree a few yards from the guard post, confident that Malachi would hit exactly what he was aiming at and nothing else.

The GAU-12 spat about a hundred rounds through the heavy-gun position, then moved on; Karr got up and started running through the guerrilla camp's perimeter, making a beeline for the pair of huts a hundred yards away. Puff/1, meanwhile, blasted away at the heavier emplacements on the northwest.

The guerrillas began returning fire, their green tracer rounds streaking haphazardly upward. Sourin and two of his men were now a few yards behind the NSA op.

Something moved on Karr's left. He threw himself on the ground; an automatic rifle popped behind him, taking down the guerrilla.

By the time the big American had hauled himself back to his feet, the Thai Army squad had already breached the defenses and was just about at the buildings. They were firing at them, though it wasn't clear whether they had targets or not.

"Whoa, guys, whoa!" shouted Karr. "Major Sourin— Major. Hold on. We want the people inside there alive, remember?"

Sourin shouted something back at him but was drowned out by a fresh splatter of cannon from Puff. Karr jumped into a shallow revetment behind the two buildings; Sourin was a few feet away, emptying his rifle at the building.

"Damn it, we want the people in the buildings alive if

we can do it," said Karr, clamping his hand on the officer's shoulder.

"*You* want them alive," said Sourin, but he stopped firing and shouted at his men to hold their fire.

"Tommy, two men are running to the northwest toward team delta," said Chafetz.

Karr alerted Gidrey, who was with the team there.

"We have prisoners," said Foster over the radio. He was with the team sweeping in from the southwest corner.

"Good," said Karr.

The Thai major said something in Thai that didn't sound particularly respectful, but Karr chose to ignore it. He pushed forward against the edge of the ditch, holding his glasses as he scanned the buildings.

"All your posts are neutralized," said Malachi. "Heavy weapons are down."

"Can you tell me what's inside that building in front of me?"

"Coming over it now. Two—five people. Weapons."

"Beam me the image." Karr took out his handheld, staring at it as the image downloaded. He showed Sourin the handheld computer with its frozen-frame image. "Tell them to surrender."

"They won't," said the major.

"Well, convince them to."

The Thai commander started speaking rapidly in his native language.

"Chafetz, you getting this?" Karr asked.

"Doesn't want to take prisoners, basically."

"Look, Major, we play by my rules," Karr told him in English. "I need these guys alive. You got it?"

Sourin made the mistake of moving his gun toward the op.

"Mal, bracket us," said Karr.

"Uh—"

"Now, Mal," said Karr. He looked into Sourin's face. "Look, Major, I don't want to embarrass you in front of your men. But—"

Malachi finished the sentence for him, peppering the ground around them. To his credit the major didn't flinch.

Much.

"Get my point?" asked Karr.

Sourin frowned but then told him in Thai that he could go ahead and approach the buildings.

Chafetz supplied the translation.

"He's not happy," added the runner.

"Neither am I," said Karr. He slid off the backpack with the extra ammo and climbed up out of the ditch.

The Thai officer yelled something to him, but Karr ignored it, jumping to his feet and running ahead. The A-2's laser dot danced near the window of the hut as he ran, but no one appeared in the opening. About ten feet from the back of the building he threw himself into the dirt. Foster flopped in the dust right behind him.

"Where are you going?" Karr asked.

"Coverin' your ass."

Tommy got up to one knee and sidled to the side of the building. "You watching them for me, Sandy?"

"No one's moved."

"They dead?"

"Not sure. One was definitely hit, and another looks out of it."

"Is our guy in there or what?"

"The profiles are obscured and we can't be sure."

Karr reached into his pocket and pulled out the handheld computer. Four of the five men were huddled against the opposite wall, but one guerrilla was about three feet away from him, just on the other side of the wall near the opening.

"Give me the Burmese words for *surrender*," Karr told Sandy as he slid a grenade from his pocket.

Foster pointed his M4 rifle toward the window; there was no door on this side of the building.

The translator came on the line with the phrase, which sounded like *"cul-osh-dik"* repeated twice.

Karr tapped Foster's arm. "Don't breathe. It's one of the

gas grenades," he told him as he reached up and dropped the grenade through the open window. "Take about ten, twenty seconds to wipe them out."

"*Cul-osh-dik,* cul-osh-dik," tried Karr.

The grenade exploded. Foster started to jump up, but Karr grabbed him.

"No. Hang on."

"They're still not moving," said Sandy. "Okay, one just fell over. They're out of it."

"Let's get the other building and then come back," Karr told Foster.

"Two men. They're pointing their weapons in the other direction," said Chafetz as they ran toward it. "Not going to be your target." The computer had compared the profiles it saw on the infrared camera and decided neither man was big enough to be Kegan.

"Gotcha." Karr turned to the Marine. "Flash-bang? I go through the door."

Foster nodded. He took a grenade and dropped it through the window.

"They're moving," said Chafetz just as it exploded.

In the same instant, Karr leaped through the nearby door, his shoulder muscling the flimsy panel aside. The A-2 roared and the two guerrillas sprawled back on the ground.

Karr took a long, slow breath, the tension draining away now that the guerrilla camp was secured. He and Foster checked the hut. Back outside, Karr pulled a lightweight respirator and mask from the large flap pocket on his thigh. The gas should have cleared out of the first hut by now—it was a fast-acting Demerol derivative cooked up specially by the Deep Black chemists—but there was no sense taking chances.

"That little gun is pretty damn loud," said Foster, pointing at the A-2.

"Yeah," said Karr. "I think it really works by scaring the shit out of people."

He smiled, then, with the mask on and gun ready, went to inspect the other hut.

50

"What the hell is going on?"

"Miss DeFrancesca, you're going to have to calm down."

"Don't call me miss. What the hell is going on?"

Rubens placed his palms together before his chest, pressing them together as he relaxed his shoulders. He'd decided before the conversation started that he would be patient.

"There's a possibility that you have been infected with a man-made bacteria," Rubens told her.

"God damn it." Lia paced on the screen, walking across the white linoleum. "I knew it."

She and Dean had been evacuated to an American air base in Germany, where a set of trailers was equipped for medical isolation. The facilities were not quite as elaborate as Rubens had been told, but at this point they would have to do.

"We are working on finding the cure," added Rubens.

"You knew it all along," she said, turning toward the camera.

"That's not correct," Rubens told her. "We only began to suspect recently."

"How recently?"

"Recently."

"You're a bastard."

"Such language, Lia, really. Did they teach you that in the Army?"

"Screw off." She kicked at the linoleum on the floor,

twisting away from the camera and then back. "Where's the antidote? That's what this is about, isn't it? Kegan sold them the bacteria and promised to give them an antidote."

"You're jumping to conclusions. We don't know that he sold them anything. We do believe, however, that he did have a cure for this disease. So we're pursuing leads to that effect."

"How?" she snapped.

"Mr. Karr is running it down as we speak."

"I want to help him."

"Not possible at the moment," Rubens told her. He wondered what her reaction would be if he said that they weren't even sure yet whom Kegan had been dealing with.

Lia looked down at the floor for a moment, then raised her eyes back at the video camera transmitting her image. The anger had vanished from her face—not a good sign, Rubens knew.

"I can get out of here, you know."

"Lia, I'm sure you can."

Not only were there four guards on each of the two windows, but there were a dozen men at the only door, and another six or seven milling around the sides. The outer fence ringing the trailers was surrounded by a company of soldiers, several machine gun–equipped Humvees, and at least one M1a1 tank. But Rubens had no doubt Lia was correct.

"Dr. Lester is en route to examine you himself," added Rubens in what he hoped was a conciliatory voice. "He should be there within a few hours."

"Who's Lester?"

"He's with the CDC. There will be some blood tests, and the results should be pretty clear. Believe me, this has our top priority."

"Oh, peachy."

"As we speak, Johnny Bib and his team—"

"Oh, God, not *that* nut."

"Johnny's team is tracking down the construction of the organism as well as this so-called antidote." Rubens realized belatedly that the word *so-called* was an extremely poor choice on his part. He rushed to continue. "We have some very good ideas about it. And since the man who's the center of the attention here is a friend of Mr. Dean's, I'm confident that once we apprehend him he will be more than glad—he'll be anxious to help."

"What's he going to do if he's dead? You hear him in there?" Lia gestured to the other room. "He's groaning."

"Is his IV set up correctly?"

"You think I'm a nurse?"

"I was under the impression your background included extensive medic training."

Lia growled and disappeared into the other room. Rubens understood that she would not be returning anytime soon.

"What do you think?" asked Telach.

"I think we'd better see if they can spare some more soldiers for the perimeter guard," said Rubens.

51

"I thought we were looking for pigs," Karr told the Art Room. "I have plenty of pigs."

"We have new information," said Chafetz. "Apparently, Dr. Kegan was investigating texts that concern ancient folk cures for rat-bite fever. The cures mention a particular type of fungus that grows on strangler figs."

"Figs, not pigs?"

"It's a type of tree. It grows around other trees. The fungus grows in the crack. But not every crack. I'm downloading information for your computer."

Karr sighed and sat down in front of building one. Two of the men inside had been dead, hit by shrapnel or bullets as the assault started. The other three were sleeping, their hands and legs tightly bound, a few yards away. All were Burmese; there was no sign Kegan had ever been here.

"This still sounds suspiciously like a wild-goose chase," he told Sandy. "More and more."

"Can you look for those trees?"

"If I have to."

"We have some experts who are going to come on the line and help," she told him.

Karr unfolded himself from the spot and checked his watch. It was now getting close to 4:00 A.M. He had two hours, maybe a little more, before he'd have to leave for the rendezvous.

"Talking to yourself again?" asked Foster.

"Somebody's got to. Do me a favor: go through building two again and see if you see any plant stuff."

"Like marijuana?"

"No, more like a fungus kind of thing."

"Mushrooms?" asked the Marine.

"Yeah. Here, hold on a second." Karr took the computer and clicked into the pictures that were being downloaded. The fungus looked like crumbly brown rocks with white diamonds shot through, the top arching like a sawed-off mushroom. "Something like this. But hell, if you see anything close, let me know."

Karr worked his way slowly through building one, listening as a pair of scientists began explaining what they were looking for and why.

"You can give me the abbreviated version," he told them as they segued into cell skin barriers.

"Basically, we're looking for something that is a natural penicillin," said one of the scientists. "Penicillin interferes with the bacterial wall, and that causes all sorts of problems for them. This fungus is probably almost the same thing."

"Well, different, but the same," said the other expert.

"Oh sure, now I understand," said Karr.

There were training manuals, rocket-propelled grenades, and enough ammunition to keep a regiment supplied in a weeklong firefight, but no fungus, no bark, and no plants that Karr could see. He went outside and hiked over to the pen where the animals had been kept.

"It all begins and ends at the cell wall," said the scientist in a flourish. "Imagine if your house had no walls or roof. Water would rush in—swoosh, you'd be wiped out."

"Actually, we're guessing that it's attacking the cell wall. It may be protein synthesis," said another scientist.

"Give me the bottom line, guys," said Karr.

"You need to find the fungus. It's probably a cure for the disease. See, it's very similar to penicillin, except that the bacteria is resistant to penicillin. Penicillin, remember, is also a fungus."

Ordinarily that would have provoked some sort of joke from Karr, but he felt too tired and drained to even respond. He finished his search of the area without finding anything that looked remotely like a mushroom. He met Foster back at the hut, also empty-handed.

"Lot of old weapons," said the Marine. "No trees, though. No plants. Hey, look who finally got here."

He gestured toward Gidrey, who was walking into the camp with the Thai squad he'd been working with.

"Stinking jungle's thicker than a whore's bush," said Gidrey.

"You'd know," said Foster.

"You see any fig trees?" Karr asked.

"Figs?"

"Twisted ones," the NSA op told him, explaining.

"Jeez, I don't know."

"All right," said Karr. "Come on with me and let's have a look. We got some time before we have to leave for the helicopter."

52

Keys stood before him in a surgical gown.

"You're going to be okay, Charlie."

"Keys—what do I have?"

"Fever. Fever!" Keys started to swirl around in the room. Dean blinked and he was in the middle of a basketball court, heading down on the left side of the court as Kegan dribbled ahead. Dean knew the ball would be coming a second before it squirted in his direction; he grabbed it and leaped in the same motion, laying the ball into the hoop.

Except it didn't quite go in. It rolled and rolled around the rim. Dean stayed suspended in midair, watching it as it twirled and twirled.

Then his stomach began to tighten.

He saw Keys as a doctor again, standing before him, sweating himself. They were in the jungle.

"I can't cure all these people," said Keys. "I can't cure them. They call me the Good Doctor, but I can't cure them."

"Cure me," said Charlie, grabbing for him. "Cure me."

Keys took a step back. They were sitting in his living room in Athens. The dead man lay on the floor behind the desk. Every so often Dean would glance over, but Kegan seemed oblivious to the body.

"That was the best time of my life. And the worst. They killed her. Changed everything for me," said Kegan.

"Yeah," said Dean. He knew what Kegan was talking

about—and yet the exact memory stayed out of reach, back in his brain.

"You'd be amazed. These people had none of the basic medicines, nothing. We trained some good nurses, though," said Keys. "She was one of the best."

"Who?" said Dean.

"They killed her, though."

"Who?"

53

By the time Rubens returned to his office, Hadash had called over twice for an update. Rubens began to pick up the phone but was interrupted by a knock on his door. Only one person in the agency would knock on his door without an appointment—Rubens looked up and saw Vice Admiral Brown, the Director.

"George Hadash has been calling over," said Brown. "He wants you to update the President."

"Okay," said Rubens.

"They want you to do it in person."

"It's not a particularly good time to do that," said Rubens. He wanted to check with the medical people, find out about the autopsies, push the researchers to make the link between Dean's captors and UKD—or the Russians, or anyone.

"It may be worse in a few hours," said Brown. "Apparently the *Post* has caught wind of some of the disease cases. Update me as well. There's a helicopter en route."

Rubens wanted to ask Brown about the Secretary of State, but the admiral spent the entire flight on the phone. They landed on the White House lawn, hustling inside quickly and walking briskly to the President's office in the West Wing, where President Jeffrey Marcke was meeting with Secretary of Health, Education and Welfare Debra Jodelin, Surgeon General Peirs Fenimore—and Secretary of State James Lincoln.

"Admiral, very good of you to come," said Marcke, who leaned back in his chair. "Billy, I'm glad you're here—you can answer some pressing questions for us."

Stifling his displeasure at being called Billy in front of the others, Rubens took a seat. Westhoven from the FBI and a CDC official Rubens didn't know very well came in almost on his heels; Westhoven kept his eyes pasted on the carpet, seemingly resigned to being made the scapegoat.

Rubens took over the meeting, very briefly laying out the most obvious points: they were trying to track down a doctor who had disappeared who was somehow involved in the manufacture—the possible manufacture—of a synthetic bacteria.

"A killer bug," said Dr. Fenimore, the Surgeon General.

Jodelin winced.

"That may be an overstatement," said Rubens.

"There are a hundred people sick with it in New York already," said Fenimore.

"I took the liberty of updating myself on the way over," said Rubens. "We have only twelve confirmed cases."

"That's not what the newspaper reporter told me," said Fenimore.

"Well, with all due respect to the fourth estate . . ." Rubens began. He paused as the President laughed. ". . . they do tend to exaggerate. We are confident of those diagnoses. There are a large number of cases that have to be checked, but so far it's been running less than one out of ten confirmed. And they can all be traced back to Athens, New York, and the doctor in question in some way."

"I've spoken to Dr. Lester," said Jodelin. "There are a cluster of cases in New York City with similar symptoms and no clear connection, and he is very concerned."

"As am I," said Rubens. "Nonetheless, I'm sure he told you the cases there have not been confirmed."

"How long will that take?" asked the President.

"It's ongoing. The hospitals are following a very strict protocol," said Jodelin.

"Why is Dr. Lester en route to Vienna?" asked the Secretary of State.

Rubens glanced at the President before correcting Lincoln, saying that Lester was going to consult with agency personnel in Germany.

"Consult? I understand they're in quarantine," said Fenimore.

"A precaution," said Rubens. "We try to err on the side of prudence."

There was a knock on the door; George Hadash entered—with Sandra Marshall in tow.

Looking as beautiful as ever, unfortunately.

They all exchanged greetings. Hadash and Marshall had apparently spent the last half hour trying to gauge how much the *Post* knew about the case, and whether they were serious about printing a story.

The answers were "not much" and "very."

"Panic in the streets," said Fenimore.

"They'll look foolish if they print a story along those lines," said Rubens.

"They don't think so," said Marshall. "And frankly, the facts may bear them out."

"Any sort of publicity like that may jeopardize our people," said Rubens. "And prevent us from getting a cure for this."

"How close are we to a cure?" asked Lincoln.

"We're not sure," said Rubens. "We have some circumstantial evidence about what the cure may be, but we haven't quite found it."

"What is it?" asked Fenimore. "A drug?"

"A type of fungus that acts like penicillin. Apparently the disease was bred to be resistant to regular penicillin. Well, we don't actually know that yet," Rubens said quickly. "We're speculating."

"This wasn't in the earlier report," said the Surgeon General.

Rubens emphasized that he was only guessing that it was penicillin-resistant. "It's only been a day and a half. The doctors are not yet in a position to really know that much about the disease." He looked at Jodelin. "They've done an excellent job, under the circumstances."

"The problem is," said Jodelin, "excellent may not be enough."

Westhoven shifted in his seat but didn't say anything. Rubens decided to throw him a bone, on the off-chance that the FBI man survived the fallout.

"The FBI has been heavily involved," said Rubens. "Doing a lot of work."

"Anything new, Bill?" asked the President.

Westhoven shook his head. "Mr. Rubens covered it."

How come he's Bill and I'm Billy? wondered Rubens.

"The information the NSA has must be shared," said the Surgeon General.

"The CDC has been with us every step of the way," said Rubens, deciding not to get into the difference between Desk Three and the NSA. "Every step of the way."

"That's correct," said Vice Admiral Brown. "Given that the matter only came to light a few days ago," he added, sticking up for his agency, "we've done a remarkable job just to get this far."

Rubens glanced at Marshall. She had a bit of a smirk on her face.

"So how do we handle the press without jeopardizing Billy's mission here?" said the President. "Because, really, if Desk Three can't break this very quickly, we're all in a lot of trouble."

The Surgeon General suggested they tell the news media everything they knew.

Really, thought Rubens. *How did someone so naive get into government in the first place?*

"I think that's out of the question," said Marshall. "On the other hand, they do know a good deal. I would say as soon as the *Post* puts this on their Web site, New York will be crawling with reporters."

Rubens indulged in a long glance at her face, his eyes trailing down to her crisp blue suit jacket.

Enough, he warned himself.

"Depending on how it's spread, within a day we may have a thousand cases," said Jodelin. "In that case, we'll be lambasted not only for not dealing with it but also for not leveling with the American public. Remember the furor over anthrax? And that was just a few cases."

"The situation now is different," said Rubens.

"Sure. It's worse."

"Potentially, yes," said Rubens. "That's why the operation has to receive priority."

"Maybe Homeland Security rather than CDC should take the public lead on this," suggested President Marcke. "While still emphasizing that we believe it's a natural outbreak, or rather, emphasizing that we don't exactly know what is," added the President, correcting himself, "we could still make it clear that we're taking it very seriously. Then no matter what happens, we can't be roasted."

Rubens watched Marshall closely as she replied, saying that the Director was still in Texas on his retreat, but if necessary she would be happy to deal with the media.

After conferring with Billy, of course.

Billy. God, there was no escaping it now.

"We can arrange something," said Rubens. "Mr. Westhoven might want to be present as well."

"How much more time do you need before you solve this?" asked Marcke.

"We're analyzing a lot of data right now. But whether that's going to lead to a cure, I don't know." Rubens looked at the Surgeon General. "Potentially, if this germ really is resistant to penicillin and there's no other cure—"

"Depending on how it's spread, it would be a true disaster," said Fenimore. "An incurable epidemic—it would make AIDS look like an outbreak of food poisoning."

"Let's move then," said the President. "Billy, Bill, work this out with Ms. Marshall. In the meantime, I want worst- and best-case scenarios."

Lincoln and Hadash made no move to get up as the others filed out. Marcke asked Brown to stay as well. Rubens couldn't help but think they would be discussing the Secretary of State's plans—but of course there was no way to ask.

"What's this about Internet DNA?" asked Jodelin after Rubens had carefully delineated the minuscule amount of information Marshall could share with the media.

"A bold initiative to increase Internet security," said Marshall so quickly it could have been a setup.

"The President seems in favor of it," said Fenimore.

"He mentioned it to you, too?"

"Yes. There might be some benefits vis-à-vis medical information," started the Surgeon General, segueing into a pet project of his, on-line medical records instantly accessible to patient, doctor, and emergency room.

Vice Admiral Brown knocked on the door. Rubens gave his regrets and started to leave. As he reached the hallway he heard Marshall telling the others that the proposal was almost ready for the President.

"Only Billy is opposed," she said. Rubens pretended not to hear.

"Marshall's a real climber, isn't she?" said Brown on the helicopter ride back.

"Ambitious," answered Rubens, looking for a way to turn the conversation toward the Secretary of State.

"You know what her boss Johnson is doing, don't you?"

Rubens replied that it was a rather poorly kept secret that he was rounding up support—and donations—for a run at the Texas governorship.

"Yes. Good riddance, I would say," added Brown.

"You think Marshall will succeed him?" asked Rubens.

"Of course. And she'll be just as bad," said Brown. "But at least pleasant to look at."

Pleasant or not, Rubens thought Marshall would be a much more formidable problem than Johnson, especially if she remained close to Hadash and Marcke.

"I've heard the Secretary of State was thinking of leaving," he said as the helicopter began to descend. He hated to be so blunt, but it was clear that he had to take his shot now.

"Who told you that?" asked Brown.

Rubens couldn't tell whether Brown was being evasive or not.

"There are rumors."

"Well, keep them to yourself," said Brown.

"They're true?"

Brown didn't answer. Rubens had no choice but to drop it as the helicopter touched down.

54

"I'm not saying there's no fig trees here, but if there are, I can't find them," Karr told Chafetz as he walked through the camp.

"Kite packed away?"

"Yup."

"Have you killed all the pigs?"

"All but the one we're taking back." He'd also taken blood and tissue samples from each for analysis.

"Buried 'em?"

"You know, you're starting to sound a little like my mom before going on a camping trip."

"I'm just tired."

"Hey, that was a compliment," said Karr. He could definitely sympathize with her. He hadn't slept now for more than twenty-four hours. His normally robust body was turning against him, weighing him down so badly his fatigue felt like a physical thing clamped over his head and chest.

Sourin and his men were waiting at the far end of the camp, near where they had launched the assault. The Thai major had gotten over his earlier crankiness and hadn't objected to the burial of the men and pigs they'd found.

The promise of an unspecified "burial bonus" might have had something to do with his heightened spirits, but Karr preferred always to look on the brighter side of human nature, and put it down to the fact that the major and his men were glad to be going back to camp with the satisfaction of a job well done.

"Your helicopter's en route. It's a replacement—the Special Forces units had to punch over east," added Chafetz. "Things are heating up over near Cambodia. Replacement is a Thai military helicopter. Sorry."

"Not a problem," said Karr. "As long as it comes."

"It will."

Sourin ran scouting parties and had teams flanking them as they walked to the landing zone. Karr tried looking for fig trees, though it was becoming a struggle to keep his eyes open. He felt incredibly cold—odd, because the others were stripping off their vests and seemed to be sweating.

"What do you think about a pig roast when we get back?" asked Gidrey.

"I'd love to, but not with that pig," said Karr.

"Why not?"

"Doctors want to see if it's growing bacteria or a virus or something," said Karr.

"You don't think the guerrillas kept it around for food?"

"Doesn't matter what I think. It's what they think that counts." Tommy smiled at the Marine.

"Who is 'they' anyway?"

"The Big They," said Tommy. "The They above all other Theys. They."

"You ever stop joking around?"

"When I'm sleeping. Which I hope will be pretty soon." Karr could hear the harsh beat of the Chinook as it chomped through the air. "Here comes our taxi."

Karr slid down into a crouch as they waited at the edge of the clearing.

"Tired?" asked Foster.

"Yeah, I guess so."

"You don't look that good."

"Just tired. It's cold for the jungle."

"Cold? Hell, it's got to be close to ninety," said the Marine.

The wind from the helicopter felt good for a moment, but

then the grass and grit formed into a kind of paste covering Karr's face. He started to trot with the others, but by the time he reached the rear ramp of the big air-going bus, he had slowed considerably. His legs felt shaky.

The rotors whirled up, the helicopter shuddering. They did a slow orbit around the camp, then began angling back toward the border. Karr tried to think about the other camps he had to inspect, but he couldn't focus.

"I think I'll take a nap!" Karr shouted to Foster, who was sitting next to him on the long bench. "Wake me up when we're home."

As he turned to hear Foster's reply, something exploded above him.

"Uh-oh," said Karr, grabbing for the seat as the helicopter lurched sickeningly and began to rotate.

55

Lia twisted the washcloth in her hands, wringing the excess water into the basin. She went back to Dean's bed and laid it over his forehead.

He seemed a bit cooler at least, and he'd stopped mumbling in his sleep.

Maybe she could leave him.

She would, if she had any idea where to go.

Back to New York, get into Kegan's lab.

Karr had already been there. But really, what the hell did he know? God bless him, he was a great op, resourceful and all, but no genius. How he'd managed to sneak through RPI and get his college degree in three years was beyond her.

Legacy admission, obviously.

Lia took the electronic thermometer and placed it into Dean's ear. He was down to ninety-nine degrees.

If she got out of here, could she get back to the States? The Art Room would be tracking her.

Maybe the thing to do was to go back to Crypto City— confront Rubens—confront the Director himself. Demand—

Demand what?

Lia put the thermometer back and walked from the room pensively, still not entirely sure what to do. She paced in the hall, then went to the door. She was about to open it and step into the vestibule when the outer door opened. A man carrying a large duffel bag and what looked like an old-fashioned doctor's bag entered. He was the first person who'd come in without wearing a moon suit, and Lia stepped back, waiting to see if he'd come in.

He saw her at the glass door, waved, then pointed at the door.

"It's not locked," she said.

He didn't hear. She scowled but opened it for him.

"Better stand back. I'm highly contagious," she told him.

"Maybe," said the man. "But probably not."

His hair had started to gray, but he was fairly young, early thirties at most. Lia stepped back as he shut the door.

"Where's the patient?"

"Other room."

He nodded but then took a step toward her, peering at her eyes. "How do you feel?"

"Who the hell are you?"

"Lester. CDC. I'm a doctor." He stuck his hand out to shake. Lia scowled at him without taking it. "Good idea," he said. "A lot of germs are passed that way."

"What's going on?" she asked.

"I don't know for sure. Stick out your arm and I'll take some blood. Then we'll have a look at the patient."

Dean felt the knife jab his arm.

Needle, not a knife.

Thick needle, attached to a small vial.

"Damn!" he yelled, pulling himself upward.

"Sorry. I'm slightly out of practice," said an apologetic voice next to him.

Still unsure where the border between sleep and consciousness was, Dean pulled himself upright.

"Grab this one," said Kegan, holding out the test tube to Lia.

She took hold of it. It nearly slipped through her latex-clad fingers. The man at his side had slid another tube into the needle; blood was thumping into it.

"Mr. Dean, my name is Dr. Lester. I work for the CDC. I'm a disease expert. Well, that's what my job description says. I kind of ended up a bit of a jack-of-all-trades."

"What do I have?"

"We're going to find out. For now I'd like to hear your symptoms."

"Stomach feels like crap. Head's light. I have—I had a fever." Forgetting his other arm was attached to an IV, he started to raise it to his head. The bag jostled on its holder nearby and he stopped. "I think I have a fever."

"Actually, we just took your temperature and you're pretty close to normal."

"Pretty close," sneered Lia.

"Does this have to do with Kegan?" Dean asked.

"Let me finish taking the blood and then run the tests. We can talk when I'm done," Lester said.

"How many days is that gonna take?"

"Just a few minutes. I'll say one thing: your agency has some amazing resources."

Dean grunted. Lia came over and propped a pillow beneath his head.

"No kissing," warned Lester, his voice suddenly stern. "No body fluids."

"He's not much of a kisser anyway," said Lia.

Dean laughed and realized he was feeling a lot better.

A half hour later, Lester came into the room with a grin on his face. He wasn't wearing the gloves anymore. Lia, still scowling, curled her arms in front of her chest and fell into a metal chair nearby.

Did I infect her? Dean thought to himself.

"Mr. Dean, tell me what you last had for dinner," said the doctor, pulling over the other chair and sitting down.

"Some sort of beef thing with this white gloppy sauce," said Dean.

"What else?"

Charlie recounted the meal he'd had after Lia picked him up. Potatoes, some horrid cabbage, beer, two pieces of chocolate ganache cake.

"You packed it away," said Lester.

"I hadn't eaten for a while."

"Something you ate gave you clostridial food poisoning and gastroenteritis."

"And the fever?"

"Part of it, I'm pretty sure," said Lester. "Unusual, but part of it. I suppose it could be a generic virus, but in any event, I tested you for the synthetic rat-bite fever bacteria and you don't have it. Neither does Lia."

Lester explained a CDC team had isolated the bacteria that had sickened Gorman and the other confirmed case in New York. While they still had many more questions than answers, they could at least identify the bacteria by relatively simple tests—thanks to help from Desk Three and the NSA.

"So you can cure it then?" asked Dean.

"Not by a long shot, not yet. Gorman died a few hours ago."

"How'd he get it?" asked Dean.

"I don't know. That man you found in Dr. Kegan's house—did you touch him?"

Dean shook his head.

"Touch the blood?"

"I know better than to mess up a crime scene," said Dean.

"You could say the same for Gorman."

"The guy was shot."

"Yeah, but he had the disease. Or had had it. We're not sure. There was definitely some of the organism in his blood."

"He got better?" asked Lia.

Lester shook his head. "We don't know. Maybe he's just resistant somehow. It's possible he got better. So far, the only people whom the disease has severely affected have died. That's two. We have a bunch more very, very sick. I want to go back over what you found at the house again if you don't mind," he added. "Maybe we can figure it out together."

"You don't think Gorman just breathed it through the air?"

"Then you'd have it. And everyone who was in the house."

"How do you get rat-bite fever?" asked Dean.

"Rat bites you."

"Maybe you'd better check my blood again," said Lia. "Everybody I work with is a rat, present company excepted."

56

Johnny Bib waited as the small Bell helicopter hovered over the garage. The door on the left side opened and a bundle was lowered slowly by rope. When it hit the ground, Johnny ran forward, thinking he'd untie it. Instead, the man in the helicopter let go of the rope and it fell down on Johnny's head as the chopper whirled away.

This would not have happened to him had he taken his mother's advice and learned to play the piano when he was five, Johnny thought to himself. It was a mistake he'd paid for all his life.

The bundle proved to be a large duffel bag, so packed that Johnny had to drag it along the ground to get it inside. He found the encrypted phone at the top and dialed into the Art Room.

"It's Johnny Bib," he said. "I thought I was going home."

"Johnny, we have a lot to do," said Rubens, who was in the Art Room. "You're already in the house and—"

"There's no more information here."

"I'm going to let Chris Farlekas talk to you," said Rubens. "He may have some ideas."

"Yes, sir."

"Hi, Johnny. How are you?" said the Art Room supervisor, coming on the line.

"Lousy."

"Sick?"

"Just lousy."

"Come now. We need you to be strong."

Farlekas was fond of "Win One for the Gipper" crap. He didn't understand mathematicians at all. He probably couldn't even balance his checkbook.

"Forty-three dollars and seventeen cents."

"What's that, Johnny?" asked Farlekas.

"My checking account balance."

"Uh, okay. Listen, I'm going to put Dr. Chaucer on-line. We had some ideas."

The line clicked.

"Hello," said Chaucer. "The line's secure now, right?"

"In a manner of speaking. Technically, the encryption used in these phones is hardly tamper-proof. As was shown by the Dalton-Blitz paper of 2003, working—"

"Actually, I was wondering if we could turn our attention to the disease," said Chaucer. "It would be helpful to understand the vector. If you could look through his papers for articles on disease, perhaps."

The room seemed to light up. Finally the doctor had said something that made sense, thought Johnny Bib.

"What sort of vector?" asked Johnny.

"That's exactly the question," said Farlekas.

An odd sound behind him caused Johnny to jump. "A cat," he said involuntarily. "I hate cats!"

"Dr. Kegan has a cat?"

"It's right there," said Johnny, pointing. The fur ball finally got the message and retreated.

"Don't pet it. Don't pet it at all," said Chaucer.

"I don't intend to."

"Is that it?" asked Farlekas.

"It could be. We're going to have to capture it."

"Not me," said Johnny Bib.

"Someone has to."

"I'll fly to the moon first."

"That may be your next assignment," said Rubens, breaking

into the line. "If you don't do what Dr. Chaucer and Mr. Far-lekas tell you to do, precisely and expeditiously, you will be on the moon."

Rubens agreed with Chaucer that having Johnny Bib handle the cat was too dangerous. Fortunately, the cat's hunger and a can of tuna fish made luring him into a room where he could be quarantined relatively easy. One of the CDC teams was nearby, interviewing residents; they were detailed over to the house, along with a pair of state troopers, two animal control officers, and a special hazardous materials unit with contamination suits. In the meantime, Rubens had Farlekas contact Lester in Europe. Rather than the doctor, however, Lia came on the line.

"Why are we still in isolation?" she demanded.

"Miss DeFrancesca, always a pleasure. Put Dr. Lester on the line, please."

"When the hell are we getting out of here?"

"Lia, we can work out your personal issues—"

"Personal issues?"

"Put Dr. Lester on the line," he said.

"Quite a pistol," said Lester when he finally took the phone.

"Quite. Would a cat be a potential host?"

"Possibly. At this point, I wouldn't rule anything out."

"Is Dean off the hook?"

"Probably just food poisoning. As I told you while I was en route, the fever was never that high. I can ask him about the cat."

Rubens looked up. Farlekas was waving at him from the front of the Art Room.

"Excuse me, I have to speak to one of my people. Here's Dr. Chaucer." He clicked the line over to Chaucer, then went down to Farlekas.

"Tommy's helicopter went down. We're not sure what the hell's going on over there."

"You have a location?"

"They barely got off the ground. They're a good fifty miles inside of Burma. There are three guerrilla camps close enough to throw rocks at them. One other thing," added the Art Room supervisor. "Right before he got on the helicopter, he said he didn't feel too good. He thought he had a fever. Somehow I don't think we'd be lucky enough to have two cases of food poisoning on the same mission."

57

By the time Karr's head stopped spinning, he'd managed to crawl out of the helicopter, pulling Foster with him. Gidrey hunched a few yards ahead near the trunk of a tree, pistol out and pointed toward the jungle. The helicopter had pitched itself into a ravine and they were down next to a shallow pond, looking up at a slope that left them at a distinct disadvantage if attacked.

The Thai soldiers were struggling from the helicopter. Karr put his hand to his head as if to help his eyes focus as he tried to puzzle out where Sourin was.

"We gotta get out of here," said Gidrey.

"Yeah." Karr stood up, checking himself for wounds like a hiker might look for ticks. When he realized he wasn't hearing the Art Room he reached to the back of his belt to hit the send unit; he pressed his fingers over the belt loop where the unit could be turned on and off by pressure, but nothing happened.

It was possible the battery, which was integrated into his belt, had drained. He started back for his knapsack in the helicopter, but Gidrey grabbed his shirt.

"I think it's gonna blow," he said.

"I need my gun," Karr said.

"Come on," insisted the Marine. "It's on fire."

An automatic rifle began blasting in the jungle maybe fifty yards away. Karr pushed Gidrey out of the way and went back to the chopper, ignoring the rifle shots. He picked his way past the twisted rotors and bent fuselage, looking for the crease he'd squeezed through. There were a dozen or more bodies inside. As Karr started to punch into the darkness, a mortar or rocket-propelled grenade exploded on the far side of the ravine. The wrecked helicopter shook all around him; he couldn't see his backpack, or his A-2 for that matter. The spot where he'd been sitting had been pinched tight by the crash landing.

"How the hell did I get out of that?" he said aloud.

Another mortar round answered, this one close enough to throw a small hail of dirt against the wrecked fuselage. Karr grabbed one of the Minimis from the hulk, scooping up two mags of ammo before turning back to find Gidrey. His chest and legs were pounding him, though he hadn't been shot there; though his head had settled a bit, he still felt as if he were moving inside a long hollow tunnel.

Gidrey had Foster slung over his shoulder. Karr started to trot up the hill to him but quickly ran out of breath.

"We got to get the hell out of here," said the Marine. "Thais are going that way."

Karr pulled his handheld out, jogging the map button. He didn't have a live feed; without his com system working he had only what the small computer itself could store.

The automatic rifle fire stoked up. He pulled up his machine gun and half-walked, half-stumbled up the ravine back to the two Marines. The Thai soldiers had fanned out already—or perhaps just run off—and he couldn't see any as he hunkered down behind a pair of boulders.

"There," warned Gidrey.

Burmese guerrillas ducked between the bushes a few yards away. As one of them lowered his rifle, the NSA op blew apart his midsection with a burst from the Minimi, fired from his hip. He twisted left and put a stream of bullets through the head of another guerrilla a foot or two away. His scalp seemed to sheer off, blood exploding upward as the force of the slugs pushed the rest of him into the compost.

"We got to get the hell out of here," said Gidrey.

"All right." Karr pulled his glasses out, using them to look for warm bodies. There were two, maybe three men roughly sixty yards straight ahead; they looked like shadows and it was impossible to tell whether they were guerrillas or Thai soldiers who had escaped from the downed helicopter.

Something exploded back by the helicopter.

"They have a mortar," said Gidrey. "Zeroing in on the chopper."

The three figures began moving toward them, then disappeared, the view blocked by rocks and vegetation as they worked their way to the left. Karr pulled off the glasses and pointed for Gidrey, who now had a pistol in each hand.

"I can't tell if they're on our side or not," Karr warned.

"Better safe than sorry," said Gidrey.

Something black moved twenty yards away. Karr fired into it, spraying bullets all around the area. There was no return fire.

Foster started to moan. Gidrey patted him reassuringly, then spun to his right and fired three bullets point-blank into the chest of a guerrilla who had managed to crawl out of the jungle ten yards away.

"Time to move on," said Karr.

"Past time," said Gidrey.

"Northeast," said Karr. "They're coming from the south and there's another base a couple of miles west. There's a field we can get rescue choppers into five miles that way."

"You think we're going to be rescued?" said Gidrey.

"Dad'll come for us." Karr smiled weakly. "I got the keys to his car."

58

The flavor of the soup leaned heavily toward the metallic, but Dean sipped it off the spoon anyway.

"You look like Little Red Riding Hood," snickered Lia, sitting across from him at the table.

"Thanks." Dean left the towel draped over his head and took another sip of soup.

"You know, maybe you should let your hair grow." Lia came over and started playing with the towel, arranging it as if it were a mop of hair. "You'd look good as a hippie."

"Probably come in gray," said Dean.

"Oh, Charlie, you're not that old," said Lia. She ran her fingers across the back of his neck, which still felt damp from the shower.

"I could dye it. I always wanted to be a blond."

She slid her hands across his shoulders, starting to knead his muscles. Dean let himself lean back against the chair, his lats gradually relaxing. Her hands worked downward, then around to his chest.

He took another sip of soup.

"I could use a backrub," she told him.

"Yeah?"

"It'd be nice," she said, sliding her fingers up to his neck and then brushing his chin lightly. "Very nice."

"Might be," he said, taking another sip of soup.

Lia took the spoon from his hand and set it on the table. Dean didn't need any more hints—he pushed up and let her fold her body into his. The towel fell off his head.

"You think they got this place bugged?" he asked her.

"Of course."

She moved backward from the table. Dean put his hands over her thighs, then brought them up to her pants and unbuttoned them.

"Let's go in the bedroom," she said as he slid them down.

"My idea exactly," said Dean, but rather than moving he pulled off her black T-shirt and ran his hands over her bra. He slid his fingers under the top, rubbing her left nipple, then moved up to pull the straps down from her shoulders. He pulled the cloth gently away from her breasts.

"The bedroom," she whispered.

"Yeah," said Dean, putting his mouth on hers.

Something started to beep.

"Fuck," said Charlie.

"Not now," said Lia, pulling her straps up. "I told you the bastards were listening."

Dean would have ignored the summons, but Lia had already donned her T-shirt, going to the video conference area and snapping on the send unit.

"We interrupting something?" asked Rockman. He wasn't on-screen. The communications system in the trailer was part of the DoD network and arguably among the most secure in the world. Nonetheless, it wasn't the NSA's and therefore protocol called for communications from the Art Room to be voice only.

Unfortunately, the protocol didn't play both ways.

"Hot steaming sex."

"Great," said Rockman. "We'll roll tape."

"Where the hell have you been?"

"We're handling a difficult situation in Asia," he said. "I can't give you other details."

"Tommy?"

"I can't give you other details."

Dean walked over to the area covered by the video camera.

"What's the status of the disease?" Dean asked.

"Roughly two dozen confirmed cases, with a bunch more probables."

"A bunch?"

"I don't have the details," said Telach. "Feeling better?"

"Much. How come I don't have it?"

"We're not sure. I can't get into specifics."

"Did you find Kegan?"

"Charlie, you have to remember that the communications system we're using is not of the same caliber as our usual network."

"Oh, come on," said Lia.

"I have to follow the rules," said the Art Room supervisor. "We have an update for you, and new mission data if you're up to it," said Telach.

"We're up to it," said Lia.

"We're going to set up a conference call with some of Johnny Bib's team and the bio experts, probably in about a half hour," said Telach.

"You can do that, but you can't tell us about Tommy or Kegan?" said Lia.

"Mr. Karr is all right," said Rubens, coming onto the line. "We will give you a full update as soon as you're on the secure network. Reactivate your communication devices and you can participate in the conference call."

"Did Kegan make this thing?" asked Dean.

"The conference call will begin in thirty minutes," said Rubens. "Be ready."

"We will be," said Dean, grabbing hold of Lia's arm.

"The bacteria is definitely man-made, and was definitely designed to resist penicillin-related drugs," said Dr. Chaucer. "Its transmission is through bodily fluids, or at least we're guessing it is. The cat was a host. What we don't understand is how it gets from the skin into the bloodstream, since there didn't appear to be bites. But it's not as contagious as, say, a flu virus would be."

"Does that mean it wasn't intended as a biological weapon?" asked Dean.

"Impossible to say. Frankly, if you were trying to use an agent like this as a weapon, you wouldn't want it to be too contagious; otherwise you'd eventually die from it yourself."

"Unless there was an antidote," said Dean.

"Right."

"And there is one."

"We don't know that yet, Charlie," said Rubens.

"It still very possibly was an accident," said Lester, who was speaking via a secure connection on a military aircraft headed back to the States. "We haven't completed the autopsy on the cat, but the most likely course would have the cat catching it from the man who had been killed at Dr. Kegan's, then infecting the others. If the man had it and was carrying it when he arrived, that would explain the cases outside of Athens."

"Probably the two men in New York City sheltered him," said Segio Nakami. "If they shared drinking or eating implements, had sex, any sort of intimate contact like that."

"Gorman didn't sleep with the cat," said Dean sarcastically.

No one laughed.

"The effect of the host on the organism remains to be seen," said Chaucer. "Again, we're making guesses here based on incomplete data."

Dean leaned back in the chair, his legs resting on the floor. Lia had her shoes off and was running her feet up and down them, teasing him.

"Is it always fatal?" asked Dean.

"Not enough cases to tell," replied Lester. "So far, though, the answer has been yes. Of course, in terms of a disease outbreak, we're at a very early stage—an incredibly early stage. We're basically there at birth. That's unheard of."

"Maybe we're not," said Rubens. "It's possible this has struck before and hasn't been recognized."

The experts began talking about that possibility. For Dean, the real question was whether Kegan had invented the bacteria.

And if so, why?

Money.

No.

Why?

He wouldn't have.

"There's a two-week gap in Kegan's whereabouts six months ago that we're looking at," said Segio. "If we can find another outbreak, we might link the two."

"Excuse me, what did you say?" asked Dean.

"It's possible that Dr. Kegan was working on the bacteria elsewhere," said the Desk Three analyst. "Because while he could have used the facilities at either his school or the Hudson Valley lab, we've come up with nothing definitive there."

"He may just have been very careful," said Chaucer.

"He wouldn't do this," said Dean.

No one spoke for a moment.

"The other theory would be that UKD came up with it," said Segio finally. "And that for some reason they believed Dr. Kegan could cure it. And that they need a cure. The man in his house must have been their emissary. Instead of going with him, Dr. Kegan killed him."

That didn't fit particularly well, Dean thought. The people who had contacted him didn't refer to the incident at all.

"We have linked the people who contacted you to UKD, Charlie," added Rubens. "Thanks to Hercules. His actual name was Fedor Mylonas and he was a scientist and professor in Athens until a few years ago when he was involved in a pornography scandal with one of his students. Radoslaw Dlugsko contacted him roughly six weeks ago and he seems to have been doing some work for him. His area is bacteria, but the Greek military has a file on him, so he must have been familiar with weapons programs in some way."

"Dlugsko is the arms dealer?" asked Lia, looking at Charlie.

"That's his main claim to fame," said Rubens. "He also runs a lucrative business selling stolen antiquities."

"He has the bacteria?" asked Dean.

"We're in the process of figuring that out."

"How does Thailand come into this?" asked Dean.

"That's where Kegan seems to have gone," Rubens told him.

"Why?"

"Perhaps seeking a cure or an antidote. But we were hoping you might shed some light on his specific whereabouts," said Rubens. "He's been there before, but we haven't found any photos or anything of that nature among his personal belongings. Did he mention any area in particular?"

"Yes," said Dean. "Long time ago. When he was just out of school."

"When he was just out of school?"

For the first time since Dean had met Rubens, the Desk Three director seemed surprised. Dean told him about Kegan's stint as a WHO doctor. Apparently his résumé did not list his months in Thailand along with his longer stays in Malaysia and the Philippines.

"Interesting," said Rubens.

"What time were you talking about?" Dean asked.

"He was there eighteen months ago," said Rubens. "For two weeks."

"You sure? Eighteen months ago—I think he would have told me."

"As far as ever going back to Thailand, were there other times?" asked Rubens.

Dean shook his head, looking at Lia. "Not that I know."

"That's where Tommy's working on locating him?" asked Lia.

"Along those lines. He's still in the bush with the Thai forces across the border."

Dean glanced at her. Lia shook her head. It was clear that Rubens wasn't giving them the whole story.

"What do we do now?" asked Dean.

"We've tracked Hercules' travels over the past month and we're reviewing intercepts related to those cities," said Segio. "We're still in the process of sorting everything out, but the theory that we have is that Hercules brought the bacteria with him to labs. We have two wire transactions that back this up, though we still need more details."

"We'll get them," said Rubens. "In the meantime, we want to get people in place to move quickly once we have the details."

"Makes sense," said Dean.

"I'm glad you feel that way, Mr. Dean. If you feel up to traveling, I'd like you and Miss DeFrancesca to head south to the most problematic location."

"Fine."

"Where are we going?" Lia asked.

"Syria. Your plane should be waiting on the tarmac."

59

Karr and Gidrey took turns humping Foster through the jungle, working their way across a pair of hills. While his com system still refused to work, Karr was confident that he was being tracked by the Art Room and figured that they'd eventually send a rescue team. The problem was to get to a place where a rescue would be easy.

They also had to stay alive long enough to be rescued.

The second time he took Foster over his shoulder, Karr nearly slipped with the weight. He got only about a hundred yards, then practically collapsed against the trees. Barely holding himself up, he slid Foster down. The Marine groaned.

"Wow," said Karr. "I'm dizzy as hell."

Gidrey said something that Karr couldn't quite decipher. He slid down against the tree, trying to focus his thoughts. His body felt as if it had been pummeled.

"I can carry Foster but not you," said Gidrey. "Maybe you'd better rest awhile."

"If I rest I don't know that I'm getting back up," said Karr. He held out his hand; Gidrey pulled him to his feet.

"I'm no doctor, but I'd say you got a monster fever."

"Really? I feel like horseshit."

"You shoulda taken a flu shot, man. Flu shots keep that crap from happening."

"Yeah, next time." Karr exhaled as slowly as he could, trying to force his body into concentrating. The tiny hamlet he'd pointed them toward lay down the slope at about three o'clock, roughly two miles off. He thought of sending Gidrey there by himself but decided that wasn't the best solution; the Art Room would be tracking him, not the Marine.

"All right, let's go," said Karr. "We got to get to that field near the village before nightfall."

"Christ, it better not take us that long," said Gidrey.

"At this point, if we get there this year I'll be happy," said Karr. He tried to smile but couldn't quite pull it off.

60

Johnny Bib stared at the Escher print in Dr. Kegan's kitchen, trying to work out the topographical solution to the visual puzzle. Two spheres seemed to exist within each other, but the mathematician knew this was just a metaphor for the formula that allowed a five-dimensional space to be conjured into a three-dimensional object.

Unless it was supposed to be a two-holed doughnut in four dimensions. In that case, it would be a clever reference to the Poincaré Conjecture.

Or was the artist simply depicting a doughnut and a sphere coexisting: a metaphor for the universe stated in its two essential shapes?

The secure sat phone rang as Johnny debated the point.

"Johnny Bibleria."

"Yes, Johnny, I was hoping it would be you."

Johnny sensed that Rubens was being satirical, but he wasn't quite sure.

"Are you familiar with Escher?" Johnny asked him.

"Of course. Listen, Johnny, I need you to come back to Fort Meade and help out your team. We've been trying to link the man found there with UKD and we're having a devil of a time. It was hard enough linking the Greek that met Charlie Dean with them, but this man. I need more information on the Dulugsko group—"

"Dlugsko," said Johnny, correcting Rubens' pronunciation. "It's Polish."

"Since you're not coming up with anything further there," said Rubens, "I'd like you to get back. I have a helicopter en route."

"I was just examining this Escher print," said Johnny. "I realize it's a metaphor."

"What are you talking about?"

"Poincaré."

Poincaré was a famous mathematician who had posed a simple—or seemingly simple—question about spheres. No one had been able to prove that his guess about the answer was right. It remained one of math's great problems—but Rubens couldn't imagine what its relevance was here. "What the hell are you getting at?"

"Two essential shapes, sphere and doughnut. They don't go into each other."

"I don't need a lesson on topology, for christsakes."

"Unrelated. Is that the metaphor? Yet they coexist."

Baffled, Rubens said nothing.

"Was the man meant to poison him? But then it couldn't have been our Polish friend, since he wanted something," said Johnny, gazing at the print.

"I'm going to send a helicopter, Johnny. I want you back here."

"A helicopter? I don't want to fly."

"You must. There is no other option."

Johnny Bib closed his eyes. There was no arguing with Rubens when he spoke in that sort of tone.

"Okay," said Johnny Bib. "But . . ."

"But what?"

"Would anyone mind if I brought the Escher print?"

"Take the whole wall if you have to. Just get down here."

61

It took two hours to walk the two miles to the village but seemed considerably longer to Karr. The pain in his body surged and then dropped off, only to surge again. His fever likewise seemed to wax and wane, occasionally replaced by violent chills. He started shaking uncontrollably as they reached the edge of the field.

"Gotta rest," he told Gidrey. He went to sit and sprawled on the ground.

"You okay?"

"I'm real thirsty."

"I'll be back," said the Marine. "Give me your gun."

"Uh-huh."

Karr closed his eyes, resting his head in the thick weeds. Warmth seemed to wrap itself over his face, a blanket covering his body.

His mind drifted; he thought he heard Lia calling to him.

"Hey, princess, what the hell are you doing?"

"Looking for you, asshole."

"That's sweet."

"You're dying, Tommy Karr."

"Screw that," said Karr, the wave of heat once more rushing up from his chest. "Just taking a nap."

62

"They're in a small village about seventy kilometers from the border," said Sandy Chafetz. "One group of guerrillas seems to be following their trail, but it's not clear."

Rubens pressed his arms together in front of his chest. "Let's get them out of there," said Rubens.

Chafetz looked up at Telach, who was leaning against the runner's consoles. The Art Room supervisor looked spent, as tired as Rubens had ever seen her.

"I'm working on it, chief," said Telach. "The Army has all the resources over in the other end of the country."

"What other resources are available?" asked Rubens, knowing the inevitable answer.

"CIA has some contract people. But I have to talk to Deputy Director Collins."

The one thing that Rubens hated more than having to draw on CIA assets was having to go through Collins to get them. Collins, who headed the Operations Directorate, had been in the running to head Deep Black and still felt she should have had the job—and that the organization should have been part of the CIA.

"Boss?"

"Yes, of course, go ahead."

"I have the Puff/1 en route. It'll keep an eye on them until we can get in there."

"How long?"

"Few hours maybe. I'll know soon."

"It'll be nightfall."

Telach pursed her lips.

"Why isn't his radio working anyway?" Rubens asked.

"Most likely the battery died. The charge isn't indefinite and he didn't have a place to recharge in camp. Obviously, we'll have to look into it."

"Oh, very well," said Rubens. "I have to go upstairs. Keep me informed."

"Yes, boss."

Rubens ignored her tone and left the Art Room, passing through the elaborate security chamber and the manned checkpoints to return to his office. While Desk Three operations tended to consume a major portion of his time, Rubens had a large number of other responsibilities as the number-two man in the agency. Nearly two dozen phone messages and twice as many E-mails were waiting for him on the secure systems. Several had to do with meetings he'd had to blow off and there were a fair number of useless updates on projects that were going nowhere, but nonetheless it took time to wade through them all.

One of Rubens' administrative assistants, meanwhile, had organized a queue of reports in his secure computer system—urgent, more urgent, and ridiculously urgent. Rubens was just starting to take a look at the items in the last category when his outside phone buzzed. He picked it up and heard Sandra Marshall tell him things had gone well with the media.

"A home run," she said.

"That's very good," said Rubens.

"Are you going to make the working group meeting in the morning?"

"It looks tight," he answered. He'd already decided he'd rather try getting some sleep downstairs than sit through the session, but he was suddenly feeling as if he didn't want to disappoint her.

"We are going to be preparing a final report on the Internet DNA," she said. "Are you still opposed?"

It truly did pain him to have to disagree. This was, of

course, uncharacteristic. Rubens examined the emotion—partly it was because, politically, it was never a good idea to step on someone's pet project, which this obviously had become. But partly—*good God*—he was having actual feelings for her.

A very dangerous area.

Why should he oppose the report? The President liked the idea; it would be floated out to Congress whatever William Rubens said. All the committee wanted to do was authorize a study, after all. Why draw a line in the sand on something that surely would die eventually on its own?

Because it was the right thing to do?

"I was thinking maybe we would have dinner," she suggested. "And I could explain my position."

Rubens started to object.

"I had in mind my place later this evening, if that is convenient," said Marshall. Her tone was formal, but then she added, in a voice that seemed to come from someone else, "Please?"

A strange weakness came over him. Fatigue? Misplaced lust or, worse, sympathy? Interest?

"What time should I be there?" he asked.

63

The path toward Tommy Karr's locator took Puff/1 over the helicopter wreckage, and Malachi slowed momentarily to let the sensors get a good look at the site. It took all of twenty seconds, but it threw off the ReVeeOp's rhythm; the slow aircraft just couldn't synch with G*ng*f*x. He started flipping through his Mp3 index to find a better beat, heading down toward the golden oldie section before settling on Beck.

The helicopter seemed to have been taken down by a shot on the rear engine area; that argued for a heat-seeking missile. Several bodies lay near the wreckage. The guerrillas had split into two groups. One continued to harass what was left of the Thai Army unit moving in the direction of the border. The other, about a dozen men, shadowed toward Karr's locator.

"We got what we need," said Telach from the Art Room.

"Yeah, roger that," said Malachi, pushing his speed control back up to max, such as it was. The robot airplane had a tendency to nose down slightly as the engines revved, but he was 12,000 feet above ground level and had plenty of room to deal with it. Careful not to overcorrect—the drone would gallop up and down like a roller coaster if he did—Malachi pushed his joystick to the right, nudging the remote aircraft into an arc aimed at giving him a good position between the guerrillas and the NSA op.

"Satellite has those guerrillas getting close," warned

Sandy Chafetz, Karr's runner. "I'm losing sat coverage in about ninety seconds."

"Roger that. I'm still about zero-three minutes from the area," said Malachi. "If I can find my rhythm."

"You'd better find it," snapped Telach. The Art Room supervisor was edgier than normal, not a good sign.

A blue dagger marked out Tommy Karr's position near an open area beyond a small hill. Malachi started to swing south of it, toward the red dots that the computer had used to mark the guerrillas' position as they followed.

The marked positions were actually about 205 seconds behind real time. That was the overhead imposed by the system as it transposed data from one set of sensors to another, integrating the satellite information with the other inputs, in this case primarily the robot aircraft. A three-and-a-half-minute gap didn't seem like much, but a well-conditioned runner could cover more than a half-mile in that time, and even an armed soldier in rough terrain could move a quarter-mile without breaking much of a sweat. For that reason, Malachi would rely on Puff's native sensors as his primary indicators once he was inside the target area.

The ReVeeOp pushed Puff/1 through some unexpected turbulence as he continued on course. There was some speculation among the jocks at Space Command—the Air Force unit that controlled some of Deep Black's remote aircraft—that the next generation of remote gunships would be designed to stay airborne for twelve to eighteen hours and that there would be enough of them to provide global coverage twenty-four/seven. The idea wasn't necessarily popular, however—blanket coverage on that order would require even more automation than currently employed, which meant computers, not ReVeeOps, would be controlling most of the flights.

Malachi had a better solution—space vessels with rail-guns, fueled by plasma gases heated in reentry. That looked to be ten years down the road, at least.

He'd be in his thirties. Ready to hang it up.

Wow.

"Got some action coming out of that village toward our guy," Malachi told Sandy, going over to Puff's sensors. "Uh, three, four people. One of 'em with a gun."

"Yeah, we're looking at it," said Sandy.

"You want me to stay on them or check out the guerrillas?"

"Line up a shot," said Telach. "I don't want to take any chances."

"May be one of the people who were with Karr earlier," suggested Chafetz.

"You sure?" asked Malachi.

"Just line up the shot," said Telach. "We'll make the call."

Karr heard someone calling to him. He thought the voice was coming from the Art Room; he snapped up, put his hand to his ear.

No, it was outside, a real voice—back from the village.

His Marine.

Karr heard something else, the light fanlike noise of a robot gunship. The Art Room had obviously tracked him here.

They wouldn't know Gidrey was on his side.

"Gidrey!" he yelled. He pushed himself to his feet. Blood flew from his brain and he felt himself tremble.

"Karr!"

"Stay where you are," said Karr.

"What?"

"Stay there."

"I got some help."

Karr took a few steps toward Gidrey, his balance precarious. How the hell could he tell them Gidrey was on his side? With his radio out, there was no way to communicate with them.

Of course there was. He knew there was. He just couldn't remember it.

Marie Telach stared at the large screen at the front of the Art Room showing the radar image from the belly of Puff/1.

Karr was between two groups of people. The one to the south was almost definitely a guerrilla force; they were now about a half-mile away. To the immediate northeast, less than a hundred yards from him, was a second group. The vegetation made it impossible to use the optical camera to see them.

They had the synthesized view in a window in the corner. The northeast group wasn't on it.

Friends or foes?

One of the people who'd been with Karr earlier was missing from the synthesized screen. But there was no way to know until it was too late if he was with the other group.

It wasn't the computer's call anyway. It was hers.

Karr had to be protected at all costs.

"Marie?" asked Sandy.

Better to kill allies or even friendly civilians than to lose her man.

"Malachi, target the group at the northeast."

"Got 'em. I'm locked."

"Fire on my signal," she said, staring at the screen.

Karr could hear the Puff/1 banking above them, undoubtedly ready to shoot.

He had to talk to them somehow.

He pulled out his handheld computer. The unit had to be plugged into his com system for instant messaging and serious downloading; at the moment it was just another handheld—albeit one on steroids.

They'd see it, though.

"Yo, Marine," said Karr.

"What?"

"Catch," he said, throwing the computer in the direction of the shout.

Malachi moved his thumb back and forth across the red button at the top of the thick joystick controller, waiting to fire. The target designator was locked on, the gear constantly computing the exact angle as the gunship circled overhead. He had the option of giving a verbal order but liked the old-fashioned trigger better; it was faster.

He leaned toward the screen, waiting for Telach's order.

The group was moving toward his man.

Something flickered on the infrared feed.

"Fire," said Telach.

But Malachi didn't. Karr had thrown something toward the other group.

"Magnify object," he told the computer.

Grenade?

No. Karr's handheld computer.

"Don't fire! Don't fire!" yelled Telach.

"I'm with you," Malachi said, drawing a breath and staring down at his hand, making sure it obeyed.

64

Dean looked away from the small computer screen, his eyes starting to cross with the bad light. The Art Room had downloaded information about the target they were heading toward, along with instructions on how to operate the spectrometer and other gear that had met them at the airport in Italy. The tech manual seemed to have been written in Chinese, then translated into Russian before being put into English.

Lia claimed to already know it all. Which confirmed for Dean that he'd better struggle with the instructions.

She was sitting two rows in front of him. They had different covers for the mission. He was supposedly a Canadian archaeology professor; she was a French tourist with a shadowy past linking her to arms dealers. His was by far the more dangerous cover.

Their target was a prep school favored by foreigners in the northern area near the coast of the Mediterranean, about five miles from Latakia. Dean would visit the school as a prospective parent. According to his back story, he was working on a book on hunter-gatherers, which included the Nafutfians, who'd inhabited Syria somewhere around 10,000 B.C.

How could Keys have done this? And where was he?

"Something to drink, sir? Wine perhaps?"

Dean looked up into the smile of a stewardess.

"Sure," he said, but when he felt his stomach rumble, he

changed his mind. "Maybe just some water," he told the young woman. "Or better, coffee."

He'd need some sort of artificial stimulation to get through all this reading material.

65

Marie Telach felt a tremor run through her body as the gunship circled south.

She'd nearly killed one of the Marines.

"God, help me," she whispered to herself. "Thank you."

"Marie, that helicopter we were counting on is still on the ground," said Sandy Chafetz from her station. "They have some sort of mechanical problem."

Telach turned to the runner, not quite comprehending. Fatigue and shock over what had nearly happened had temporarily blanked her head; she couldn't think straight.

But she had to.

"What sort of problem are they having?" Telach asked.

"Bad oil pressure or something. I don't know if it's bullshit or not, but they refuse to budge. What should we do?"

"Where's the asset we had as backup?"

"Navy helicopter. Won't get there until nightfall. Might be safer to wait until morning, when we get the Special Forces people in. They said they'd have a Blackhawk ready to go at first light."

Another decision she had to make. Could she trust her judgment?

"Marie?"

"I want him out of there as soon as possible," Telach told

the runner. "ASAP. Have them get in there even though it's dark."

"Your call."

"Yes, it is," she said, but it was only a whisper.

66

Gidrey had managed to find what passed for a doctor in the Burmese outback: an old woman who seemed to have been trained as a nurse or maybe as a witch doctor. She and another man in the party that had come out from the small hamlet seemed to know a few English words, including *Red Cross*. Between that and their gestures, they made it clear that Foster's wounds had to be cleaned. Karr brought them with him to the field, where he waved his arms and made sure the Puff/1 got a good visual on him and the group so the Art Room knew these were friends. Then, drained and tired and sick, he let the others help him to the village.

With one exception, the huts were made of some sort of straw or vegetation. The lone exception was a metal shack with a Buddhist statue at the front; it served as a temple and a common building, and it was there that the Americans were brought. The old woman pulled a small piece of shrapnel from Foster's leg, then prepared to pour liquid on it. Gidrey stopped her, taking a whiff from the bottle to see what it was.

"Smells wicked," he told Karr. "What do you think?"

"I think if they were going to kill us they would have been a hell of a lot more direct about it," said Karr. He shrugged. "She seems to know what she's doing."

Gidrey nodded. The woman poured the liquid, which had an immediate effect—the Marine practically jumped from the bed where he'd been laid.

"Nothing like ol'-fashion' medicine," said Karr.

A bedroll was laid out for him on the floor. He lay down, gazing at the odd mix of items near the wall—carved drinking gourds and an empty television set, its picture tube gone.

The woman bent over him and started talking in rapid-fire Burmese. Karr shook his head. She repeated what she had said, a little slower and louder. He smiled, then held up his hands. She put her hand on his forehead.

Karr put his hand over hers, gently removing it.

"Thanks. I'll be okay," he told her.

She pointed at his stomach.

He looked down. "You telling me to lay off the nachos?" He glanced up at Gidrey. "Man, these doctors are all alike."

The woman disappeared for a few minutes; when she came back she had a small bottle, which she obviously wanted him to drink. When Karr didn't take it, the woman began talking very quickly again, no doubt urging him to be a big boy and swallow it down. She reminded him of his Scandinavian grandmother, whose words were similarly indecipherable yet just as obvious.

"How much?" he asked, taking the bottle.

She put her finger on the bottle. Karr took a slug. The taste of the medicine—if that's what it was—nearly killed him.

"Whoa," he said. His throat constricted and his eyes watered.

There was gunfire in the distance.

"What the hell?" said Gidrey.

"Wait," said Tommy. "That's just the Puff, taking out the guerrillas."

"I'd better go check."

"Not unless I go with you. They may not know it's you."

"I think you ought to rest."

Karr tried to push up from the seat, but there was no way he was moving.

"All right, listen—take my handheld computer," Karr told Gidrey. "Keep it out where they can see it."

"Where who can see it?"

"The Puff—the UAV gunship. Or the Kite they took over

or there's a satellite overhead or something. They're watching us, believe me."

"All right," said Gidrey reluctantly.

"Make sure they can see the computer clearly. And don't try turning it on," added Karr. "If you do, it'll check your thumbprint and it'll blow itself up."

"Really?"

"Really."

67

Sandra Marshall lived in what passed for a modest condominium development in suburban Virginia—though anywhere else it would have seemed opulent indeed. Green marble slabs, walnut-stained wainscoting, embossed wallpaper, and two-tone paint on the walls; chandeliers and recessed lighting; cool Italian marble and elaborate oak inlays on the floor—the materials alone would have paid several government workers' pensions for a lifetime. Rubens, who had grown up with wealth, wasn't impressed by the setting, but he was somewhat surprised when Marshall greeted him in an apron. It wasn't for show, either—there were some light stains, and her face was flushed from working over the stove.

"I'm glad you could come," said Marshall, taking his arm. Her perfume wafted through the air as they walked through the corridor past the library and parlor, down toward the kitchen.

"My pleasure."

"I thought we'd eat in the kitchen," she said. "If that's okay? The dining room is too formal, and it's just the two of us. All right?"

"Of course," said Rubens.

So she really was in love with him, he realized. He'd been trying to fight off the idea—banish the possibility—the whole way over. Perhaps he'd been trying to fight it off from the moment they first met.

Rubens ordinarily did not trust love. It made one vulnerable. Oh, far worse than that. Far, far worse.

"Cocktails first, or should we start with wine?"

"I don't like to drink too much," he said.

"I agree." She went to the island in the kitchen, which stood under a collection of enough copper pots that the Treasury could tap her supply for a year if the Mint ran short of pennies. She produced a bottle of cabernet. It was Chester Valley—an inexpensive and not very well-known label that Rubens himself had come across only recently.

He dismissed this as a coincidence, though a very promising one. He sipped the wine as Marshall presented an *amuse-gueule,* a mini-appetizer in this case made of foie gras and caviar served with poached pheasant eggs.

From there, dinner got involved; Marshall even flamed the beef medallions with a touch of port. Rubens ate well when he ate, but rarely had he tasted a dinner like this—and surely no one had cooked one for him under such circumstances.

She *was* in love.

And he?

"What a dinner," he said as he finished.

"I thought the meat slightly overdone," she fretted.

That was obviously a put-on, but Rubens couldn't ignore his cue.

"Nonsense. Perfect," he said.

"Really?"

Her voice was sincere. The poor creature was actually insecure.

"You could open up a restaurant, I assure you," said Rubens.

She got up, pulling the plates away.

She was in love, but he wasn't, he decided. And his duty was to reject the Internet biometric DNA proposal.

"So. You wanted to discuss business?" he asked.

"Oh, we can put that off."

"I really have to get back to my office," Rubens told her.

Marshall reached behind her back for her apron. For a second Rubens thought she was going to pull off her skirt as well.

"Let's have a little cognac in the library, shall we? It's so much more comfortable."

"I can't really drink much."

"A small glass? You only had half a glass of the wine."

It was true, and Rubens did like cognac. He got up and went inside, even though he knew he should leave. He was torturing her, really—he had to say no.

Actually, he was torturing himself. She might not be a knockout beauty, but she was attractive. She was a good cook, much smarter and deeper than he had thought . . .

Rubens slid into one of the leather club seats. Marshall presented him with a tray and two small cognac glasses.

"To Homeland Security," he offered.

As the words escaped his mouth, he realized that if he wasn't in love he was at least in trouble. Never in his life had he said something so lame and ridiculous.

She smiled and clinked his glass gently.

Rubens took a sip. At the first taste, he knew he had been had.

The cognac was clearly Luc Ugni, the distinctive product of a tiny château in the heart of the region. The bottle would have been one of 300 the tiny vintner allowed on the market each year—a fact Rubens knew because his family was allotted two.

Son of a bitch! I'm being played like a violin. What a fool I am!

"Do you like the cognac?" she asked, playing the unsure hostess again.

"Of course I do," he said. "And I can't support the ID proposal under any circumstances. It's not a good idea."

"Oh, you don't think that's why I invited you, do you?" She started to laugh.

Rubens did his best to smile back.

"Well, your support would be useful," she said: "But that's all right."

He waited, watching her.

"On the other hand, if you decided to actually oppose it . . ."

She let the sentence hang there.

"I've already expressed my views, and will if asked," he told her.

"As a cabinet member—"

"I'm not a cabinet member."

"I was referring to myself," she said. "I would be in a position to push for your elevation. You do want State, don't you?"

Finally she had dropped all pretense. They were two animals confronting each other in the jungle, tiger and tigress. Rubens felt himself relax. This was so much easier to deal with than love.

"If I were offered the position to serve our country in that capacity, I would certainly welcome it," he said.

"I can guarantee you'll be offered it," she said. "Unless you're my enemy."

"And I'd be the enemy if I spoke out loudly in opposition of the study?"

"Would you like more cognac?"

68

Every time Karr thought he was feeling better, a surge of dizziness and pain shot through him. The old woman stood over him periodically, shaking her head; twice she had him drink more of her magic elixir.

When it was so dark that Karr could no longer make out the lines in the walls, a helicopter chattered in the distance. Karr surprised himself by managing to get to his feet. He shook Foster, who opened his eyes at him.

"We got to hit the road," he told the Marine.

Foster growled and closed his eyes but turned over and got to his feet. They were about halfway down the trail toward the level field when Gidrey came up with four U.S. sailors dressed in battle gear. Between their armor and guns they could have subdued a battleship.

"Bus here already?" said Karr.

"Navy sent the shore patrol," said Gidrey. "Corpsman's right behind us."

"Mr. Karr?" said one of the sailors.

"That's my dad. I'm Tommy."

"Sir, we're supposed to ask you to wear a special mask and avoid sharing any bodily fluids." He put down a large case and then stepped back. "Could you direct Corporal Gidrey to do so as well? And Corporal Foster, sir."

A wave of dizziness hit Karr as he bent to the case. He knelt over it, then snapped it open. The case contained what looked like firemen's helmets and visors. Each unit had a large chin portion that snapped onto the sides; this part extended over the visor. There were respirator filters at the bottom of this part.

"I ain't wearing no gas mask," said Gidrey.

"Yeah, all right," said Karr. "Come on, Gidrey, Dad won't let us borrow the car again if we don't wear these masks."

"They think we're sick?"

"Probably just being cautious," Karr told him.

"What about them?" asked the Marine, pointing to the villagers who'd come up to see what was going on.

"We're just supposed to take you out of here," said the sailor. "After you put the masks on. I'm sorry. Those are our orders."

"I'll make sure they're taken care of," said Karr.

He turned back toward the knot of villagers who'd gathered behind them. "Thank you. Thank you very much," he said, bowing his head as a sign of respect though the rushing blood unsettled his balance. "Thank you."

The old man, who knew a few words of English, nodded as well. The nurse pushed through from the back, thrusting a bottle in his hands. "Red Cross," she said. "Red Cross."

"So I'm supposed to take this? What, like every hour or two hours or what?"

The man said something to her and she started talking quickly.

"Hold a second." Karr took out his handheld computer and hit the voice recorder as she jabbered away.

"We'll be back," he promised when she was done. "Red Cross."

"USA," said the woman, smiling.

"Yeah, USA." He smiled back at her, took a swig of the medicine, and headed toward the waiting helicopter.

69

Rubens' belated realization that he had underestimated and misjudged Ms. Marshall served as a proper chastisement, and by the time he had reached Crypto City from her apartment he had completed a dozen phone calls, gathering the background information that he surely should have compiled earlier. The most informative source proved to be a member of the fourth estate, who was somewhat sympathetic toward Rubens thanks to a handy tip in an earlier domestic matter Rubens had had some firsthand knowledge of. After consulting with a professional gossipmonger, the reporter was able to run down a long list of connections to political donors. More interestingly, he provided the tidbit that Ms. Marshall had filed for bankruptcy a few months before coming east, apparently undone by some poor real estate investments and, it was rumored, a fondness for illicit mind expanders.

Rubens dismissed the drug rumor—clearly Marshall was too much a control freak to allow herself to indulge on a regular basis. But the financial connections accounted for her influence as well as her motivation. And among those connections were two firms with projects in Internet security.

Both had done work for the NSA. Hence the importance of his opinion. Neither had done a particularly competent job, hence the likelihood of his negative opinion being shared vociferously—not so much on the study but on who would do the study.

The most obvious things were always the most difficult to find. Another lesson.

Rubens was not such a political naïf that he was shocked by the motivations involved. On the contrary, he would have been surprised had avarice not been involved. No, surely what was significant was not the motivation but the boldness of the threat and the corresponding promise. For it implied the ability to affect presidential decisions far beyond the normal scope enjoyed by someone like Ms. Marshall or the political donors associated with her, for all their dollars.

There was the possibility that it was mere bluff, an overplayed hand clumsily put forth by a newcomer unskilled in the Machiavellian arts.

Rubens knew Marcke through Hadash; their association went back more than a decade. Marcke had his peculiarities and normal political vulnerabilities, of course, but his personality suggested strongly that he would make up his own mind about cabinet appointments and any attempt to unduly influence him—especially by a campaign donor—would be met with considerable animosity.

But then Marshall's threat was of a negative nature—a veto. From what Rubens knew of Marcke, a direct move to nix a choice would surely provoke a strong reaction. To be effective, the move would have to be more subtle—a whisper of disapproval, a hint of scandal.

Rubens had no skeletons in his closet, and Marshall and her backers would clearly know that. Any attack on him would have to be at once subtle and direct. Someone in the Senate determined to block the appointment—that would be the proper tactic.

Rubens ran through the roster of possible suspects as he drove back to Crypto City and headed toward the Art Room in the basement of the Black Chamber, the most secret lair in the world. Melfi from New Jersey—a liberal with real power on the Senate Banking Committee. But the banking connections argued against him; he had no need of Marshall's ilk. And Rubens and banking people in general got along fine; genetics, after all, could not be fudged.

The woman from Georgia—hadn't he snubbed her at a recent reception? What was her name? He couldn't remember; he was blocking it out, along with her face.

God, to forget a senator's name at a time like this.

Rubens waited impatiently in the security chamber leading to the Art Room. The sensors did not take his identity for granted; he was not only checked for bugs and electronic devices, but the sensors also sniffed his clothes for untoward chemicals. Cleared through, he strode into the control room, still somewhat distracted by the need to find an enemy among the Senate.

"Karr's been quarantined at the base," said Chafetz. "Doctors say he's in very good shape."

"Does he have it?"

"Oh yes, he's got it," said Chaucer. The scientist got up from his station a row away, rubbing his eyes. "But we think he may have found the cure as well. His fever's dropped back to normal, he has only a few welts, and the bacteria is gone from his saliva. The cure is remarkable—it is like an antidote, truly."

Karr had arrived at a military hospital near Phitsanulok in the central plains of Thailand. While the results so far were only preliminary, it was clear that he both had had the disease and was well on his way to being over it.

"It would fit with our working theory," explained Chaucer. "Kegan came into the area looking for a fungus that is related to the penicillin family. The books that Mr. Bibleria located relate to cures such as this, and in checking Chinese texts related to rat-bite fever we found a mention of cures in what we now call Thailand. We need a chemical analysis, of course."

Rubens realized it fit together nicely—a little too nicely. As a mathematician, he had been trained to find simple answers to complex problems. But as a spymaster, he had found the world generally preferred complex answers to simple problems.

Such as the situation with the Internet DNA?

A bluff. Surely she was bluffing.

"Have you told Tommy about this?" Rubens asked Chafetz.

"We don't have a secure link yet," said Marie Telach, just joining them. "Apparently the battery in his transmission unit ran out and his spare hasn't been recovered. How much of a quarantine do we need here? The two Marines are with him and they're making noises about busting out."

"They'd better not do that," said Chaucer. "We're still not positive that it's only transmitted via bodily fluids."

"Do they have it?" asked Rubens.

"Not according to the tests."

"Release them then."

"Now wait on that," said Telach. "If we're wrong, we could be unleashing an epidemic."

Rubens noticed that her lower lip was quivering. It quickly stopped, but he continued to stare—he'd never seen that happen before, and the Art Room supervisor had worked for him for years, since well before the advent of Desk Three.

"We have to be cautious," she added.

The tremor again.

"Very well," said Rubens. "Keep them under observation for the time being."

He turned back to the doctor. "How does this fungus work?"

"Basically it's like a natural penicillin," said the doctor. As he started to explain, Rubens remembered something Dean had mentioned when talking about Kegan.

"How would he know about it?" Rubens asked.

The expert shrugged. "Probably came across it somehow. Accident."

"Could it cure cancer?"

"Cancer?" The scientist laughed. "I doubt it. Well, you know." He shrugged. "People might say it did."

"Tell me about pancreatic cancer. What do they do for it?"

"Nothing that works."

"You sure?"

"Well, I'm not positive. I can check. Is it important?"

"Probably not," admitted Rubens. "Don't waste your time."

70

A man known to be employed by Mossad, the Israeli intelligence agency, started trailing Lia at the airport; while not entirely unexpected, this complicated their arrangements as the two Desk Three ops made their way north toward the school. Rather than using the agency-retained driver, Lia had to opt for a bus. This meant, in turn, that she had to make some adjustments to her wardrobe; she pulled on a pair of scarves in the ladies' room of the station, carefully placing a pin that contained a video fly at the rear of her hair.

The Art Room ID'ed the agent as Yacoub Bahir Ben Rahimat, a Syrian Christian who was technically a free agent but in practice a Mossad gofer. It wasn't immediately clear how the Israelis had glommed on to her, though the fact that he was being used suggested that it was a local deal—the Syrian secret police were also trailing Lia.

Wearing her scarves and jeans—along with a lightweight bullet-proof vest—Lia approached the ticket window and asked, first in French, then in somewhat halting Arabic, for her ticket. A half hour later she found herself wedged between two evil-smelling old ladies traveling with a pair of six-year-old she-devils. The children were playing a game of tag, darting back and forth in the seat, trampling on her legs.

"Mother of God, how long?" she groaned, as if to herself.

"Another three or four hours," said Rockman. "Syrians

gave up on you. Couldn't figure what you were up to. Don't worry; we'll reload up north."

"Mmmmph."

"What's Syria like, anyway?"

"Mmm-mmmph."

"Happenin' place, huh?"

One of the girls poked her in the shin. Lia grabbed the little devil by the shirt and raised her up to eye level. The two old ladies stopped their chattering.

"Mon chou," she started, speaking in French; *chou* normally meant "sweetie," but the inflection here implied anything but. "If you don't stop tripping over me I'm going to pluck out your eyes and eat them for dinner. You want that?"

The little girl furrowed her eyes—then started to laugh.

Realizing everything she did was being recorded, Lia let her go.

71

"Marie is seriously worried about you," Chafetz told Karr when the link with the Art Room was finally made.

"Hey, can I talk into this thing?" Karr asked. He was using what looked like a Raytheon AN/PSC-5 radio, a standard unit used in the field.

"Reasonably secure," answered the runner. "But keep your voice down. Some of the exterior security is being provided by nationals."

"Bet they'll understand about as much of what I say as I understand what they say." He pushed around to sit up in the bed. Unlike in the States, the hospital bed didn't adjust. In fact, it was far too small for his frame; Karr's feet bumped against the metal frame, and if he rolled over he'd find himself on the floor. "That reminds me—I have some stuff on the handheld for you to translate."

"We have a backup battery unit en route. Should be there any minute. I have some questions for you," added the runner.

"Fire away."

"Did you pet a cat when you were at Kegan's house?"

"Cat petted me," he told her. "Sweet little thing."

"Lick your hand?"

"You going to ask if I kissed it next?"

"Yes, as a matter of fact."

"It did lick my hand, and no, I didn't kiss it."

"Good," said Chafetz. "Very good. That's how you got

S. moniliforms. Dr. Chaucer can explain the theories. Hang on."

There was a knock on the door.

"Yeah?"

"Delivery."

"Delivery?"

"They're still treating you as if you're in isolation, Tommy," said Chafetz. "Can you get out of bed and get the boxes? The batteries and the other gear you need are in there."

Karr got up out of bed, his joints stiff and his muscles aching. He had to pull the bag of fluid with him across the room, and by the time he got to the door the person who had knocked was long gone. Two metal footlockers with digital locks were in the hallway. He lifted them up, bringing them back inside.

Obviously, his strength was returning, he realized. The lady in the village had cured him.

"So, Sandy, are you going to give me the combination on these?"

"I was thinking I'd make you guess."

"Let's see, twelve numbers. Ought to take me what, three years?"

"Well, you must be feeling better. You're starting to joke around again."

"Still hurts when I laugh, though."

The runner gave him the combination. Inside one of the lockers was a new battery unit for the com system. Once he had it on, he lay back on the bed, listening to Chaucer talking about possible vectors and epidemic surges—and the miracle of penicillin.

"What we're not sure of yet is whether the disease was engineered to be resistant to specific antibiotics," he added, "or if it was made to be vulnerable to just this one."

"How can you tell?"

"We may not be able to," said Chaucer. "You don't seem to have much of a rash," he added.

"Am I supposed to?"

"In the natural version of the disease, yes. How are your joints?"

"Stiff." Tommy looked at the undersides of his forearms and wrists. "I have some dark things like welts on my arms. Blotches. Raised a little."

"Very minor compared to the natural version. I wonder if that was programmed in. The arthritis seems milder too, but it may get worse."

"I have arthritis?"

"The joints swell up. You'll get better. It seems as if the disease was engineered to increase some of the earlier effects of the disease, but it's not clear whether that diminished the after-effects or if the designer did that on purpose for some reason. I'd love to talk to him—after he's put away. Anyone who can do this is pretty dangerous."

"Bottom line here, though, is I'm going to be okay?" asked Karr.

"If what the woman gave you was made from what Kegan was looking for, then it's a good guess. Drinking a cup of that would be just like taking a shitload of penicillin."

"That a scientific measure? Shitload?"

"It's between a tablespoon and a gulp," said Chaucer.

"How long am I in for?"

"Well, we'd like to keep you isolated for a few weeks while we work all the possible permutations out."

"Weeks?" Karr laughed.

"We may settle for less. According to the tests, you're no longer contagious. But—"

"Why is there a *but*?"

"We don't have much experience—we don't have any experience really—with this specific disease. We're really still learning about it."

"I'll make you a deal. You set me free and I'll go back and grab some more of this stuff. We can cure the world."

"It's not my call," said Chaucer.

"You do want the stuff, right?"

"Absolutely."

"Tommy—we have the translation of those snippets you recorded," said Telach, breaking in. "She told you there were other people who have the same thing, and that the liquid she gave you would cure the disease in just a few hours. Tommy, I have to talk to Mr. Rubens about this, but she mentioned another white person was in the area recently. It may have been Dr. Kegan."

72

Dean watched the Mossad agent watch Lia as she got off the bus and retrieved her luggage. Both Dean and the Art Room had checked around for a trail team but found no one. According to Telach, Lia's supposed status as a tourist of dubious background shouldn't attract all that much attention from Mossad, since the Israeli secret service had all of the important arms networks in Syria pretty well figured out; even Deep Black had trouble getting things in and out of the country without the Israelis knowing about it.

Trouble being a relative term.

But if that was the case, what was up with Yacoub?

"She's getting into the taxi," Dean told Rockman. "Yacoub's behind her," he added. "Getting his own cab."

"Yeah, we see it. All right. You're at the same hotel. She's Five-fourteen; you're Three-twelve. Already preregistered. Give her five minutes, then go on."

"You don't want me to trail them?"

"The hotel's only a mile away. She won't get lost," said the runner. "If you burn your cover we're going to have to start from scratch. Let her go on."

Dean waited three minutes before telling his driver to go along to the hotel. Even so, it appeared that Lia beat them by a considerable margin; she'd checked in and was upstairs before Dean got to the front desk.

The desk clerk's English was passable, and after handing

over his credit card, Dean found himself being led by a bell-hop to the elevator.

"Charlie—where's Yacoub?" asked Rockman in the elevator.

"Don't know."

The bellhop turned and gave Dean a puzzled glance. He smiled.

"Something's up."

Dean reached across and pressed the elevator button for the fifth floor even though the bellhop had already pressed 3.

"Go on to your room," said Rockman. "We'll give you more instructions."

The door opened on 3. Dean reached into his pocket and took out some of the Canadian money he was carrying, stuffing it into the bellhop's hand.

"Go," Dean told him. "I'll be along. Go." He reached to hit the DOOR CLOSED button.

"Charlie, what are you doing?" asked Rockman. "Go into your room. Stick with the program."

By the time the elevator opened, Dean had taken out the small Sig pistol he'd been given as a personal weapon. He ran down the hallway toward Lia's room, rapped twice on the wooden door—then used his leg to kick it open. He dived to the floor, rolling around the empty room.

"She's not here," said Dean.

"No kidding," said Rockman.

"Where is she?" asked Dean, jumping up.

"Look, Charlie, this is a complicated situation. We don't have time to explain everything to you," said Telach.

"Screw yourself, Marie," he said, running back into the hall.

73

Rubens stared at the grid position screen, which showed Lia moving out of the hotel.

"Are we sure of Yacoub Bahir Ben Rahimat's loyalties?" Rubens asked Telach.

"The only way we can be sure is to ask Mossad."

Rubens did not want to risk the loss of one of his people. And there were definitely points to be gained in telling a fellow intelligence agency that one of its foreign agents was more foreign than it believed. But inadvertently tipping the Israelis off to the bacteria would have untold consequences. He couldn't do so without Hadash's—and the President's—direct authorization, and probably consulting with State as well.

If he were Secretary of State, what would his call be?

"Keep a close eye on the situation," he told Telach. "I'll talk to the Israelis."

"Boss?"

Rubens turned and looked up toward Chafetz.

"Yes, Sandy?"

"What are we doing with Tommy? I have him on the helicopter, but you said to wait for your approval. Can he go over the border or not?"

Rubens looked at Telach. "The doctors cleared him?"

"They say he's no longer contagious. It's also a pretty good bet that the people up in that village were already exposed, and have some sort of immunity. He wanted to be part of the team going north, but I told him he needed your okay."

Rubens turned back to look at the map indicating where Lia was being taken. He found following two halves of the operation invigorating—switching from one segment to the other kept his mind fluid.

He'd have to talk to Mossad and make sure about Yacoub Bahir Ben Rahimat. Which meant talking to Hadash. Which would also give him an opportunity to sound Hadash out about Marshall and asking directly about the Secretary of State matter. Hadash was sure to have a considerably more developed perspective than Brown had had—and be much more willing to discuss it. The National Security Advisor might use fewer words and yet prove twice as revealing.

What if he found that Marshall had succeeded in buying off Hadash himself? A Hadash veto—that would truly stop him.

Good God—*Hadash*?

The operation to gather the drug had to proceed one way or another. Karr was their best bet at getting the antidote. The villagers would trust him.

"Have Tommy go ahead," Rubens told Telach. Then he pointed to the map. "Help Mr. Dean trail Lia, but please put a collar on him. You'll do well to remind him of the line between personal initiative and running amok. It looks from your screen that he's tearing through the hotel. That won't make his cover story any more believable."

74

Karr wrapped his hand around the strap next to the seat in the back of the Sikorsky. He was all alone in the chopper, one of several precautions the doctors had asked him to follow just in case they were wrong about the tests and he was still contagious. The NSA op was supposed to keep several feet from everyone he came in contact with, not touch them, and not let them touch anything he touched. He wore gloves, a special set of rubber boots, and layers of pants and shirts that were supposed to keep his sweat from contaminating anyone.

"How you feeling, Typhoid Mary?" asked Chafetz.

"Just dandy," he said. "Even had solid food for lunch."

The helicopter banked so sharply Karr nearly fell out of his seat. A Thai patrol had run north a few minutes before and Puff/1 was flying shotgun just ahead, but the guerrillas had already demonstrated that they were adept at taking down flying objects. It took nearly twenty minutes to weave across the border and reach the village. Karr stared out the window. It was a good thing he was feeling better, though; the zigzag route would have done a number on his stomach otherwise.

He stepped out of the helicopter, steadied himself with a huge breath of air, and started toward the hamlet. He nodded at the Thai military people who'd put down earlier; all of them were wearing surgical masks. Contrary to popular belief, the masks offered little, if any, protection against most infections and were undoubtedly of little value here, where the disease was spread through saliva coming in contact with the skin. It was difficult, however, to argue with the psychological value.

The doctors reasoned that, since Karr had already been here, it was unlikely that he would infect any of the villagers even if they were wrong about him being contagious. Nonetheless, he followed the protocol they had outlined, making sure to stay at least six feet from them. The doctors with the company fanned out, preparing to administer tests to see if anyone had been infected earlier.

"I came for a refill," said Karr, smiling and waving as the Burmese nurse appeared from the village. She was frowning; Tommy quickly gathered that she was suspicious of the soldiers.

As Karr started to explain why he was back, Chafetz warned him that the interpreter wasn't translating his words properly. He dismissed the man and began trying to repeat what the Art Room Thai expert told him to say. But his pronunciation left a great deal to be desired, and while it greatly amused the nurse to be called "a young cake," Karr realized after a few minutes that he wasn't going to be able to talk to her this way. Finally he hit on a solution.

"You have a Burmese language selector on Speaker ID?" he asked, referring to the neural Net program that could translate intercepts in real time.

"Of course," said Rockman.

"Why don't you use it to translate my questions into her language, then beam the characters down to my computer?"

"I don't know if that'll work."

"Well, find out," said Karr, smiling at the nurse.

He gave up asking technical questions and started asking the woman about herself. Her face turned sad; she told a story about being chased out of Loikaw due to her husband's profession nearly thirty years before.

"What was his profession?" Karr asked.

"He was a doctor," the translator told him, relaying what she said. "Anyone educated, they were persecuted. The way she's talking about him, he's long dead."

Karr nodded as the woman added details about her family and friends, all lost. He might not understand the words she used, but the meaning of what she said was clear, and even his naturally buoyant spirit was weighed down with the tragedy of a life torn to bits by a dictator's paranoia.

"We got it," said Rockman. "We have the character set and we can make it work. We're just double-checking everything before downloading. You'll have to put the unit down and walk away from it. Tommy? Hey, are you there?"

"I'm here," said the agent somberly. "Go ahead."

75

By the time Charlie Dean figured out where the back stairs were, Lia had already been packed into a car. He got out of the hotel just in time to see the vehicle, a small white Toyota, pull off. Dean ran after it like a madman. A motor scooter shot out of the intersection on his left as he ran into the street. Dean thought the man was coming to knock him down; by the time he realized he wasn't, he'd already thrown himself at the bike. Dean, driver, and vehicle tumbled to the pavement. Dean grabbed the teenage boy who'd been riding the bike and tossed him away like a candy bar wrapper. Then Dean scooped up the scooter and took off in the direction of the car carrying Lia.

"Turn left at the second intersection," said Rockman.

"Why did they take her?"

"We're not sure, Charlie. It may be routine; it may be more interesting; we'll have to see how things go. She's not in any danger."

"Bull."

"Charlie, you have to trust us," said Telach. "Just relax. Slow that bike down. You're going to crash."

"Screw that."

"Look, we can see the situation from here. We know what's going on. We'll tell you where to go."

"You think you can see better than I can? You think your satellites and intercepts and fancy gear tell you everything?"

"I didn't say that."

Part of him knew he was reacting emotionally—something that was not merely unprofessional but potentially deadly. If he'd still been in the service, a phalanx of Marine noncoms would have lined up to kick his butt. You followed orders; you stayed with the program. Otherwise, you died and your friends died.

On the other hand, his service and experience, in Vietnam especially, had taught him to be skeptical of superiors, especially ones who tried to micromanage situations. The Art Room was all about micromanaging, in his opinion.

He wasn't in Vietnam. And Telach wasn't a second lieutenant trying to make her bones.

Still. They trusted their technology too much.

And something else. He cared for Lia in a way that made him reckless.

Dean backed off the gas, slowing to take the turn through the intersection. A block later, he found the street blocked with traffic. It was a struggle not to go up on the sidewalk and whip through.

Yacoub seemed to be on very friendly terms with the people at the police station. The loyalties of the police were not in question—all were card-carrying Ba'athists, fervent followers of the Nazi-like prima donna running the country. Lia soon found herself sitting in a small room, flanked by a Syrian who obviously had a thing for garlic. Yacoub disappeared; Lia studied the picture of the Syrian President on the wall, wondering how he would look with devil horns.

"We're with you," said Telach in her ear. "Let's see how far this goes."

Just peachy, thought Lia.

A few minutes later, the door opened. A man in an army uniform came in and sat down. He gave her a grim look, introduced himself as Lieutenant Abbas, and asked in heavily accented French for her passport.

Lia took it from her pocket and threw it on the desk. The lieutenant scowled but picked it up.

"Welcome to our country," he said in English.

"*Oui.*"

"I don't speak French very well," he said. "*Anglais?*"

"*Oui,*" she said, with the sneer only a Frenchman would use. "I can speak it if I must."

The lieutenant smiled sympathetically. "We all do things we don't like."

"*Oui.*"

"Which way now?" he asked when the traffic opened up.

"Take your next right," said Rockman. "She's in the police station."

"Damn."

"No, Charlie, it's fine. We can hear what's going on. Please—don't attract attention to yourself."

"Yeah, I know," said Charlie. "Okay."

"A French arms dealer in my city," said the Syrian. "Why is that?"

"I like the beach," answered Lia.

"The beach is thirty miles from here."

"I was misinformed."

"You are French? Or Vietnamese?"

"Does it matter?"

"Your passport says French."

"Then I'm French." Lia's back story indicated that her parents had fled Vietnam shortly before its fall to the Communists, but that she had a wide range of contacts there. A small file on the Interpol network—compromised by the Syrians, though they did not appear to have real-time access to it—duplicated the back story.

"Are you here as a buyer or a seller?" asked the lieutenant.

"A trader," said Lia.

The Syrian shook his head. "A buyer or a seller?"

"A buyer," decided Lia.

"Very unlike the French, to buy when they can sell."

"What I'm trying to buy isn't available in my home country. It came through Austria."

There was a slight twitch on the Syrian's face.

"Perhaps, if you are very good, someone will contact you," he said.

"Great." Lia got up. The guard behind her started to grab for her, to push her back into her seat.

On another day, another mission, Lia might have accepted the gesture in stride. Today, however, she was too tired, too worn, to hold her reactions in check—she threw the man over her shoulder onto the lieutenant's desk.

Then she figured, What the hell.

Lia vaulted over the side of the desk and confronted the lieutenant directly—with her custom-made Kahr pistol in his neck.

"Let's just decide right now that I'm very, very good. *Comprende?*"

He managed to smile before she flattened his windpipe with the butt of her fist.

"*Comprende* was a bit over the top," said Rockman as she walked down the front steps onto the street.

"I got jet lag. What can I tell you? And tell Charlie Dean he stands out like a sore thumb in that bazaar over there. If he's going to back me up he's going to have to work on his act."

76

At first, Karr thought the woman had misunderstood or the translation had been bad. He had the translator rephrase and repeat the question twice.

She had treated men with a similar disease four or five weeks before; an entire village had been infected.

And a white man, an American, had come into her village about three weeks ago.

"All right," Karr said. "Where exactly is this place?"

It was a guerrilla camp, not a village, though the description was not that far wrong. Karr counted eight buildings on the sat picture, and the analysts believed there were at least two more in the bushes.

They also believed the camp was abandoned. It was the one they'd ID'ed earlier affiliated with the Crescent Tigers.

"If they got the disease, that would account for the fact that they abandoned the camp and have almost completely disappeared," said Chafetz. "Except for maybe five or six people, including the ones who followed you in Bangkok."

Abandoned or not, they weren't taking chances. Rubens convinced whomever he needed to convince that this was important, and besides the Thai Army unit that had accompanied Karr to the old woman's village, a company of U.S. Army Rangers took control of the area. Heavily armed gunships led the way, and after the perimeter was secured a specially equipped NBC unit rappelled into the central part of the village, checking it before clearing the rest of the unit inside. All these precautions spooked the Thai soldiers, and Karr had a hard time talking the pilot into dropping him off. As it was, he barely dropped into a hover as he skirted into the landing area, a clearing just below the main area of the camp.

"You'd better stay back," said one of the soldiers as Tommy walked up the hill. "Hasn't been cleared yet."

"It's all right," said Karr. He held up his hand spectrometer. Unlike the bulky gear the unit attached to the Rangers carried, Karr's handheld "sniffer" could sort chemical and biological compounds. It was also sensitive enough to detect extremely minute amounts of material at a safe distance. Most of the work was actually being done back in Crypto City; his unit was essentially a very sophisticated nose communicating its tickles via his com system. The data stream was so thick he couldn't even talk to the Art Room while it was being used.

Karr got a *bing,* an audible alert piped from the units when a detection was made. He stopped, moved to his right. Another *bing*.

He pushed the button on the wand to stop the transmission.

"That burial spot we told you about," Chafetz said. "Why don't you take some readings?"

"Why not?"

Karr walked to the right, past a series of tree trunks that had been felled as part of defenses. The Art Room had ID'ed a minefield and booby-trapped area about a hundred yards farther in the jungle. The area just above that had been cleared and dug recently; Karr knelt down, examining it. The dirt had been packed down for a few weeks but not much more than that. He took pictures and chemical samples, then moved back toward the village area, where the men in the special suits were still conducting their methodical inspection.

Two of the buildings had been destroyed by explosive

charges strong enough to obliterate their roofs and most of their sides. Karr went to them first; the sniffer confirmed that there had been people killed inside them, though by now the ruins had been fairly well picked over. Karr poked around carefully, looking for some part of the bomb or igniter, but found none.

"We're still looking for labs," said Chafetz. "Nothing the Rangers have been in fit."

"What about that burial site?"

"Not getting the right chemical hits. Look up at that knoll to the west, beyond the large building with the thatched roof."

"They all have thatched roofs," he told the runner, though he knew what she meant.

One of the Rangers in a chemical-protection suit tried to block his way, but Karr just waved him off.

"I already got it," Karr told the specialist. "I'm fine. Trust me."

Before he went to the knoll, Karr walked into the building. Dried blood was splattered on the walls and tables that lined the open hall, and there were smears along the floor. He took pictures and looked through the building. The kitchen area looked so neat he was tempted to turn on the stove and make himself some tea.

A small radio unit lay next to the wall in the outer vestibule. It was an igniter, the sort used in a commercial construction operation to detonate rock-blasting explosives by remote control. Karr picked it up and held it in his hand as he went to the knoll.

"Definitely bodies buried there. Burned, most likely," said Chafetz.

"Lab equipment?"

"Have the Rangers bring over that radar unit and we'll take a better look. Doesn't seem like it, though."

"Yeah, okay. In the meantime I have some pictures to send you. And information on a command detonator, looks commercial."

"Serial numbers?"

"Yup."

"Good deal."

Karr uploaded the data, then went and found the head of the Ranger unit. As the soldiers hauled their gear up, Karr took a breather, walking back to the middle of the camp and sitting down on a rock at the side of what had probably been an assembly area. He reached into his pocket for his small flask of water, took a long swig, then another.

Camp gets sick but doesn't make the bug.

Then it gets blown up.

The survivors track him.

Oh, he said to himself.

Oh.

A lanky captain appeared before him, hands on hips.

"Mr. Karr?"

"Tommy." The NSA op rose and shook the captain's hand.

"Good to put a face with the voice," said the Ranger captain. "What else do you need?"

"Two cemetery sites that we'll want to secure, those buildings that were blown up, and that long building with the tables in it, the mess area. Forensics team will be here a few hours."

"Yes, sir."

"I need a favor."

"Yes, sir."

"You think one of the helicopters could take me back to Bangkok? Seems I have some unfinished business there."

77

At 3:00 A.M., even Washington, D.C., seemed like a ghost town, deserted and eerie. The streetlights seemed to glow brown instead of yellow, and the blinking traffic lights did more to create the fog than cut through it. Rubens and his entourage—his car was sandwiched between two vans packed with an NSA Black Suit security team—raced through the streets, veering up Pennsylvania Avenue. They were going not to the West Wing but the White House itself, summoned by Marcke for an in-person update.

One of the night staff had forwarded a copy of the executive branch's daily news summary of headline stories appearing in the morning papers and on the morning news shows. "Killer Epidemic" led all the major papers. An unnamed CDC official—undoubtedly Lester—was booked on all three networks.

Crisis makes the man, Rubens thought to himself as they drove. It was an idea he firmly believed. Indeed, he had lived it, welcoming the challenges that came with responsibility. William Rubens had thrived on crisis and had reason to believe that he handled grave stresses well. And yet some crises were too much for any man. Some problems were beyond solution; a tidal wave was best not confronted but merely survived.

In politics, those who succeeded generally chose the latter path. The best way to Secretary of State surely led in that direction—go along, go along, get past this, stay away from that. Survive.

No, Rubens decided, he was not a man who settled for survival. Nor was that what was needed now. The threat would be conquered, or he would be conquered by it.

Rubens left his security team outside and went up the stairs, his feet shuffling against the stones and then gliding across the carpet. The President was waiting with George Hadash in the Blue Room. The large room in the center of the first floor of the house was more often used by tourists than the President, but the staff had brought in some coffee urns and arranged the chairs in a semicircle. Rubens might have thought he was back at school, sitting in one of Hadash's informal seminars on the intersection between diplomacy and technology.

"The secretaries of state and defense are on their way," said the President, who took a cup of coffee and sat on one of the chairs. "Health, CDC, Ms. Marshall—they're coming as well. But I want you to give me the full story first, Billy. What's the situation?"

"Man-made disease sold to a syndicate run by Radoslaw Dlugsko, a Polish weapons trafficker who among other things operates a front company called UKD. We've tracked three probable sales. One was to a Swedish company. We've compromised their computers and done a physical check on the shipment. We believe the bacteria in question wasn't involved, but to be safe I'd recommend alerting their authorities. We're in the process of completing the same procedure on an operation in Syria. We hope to have further data on that very shortly. But in the meantime, we have the last shipment tracked to a facility in Russia. According to our information, it's to be shipped to a military base within six hours."

"Where exactly?"

"Chechnya."

"Chechnya?"

"Yes. Two weeks ago, the Third Battalion of the Second Armored Division/Special moved to that base. That unit is trained to deal with NBC warfare."

"They're planning to use it in an operation?" asked Marcke.

"I don't have intelligence on that," admitted Rubens. "But we cannot take the chance."

"Do you think the Russians would indiscriminately use biological weapons?" asked Marcke.

"They may feel that, because of the way the disease is spread, it's not indiscriminate. It's liquid contact on the skin. It can be passed by person to person apparently through saliva contact—but we're still working on the exact mechanics."

"Go over the outbreak in America," said Hadash. "Now, before the others get here."

"At last count, there were fifty-three confirmed cases. We have a test. And we have a cure."

"A cure?" said Hadash.

"An Asian fungus that works like penicillin. It cured one of my agents. We're in the process of having it shipped back here for both study and use."

"How many of those fifty-three are going to die?" asked Marcke.

"Probably all of them," said Rubens, resisting the temptation to hedge.

"How many more people are going to get it?" asked Marcke. The President wore a blue oxford shirt with rumpled tan pants and Docksiders—about as dressed-down as he got. In contrast, Hadash was dressed in his normal business suit.

"Until we know for sure how it's spread, it's impossible to say how many cases we'll get," said Rubens. "But if the latest theories are right, then we should start to bring it under control soon. Dr. Lester is pretty confident that that's going to happen. The wave that we're seeing now are mostly medical people who weren't aware of what they were dealing with. That will stop."

Marcke nodded, though Rubens could tell he wasn't entirely convinced. The media reports exaggerated the confirmed cases fourfold, and though the President had been told they were wrong, the specter of a widespread contagion was difficult to shake.

Precisely why they must act decisively, thought Rubens. And precisely why he must lay out the situation forcefully, without sugar coating, with a definitive plan.

"Even though we will contain this outbreak," he told the President, "it remains a very dangerous weapon. If we lost the Russian strain now, there's no telling where it would end up."

"I agree," said Hadash.

"Where is it?" asked Marcke.

"Moscow," said Rubens. "A lab in the basement level of Botkin Hospital."

78

Walking up the steps to the Syrian day school, Dean wondered what effect all these guards might have had on his own
education. Besides a pair of policemen at the gate, there
were several knots of supposedly private guards in nondescript uniforms posted along the driveway and in the infield
of the small circle in front of the steps to the main building.
Dean saw at least two men on the roof. The rifles the men
had were AK-47s, old but in excellent repair, their wooden
stocks gleaming. The driveway had obstructions so no vehicle could get close to the building, and Rockman told him as
a "point of information" that there were mines implanted in
the roadway and at least one antitank weapon trained on the
approach. The security was not considered excessive—in
the Middle East, Western children were always potential targets for extremists—but Desk Three had already determined
that the private security force wasn't private at all but rather
a special unit of the Ba'ath Party's own army.

A large wooden table, its top inlaid with dark and light
wood, served as the reception desk in the open vestibule just
beyond the doors. A large cupola behind the desk made the
secretary's words echo as she addressed Dean in English,
welcoming him to the school. A man in his early twenties
stood nearby, apparently Dean's tour guide.

Dean adjusted his glasses—they had a video transmission
set in them—and gave the little prattle he'd rehearsed about

how great an opportunity he had before him if the educational aspects for his two children (stepchildren, adopted, second marriage, great kids) could be worked out.

The secretary waxed eloquent in response, telling him about the quality of the professors, who in any other country would be teaching at top universities. The amenities included a tennis court, swimming pool, and around-the-clock guards.

Dean smiled and nodded, nodded and smiled. After a few minutes he interrupted the woman, taking out a small inhaler.

"Asthma," he said apologetically. "This climate is supposed to be good for it."

The secretary smiled sympathetically and went on with her spiel. Finally, she called over Ahmed, a graduate of the school originally from Egypt. Dean knew that to be false—the man was a low-ranking Syrian intelligence officer—but nonetheless played up the concerned parent angle as they moved through the building. Athletics appeared to be the school's Achilles' heel; the soccer team had finished no higher than third in the national association contests over the past decade, a fact that made the guide hang his head in shame.

As Dean continued his tour, the sniffers in his coat were sending data back to the Art Room. Every so often he stopped and slipped a small black dot from his pocket onto the wall. The dot, of course, was a fly, sending audio back to the Art Room.

"You want to look at that music room more carefully," said Rockman. "It accesses the east wing. We need you to get inside."

Dean followed as his guide took him upstairs past a series of classrooms where the students were learning math. The east wing was perhaps 200 yards away.

"Is the music teacher available?" he asked as they walked down the hall toward the auditorium. "My oldest—my wife's oldest really—is very interested in music. He plays the violin and piano."

"I'm afraid the teachers are on holiday." Ahmed smiled at him. "As I explained earlier. Our semester doesn't begin for two weeks."

"Oh yeah, sorry. Can we look at the music labs again, at least? I'll check out the piano, that sort of thing."

Ahmed smirked at him but then nodded. They continued to the end of the hall, then back down the stairs. Dean started for the room on the right.

"No, it's this way," said Ahmed, gesturing to the left.

"Oh, I thought it was right."

"You are mistaken, Mr. Dean," said the guide, pulling a pistol from his pocket.

79

Lia got up from the café table, sliding the coins for the tip under the saucer. She opened her pocketbook and took out her makeup case, examining her lips—and her Syrian tail—before leaving the small restaurant.

"He's with me."

"We can see him," said Rockman, who had a video feed via a small fly attached to her bag.

Lia disliked pocketbooks, especially monsters like the one she had slung over her shoulder. She grumbled to herself as she made her way outside and then down the street, still waiting for the incompetent Syrian intelligence agents to get their act together and approach her. Finally, a young woman approached from the crowd of tourists at a small shop on Lia's left.

"Ms. Ki?" she said.

"Finally," said Lia. She saw the car approaching from the left and started toward the curb. *"Parlez-vous français?"*

The woman shook her head.

"Merde. I have to speak English?" said Lia.

"Or Arabic."

"My English is better than my Arabic. Come on."

"I am to check you for weapons first."

Lia scowled at the girl but took the Beretta out from under her knit shirt.

"And your bag."

"Fine," she said.

"You have a small gun on your leg."

"That stays with me," said Lia.

The young woman pursed her lips. A pair of white Renaults had just stopped at the curb, holding up traffic; four men got out of the second car.

"I really must insist," said the Syrian.

"No."

The Syrian agents nearby were all clutching their jackets, as if experiencing a group heart attack.

"Lia," hissed Rockman in her ear.

"Oh, all right." Lia undid her trousers and reached down to the gun, strapped at the top of her left thigh. "I'd better get this one back. I paid a fortune for it."

The young woman took the weapon, nodding to the security people in the street. Lia got into the back of the lead car.

"Your English is very good," said the young woman, sliding in next to her.

"I practice a lot when I'm pissed off," Lia told her.

80

Rubens leaned back against the wooden chair, an ornate French piece that had allegedly been brought to Washington by Jefferson, though that provenance seemed highly unlikely. It was, however, very old, and Rubens felt it creaking and shifted his weight forward.

Marcke got up and began pacing back and forth. One of the President's assistants appeared at the door to tell him that the others were waiting outside; Marcke waved him away, wordlessly telling him to keep them waiting.

Hadash, meanwhile, remained in his seat, his legs spread and his arms hanging down between them. He alternately cupped and uncupped his hands.

"Billy, you're recommending blowing up a hospital," said the President. "And potentially starting a world war with Russia."

"With respect, sir," said Rubens, "the plan won't destroy the hospital, just the lab. We'd use F-47Cs. We've penetrated Russian airspace before without detection. If we want to eliminate the bacteria, this is the time and place to do it."

"If we have a cure, the bacteria is useless," said Marcke.

"If it works," said Hadash. "There's no guarantee yet that it does."

"I think it does work," said Rubens. "But we don't know how much we can make, or how fast. As a natural substance, it's pretty rare. We're not sure we can get enough to take care of even the confirmed cases in upstate New York. And that's if the disease proceeds in the manner Dr. Lester projects. In any event, having a cure does not eliminate the potency of the disease, or the threat. We can fight anthrax, after all. That doesn't make it any less dangerous."

"I agree that with or without a cure, the bacterial agent is a big problem," said Marcke. "But not a reason to go to war."

"If you had a chance to eliminate weaponized anthrax from the planet, wouldn't you take it?" asked Rubens. He glanced at Hadash. "Wouldn't the risk of collateral damage be worth it?"

Neither man said anything.

"This isn't an act of war," said Rubens. "It would be a preemptive strike against a threat not just to us but the entire world."

"On the contrary. I would consider a Russian attack on a hospital in Washington or anywhere else an act of war," said Marcke.

"We're not hitting the hospital. Only a small portion of the lab beneath it. We can put a two-thousand-pound bomb down one of the ventilation shafts," said Rubens. "The attack will appear to have been launched by separatists using a remote detonator. There'll be radio transmission for the Russians to overhear."

Marcke stared at him.

"It's doable. We can blow it up with no fingerprints. The odds are that no innocent people would die," added Rubens.

"You can guarantee that?" asked Hadash.

"I can say with ninety-eight percent certainty, yes."

"That leaves a two percent chance of a world war."

"There's another risk," said Rubens. "If the bacteria is shipped to Chechnya and the Russians lose control of it, it will undoubtedly be used. The disease will spread throughout Russia, and then Europe, and then here. We'll have lost the easiest chance we had to contain it. And if the so-called antidote turns out to be as effective as we believe, the results will be beyond catastrophic."

"Show me the details of the plan," said the President, pointing to Rubens' briefcase. "Then we'll let the others in."

81

"What is this?" insisted Dean, looking down at Ahmed's pistol.

"You are an Israeli agent."

"What the hell are you talking about?"

"Through that door there, and then down the stairs," said Ahmed. "Come on."

"Men coming down the hallway," warned Rockman.

Ahmed started to grab him. Dean threw his forearm into the young man's neck; in the same breath Dean smashed his heel into Ahmed's foot and then kneed him. The gun clattered away. Dean pushed the sniffer he'd been holding in his hand over Ahmed's nose, giving him a dose of a quick-acting Demerol derivative; the drug would make a 150-pound man sleep like a baby for four hours.

Dean grabbed the pistol and aimed it point-blank at the doorway just as the two guards entered.

He fired, once, twice, three times—the pistol just clicked helplessly, its magazine empty: Ahmed had obviously been under orders not to harm him.

For a moment, Dean and the guards exchanged looks of shock, compounded by awe. Then Dean threw himself into the closest man, bowling him and his companion over onto the floor, Dean grabbed at one of the rifles, managing to wrest it free and drive the barrel into the man's neck and chin. Then Dean rolled free, slamming the butt end of the gun into the side of the man's head.

Dean was just getting up when he heard the click-clunk of an automatic weapon being locked and loaded.

The other guard was holding his gun perhaps five inches from Dean's head and jabbering something.

"Okay," said Dean, letting go of the other rifle. He held his hands out, then started to cough. "Okay."

The man motioned with his gun for Dean to step back. Dean coughed again, then pointed to the inhaler on the floor. He motioned that he needed it.

The man was unmoved.

"The word," said Dean. "Inhaler. Jesus."

The Art Room translator responded, *"Inhaler."*

The English word served in Arabic as well.

Dean was dubious but kept pointing and repeating the word. Finally, the guard stepped to it and kicked it at him.

"Thank you," said Dean. He picked it up and fiddled with it, then took a breath—and began coughing even more uncontrollably. The guard poked him with his rifle, prodding him toward the door.

Dean pressed the button on the inhaler, sending a spray of the Demerol solution flying about ten feet—in the wrong direction. Poked again, he cursed and coughed and then got the spray in the man's face, grabbing for the rifle at the same time. The guard pushed hard enough to knock him down—but then the drug took over, and he fell to the ground.

"Inhaler's the right word?" said Dean, grabbing the rifle.

"I wasn't sure, so I guessed," replied the translator. "A lot of medical terms come straight over."

"You guessed?"

"It worked, right?"

"Okay, Charlie, back across the hall," said Rockman. "There's a door at the far end of the music room. Combination lock—we've already defeated it. Don't worry; we're inside their computers. We have a good handle on this."

"That why you let the guards nearly kill me?"

"Their brains aren't wired into the system," said the runner dryly.

Dean pushed into the room, running past the collection of

instruments, a rifle in each hand. The stocks folded up along the bodies of the guns, making them look and feel more like large pistols than assault rifles.

He slapped the door open and went into the hallway. The network of security cameras didn't extend past the classroom wing, which meant he could proceed easily without being detected. On the other hand, it also meant that the Art Room couldn't tell him where any other guards were.

"Take the right hallway to the end, into the vestibule," said Rockman. "Go downstairs. Ready with the grenade. We're locking the doors behind you. It'll only slow them down, so keep moving."

"No kidding."

The door opened into a hallway flanked by laboratories on either side. The door was metal; Dean stopped outside and took out an inch-thick disk from his jacket, putting it against the panel. But before he could push the slider on the back and activate the unit's radar, the door began to open. Dean stepped back, then grabbed the person and threw him down as he came through.

Her down. It was a woman. He clamped the inhaler over her nose before she could scream.

"Radar," said Rockman.

"We don't have time to screw around," said Dean, jumping up.

"Radar. Stay with the program, Charlie Dean. We need to see inside that wing."

Dean pushed the radar on and waited for the Art Room to analyze the inputs.

"Clear. Go."

"Charlie," said Telach, breaking in. "Walk calmly to the very end of the hall; throw your grenade into the room at the right. Just stand there and wait."

"Yeah, yeah, yeah."

"Charlie, we need you to follow directions."

"I'm doing it."

"Then go."

Two of the rooms were open, and Charlie could hear the

scientists inside talking. But no one noticed him as he passed, or at least no one had time to react before he reached the end of the hall. The door was open; he rolled the grenade inside and stood back.

There was a shout and some yelling. Something crashed inside.

"Wait sixty more seconds or it will knock you out, too," warned Telach.

"Heads up!" warned Rockman.

Dean pulled the rifle up as someone in a lab coat came out of one of the labs he'd passed. A burst of rifle fire sent him back into the room.

"Go, Charlie. Go," said Rockman.

Dean spun into the room, stepping over two bodies in lab coats. He moved around a bench stacked with autoclaves but found his way blocked by a row of minirefrigerators that reached nearly to the ceiling. He had to backtrack and move down the row to the right.

"The petri dishes at the far end of the room," said Telach. "On the right. Your sniffer's got a good hit. This is it."

Dean reached the bench, where what looked like a strange knickknack cabinet held about fifty small, round dishes used to grow bacteria or other organisms. The cabinet had climate controls and a set of locks.

"Charlie, drill through the glass. We've compromised the alarms and the explosives," said Telach.

"Explosives?"

"We'll explain later. Just go."

Dean took his pocketknife out and held it against the glass. When he pressed the Swiss insignia on the side, a diamond-tipped drill began to revolve at high speed. It whined; the glass cracked before the drill made it all the way through.

"Now what?" asked Dean.

"You're okay. Tape the crack, then put the gas in. Go," said Telach.

Dean pulled off his sport coat and stripped the cartridge from beneath the armpit, pulling the long bladder of poison gas out with it. He had trouble getting the stopper set right around the cartridge opening and finally jammed it in.

"Get away from there now, Charles," warned Telach. One by one the fans on the petri holder began revving at high speed, their instructions commandeered from the Art Room. "On the other side of the room."

Dean got behind the counter. The chlorine gas would kill any bacteria on the outside of the dishes. While he was waiting, Dean stripped out the containment bags from the lining of his coat, along with a set of gloves.

"Go. Don't breathe too deeply," said Telach. "You can break the glass. Be expeditious."

Yes, thought Dean, *expeditious.*

When Charlie had the dishes in the bag, Rockman directed him to put them in a small carrier at the far end of the room. The unit looked like a small musical instrument case; it was lined with insulation.

"Good. You have exactly three minutes before the Mossad people arrive," said Rockman.

"That much? I can hear the helicopter already."

"The second door on your left is an emergency staircase to the rear of the building. Take it. The car's waiting on the other side of the wall."

82

Lia was led to a library inside the low-slung building that sat in a compound owned by Umar Ibn Umar, a cousin once removed from the Syrian President. Umar was seated on a leather club chair, pretending to be absorbed in a book. He dawdled over a page for several minutes, nodded to himself, then finally rose, rolling a thick cigar in his fingers.

"I'm glad you could come," Umar told her.

If there was one thing that Lia hated—hated—it was cigars. Especially when they were smoked by slick-haired fat boys who wore pinkie rings and thought they were James Bond.

"I had nothing better to do," said Lia. "Apparently the beach isn't very close to my hotel."

"Beach?"

"False advertising."

He gave her a faint, token smile. "Would you like a cigar?"

"Only to break it in half."

"Very good cigars. From Cuba."

"I'm sure Fidel rolled it himself."

"So what precisely is it that you'd like to buy?" asked the Syrian.

"Disease," said Lia. She saw no point in playing this with any degree of finesse, despite the advice Rubens and Telach had given her last night.

The Syrian laughed. "You can pick that up in any slum."

"I'm looking for a very specific type," she said. "The kind that comes from rats."

"Interestingly enough, we are in the market for that ourselves," said the Syrian. He went to a sideboard and took the top off a crystal bottle filled with what looked like whiskey. "A drink?"

"Does that come from Cuba, too?"

"America, actually. Jack Daniel's. The Americans know how to make bourbon particularly well."

"They have to get something right."

He filled the glass nearly halfway, then took a very tiny sip.

"I understand you've dealt with my Austrian friends," said Lia.

"You keep calling them Austrian. I don't know anyone from Austria."

"Radoslaw Dlugsko. UKD," whispered Rockman. "He's Polish; the company is allegedly based in the Ukraine. Austria was just a convenient stop."

Lia wanted to reach up through the satellite and slap the runner.

"I know them from Austria," Lia told the Syrian. "Actually, the principal I met with was Greek."

Umar Ibn Umar took a long, thoughtful pull on his cigar. "Why aren't you dealing with them?"

"The Austrian police put them out of business two days ago. Very inconveniently, since I have a buyer lined up. An important buyer. I feel an obligation to carry through with my arrangement."

"Austria is not familiar to me," Umar Ibn Umar said, waving his hand as if dismissing the existence of UFOs or unicorns.

"And UKD?"

He shook his head.

"Oh, well," she said, calling his bluff. "I'll be off."

She got to the hallway before he called her back.

"Perhaps we can deal with your client directly," said the Syrian.

"Not possible."

He frowned. Before he could say anything else, the phone rang. The Syrian picked it up, but there was no one on the other end.

"Sorry about that," whispered Rockman. "We got to it a second too late."

Well, just peachy, she thought to herself.

"We're moving to get more backup," added Rockman. "You'll be all right."

Even more peachy.

The Syrian gave the phone a quizzical look, then hung up. "As I was saying, perhaps we can deal with them ourselves."

"The people I'm dealing with aren't as free to move around as you and I," said Lia. "It'll be much easier for all concerned if you simply sell the bacteria to me. You've probably grown twenty pounds of it already."

"Hardly." He considered his cigar ash. "What do you know about the disease?"

"It's a type of rat-bite fever that has no cure," said Lia. "It's the perfect assassination weapon."

Umar Ibn Umar smiled. "Perfect for many things. But there is a cure. We've been promised it."

"What? Penicillin?"

"No, it's supposedly resistant. However, we have questions about the potency of the bacteria. It doesn't seem to actually work."

"Doesn't work?"

"No." A second phone began to ring—it was a cell phone.

"Jam it," said Lia, talking to the Art Room.

Umar Ibn Umar gave her an odd look as he took the phone from his pocket and put it to his ear.

"Interesting," he said. "Why would my phones stop working?"

"Why doesn't the disease work?" asked Lia.

"Your Israeli masters haven't told you?" Umar Ibn Umar

took a pensive puff. "I would have thought you were high-ranking enough to be in on their secret."

"Guards behind you," whispered Rockman. "Their guns are out."

"Thanks, sweetie," she said.

83

"Charlie, we're moving the rendezvous point and going with a backup plan," Telach told Charlie after he got in the car. The driver, a Brit named Jack Pendleton, started away smoothly. Pendleton was a member of the British Special Air Service, or SAS, the Special Forces military branch trained in covert operations. Assigned to Middle East duty, he had been "borrowed" by Desk Three. Even though he was an ally, Dean had to take out his sat phone and pretend to be using it as cover when talking to the Art Room; Pendleton wasn't cleared to know about the com system, let alone the rest of Desk Three's technology.

"You with me, Charlie?" asked Telach.

"Yeah, I'm here. What's going on?"

"I'm going to explain everything to you, Charlie, but first we have to get that sample safe. That's our priority."

"What's wrong with Lia?" he demanded.

"She's okay. Follow my directions. Have the driver turn at the second intersection."

Dean leaned forward in the seat. There was no question that the sample he had stolen was extremely important. But so was Lia.

He knew where she'd gone. They could just drive straight there, then make the rendezvous.

Unless he didn't make it.

"The turn's coming up, Charlie. You have to trust me."

"Turn here," he told Pendleton.

"That's going to take us out of the city," said the driver.

"Yeah," said Dean.

The houses thinned quickly. They began climbing up the hillside. Dean could see the Syrian's walled compound in the distance.

Lia was there. In trouble.

Duty or love—which was more important?

"Next left, Charlie," said Telach.

If they went straight, they could get down to the compound.

I'm not a Marine anymore, Dean told himself. I don't follow orders blindly.

Hell, he hadn't done that as a Marine.

But he had the driver take the turn.

"Next right," said Telach.

"Where's Lia?" demanded Dean.

"She's okay. We'll have you back her up in case the Israelis don't get there quickly or something goes wrong. But first, you hand off the sample."

"If she's in trouble, every second counts."

"I'm well aware of the constraints," said Telach.

Constraints?

Jesus!

"All right. Stop on the side of the road," said the Art Room supervisor.

They pulled over. Dean opened the door. "I'm going to leave the pack here."

"No," said Telach. "Thirty seconds. A woman on a bicycle."

Dean got out of the car and waited. Sure enough, what looked like an old woman dressed in a black chador soon rounded the curve.

"She's going to say something to you in Arabic," Telach told him.

"What do I do?"

"Nothing. She has orders to shoot you if you do anything."

The woman approached the car, stopped, then repeated a long phrase twice.

"Give her the sample; go ahead," said Telach.

Dean reached back into the car and took out the small insulated bag. The woman took it without comment and began pedaling away. Dean saw an airplane banking above.

"It's ours, Charlie," said Telach. "Now go ahead; go over to the compound. We're still assessing the situation."

Inside the car, the driver was suppressing a laugh.

"What's so funny?" asked Dean.

"The hag said you have tiny balls and couldn't fuck a cat. Anyone who understood her couldn't have helped but react. That's how she knew you were the right contact."

"Everybody's a comedian," said Dean.

There were a half-dozen men at the entrance to the compound and two guards on the western fence, nearest the town. But the southeastern side was uncovered.

"When are the Israelis getting here?" Dean asked.

"They're on their own schedule," said Telach. "But I'd say within a half hour."

"Too long. I'm going in."

Telach didn't answer right away. "All right," she said finally. "Get as close to the wall as you can. What weapons do you have?"

"I have the AK-47 I took from the school, and an M4 in the trunk."

"All right. Wait until the aircraft attacks the main gate. When it does, go over the wall."

"Then what?"

"It depends on what they do. You'll have to trust us."

"I really wish you'd stop saying that."

"I will when you start doing it."

"I'm here, right?"

Lia followed the guards to the back of the house, expecting to be led to the bunker they had ID'ed below the back of the building. But instead they led her outside to a side garden and left her. She looked around. There were guards at the far end of the compound and back in the house, but otherwise she seemed to be alone. Lia took out her handheld computer and thumbed up the bug scanner; she wasn't even under surveillance.

"What's going on?" she asked Rockman.

"Umar the son of Umar seems to have bought your act," said the runner. "In any event, it's clear you're not Jewish, so he's confused."

"Does he know about the Israeli raid?"

"Not yet. We think there's a messenger on the way. Definitely time to leave. We have Dean outside. We're going to launch a diversion and you can get over the side wall. I'll guide you."

"I have to get the dongle into the computer in the bunker," she told the runner. "Go ahead with the diversion and tell Charlie I'll be along in a minute."

"They'll kill you if they find you."

"The second entrance is back beyond the pool, right?"

"Lia—"

"Are you going to help me, or do I have to figure it out for myself?"

The missile that exploded at the gate shook the ground so hard that Dean fell against the wall. By the time he got up and over the top, Pendleton had jumped onto the other side, thoughtfully leaving his jacket over the sharp shards of glass that lined the top. Dean heard a crack of rifle fire as he jumped; he rolled onto his shoulder and up, looking for a target. But the gunfire had come from the front of the building, one of the guards there firing in panic.

As Dean got up, the ground shook again. There were shouts from inside the house. Dean saw the Brit kneeling a few yards away; he whistled to him and then started running toward the building.

"Where is she?" he asked Rockman.

"She's inside the bunker beneath the house. Go to your

right. You'll see a large garden. Down the steps, keep moving to your right. Around to the pool house. She left the door
open for you."

"She left the door open for me?"

"She's a lot more sentimental than she seems."

84

Malachi Reese leaned back from the console, waiting as the commander of the mission cleared his F-47C bird from the engagement area. Malachi had the second plane in the formation; the unmanned fighter had a pair of 2,000-pound selectable GPS/laser-guided missiles under its wing, ready to fire.

But no target.

"Hang tight, Mal," said Train—also known as Major Pierce Duff, the mission commander. "Orion has some good snaps for us—no more resistance there."

"Yup on that," said Malachi.

"Get into position for the bunker shot," said Train.

"On it."

A targeting reticle had opened in the middle of Malachi's main screen. It boxed the back portion of the Syrian intelligence agent's house with a yellow square. At this point, Malachi could launch his two air-to-ground missiles with 98.9 percent confidence that their GPS systems would take them within eighteen inches of the center of the square, striking within .4 second of each other.

"Hold off," said the commander. "We have people in the bunker. Our people."

Malachi held his stick lightly, staying on course. While in theory he could launch from anywhere within a twenty-four-mile oval fire zone, his best aiming area was somewhat more limited; he'd run out of it in about ninety seconds and have to slide back in the formation. Truck had already taken direct control on the backup plane and would have the next shot.

"We're just going to hold here," said the commander. "We may not have to be firing at all. Mal, you copy that?"

"Roger that. I got it. All dressed up and nothing to blow."

"Don't sweat it," said Whacker, who handled the weapons systems for the four-man team that flew the birds. If the GPS failed for some reason, he could use a laser system to put the bomb on target. He could also launch the weapons himself, if authorized by the pilot or commander. "You'll get some action."

"Still got plenty of time here," said Riddler. He worked the electronic countermeasures, or ECMs. The remote-controlled attack aircraft were flown from a bunker at Crypto City by four-man teams, who together handled any-where from four to eight planes with the help of computers. The computer system and crew arrangements were neces-sary partly because of the slight but significant lag time in-volved in communicating commands over the network. The automated flight control systems actually did much of the "real" flying and fighting. Typically, two men served as pi-lots, with another taking offensive weapons—usually air-to-ground bombs, though they could fly interceptor missions as well—and another handling the defensive gear. All four men were actually cross-trained and could handle any of the oth-ers' tasks.

"Israeli fighters now zero-five off," said Riddler, adding their approach and speed. The Israelis had not been in-formed of the Birds' mission; the four planes were too stealthy to be picked up by Israeli radar at present. "Going to have to decide what we're doing here, chief. They're coming hot and look like the 'shoot first, say prayers later' types."

"All right, let me talk to Telach and see whether we want to give these guys a heads-up or just blow out of here," said Train.

85

Lia pushed against the wall as she heard someone at the far end shout in Arabic. Two men ran from the front room into the hallway and then into the access chamber and outside.

The bunker looked more like the basement of a well-appointed middle-class home than a bomb shelter or backup military headquarters. A beige Berber carpet covered the floor; the walls were covered with plasterboard painted a muted damask.

The computers she had to tap were about midway down the hall. As Lia moved up the hallway she heard someone talking. Not sure exactly what was happening, she ducked into a nearby room, which turned out to be an oversize linen closet. Towels, sheets, and pillows filled the walls on the left. The rest of the room was empty.

Lia pulled a pile of the towels out, carrying them in front of her as if she were a housemaid. She took a breath, then went back into the hallway.

"Lia?" asked Rockman.

"Got it covered," she said.

The door to the computer room was open. Lia swung inside, back to them, as a towel dropped to the floor. One of the two men inside got up, starting to question who she was. As she turned toward him the wall flashed and exploded— the result of a lipstick-sized mini–flash-bang grenade Lia had slipped into the towel.

Stunned, the man closest to her went down with a quick chop to the side of the head. Lia jump-kicked the second man as he rose, or tried to, from one of the desk chairs near the computer. A second kick rendered him unconscious. Lia went back to the first man, just rising from the carpet. Two sharp kicks from her heel ended the effort. Neither man had been armed, unfortunately, and there was no door to the room.

The computers were late-nineties PCs. One had just connected via modem to some other database; a prompt flashed on the screen requesting a password. Lia connected the dongles via the serial port, using a second adapter.

"Go," said Rockman. "Get the hell out of there!"

But it was too late. As she hopped over the bodies and ran for the door, two of the Syrian bodyguards and the woman who had brought her here came down the hallway.

Dean and Pendleton were nearly to the pool when the ground in front of them began percolating with small-arms fire. They threw themselves down onto the patio, rolling behind a low wall that provided scant cover.

Chips of concrete flew around Dean as he hunted for a target. He pushed to his right, saw something move, and fired. The sky vibrated fiercely—Dean threw himself into the vibration, running to the pool building as he emptied the AK-47 into three figures in green running toward him. He dived behind the building, rolling on the ground and then scrambling back, swimming through the rumbling air that had enveloped the world. From the edge of the building he saw two of the guards advancing, their rifles flaring. He popped in a new magazine and took them with two presses of the trigger. But the magazine had been nearly empty and the gun ran dry after a pair of bursts.

"Cover me!" he yelled to Pendleton, launching himself back up across the patio toward the two guards. Just as he reached the closest one, another Syrian came out from the back of the house; Dean tried scooping up the AK-47 but dropped it, then threw himself down as well. By the time he got the gun in his hands and rose to his feet, Pendleton had burned though his own magazine. The Syrian lay on the ground, blood burbling from his neck.

"We have to get into the bunker there," Dean told Pendleton. The SAS sergeant bent and grabbed two mags from the dead man, tossing them to him.

"More men, coming around the north side of the house," warned Rockman.

"Come on back to the pool house and watch my back," Dean told the sergeant. "There's two guys coming up from around the side of the house there."

"How do you know?"

"God told me."

As Lia stepped out into the hallway, she saw that the Syrian woman had her handbag over her shoulder.

"I'd like that back, please," Lia said.

"We'll bury it with you, Jew."

"Now do I look Jewish?"

One of the two men poked her breast with the nose of his gun and leered. Lia stepped back but didn't make a grab for the barrel; the others were too far for her to be certain of getting the gun and shooting them in time.

"You'll tell us exactly who you're working for before we kill you," said the woman.

Lia took another step back, her right elbow now at the doorjamb of the computer room.

"You're getting all this?" she said to Rockman.

"On your signal."

Before she could give it, the door at the far end of the hall behind her opened.

"Lia!" said Dean.

"No," said Lia.

The guard nearest her started to jerk his rifle toward Dean.

"Now!" screamed Lia, grabbing the gun and throwing herself sideways into the computer room. "Duck, Charlie Dean!" she yelled.

In that instant, the hallway exploded, the bomb in her purse ignited by the Art Room.

86

By the time Karr got himself situated in Bangkok, the Art Room had managed to track the detonator he'd found in Myanmar to a manufacturer in Singapore and from there to Taiwan. From there it had gone to Thailand, purchased by a Royal Thai Construction Company—owned by a holding company that also owned the Bangkok Star Imperial Hotel, the same hotel Karr had visited upon his arrival.

"Kinda symmetrical," Karr told Telach.

"I know. On the other hand, as Johnny Bib himself pointed out, a handful of big companies own everything anyway, so there'd be connections somehow."

"He didn't tell you how many companies?"

"Actually he did. But the number is suspiciously prime."

Karr laughed and checked his watch. It was going on six.

"Think I can catch Mr. Bai before cocktails?"

"He's there. But once the ball starts rolling—"

"It'll gather no moss."

87

Dean flew backward against the wall, his head rebounding against the concrete. His right knee collapsed and he fell in a tumble to the carpet. Smoke and dust choked his lungs; he coughed, rolled over, grabbed for his gun.

Something snapped it down out of his hand.

"Christ, Charlie Dean, you are the original bad penny. Always showing up at the wrong place and the wrong time."

Dean looked up into Lia's face. "That's how you thank me for coming to save your butt?"

"The day I need you to save my butt is the day I buy myself a fuzzy pink bathrobe and rabbit slippers," she said, pulling him up. "Let's get the hell out of here before the Israelis get here and blow the crap out of this place."

88

Rubens avoided glancing at his watch as the discussion continued. It was now early morning in Moscow; they had just under four hours to strike.

And he had just over twenty minutes to give the order.

Technically. In reality, Rubens had foreseen the possibility that the discussion might continue past the optimum moment and so had instructed Telach to have the strike aircraft ready. To keep operational secrecy—and to prevent accusations that he had jumped the gun later on—he had also told her to use the crew from the Syrian mission, giving them information only on an as-needed basis. The final strike order would be given only if he approved it.

"I think Mr. Rubens is a warmonger," said Sandra Marshall.

Even Rubens had to take notice of that. He looked up at her as she continued, telling the President that the national situation was well on its way to being under control. Attacking a hospital was uncalled for.

Her position was eminently reasonable, calmly presented, and in its way entirely logical.

She was quite good, Rubens realized. Quite good.

"Preemptive action may well be justified," said Debra Jodelin. "But there is a lot of risk to innocent people there. Can't you strike the bacteria while it's being transported?"

"We have a much better chance here, much better," said Hadash. "Hitting a moving object can be quite difficult, especially when you're launching your weapons from sixty or seventy thousand feet. We would run the same risks of collateral damage, with a much higher chance of failure. Considerably higher."

"What if the bacteria survives the attack?" asked Jodelin.

Before Rubens could open his mouth, the Secretary of Defense, Art Blanders, jumped in.

"The weapons they're talking about using would obliterate the lab area," said Blanders. "And I assume pile debris in such a way that it could not be easily accessed."

"That's correct," said Rubens. He and the Defense secretary occasionally disagreed, but Blanders could be a very useful ally. "Without a support medium, the bacteria should die within twenty-four hours. All of their machinery will be wrecked and of course the electricity will be turned off. We'll infiltrate the recovery teams, just to be sure."

"If we strike them like this, there may be consequences," said Secretary of State James Lincoln. "Severe consequences. We should explain our rationale."

"They won't know it's us," said Hadash. He seemed to be a firm supporter of the plan, albeit a reluctant one.

"The weapons are sterile," explained Rubens. "Everything is arranged to make it appear as if it's a terrorist attack. We'll plant information so that the Russians have plenty of evidence."

"Devious," said Marshall. Her tone was closer to mocking than admiring. Rubens realized that the performance was mostly meant for him—she was showing him that she could be an enemy as easily as an ally.

Marcke, apparently mindful of the time line Rubens had laid out earlier, raised his hand to end the discussion.

"Do it," said the President. "Let's talk about what Dr. Lester should be saying on the talk shows, and then let's all take a break."

Rubens called the Art Room from inside the White House.

"We're go on the project," he told Telach.

"Yes."

Her voice sounded distant but no longer shaky. Progress, he thought.

"Where else are we?"

"We've downloaded data from the Syrians. Lia and Dean are just getting out of there; we're setting up to debrief them and run back the mission."

"Have you analyzed the bacteria from the school?"

"We haven't gotten it physically to the mobile lab yet," said Telach.

"We're positive the Swiss don't have the bacteria?"

"If you want to talk to Johnny Bib about it, I'll be happy to put him on."

"Not necessary, Marie. What about Karr?"

"Tommy's ready in Bangkok. We've tracked the detonator."

"Very good. I'll be back as soon as I can."

"I have it under control."

He considered this. Marie had been out of sorts the other day but now seemed back on her game—the sharp comeback earlier and the bristle over his hurrying back were exhibits A and B.

"You seem more yourself this morning, Marie," he told her.

"I always feel better after a sleepless night," she told him. "Excuse me, but I have a job to do."

"Very good," he said, hitting END.

89

Karr glanced up at the ceiling of the Bangkok Star Imperial, trying to catch a glimpse of himself in the gold leaf. But the shine was more luster than reflection.

"Now that's a surprise," he said, spinning around as he continued to stare upward. As he did, he bumped into one of Bai's security people.

It was a fairly hard bump. The man—who, though six-three, was still about four inches shorter than the American—fell to his knees, suddenly out of breath. Karr leaned over to help, applying a very special first-aid resuscitation technique—which resulted in the guard's Beretta pistol flying up out of his hand into the air.

Karr snatched it when it reached eye level. He stuck it into his waistband as he walked toward the office Bai used as his headquarters. Two large Asian men—they looked Chinese, but that may have been a function of the tattoos on their necks—pushed their chests out in his direction.

Their drawn pistols were somewhat more impressive than their muscles.

"Hey, guys. Remember me?" said Karr cheerfully. "I have some business with the boss."

The sentry on the right replied with a long sentence that, when translated from Thai, might be considered a travel suggestion.

"Nah, he definitely wants to talk to me here rather than

there," said Karr. "Although I suppose he can catch me *after* I talk to the defense minister. Either of you got the time? I may be running a bit late."

As the two men pressed closer to him, the door at the end of the hall opened. Bai said something to the men, who stood aside.

"Thanks," said Karr, walking inside.

"Why are you here?"

"The obvious reasons," said Karr.

He sat down in the seat near the desk, then opened his jacket. Bai immediately flashed his pistol.

"Relax. I want you to look at these pieces of paper, then decide whether you want to cooperate or not. Your call."

The NSA op pulled the documents out of his coat pocket and unfolded them. The top two were copies of electronic transfers that had been made to Bai's personal account from Hong Kong banks occasionally used by the Chinese Communist government as a conduit for external operations. One collected transactions from Bai's accounts overseas, showing that the money had indeed gone to him and his family. The next two were authorization memos connecting the transfers to arms shipments to guerrillas in Myanmar. Last but not least was the transcript of a conversation between Bai and a member of the guerrilla group known as the Crescent Tigers.

"The translation on that last one may not be that good," Karr said as Bai stared at the intercept. "They did it by computer and they had to use English because the character set was a serious pain in the ass to transmit. I mean, you know, technology's great, but it does have its limits."

Bai sat back in the seat. "What do you want?"

"Kegan. I need him now."

"I owe him too much to betray him."

"He saved your sister's life, yes," said Karr. "But that was a long time ago."

"I can't."

"You think he's worth these papers showing up in the defense minister's office? Considering all you've done for him already?"

Bai shook his head, but Karr could tell he was wavering.

"He's going to die anyway, Mr. Bai. You know that as well as I do. The other people looking for him won't be as considerate if they find him before I do. And you know they're looking for him. They followed me out of here last time I came by."

90

Malachi checked the course indicator on the lead bird, then rolled through the instrument screens, making sure the aircraft was in good shape. Train had split the team in half, giving Malachi and Whacker the two F-47s inbound for Moscow while he and Riddler mopped up over Syria and took the flight home. The commander and the other weapons officer would join them just before they were ready to hit the target area; in the meantime, this was a piece of cake. Malachi had his aircraft at 72,000 feet; their stealthy profiles were invisible to Russian radar, which was surprisingly sparse once you got beyond the border areas.

"Civilian aircraft coming out of the west toward us," said Whacker. He ran down the particulars; the airplane, a Boeing 767, was flying around thirty-two thousand feet and would come within three miles of them if they didn't change course. Technically, that was probably far enough away for them to be missed, but given the fact that they were over Russia, Malachi brought his throttles up to full, accelerating briefly to get past the passenger jet.

"Looking good," said Riddler. "Getting tired?"

"Hey, no way," said Malachi. "You want some strawberry drink?"

"What's it spiked with? Caffeine or amphetamines?"

"Just sugar. Can't beat a glucose high."

"You been listening to thrash rock too long."

"Alternative music."

"I listen to alternative music. You listen to trash crap."

"Thrash. And Barry Manilow is alternative?"

"That was Frank Sinatra I was listening to the other day. A world of difference."

Malachi was about to argue the relative merits of crooners he knew nothing about when Telach interrupted from the Art Room.

"Malachi, we have a change in plans. How quickly can you be on target?"

"How quickly?"

"Balls-out."

"Uh." His fingers slammed on his auxiliary keyboard, the computer doing the number crunching.

"I can get you there in forty-nine minutes, but we'll have to self-destruct right after we shoot."

"Set it up. We're just decrypting an intercept that they're moving the shipment up." She paused, doing her own calculations. "You'll have only ten minutes to spare."

"Okay. Listen, we're going to need a precise target," he told her, bringing up the greater Moscow area on the GPS-assisted map screen. "I may be able to shave a minute off, depending on where we're going."

"Botkin Hospital. I'll have a precise map for you in a few moments, with index numbers for your target."

"Hospital?" said Malachi.

"The order is nine-thirteen-oh-three. I need you to acknowledge it and add your personal voice code."

91

There was a guard in the hall and another on the door. Karr decided his best bet was the window.

The only problem was the window was twenty stories above the ground.

He knocked on the door of apartment 22D, directly above the one where Bai had told him Kegan was holed up. To his surprise, the door opened immediately.

"Hello," he told the old woman who answered. "I'm here to wash the windows."

He walked inside as the woman stood at the door looking at him, dumbfounded—obviously she didn't speak English, much less need to have her windows cleaned.

Karr pulled off his backpack and pointed to the window.

"Got to take a look at it," he told her.

The woman began talking to him in Thai. Karr ignored her, walking to the large plate glass window at the far end of the living room.

"Double-insulated. Figures." He nodded at her, then took out the souped-up RotoZip cordless drill from his pack. The diamond tip on the bit quickly made it through the glass; he moved down as if he were working with a piece of plaster-board. He reached the bottom and turned left.

"Torque on these suckers makes it hard to get a perfect straight line, you know?" he said cheerfully. "But we're in a little bit of a hurry here."

As he turned the corner up, the bit broke.

"I hate that," he said, pulling the drill out. "Don't you hate that?"

The woman reached and picked up the phone.

"You got the phone, right, Rockman?"

"Cho's taking the call right now."

"Yeah, well, double-check, okay? You told me there was no one in this apartment."

"Sorry. The image from the Kite looked clean."

"You check on our guy?"

"I'm looking at the thermal image right now," said Rockman. The feed was coming from a Kite robot aircraft Karr had launched before coming upstairs.

"You sure?"

"Yeah, I'm sure. Smile."

Karr waved out the window at the Kite, then went back to work. He intended on using a suction gripper to pull the glass piece inside and left the right corner intact. But before he could put the gripper on—the device looked like the plunger end of a plumber's helper—the glass broke and fell, fortunately into an open courtyard.

The old woman was now talking into the telephone to a translator at the Art Room, who was telling her that the "odd white giant" who had invaded her house was looking for marauding insects. Karr, meanwhile, set an anchor in the wall. He tugged, then tugged again.

"Ready for me?" he asked Rockman.

"Let's go for it."

Tommy edged through the window space, holding on to the ledge. The Kite, meanwhile, swooped below, zooming against the window of 20D. As it hit, the small charge of explosive in its nose exploded. Karr dropped the twenty feet or so to the window so quickly that he found himself in a cloud of dust as he kicked out the rest of the window and dropped inside.

"Your right, your right," Rockman coached in his ear.

Karr swung up his A-2 as the door opened. The guard got off one shot before the fusillade of bullets from Tommy's gun carried him back out into the hallway, dead. By the time Karr got out there, the other man had fled.

"He's in the apartment, on the left. Alone," said Rockman. But Karr had already seen Dr. Kegan, sitting with a blanket pulled around him in the large chair at the side of the room.

"Who are you?" asked Kegan calmly when Karr returned.

Karr stretched his arms and shoulders and began pulling off his knapsack. "Name's Kjartan Magnor Karr. Most people, though, call me Tommy. Kind of a long story why."

"How'd you find me?"

"I had some help. You missed your meeting, Doctor. CDC and FBI guys were worried about you."

"Couldn't be avoided."

"That go for the rat-bite fever, too?"

Kegan frowned.

"Why'd you sell it?" asked Karr.

"I ran out of money."

Karr pulled over a chair and sat down.

"Want to talk to me about it?" asked Karr.

"Not really."

"Might as well, though." Karr pointed at his stomach. "Pancreatic cancer?"

"How do you know about that?"

"Well, a friend of yours mentioned it. But he was under the impression it was cured."

Kegan gave him a funny smile.

"You really don't cure that, do you? One of our doctors mentioned there really isn't a cure. Sooner or later you die. Sooner, right? You've lasted a long time."

"I'm right in the probability curve," said Kegan. "Funny how those things work."

"You found out eighteen months ago."

"Twenty-four. At first I did the treatments, you know? Not really because I thought they would work. Just because I didn't know what else to do."

"You came here for a cure?"

"No. Not really."

Karr nodded. "So you wanted to take care of the people

who'd killed your girlfriend in the seventies. Long time to hold a grudge."

"They changed my life. They ruined it." Kegan shifted in the chair, drawing his legs up under him. He'd lost a great deal of weight recently; the skin hung off his face. "Though I suppose it's at least spared her this, seeing me waste away."

"Sucks."

"You don't know the half of it. I can't eat. I can barely drink."

"Actually, I do know the feeling. Or at least something like it. I caught your disease."

Kegan stared at him for a moment, trying to see if he was telling the truth or not. "You caught it?"

"From your cat."

"Oh, Jesus."

"It's all right. The old lady's penicillin cured me. That cured the guerrillas, right? Or some of them, anyway. That's what screwed up your plan—they got better."

"I didn't mean for anyone else to get hurt. I took precautions. The disease wasn't that easy to spread."

Karr pulled out his handheld computer. "Would you mind telling me exactly what you did?"

Slowly, the doctor began to tell his story.

Thirty years before, as a young medical volunteer, Kegan had met the love of his life while a volunteer with the World Health Organization. She was killed by one of the rebel groups; he'd told the story many times to Dean.

Over the years, as the fortunes of the group had varied, Kegan had kept track. He'd gone to Thailand several times in fact, to gather more information and to consider how to take revenge. Once he'd even hired a Burmese gangster to make a hit, but by then the leader of the guerrilla group had once more fallen from grace and was in the hills.

The work on germ warfare, though he'd stopped working in the field, suggested the possibility, and his early experience with the disease had made him familiar with the organism.

Still, he had worked on it off and on for many years before discovering precisely how to do it.

And then he had hesitated. Not until the cancer did he decide. He had needed help, however, to get the disease to the guerrilla camp. He was fortunate that many of those who had known him when he was a young man owed their lives or their loved ones' lives to him. Mr. Bai had been one.

Kegan had not told Bai or anyone else what precisely he was doing. Yet somehow the Pole found out. When he contacted Kegan, he panicked and alerted the FBI and CDC.

"He had someone with the people Bai sent to the camp before you arrived," explained Karr. "He simply watched what was going on. He could tell from some of the items you ordered through Bai the nature of things. I mean, what's a hotel need petri dishes for, right?"

Kegan nodded and continued. He came to Thailand himself; posing as a sympathetic member of Amnesty International, he visited the guerrillas and poisoned them, lacing their food and drinking water. He was gone before the disease took hold.

He had to make sure it had worked, and so he sent his assistant there to check on rumors of disease.

"It worked, but you didn't get everyone because of the cure. So you had to go back. But your money was spent; you needed connections. So you talked to the Pole," suggested Karr.

Kegan nodded.

"I had already begun to negotiate when the guerrilla arrived to kill me," said Kegan. "Fortunately, he stood out rather starkly in Athens, New York."

"The man who came to your house—"

"They found my assistant here and probably tortured him. I'm not sure what's happened to him, but I'm sure he must have been the link, not Bai."

"Wait—you were negotiating?" asked Karr. "You were talking to the Pole, the guy with the company UKD, right?"

Kegan nodded. "I had no other way of getting money. I had already put two mortgages on my house."

"You sold him the bacteria in exchange for his help."

"I gave him one of the strands that had failed. I promised the medicine as well," said Kegan. "The Pole can't kill anyone. The strains are useless. They cause slight stomach discomfort. They show up in subjects, but they're not fatal. I'm not a fool, Mr. Karr. I don't hate the human race. I just hated the people who killed Krista."

92

Now what the Syrian had told Lia earlier made sense—
Marie Telach jumped to the panel, punching the line to the
piloting area.

"Malachi. Malachi. Abort! Abort!"

She could see on the screen that the timer had drained to
five seconds.

"Marie?"

"Abort," she repeated.

"Once I'm authorized I'm only supposed to abort on Mr.
Rubens' orders. You already confirmed the order."

"Stop now, Malachi," she said, her voice calm and cold.
"Stop. My authority."

"If I abort, I still have to destruct. No second chance."

"Abort! Now!"

There was a pause. The timer had hit 0.

"Yes, ma'am."

Inside the piloting pod, Malachi and Whacker didn't speak
until they were ready to start the destruct.

"Counting down," said Whacker.

"Roger that."

"I need your voice," said Whacker, meaning that Malachi
had to give the verbal authorization or the F-47s would not
blow themselves up.

"Just a second," said Malachi. He nudged Bird 2 so that it was lined up to hit the water as it destroyed itself. "Barry Manilow sucks fish."

"That's it?"

"You have to repeat word for word."

"Barry Manilow sucks fish."

The screen flashed red.

"Confirmed," Malachi told the computer. "Destruct one. Destruct two."

The aircraft blew up. The feed reverted to a feed from a Space Command visual satellite that Malachi had selected earlier as a default.

"Barry Manilow sucks?" asked Whacker.

"See? I knew you were a fan."

93

"How do I know you're telling the truth about the bacteria?" Karr asked Kegan.

"Why would I lie?"

"Why wouldn't you?"

"I'm not."

"So prove it," said Karr.

"Test the bacteria strains. Buy some from the Pole and test it. I'm sure he'll sell it. He sells everything." Kegan shrugged. "He was useful."

"He wasn't a friend?"

"I don't have many friends."

"I know one. Charlie Dean."

Kegan smiled weakly. "You know Charlie?"

"Yeah. I work with him."

Kegan looked surprised. "Charlie?"

"He found the dead man in your house. He'd come up to see you."

"Charlie? Is he—oh, God."

"He's all right. Turns out he hates cats."

"Tell him I'm sorry."

"Tell him yourself. Come on. Let's get the hell out of here. I got a helicopter waiting. Get you home—"

Kegan shook his head. "Too late now."

"Nah."

"I'm afraid it is." The scientist pulled the pistol up from below the blanket.

"It'd be better for everybody if you didn't shoot me," said Karr, though he was wearing the carbon boron vest beneath his shirt.

"Everybody?"

"Well, me." Karr laughed. "What do you think?"

"Tell Dean it was all in the wrist."

"What was that?" asked Karr.

Rather than answering, the doctor put the gun into his mouth and fired.

94

Rubens reached the Art Room as the birds disintegrated.

"What's the situation?" he asked Telach.

"I aborted the strike on the hospital."

"What?"

"Tommy found Kegan. The Russian strain is a fake. So was the Syrian. We have the lab tests," said Telach.

"You countermanded my order without calling me?"

"I had five seconds to make a decision. I made it."

Her lower lip trembled slightly as she continued, but the tremor wasn't anything near as bad as the other day. Rubens listened without interrupting, realizing even before he heard all of her reasoning that she had made the right decision.

With all its high-tech gear, satellites, and fancy gizmos, at its core Deep Black was no different from any other organization. Its success depended on the ability of its people to make judgments and execute at the moment of crisis. Rubens knew that; his main asset as head of Desk Three, his real ability, was in finding the people who could do that. He had personally selected everyone in this room and all of the field ops as well. He was a phenomenally good judge of character.

So how had he failed to figure out what Marshall was up to?

A momentary blip, a necessary reminder that he was not perfect.

To be humble was the most difficult and yet important task, one he would struggle with his whole life.

Telach, too, had struggled. But she was over it, beyond whatever had troubled her.

"Very well," Rubens told her as she finished. "You did well."

"Thank you, boss."

Her voice seemed uncharacteristically tender. Rubens turned away quickly and looked around the Art Room. "Where do we start?"

Nearly twelve hours later—after debriefing the teams, calling the President, calling Hadash, spending a long lunch with Brown—William Rubens leaned back in his office chair and closed his eyes. He'd come upstairs to see to his paperwork so he could take the next few days off, but even the most routine memorandum was beyond him. Dr. Lester called him to confirm that the epidemic had begun to abate, with no new cases reported in the past twenty-four hours. The first shipment of the medicine was just arriving from Thailand; many of those already infected would die, but the disease itself no longer presented the outsize threat they had mobilized against.

"Due to your people," added Lester.

"Yes," said Rubens. "Thank you."

A moment after he hung up, the phone rang again. He looked at the receiver for a second, then reached over and picked it up.

"Rubens."

"Marshall."

"Yes?"

"You're very good," she said. "Far better than I gave you credit for."

Another time, he might have strung her along for a while, but now he simply said he was tired.

"You had lunch with Lincoln?" she asked.

"Admiral Brown happened to have an appointment with him."

"Which you arranged?"

Rubens didn't answer. He had, in fact.

"And you urged him not to resign."

"I told him he would be a fool."

"Do you actually think you can influence him?"

"Maybe. Maybe not."

"You told him you didn't want the job?"

"Yes, as a matter of fact. And apparently loudly enough to have several people nearby hear."

"What was the purpose of that? Some sort of trick?"

"To remove temptation," he said.

"You honestly don't want to be Secretary of State?"

Of course he did. But he couldn't.

"No," said Rubens.

"I take it this means you're holding to your position regarding biometric IDs."

Actually, he had gone beyond that, drafting a detailed memo on the proposal and who stood to gain from it, along with financials on the two companies that included information about key stockholders. The memo—unsigned and mailed from Reston, Virginia—would find its way to the professional gossipmonger tomorrow. A payback, and an investment.

"I'll remember this, Billy."

Rubens winced. He hated to be called Billy.

95

Dean sat fitfully as the woman at the lectern, the local village historian, recounted how helpful James Kegan had been over the years, donating money, expertise, materials, and sweat equity as the group restored one of the old homesteads for use as a museum. It was a side of Kegan Dean barely knew.

Keys had had a whole life here that Dean really didn't know. He'd talked at the local elementary school at least once a year, brought the kids down to his lab for a tour, judged the science fair. He'd been on the library board—not with the best attendance, the head librarian had felt compelled to note, but always willing to man the refreshment table at the annual fund-raiser, a thankless task.

The church was filled with people who remembered Keys for dozens of similar thankless tasks. Dean had missed the funeral, which had been held near his research institute; the church had been filled there as well, packed with scientists from across the world. Somehow, this one, with its halting and corny speeches, felt more comforting.

No one at either service knew the exact circumstances of Kegan's death, let alone what had led to it; Rubens had seen to that. Dean tried to thank him, but the Desk Three Director shook his head.

"It's a matter of national security, not a favor," said Rubens. "I don't do favors."

Dean smiled at the memory. Something else from the

meeting came to him—a question not from Rubens but, from Marie Telach.

"Did you know him well, Charlie?"

"Once," he'd told her.

Once.

Was it a lie? The James Kegan he knew was a bit—what was the word—patronizing toward the people who lived in the town around him.

These people didn't really know Keys. They certainly didn't know Dr. Kegan. But what they did know was important to them.

And the same with Dean. Keys had a hell of a jump shot once. And he was a great guy to talk to late at night, when the summer was just starting to cool down. You could talk about anything—women especially. Keys was the one person whom you could talk about love with and not feel goofy or embarrassed or part of a Hallmark ad.

It must have killed him all along. All along. Yet he'd never admitted it all.

You really didn't know me at all, did you, Charlie Dean?

No, he thought. But he did know some things. And he'd been right in the end.

So he'd known the most important thing. At least to him.

"And now, for a few words on our friend when he was a young man," said the minister, taking over, "I'd like to call up Charlie Dean."

Dean got up and walked slowly to the front. The first words stuck in his throat.

You really didn't know me, but you were a good friend anyway.

"Jimmy Keys—that's what we called him," managed Dean. "He had the sweetest jump shot you ever saw."

Read on for an excerpt from the
next book by Stephen Coonts

WAGES
OF SIN

A Tommy Carmellini Novel

Coming soon from Orion

"Whatcha gonna do when they come for you, bad boy?"

When Dorsey O'Shea walked into the lock shop that morning in October, I was in the back room trying to figure out how to pick the new high-security Cooper locks. I saw her through the one-way glass that separated the workshop from the retail space.

My partner, Willie the Wire, was waiting on a customer. I don't think Willie recognized her at first—it had been two years since Dorsey and I were a number, she had changed her hair, and as I recall he had only met her on one or two occasions—but he remembered her as soon as she said his name and asked for me.

Willie was noncommittal—he knew I was in the back room. "How long has it been, Dorsey?"

"I really need to see Carmellini," she said forcefully.

"You're the third hot woman this week who has told me that."

"I want his telephone number, Willie."

"Does he still have your phone number?"

That was when I stepped through the shop door and she saw me. She was tall, with great bones, and skin like cream. "Hey, Dorsey."

"Tommy, I need to talk to you."

"Come on back."

She came around the counter and preceded me through the doorway to the shop. I confess, I watched. Even when she wasn't trying, her hips and bottom moved in very interesting ways. But all that was past, I told myself with a sigh. She had ditched me, and truth be told, I didn't want her back. Too much maintenance.

In the shop, she looked around curiously at the tools, locks, and junk strewn everywhere. Willie wasn't a neat workman and I confess, I'm also kinda messy. She fingered some of the locks, then focused her attention on me. "I remembered that you were a part owner in this place, so I thought Willie might know where to find you."

"Inducing him to tell you would have been the trick."

Obviously Dorsey had not considered the possibility that Willie might refuse to tell her whatever she asked. Few men ever had. She was young, beautiful and rich, the modern trifecta for females. She came by her dough the old-fashioned way—she inherited it. Her parents died in a car wreck shortly after she was born. The grandparents who raised her passed away while she was partying at college, trying to decide if growing up would be worth the effort. Now she lived in a monstrous old brick mansion on five hundred acres, all that remained of a colonial plantation, on the northern bank of the Potomac thirty miles upriver from Washington. It was a nice little getaway if you were worth a couple hundred million, and she was.

When I met her, she was whiling away her time doing the backstroke through Washington's social circles. She once thought I was pretty good arm candy on the party circuit and a pleasant bed-warmer on long winter nights, but after a while she changed her mind. Women are like that . . . fickle.

I had the Cooper lock mounted on a board, which was held in a vise. I adjusted the torsion wench and went back to work with the pick. The Cooper was brand-new to the market, a top-of-the-line exterior door lock that contractors were ordering installed in new custom homes. They were telling the owners that it was burglar-proof, un-pickable. I didn't think there was a lock on the planet that couldn't be opened without a key, but then, I had never before tried the Cooper. What the hell, I would see one sooner or later on a door I wanted to go through, so why not learn now? I had already cut a Cooper in half—ruining several saw blades—so I knew what made it tick. I had had two pins aligned when Dorsey came in, and of course had lost them when I released the tension on the wrench and walked around front to speak to her.

She eyed me now as I manipulated the tools. "What are you doing, anyway?"

"Learning how to open this lock."

"Why don't you use a key?"

"That would be cheating. Our public would be disappointed. What can I do for you today, anyway?"

She looked around again in a distracted manner, then sat on the only uncluttered stool. "I need help, and the only person I could think of asking was you."

I got one of the pins up and felt around, trying to find which of the others was the tightest. The problem here, I decided, was the shape of my pick. I could barely reach the pins. I got a strip of flat stock from our cabinet and began working with the grinder.

"That sounds very deep," I said to keep her talking. "Have you discussed that insight with your analyst?"

"I feel like such a fool, coming here like this. Don't make it worse by talking down to me."

"Okay."

"It's not that I didn't like you, Tommy, but I never understood you. Who are you? Why do you own part of a lock shop? What kind of work do you do for the government? You never told me anything about yourself. I always felt that there was this wall between us, that there was a whole side of you I didn't know."

"You don't owe me an explanation," I said. "It was two years ago. We hadn't made each other any promises."

She twisted her hands—I couldn't help glancing at her from time to time.

"Why don't you tell me what's on your mind?" I said as I inspected my new pick. I slipped it into the Cooper, put some tension on the torsion wrench, and went to work as she talked.

"Every man I know wears a suit and tie and spends his days making money—the more the better—except you. It's just that—oh, hell!" She watched me work the pick for a minute before she added, "I want you to get into an ex-boyfriend's house and get something for me."

"There are dozens of lock shops listed in the Yellow pages."

"Oh, Tommy, don't be like that." She slipped off the stool and walked around so that she could look into my eyes. She didn't reach and she didn't touch—just looked. "I feel like such a jerk, asking you for a favor after I broke up with you, but I don't have a choice. Believe me, I am in trouble."

Truthfully, when she dumped me, I was sort of subtly campaigning to get dumped—but I wasn't about to tell her that. And you don't have to believe it if you don't want to.

I glanced at her. The tension showed on her face. "You're going to have to tell me all of it," I said, gently as I could. At heart Dorsey was a nice kid . . . for a multi-millionaire, which wasn't her fault.

"His name is Kincaid, Carroll Kincaid. He has a couple of videotapes. He made them without my knowledge when we were first dating. He's threatening to show them to my fiancé if I don't pay him a lot of money."

"I didn't know you were engaged."

"We haven't announced it yet."

"Who's the lucky guy?"

She said a name, pronounced it like I was supposed to recognize it.

"So why don't you ask him for help?" I said.

"I can't. Tommy, even if I pay blackmail, there's no guarantee Kincaid would give me the only copies of the tapes."

"So you want me to break into his house and get the tapes?"

"It wouldn't really be burglary. He made the tapes without my permission. They are really mine."

Amazingly enough, when we were dating, the thought never crossed my little mind that she might have a stupid stunt like this in her. I made eye contact again, scrutinized every feature. I decided she might be telling the truth.

I was trying to think of something appropriate to say when I felt the pick twitch and the lock rotated. It was open.

I put the tools on the table and was reaching for a stool when she moved closer and laid a hand on my arm. "Oh, Tommy, please! Blackmail is ugly. I really am in love, and it could be something wonderful. Kincaid is trying to ruin my life."

I reflected that sometimes having money is really hard on a girl, or so I've heard. And the prospect of burglary always gets my juices flowing. She gave me Kincaid's address. I made sure Dorsey understood that I wasn't promising anything. "I'll see what I can do." She gave me her cell phone number, started to kiss me, thought better of it and left.

I sat wondering how that kiss would have tasted as I listened to her walk through the store. When the front door closed, Willie came into the workshop.

"I don't know what you got, Carmellini, that drives all the chicks wild, but I'd sure like to have some of it. They're troopin' in here all the time wantin' to know where you are, what you're doin'—makes a man feel inadequate, y'know? Maybe you oughta open a school or somethin'. Sorta a public service deal. What'd'ya think?"

"I got the Cooper opened."

"How long it take you?"

"I wasn't timing it. I was—"

"Three minutes for me," Willie said with a touch of pride in his voice. "'Course I wasn't looking at a dish like that when I did it. What does she want you to do—steal the silver at the White House?"

"I can beat three minutes blindfolded," I told Willie, and by God, I did. And I had to listen to a lot of his B.S. while I did it.

I went into Kincaid's place the following night. There was no one home and he forgot to lock the back door. When I found that the door was unlocked, I sat down at his backyard picnic table while I thought things over. For the life of me, I couldn't see what Dorsey would gain by setting me up. Dorsey was waiting in my car halfway down the block with a cell phone—she was to call me if Kincaid returned while I was in the house.

If she was playing a game, it was too deep for me, I concluded. Even smart people forget to lock their doors.

I opened Kincaid's back door and went inside.

After thirty minutes, I was certain there were no home-made videotapes in the house, although I did find three high-end videocams and a dozen photographer's floodlights in the bedroom, which had a huge round bed in the center of the room and electrical outlets every three feet around the walls. This guy was more than kinky—he was set up to make porno flicks.

So where were they? There were boxes of videotape—all unopened, still wrapped in cellophane. Nothing that looked like it had been in a camera.

I was going through his files at his desk in his den—he was reasonably well organized, I must say—when I found a receipt for a safe deposit box at a local bank. From the amount he paid, he must have rented a large box. The receipt was a month ago. The box key wasn't in the desk and I didn't expect it to be.

I couldn't find a receipt or record that hinted that he owned a storage unit. He might have stashed a suitcase full of stuff at a friend's house, but I doubted it. These days everyone had curious friends. His car was a possibility, though an unlikely one. If some kid took it for a joyride, he could be ruined. Of course, he could have delivered the tapes to whatever lab processed them into movies. But if he did that with a tape of Dorsey and some porno kings, why try to blackmail her?

Dorsey was chewing her lip when I got into the car. "No videotapes," I said. "Has a nice little home movie setup, but no tapes."

"I could help you look. They must be there."

"They aren't. He didn't even lock the back door." I started the car and got it rolling down the street. "He's set up to film some hot porno action. The raw tapes would have to be digitized and edited, and the equipment for that isn't in the house."

Her color wasn't good. She didn't meet my eyes.

"When did he first approach you demanding money?"

She thought about it. "Three weeks ago, I think. Labor Day weekend. I had some friends over for a small party and he showed up unannounced."

The time frame seemed to fit. I decided the safe deposit box was a definite possibility.

I don't make a habit of burgling houses for ex-girlfriends, even if they are beautiful and rich and being blackmailed. During the day I work for the CIA. It isn't something agency employees talk about and I had never mentioned it to Dorsey. I think I did once mention that I worked for the General Services Administration. She probably thought I was some kind of maintenance supervisor. Maybe that was the story I told her—I don't quite remember.

Usually I worked overseas, breaking and entering for Uncle Sam, planting bugs, stealing documents, that kind of thing. Every now and then I did a few black-bag jobs stateside for the FBI, strictly as a favor, you understand, one federal agency helping another. I sometimes heard rumors that the CIA asked the FBI to ask for my help on domestic matters, but being a loyal employee, I immediate discounted and forgot those ugly whispers. In those days I was just another civil servant beating in time, working toward that happy retirement on the old fifty-fifth birthday, followed by a life of golf and restaurant meals courtesy of future taxpayers.

After my abortive inspection of Dorsey's ex-flame's house, I took her back to her car and dropped her. She was in a foul mood, chewing her lip.

I waited until she got inside her vehicle, then drove away to find a bar. As I swilled beer, I compared how I had felt two years ago when she dumped me and how I felt walking through the porno guy's digs.

Oh, well.

. . .

A few days later I had to leave work after lunch for my annual physical, so after the doc finished with the rubber glove, I took the rest of the day off. I went by the neighborhood bank where Kincaid had his box, parked, went in, and rented one for myself.

It was a typical suburban branch bank, with a drive-through window and an interior lobby. A security door that had to be opened from the inside prevented people from entering the loan officers' half of the building, and that was where the small safe-deposit vault was. I filled out the form and was admitted to the vault. A bank of boxes formed each wall. The largest boxes were on the bottom row. Beside the door was a cabinet that contained envelopes holding keys for the empty boxes, and on top of the cabinet, two steel boxes containing the cards that each box patron had to sign every time he wanted into his box. A single surveillance camera was mounted high on the wall opposite the door to the vault.

My escort in the vault was a young woman named Harriet who was wearing a wedding ring and maternity clothes, although the baby wasn't showing much. I commented on that and she told me she had five more months to go. It was her first child. She and her husband were so excited.

"You're lucky we have a large box available. This is the only one. It became available last week when the lady who had it was transferred to Europe. She's with the State Department."

She gave me my key and we checked that it opened my new box. The locks for the individual boxes were lever tumbler locks, which is the universal standard in American safety deposit vaults. Each box had two keyways. As usual, she had to insert the master key which she carried into one keyway and my key into the other and turn them both simultaneously for the box to open. Fortunately Willie had a bank of four safety deposit boxes complete with their lever tumbler locks back at the shop.

I confess I was a little disappointed, although I tried not to show it. Some banks were getting into the habit of breaking off one of their master keys in the lock of each box in the vault, then admitting boxholders to the vault without an escort. Needless to say, these boxes were a breeze for guys like me to pop. I had my hopes up, but it wasn't to be. This bank was still doing it the safe, old-fashioned way.

I told Harriet I might be back in a few days to put some stuff in my new box, thanked her for her time, and departed.

Back in the shop Willie and I discussed lever tumbler locks and disassembled one from his safety deposit boxes. Lever tumbler locks require an L-shaped pick, the prong of which must be precisely the right length. I used my key to measure the length I needed and made myself three picks, each a slightly different length, just in case.

I spent the weekend practicing on Willie's locks. My best time was twenty-six seconds, but two minutes was the average. And if I hurried or wasn't paying strict attention, I couldn't get the lock to open. Willie spent some time watching me, and even opened it a few times himself.

Willie the Wire was twenty years older than me, a slim, dapper black man who had worked New York hotels in his younger days dressed as a bellboy. Finally he quit carrying the bags into the hotel for the client and specialized in picking locks and carrying luggage out—sans tip. The last time he got out of prison he promised himself an honest job, but with his reputation, no one would hire him. A friend of mine knew him and mentioned his plight to me. We had dinner a few times and he showed me a couple of things I didn't know about locks, so I bankrolled this establishment and we became partners. He knew I worked for the CIA, but we never talked about it.

That weekend as we played with the locks on his sample safety deposit boxes, he wanted to talk about Dorsey O'Shea. "This might be a set-up, man. You ever think about that?"

"Why would Dorsey want to set me up?"

"Maybe somebody who don't like you wanta burn you— how the hell would I know, man! You're the fuckin' spy, you tell me."

"I can't think of any reason under the sun."

"She look like real money. That right?"

"She's got it, yeah."

"You don't know what the hell you gettin' into, and that's a fact. This man got somethin' on her besides movies of her gettin' cock. Whoever looks at faces in those flicks, anyway? You in over your simple head, Carmellini."

Perhaps he was right, but Dorsey O'Shea didn't hang with Willie the Wire's crowd. Although being a porno star wouldn't hurt your rep in some circles, a lot of minds weren't quite that open. If Kincaid was a real son of a bitch, he could squeeze her for serious cash.

That's the way I had it figured, anyhow. On the other hand, maybe I just wanted to see if I could pop Kincaid's box at the bank. I had never done a safety deposit box before, so what the hell.

I called Dorsey on Monday morning, right after I called the agency and said I was sick. "Today's the day. Pick me up at my house at ten o'clock."

She showed up ten minutes late, which was amazingly punctual for her. I got in with her and directed her to a costume place that a friend of mine owned in a strip mall in Silver Spring. When we came out, she was wearing a dark wig and a maternity dress. We had a hard plastic shape strapped to her stomach to fill it out. I thought she looked about seven months along. I pushed on her new stomach and it felt real to me—the proper resistance and give. On the way to the bank I drove and briefed her.

"I don't know if I can do this, Tommy," she said when I finished.

"Do you want those tapes or not?"

"I want them."

"You have two choices—pay up or do a deal. Killing Kincaid will leave the tapes for the cops to find. Odds are he has the tapes in his box at the bank. He thinks they're safe there. He may have duped them—I don't know. If we clean out that box, we may get something he wants bad enough to trade for. Everything in life's a risk."

"My God!" she whispered.

"We're about a mile from the bank. Think it over."

When we pulled into the bank parking lot, she looked pasty and haggard, which was fine. Anyone who looked at her could see she was not her usual self.

"All right," she said.

I went through it again, covered everything I could think of, including contingencies.

"Make it good," I said, and handed her the small bottle I had brought with me. She made a face and drank half of it.

"All of it."

"Jesus, this tastes bad."

"All of it."

She tossed off the rest of the goop and threw the bottle on the backseat.

We went into the bank and sat outside the security door until Harriet finished a telephone call and came to open it for us. I had a leather attaché case with me, but it was empty.

A female loan officer was seated behind her desk talking on the telephone in one of the small offices off the main office area. The walls of all these spaces had large windows in them so everyone could see what was going on everywhere in the bank. The only privacy was in the vault, a series of cubicles for customers to load and unload their boxes, and the employee restrooms, which were right beside the vault. I didn't see any other employees in this area of the bank.

Dorsey and Harriet compared due dates after I introduced them, then Dorsey sat at a chair by Harriet's desk. While Harriet retrieved the master safe deposit box key from her desk, I checked that none of the surveillance cameras were pointed into the vault. They weren't.

Inside the vault, Harriet asked, "Do you remember your box number, Mr. Carmellini?"

"Number six, I think. It was one of the large ones." I pointed at it.

Harriet opened the card catalog and looked me up while I watched over her shoulder.

She removed my card from the box. "If you'll just sign and date this . . ."

I did so and handed her my key. She inserted her master key into my box lock, then mine, and opened it.

"Do you want to take your box to our privacy area?" she asked.

Before I could answer, I heard Dorsey moan, then I heard a thud as she hit the floor.

"My God!" I said, and darted out of the vault. Harriet was right behind me.

Dorsey lay face down on the floor, moaning softly and holding herself. The woman from the loan office rushed out and bent over her. Dorsey began retching.

"The bathroom," Harriet said, and grabbed one arm. The other woman took her other arm and they assisted her to her feet. Dorsey gagged.

As they went through the door of the ladies', I faded into the vault. Bless Harriet, she had left the master key sticking in the keyway of my box!

I turned sideways to the camera, and removed a halogen flashlight from my trouser pocket. I snapped it on as I aimed it at the camera. The light was so bright I had to squint for several seconds. I placed the light on the cabinet beside the card file, arranged it on a flexible wire base so it was pointed at the camera. The beam would wipe out the picture.

I knew that Carroll Kincaid also had a large box, based on the amount he had paid in rent. It took just seconds to find his name in the card catalog. He had box number twelve, and hadn't visited it since he rented it.

Leaving the lock on my box open, I used the master key on Kincaid's, inserted one of my picks and a torsion wrench in the second keyway, and went to work. After ten seconds, I decided I had the wrong size pick, and tried another.

I closed my eyes so that I could concentrate on the feel.

Perspiration beaded on my forehead. That never happens to James Bond in the movies; it was a character defect that I just had to live with.

Time crawled.

I concentrated on the feel of the pick.

Bang, I got it, and felt the lock give the tiniest amount.

Keeping the tension on the torsion wrench, I turned the master key . . . and the lock opened.

Kincaid's box had something in it. I didn't open it. I merely transferred his box to my vault and put my empty box in his, then closed the lock flap. I replaced the master key in the lock on my box, closed it, retrieved my key and the halogen flashlight, and was waiting in the lobby with my attaché case when the women came out of the rest room.

Dorsey looked as if she had been run over by something. Her face was pasty and her hair a mess.

Harriet and the other woman helped her toward the door.

"I'll get her home," I said, and slipped an arm around her. "Thank you *so* much."

Dorsey murmured something to the women, put her hand over her mouth as if she was going to heave again. Harriet opened the door, and I half-carried Dorsey through it.

I put her in the passenger seat of the car and got behind the wheel.

"You son of a bitch," she snarled. "I nearly vomited up my toenails."

"Remember this happy day," I remarked, "the next time somebody wants you to star in a fuck movie."

"Did you get the tapes?"

"I got something. I'll go back in a couple of days and get whatever it is."

"I'll go with you. I want those tapes."

"Those women have seen you for the last time. When I get the tapes, I'll call you."

She didn't like it, but she was in no condition to argue.

When I went back Wednesday afternoon, Harriet gave me a strange look. "How's your wife?"

"Better, thank you. You gotta be tough to have a baby."

She obviously had something on her mind. "After you and your wife left Monday, I had the strangest call from our security officer."

"Oh?"

"Apparently the surveillance camera in the vault stopped working while we had your wife in the restroom."

I shrugged. "Did it break?"

"Oh, no! Merely stopped working for a few minutes. They monitor them from our main office in Silver Spring."

"That is odd," I admitted. "While you were in the bathroom I used the time to put the items I brought into my box."

"The master safe deposit key was still in the lock of your box after you left."

"You have it now, I hope."

"Oh, yes."

"I really appreciate the way you and the other lady helped my wife," I said warmly. "I apologize for the inconvenience, but you know how these things are. I've written a letter to the president of the bank. I feel so fortunate that the bank has such wonderful employees."

Harriet beamed.

We opened the locks and I pulled my box from its shelf. I carried it to a privacy cubicle. There were a dozen videotapes, four whopping big stacks of cash with rubber bands around them, and a Smith & Wesson .38 revolver, which was loaded. I put a handkerchief around my fingers as I checked the pistol. The box was the best place for it, I decided; I left it there. The money and tapes I put in the attaché case.

Harriet and I chatted some more while I put the box away, then I left.

I played the tapes on a VCR I had at home. Dorsey was on three of them. The same men were on all twelve. I didn't recognize any of the other women. When I finished with the nine tapes Dorsey wasn't on I smashed them with a hammer and put them in the garbage, where they belonged.

The cash amounted to twenty-seven grand in old bills. I held random bills up to the light, fingered them, compared them to some bills I had in my wallet. It was real money, I concluded. Tough luck for Carroll Kincaid—easy come, easy go.

I met Dorsey that Friday evening in downtown Washington at a bar jam-packed with people celebrating the start of the weekend. As the hubbub washed over us, I gave her the three remaining tapes. I put my mouth close to her ear and asked, "Are any of these men Carroll Kincaid?"

"No." She refused to meet my eyes. "I don't want to talk about it."

"For whatever it's worth, you weren't the only one."

She grunted, and slugged her Scotch down as if it were Diet Coke.

"A thank-you would be in order," I said.

She laid a hand on my arm, tried to smile, got up and walked out.

I drank a second beer while I contemplated the state of the universe. On my way home I stopped by the first church I saw—it was Catholic—and went in to see the priest.

"Father, I have unexpectedly come into some serious money. I won't burden you with an explanation, but I wish to donate it to the church to use in its ministry to the poor."

The priest didn't look surprised. People must give him wads of cash every day. "As you probably know quite well, the need is great," he told me. "On behalf of the church, I would be delighted to accept any amount you wish to donate."

I handed him the money, which I had put in a shoebox and wrapped in some Christmas gift-wrap I had left over from the holidays.

He hefted the box and inspected it. "Do you want a receipt?" he said, eyeing me.

"That won't be necessary." I shook his hand and hit the road.

A few weeks later the Agency sent me to Europe, where I spent most of the winter and spring. I didn't hear from Dorsey O'Shea during my occasional trips back to the States, and probably would never have run into her again had I not gotten into a jam the following summer.